THE
DARKEST
HOUR

THE
DARKEST
HOUR

TONY SCHUMACHER

wm

WILLIAM MORROW

An Imprint of HarperCollins*Publishers*

THE DARKEST HOUR. Copyright © 2014 by Tony Schumacher. All rights reserved. Printed in the United States of America. No part of this book may be used or reproduced in any manner whatsoever without written permission except in the case of brief quotations embodied in critical articles and reviews. For information address HarperCollins Publishers, 195 Broadway, New York, NY 10007.

HarperCollins books may be purchased for educational, business, or sales promotional use. For information please e-mail the Special Markets Department at SPsales@harpercollins.com.

FIRST EDITION

Designed by Diahann Sturge

Library of Congress Cataloging-in-Publication Data has been applied for.

ISBN 978-0-06-233936-2
ISBN 978-0-06-236238-4 (international edition)

14 15 16 17 18   OV/RRD   10 9 8 7 6 5 4 3 2 1

For my Mum and Dad, sorry you never got to read it,

and for Boo, thanks for keeping me warm when I was cold

We do not yet know what will happen in France or whether the French resistance will be prolonged, both in France and in the French Empire overseas. The French Government will be throwing away great opportunities and casting adrift their future if they do not continue the war in accordance with their Treaty obligations, from which we have not felt able to release them. The House will have read the historic declaration in which, at the desire of many Frenchmen, and of our own hearts, we have proclaimed our willingness to conclude at the darkest hour in French history a union of common citizenship. However matters may go in France or with the French Government or with another French Government, we in this island and in the British Empire will never lose our sense of comradeship with the French people. If we are now called upon to endure what they have suffered we shall emulate their courage . . .

I expect that the battle of Britain is about to begin. Upon this battle depends the survival of Christian civilization. Upon it depends our own British life, and the long continuity of our institutions and our Empire.

—WINSTON CHURCHILL, HOUSE OF COMMONS, JUNE 18, 1940

THE
DARKEST
HOUR

CHAPTER 1

IT WAS THE dream with the blood.

So much blood.

Pouring from a wound he couldn't find, covering his hands, making them so wet he couldn't open his tunic. No matter how hard he tried to grip, his hands slipped and splashed in the blood.

Around him crowded gray faces, leaning and towering, looking down as he looked up, slipping and splashing, coughing and choking; he looked down for the wound and then back up at the faces.

He surfaced in his bed.

John Henry Rossett listened to the rain lashing against the window. Panic over, sleep long deserted, he listened to the rain outside and pretended.

He pretended nothing had changed and that the world was the one he'd known back when he was a boy. A boy curled under the covers listening to his father toss damp coal on the kitchen fire after a night shift. On mornings like this, if he closed his eyes and tried, he could hear the studded work boots clattering across the backyard with the clang of the dirty metal bucket coming to rest on the cobbles.

Long ago now.

Before the blood.

Before the gray faces.

A gust elbowed the window and more rain rattled on the glass like tossed gravel. Rossett shivered and opened half an eye to look at the clock on the wooden chair next to his bed. Half past four. He realized it wasn't that he'd woken early, because he hadn't woken up. He would have had to sleep to wake up, and what he'd managed for the last four and a half hours wasn't sleep.

He reached out of the bed and switched off the alarm before it had a chance to disturb the rest of the house, then pulled his bare arm back into the warmth.

He sighed, rolled onto his back, sighed again, stared at the ceiling for a moment, and then threw back the blankets. He got out of the bed and pulled on the old dressing gown that he had left on top of the bedclothes as moral support. He wrapped it around him and shuddered with the cold, then coughed a sticky wet bark full of whiskey and cigarettes.

He walked to the window, lit a cigarette from the pack in his dressing gown, and took his first drag.

His breath felt heavy. When he ran his tongue around his mouth, his teeth and his tongue felt thick and sticky. He coughed again, this time dipping his head, trying to catch some stubborn smokers' phlegm but failing.

Nobody was moving in the street outside. His little Austin sat under the lamp, looking like it was about to be swept away by the water rushing down the gutter. Rossett wondered if he'd pushed the driver's-side window all the way up or if he'd have a wet arse on his drive to work again.

He dragged on the cigarette. The reflection of the flaring orange end in the glass looked like a distant explosion, though it was only inches away. His tired eyes tried to focus, and he blinked away some sleep and heard a rattly wet cough through the thin wall. It was coming from the room next door, and Rossett decided he needed to get going before the boardinghouse came alive and a queue formed for the toilet on the landing.

It wasn't easy being a police sergeant attached to the SS in London in 1946, and Rossett didn't want to make it any harder than it already was.

He dressed and silently smoked another cigarette, sitting on the wooden stool by the window, looking at the shadows cast on the floor by the streetlamp. Eventually, he rose with a sigh and went downstairs to the small kitchen at the back of the house. Mrs. Ward, his landlady, was already up, and a fat, sweating teapot sat waiting on the cast-iron stove behind her, gray steam whispering from its spout. She nodded as he entered, silently poured him a cup, and set it on the table.

"I've only got toast and dripping," she said as Rossett reached for the teaspoon, then added, "There's no sugar or milk either, so don't bother asking."

He placed the teaspoon on the table next to the cup and wrapped his hand around the brew, more for the warmth than anything else. He wouldn't drink it, he never did; morning tea didn't agree with midnight Scotch.

"I don't see what the point is of having a police sergeant live in your house if he can't get you things," she said as she sat down across the table from him. "I barely have coke for the stove, let alone food to cook in it."

"The point is that he pays you rent; it's not his job to steal food for you as well," Rossett said flatly, blinking through the smoke of yet another cigarette.

"Trust me to get the only law-abiding copper in London."

Rossett half smiled at her and she smiled back, eyes coming alive beautifully amid the laughter lines.

One New Year's Eve, three sherries the wrong side of sober, she had told him she would wait "all my life for my Ronnie."

Ronnie hadn't come back from Dunkirk.

That was the night Rossett realized he was jealous of a dead man.

They'd danced at midnight, in each other's arms for one song on the parlor radio, eyes closed, hearts open for five minutes.

He didn't drink the tea. He stood, and she fetched his heavy raincoat from the hook on the back of the door. It was still damp from the night before, and he shivered as she smoothed it across his shoulders and then pulled it across his chest.

He tossed what was left of his cigarettes onto the table. "Fry those for now," he said as he walked out the door. "I'll see you tonight."

He sat in the car and looked at the folders lying on the front seat.

The job.

The damn job, waiting next to him, eager to get going, already sitting in the car.

Rossett wondered about the gray faces in his dream. He couldn't remember when they had first started to appear.

He looked at the files again, sighed, and then started the car.

The window on the Austin had stayed up for once, so his drive across the city wasn't as grim as usual. Few private cars were left on the roads in the near absence of fuel, so the journey only took him twenty minutes through a black-and-white London that was still half asleep and confused in fog.

As he approached the marked house, he saw three army trucks and a black Rover police car parked on the corner. He checked his watch: five thirty-five, everything on schedule.

He parked behind the third truck, nodding to the eyes that watched him pull up. A couple nodded in return, but most stayed huddled in their heavy coats and capes, arms folded like surly schoolboys outside a headmaster's office, heads sagging from lack of sleep.

He got out of the car, walked past the trucks, and banged on the misted-up window of the Rover. The door opened almost immediately, and Rossett leaned down to speak to the occupants.

His boss, Brewer, and a uniformed inspector he didn't know nodded in the half-light of the yellow bulb in the back of the car. A uniformed sergeant Rossett vaguely recalled from a previous operation climbed out the front of the car and smoothed his tunic, nodding at Rossett.

"We okay to go, sir?" Rossett addressed Brewer directly.

"Whatever you think best, Sergeant," replied Brewer, who was pretending, quite badly, to read some papers on a clipboard in an effort to stay out of the operation.

"I'll check that the men are ready to roll," said Rossett. Although Brewer didn't respond—he seldom did—he was supposed to monitor Rossett's work as a courtesy to the Met. In truth he only turned up under protest and seldom even spoke to the Germans.

"If you don't mind, Sergeant, I'll stay out of your work as much as I can. I'm sure I can trust you not to get us, or for that matter, me, into any bother?" That was all he'd said when they first met.

And for the past nine months, that was how things had stayed.

Rossett and the other sergeant stepped across the road as a pack of cigarettes and some matches came out. Rossett shielded the flame with his hands as the sergeant held the match for him to draw on. Once their cigarettes were lit, they walked the short distance from the car to the corner of the street. Rossett blew the smoke from his mouth and, staying close to the corner of the building, sneaked a glance around like a sniper into Caroline Street, their eventual destination. He quickly ducked back after he'd checked the target house.

"Anyone moving?" said the sergeant.

"No."

"It's a bloody awful morning for this sort of work."

"I've never known a good one for this sort of work."

"I don't know how you do it."

"Someone has to. It may as well be me," Rossett replied, checking his watch.

"When I was a nipper, there was a family of them used to live in our street. They weren't a bad sort, kept to themselves. Not sure I could be all heavy-handed if I met them today. I used to play football with their lad, we was about the same age . . ." The uniformed sergeant spoke almost to himself as he looked at the end of his cigarette and picked a piece of imaginary tobacco off the tip of his tongue.

Rossett stared at him for a moment and then flicked his own cigarette toward the gutter. It fell short and rolled in a half circle, hissing to a halt in a puddle.

"We get in, we hit them hard and fast. Tell your lads lots of shouting and banging, and don't let them settle or start to argue. If any of them gives any backchat, just give them a crack." Rossett jabbed his thumb in the direction of Caroline Street. "They will offer all sorts of things—money, jewels, even food to be left in the house if you give them a chance. So you make sure you let your men know, if anyone takes anything he will be on that cattle wagon faster than the Jew who tried to bribe him.

If everything goes to plan, you'll be drinking tea in the canteen in an hour and all this will be forgotten. Understood?"

The sergeant dropped his cigarette and ground it out, suddenly aware of the tiny swastika badge on the lapel of Rossett's raincoat.

"Yes, of course. I'll pass the word," he said, turning toward the trucks. Rossett watched him go and dug his hands into his coat pockets, very much aware of the tiny swastika badge himself.

CHAPTER 2

IT TOOK ANOTHER five minutes for the two SS officers to turn up, their Mercedeses contrasting with the battered old Austin and Rover as it eased to a stately stop.

When the Germans arrived in London, it hadn't taken them long to requisition the best of everything Scotland Yard had to offer. The best cars, the best secretaries, the best offices, and the best officers.

That was how Rossett had ended up sitting across the desk from the new assistant commissioner and the senior liaison officer for Einsatzgruppe Six. Prior to that day he'd been working the crime desk over in Wapping, earning a reputation as a top thief taker.

The *Oberst* had sat and silently read his file as Rossett stood wondering what was going on. The assistant commissioner had shaken his head and given him a filthy look when, after five minutes, Rossett politely coughed in the hope it would jump-start something.

When the German had finally looked up, ten minutes later, Rossett was rocking backward and forward on his heels and looking at the ceiling, his patience with the whole affair long exhausted.

"Are you in a hurry to leave, Sergeant?"

"I've important work to do, sir."

"You do, and you are going to do it with us from now on. Report to the Office of Jewish Affairs at Charing Cross tomorrow at nine."

And that was that. No interview, no chance to ask questions, no chance to turn it down: no chance, and no choice.

When he got back to Wapping, he'd found his desk already cleared and the last of the lads lingering at the station steadfastly avoiding his gaze. He realized that news traveled faster than central London traffic, and he stuck his head into his DI's office as a courtesy.

"Come in, Rossett. Take a seat."

DI Rimmer had been waiting for him. On the desk had sat two glasses of Scotch, a rare commodity since the invasion, especially the Red Label that sat between them now. Rossett recalled having seen similar bottles being carried into the station evidence store a few days earlier, seized from the docks, if he remembered rightly. He wondered how many were left there.

"You've heard, sir?"

"We've all heard. Within ten minutes of your leaving, they'd cleared your desk. For a moment, I thought you'd been up to something you shouldn't. Scotch?"

"No, thank you."

"No, of course." The DI took the bottle from his desk and slowly started to pour Rossett's glass back into it. The glass rattled slightly as he held it against the top of the bottle, embarrassing them both.

"I'm moving to the Office of Jewish Affairs, at Charing Cross."

"They were Gestapo who turned up here; I thought it best to let them get on with it." The DI didn't look at Rossett as he poured. Rossett wondered if the old man was scared, watching his words almost as closely as he watched the whiskey, making sure not to spill too much of either.

"I'll reallocate my case files."

"It's already done." The DI put the now-empty glass back onto the desk and screwed the top onto the bottle. He licked his finger and finally looked up at Rossett, tapping the same finger against his own glass. "Shame to waste it."

"Indeed."

"Murder to come by a decent drop now."

"Difficult to come by anything decent."

"Did you request the move, Rossett?"

"First I heard was this morning."

"Are you . . . do you . . . well, do you know what they're up to?"

"I think so."

"And are you happy with it?"

"It's been awhile since I've been happy with anything."

"Yes." Another sip of Scotch. "You are going to be doing a difficult job. One wonders why they chose you."

Rossett stared at Rimmer, then shifted his gaze onto the Scotch.

"Maybe they thought they could trust me?"

Rimmer followed his eyes and then took the bottle and placed it into his drawer, out of sight of anyone passing the office window.

"Will you be having a leaving drink with the chaps?"

"No."

"Probably for the best."

Rimmer suddenly looked old. Rossett watched as he seemed to shrink into the alcoholic the whole station knew him to be. He'd once been a good boss, respected, until the bottle had gotten hold of him. Now he seldom ventured from his desk. Rossett imagined his panic when the Gestapo had marched in to clear Rossett's property. He felt sorry for him; retirement was a few years off, if it came at all. Rimmer had the look of someone who wouldn't hold up long to the new wind that was blowing through the job, and the country.

"I'd best be off, sir."

"Hmm." Rimmer stared at the glass and waved his hand as if swatting a fly in slow motion.

Rossett stood and turned to leave. As he reached the door, the old man piped up one last time, "Be careful, Rossett. You'll be doing a difficult job."

"Mostly admin, I expect, sir."

"No. They'll make sure your hands will be dirty."

"I don't think so, sir. I expect they'll—"

The old man raised his hand and finally looked Rossett in the eye, for the first time in a long time.

"Your hands will get dirty, Sergeant. Take my word for it."

Rossett nodded, turned and left the office. The constables' writing room was deserted. He walked past the empty parade room and along a silent corridor. The busy station had turned into the *Mary Celeste,* except this time there was no mystery as to where the crew had gone.

Rossett knew they were choosing to avoid him. He checked his desk, now stripped bare. The only sign he had been there was the dent in the old leather chair he'd sat on for the last few years.

As he left the station, even the cleaners stared at the floor, polishing as if their lives depended on it.

Maybe my hands are dirty already, he thought as he dropped the flap on the inquiry desk behind him for the last time.

Rossett had found himself working under Major Ernst Koehler. Initially, they'd kept their distance, but over time, Rossett had come to like his new boss, with his easy smile and laid-back charm.

One night, when they were attending a planning conference in Manchester, Koehler and Rossett had sat and drunk in the hotel bar, and Koehler had told Rossett he'd been involved in the invasion of France.

"Maybe it was me who chased you across the channel?" Koehler laughed.

Rossett stared at the beer in front of him, and the German knew enough to let the matter drop. After some time, Koehler leaned across the table and clinked his glass against Rossett's.

"War does terrible things to men, John." Koehler paused, then lifted his glass, and both men drank together.

"I heard about your wife and son. I'm sorry," Koehler said, looking toward Rossett but not at him. He fixed his eyes on a distant part of the room, unsure of how the Englishman would react.

Rossett nodded silent thanks, took out a cigarette, and put it in his mouth, shifting in the chair as he searched for his matches. Koehler slid his across the table. Rossett picked them up, took his time opening them, and finally drew one out and lit it.

"Do you have family?" Rossett asked, more as a courtesy to break the silence than a genuine inquiry.

"Yes, back in Germany, Lotte, my wife, and Anja, my daughter. I miss them terribly." Koehler pulled out his wallet, opened it, and proudly leaned forward so that Rossett could see the picture inside.

Rossett barely glanced, then twitched a smile and nodded before Koehler leaned back in his seat, suddenly aware that his statement seemed inappropriate in the face of Rossett's loss.

"I'm sorry, I shouldn't have," Koehler said as he closed his wallet.

"Don't be sorry. What happened wasn't your fault; you didn't plant the bomb."

"No, but . . . well, it is thoughtless. It must be difficult enough for you without people like me sticking photos under your nose."

"Just because I lost my family doesn't mean everyone else has to forget theirs." Koehler nodded at the logic and took another drink, then signaled the waitress across the room by holding up two fingers and pointing at his pint. He swallowed and licked his lips before putting down the glass.

"Do you have photos of your family?"

"No, they were taken from me in a POW camp."

"Maybe I can get them back for you? They'll be somewhere. I'm sure if I—"

"They were ripped up and thrown on the floor." Rossett stared flatly at Koehler as he spoke, smoke spiraling up from his hand, which rested on the arm of the chair.

"Why?"

Rossett shrugged. "Because some guard thought it would be funny, I suppose. Like you said, war does terrible things to a man."

"They died before you got out, didn't they?"

Rossett nodded.

"I read it in your file, before you came. That bomb, it was—I don't know how to say it—it was . . ." Koehler looked for the word until Rossett filled in the blank.

"A massacre."

"A massacre, it was a massacre." Koehler paused again, looking for a way to push the conversation on. "What about your other family?"

"I don't have any. I lost my father before the war and my mother in the invasion. I've a brother in Liverpool, but we don't speak."

"Why?"

"Because of this." Rossett tapped the swastika on his lapel and shrugged.

"You should maybe try speaking to him again. It's been awhile now. People have started to get used to us."

"We didn't have much to say to each other before the war, and we've even less now. I don't need him. I don't need anyone anymore. I just get by on my own."

"You should come out in London with me. Maybe we can see a band or a show?"

Rossett shook his head. "I don't do that sort of thing. I don't . . . I don't do anything anymore. My life is simple." Rossett shrugged at the simplicity of his statement and then shook his head again. "I'm like a monk." He managed a half smile at Koehler, who smiled back, somewhat sadly.

The waitress appeared and placed two full pints in front of them. Rossett ignored her. Koehler flashed her a charming smile that caused her to smile back and tap at her hair with her free hand.

"Keep the change." Koehler flashed the smile again and placed some coins on her tray, then watched her walk away from the table. "Is that why you came to work for us?"

"Is what why?"

"The resistance bomb, killing your family, is that why you came to us?"

"No."

"Why did you choose to work for us then?"

"I didn't. I just did as I was told. I just do my job. If I'm told to work for the Germans I work for the Germans." Rossett shook his head as if he'd never considered the point before. "I just do my job," he repeated, as much for his own ears as Koehler's.

Koehler slid a pint toward Rossett.

"Well, John, all I can say is that I'm glad you do. I like working with you—you do it well. There are not many men in London who could do what you do as well as you. I salute you." Koehler lifted his full pint and took a drink.

Rossett watched him, then leaned forward to stub out his cigarette in the half-full ashtray that sat between them.

"Why do you do it?" he asked softly. Koehler looked at him over the top of the pint glass. "You're a soldier. This isn't fighting—this is management, dealing with a problem. Why do you do it?"

Koehler finished his gulp and then placed the pint down on the table. He leaned forward and wiped a hand across his top lip to remove a line of froth that had settled there. The German realized that he was slightly drunk, so he paused before speaking and breathed deeply, considering his words.

"I fought in France, like I said, then across the rest of fucking Europe. I made it as far as Moscow."

"I know, the Knight's Cross." Rossett pointed at his own throat to signify where Koehler wore his medal when in dress uniform.

"Knight's Cross with oak leaves," Koehler corrected with mock seriousness, wagging his finger at Rossett, who smiled in return.

"With oak leaves," Rossett parroted, picking up his pint.

"I made it to Moscow. It was crazy there, John; you haven't seen anything like it. Winter was setting in, the whole city had broken down, people were eating corpses they found in the street. Can you believe it? Corpses in the street? Animals, they are fucking animals."

"Maybe they were desperate?"

"Nobody knew what they were doing. We'd charged halfway across Russia and ended up stuck in this shithole waiting for the weather to get better, when one day I get told to start rounding up Jews. I think they were just looking for a job to give us. The men were bored, no fighting, no training. You know what soldiers are like if they haven't got something to do?"

Rossett nodded.

"Well, I set up teams, started dragging in rabbis plus Russian community leaders and civil servants." Koehler leaned forward as he spoke, warming to the subject. "I realized, sooner than wander around the city rounding up two or three Jews, I could, with a little organization, get the bastards to walk into the fucking hotel we were staying in and hand themselves over to us. And to make matters certain, I told the Russians to let it be known that I would give a bag of potatoes and a loaf of bread for each Jew someone handed in. The next day the line was around the block. Half the fucking Jews the Russians brought me were dead already, but I didn't care. It kept my men busy and the bosses off my back."

"You did well." Rossett nodded as he took a drink.

"I did brilliantly," Koehler replied as he pulled a cigarette out of Rossett's pack. He put the cigarette in his mouth and the tip bobbed up and down as he continued to speak. "I did so fucking brilliantly I got pulled out of Moscow and sent back to Berlin. People notice good work, John. You should know that, you got the Victoria Cross." Koehler lit his cigarette and gasped as the smoke went down. He watched his exhalation a moment and then continued through squinting eyes. "Next thing I know I'm in an office being told I'm coming to London to 'continue my great work with the Jewish Question.' I couldn't believe my luck. I swear to God, I nearly shit when I was told Himmler himself had taken notice of what I'd managed in Moscow. Apparently, my unit had rounded up five times more than the nearest unit. I got a promotion and this job, and to cap it all, I got to work with you, my friend." Koehler beamed across the table at Rossett, who found himself smiling back.

"Lucky me."

"So, just make sure you remember"—Koehler leaned forward again and picked up his pint—"if you fuck up and I get sent back to Russia, I'll kill you before I go, Victoria Cross or no Victoria Cross, understand?" Koehler winked and Rossett smiled back.

IT WAS KOEHLER who had convinced Rossett to join the British Nazi Party. At first, Rossett had refused, telling his boss that he had no interest in politics, that he didn't see how it would make any difference in his work. But Koehler had quietly sat at his desk one afternoon and explained that if he wished to remain with the Office of Jewish Affairs, it was best that he joined.

"If you don't, things may become difficult. You may have to leave here. You may have to leave the police. If you have no job, you'll be forced to join the National Labor Service—poor money, poor food, and always the chance that you'll be sent out east to work on the defenses against the Russians. Just sign the papers, Rossett, don't be a fool."

"I don't have to be in the party to stay in the police? I can change departments."

"Nobody will have you. You'll be out, especially after doing this job. Your hands are dirty now. Just sign the papers, it's only a formality."

Your hands are dirty, thought Rossett. The phrase seemed to crop up more and more but mean less and less the dirtier they got.

And so he'd signed, and a week later he'd stood in front of the Southeast Area Commander of the SS as he'd pinned the tiny swastika onto his lapel and handed him his party membership card. When the German had raised his arm and said "Heil Hitler!" Rossett had stiffened, but then did the same, embarrassed to hear the medals on his suit banging together as he did so.

Once he was in the party, things had changed—ever so slightly, but change they had. He started to find that sometimes when he shopped, his ration tickets weren't ripped out by the shopkeeper. One day, the butcher had slyly winked and passed his money back. Rossett had returned later that evening to pay for the goods and to explain that such favors would not be accepted.

"But Mr. Rossett, if I can make you happy with little things, well, you know . . . we can make each other happy, look after each other, you know what I mean?"

The butcher had tapped his nose and slid something wrapped in paper toward Rossett, who noted the blood soaking through and leaving a trail on the counter. He quietly shook his head and whispered, "I am the law. I live by the law. I do what's right. Mark my words and remember them."

He had then turned on his heel and left the shop, not sure if what he had said was true or not.

That night, he'd not slept a wink, and it was that night he'd opened the Scotch again.

Other things had changed. He was given the Austin and enough fuel to allow for some personal use. Occasionally, he would drive out to Southend and stare at the sea. One afternoon, he had taken Mrs. Ward, his landlady, and they'd sat on the beach drinking tea from a thermos.

After some time, he'd noticed he was crying and that she was holding his hand.

They never spoke of it again, nor had they ever again taken that drive out to the sea. It was forgotten, like so many other things.

"SERGEANT ROSSETT, GOOD morning." Koehler reached across and shook Rossett's hand, then gestured to the other man who had stepped out of the Mercedes. "This is Schmitt of the Gestapo, just arrived from Paris. I've brought him along to see how we do things here. He'll be working with us for a while."

Rossett nodded to Schmitt, who ignored him and peered around the corner of the still-silent street.

"How many are in the building?" Schmitt asked, his thick German accent contrasting sharply with Koehler's excellent English.

"About eighty," Rossett replied.

"About?" Schmitt turned and raised an eyebrow. "You don't know exactly?"

"Eighty-four. I've every birthdate, set of fingerprints, and photo in the car, plus all the relevant documentation, if you would like to see it."

Schmitt smiled and nodded to Koehler, who beamed like a proud father, and then went back to looking around the corner into Caroline Street.

"Do we expect any trouble from the other residents of the street?"

"No, but in case there is we've brought along twenty Home Defense Troops, armed with clubs. We'll get them to form up as soon as the bobbies enter the house."

The Home Defense Troops were mostly made up of ex–British Union of Fascists members and a few thugs who just liked cracking heads. Many had been interned at the start of the war, and they had quickly joined up as soon as Mosley had moved into Downing Street. The incoming Germans had organized them with uniforms and, at first, a mostly German command structure.

They tended to be unarmed and, in some areas, worked alongside the regular police, their sky blue uniforms with red shoulder flashes contrasting sharply with the somber serge of the British bobbies.

The farther north you went, the fewer Home Defense Troops there seemed to be. North of the demarcation line, which stretched from Liverpool to Newcastle, they were virtually nonexistent. North of the D line, the country was governed by the Northern Assembly, which operated under the British Nazi Party. It was demilitarized in theory, but Rossett knew that there were a few thousand German troops up in Glasgow; he'd seen the trains full of them one night leaving Nine Elms goods yard. Rumors abounded of another base centered on the Luftwaffe station in Lossiemouth. And, no doubt, there was a German naval base guarding what was left of the British Navy stuck in Rossyth.

The Germans had gotten everywhere.

The Home Defense Troops' command structure had gradually evolved to accommodate ex–British officers who had come over to the cause, and as time passed, they had become more disciplined. Many new members had joined for the extra rations and security the organization brought.

Rossett had noticed that the Germans still hadn't armed the group, though; old suspicions died hard.

"Are we ready to proceed, Sergeant? I have an important meeting at nine," Schmitt said, still peeping around the corner.

"I'll have the men fall in." Rossett nodded to the uniformed police sergeant, who was now standing some ten feet away at the back of one of the wagons. He, in turn, whistled softly, and the HDT and police started to climb down from the back of the trucks. Everyone was silent, aware that the two Germans had arrived. From the area car, the two inspectors appeared. Both happy to let Rossett deal with the situation, they crossed the road to watch proceedings from afar.

Rossett watched them and silently shook his head; only his hands would be getting dirty again.

He walked to the rapidly falling-in groups of bobbies and troops.

"You've all been briefed, boys. Fast and thorough, understood?"

Some nodded while others drew truncheons. The HDT troops shouldered pickax handles and made ready to run into the middle of the road.

"On my whistle." Rossett held up his police whistle and stood at the head of the group. He waited a moment for the silence to fall again, took a deep breath, and blew hard.

CHAPTER 3

ROSSETT RAN AT the head of the group, the sound of their studded boots echoing off the high buildings either side of the narrow street. He arrived at the door and signaled for the first policeman to kick it in; it crashed aside almost immediately. The first few bobbies rushed past him and he turned to watch the rest and the HDT. All was going well, just as it had done so many times before.

He took a moment and then entered the hallway, waving the coppers up the stairs, urging them on, keeping them moving.

"Come on boys! Speed and noise! Come on!" Rossett shouted, and in return, the officers around him started to shout also, urging the house occupants to get out of bed and show themselves.

Rossett stepped aside as blue-clad Valkyries charged past him and up to the startled families, who, bleary eyed, were being dragged from their beds by hair and hands. It always surprised him how easy it was to motivate the men around him; maybe it was the thrill of the hunt.

Rossett turned when the door behind him in the hallway opened. He hadn't expected anyone to be in the small front room at this time of the morning. He spun and found Levi Cohen, one of the community elders with whom Rossett had been liaising for the last few months, peeking around the doorframe.

Rossett pushed open the door fully and saw that the old man was standing in tattered gray long johns. Across his shoulders was an even older, threadbare dressing gown. It struck Rossett that it was the first time he'd seen Cohen without a star of David sewn on his chest.

He pushed past the old man to look into the room. On a makeshift bed lay Cohen's wife, Martha, and two other old people. He realized they'd been sleeping near the fireplace for warmth.

"What is happening here?" Cohen was angry now, pulling his dressing gown across his pigeon chest and watching as police officers herded people down the stairs. Many of the Jews had no shoes or outdoor clothing and were complaining loudly. One passed with blood running down his face from a scalp wound, inflicted as encouragement to come quietly, the fresh red the only color in the hallway.

"Get up and get outside." Rossett spoke to the people in the bed, pointing first at them and then at the street. He then turned to Cohen. "You are being moved to more suitable accommodation. Get outside."

"But we have only just arrived; you told us to move here!"

"Get outside, Levi. Get your people outside quickly."

"You keep moving us to smaller and smaller places. How are we supposed to put up with this? Can we not have a moment to gather our things? The old people, they have no shoes!" Cohen was pointing along the hallway and out the front door to the street, where the Jews were being corralled by the HDT with their pickax handles.

"I'll arrange for their things to be brought along. Get outside," Rossett said calmly. He glanced back to the bed, where the others remained, sitting up but not getting out.

Striding across the room, he kicked at the broken wooden bed.

"Move!"

One of the old women glared at Rossett, thrusting out her chin.

"You should be ashamed!" her heavily accented voice rang out. "I come here to get away from men like you! You are a disgrace!"

A young bobby appeared in the doorway, buzzing with adrenaline. "Shall I move 'em, sir?" Wild eyed and eager.

"Yes," Rossett replied, quietly turning away from the doorway. Cohen followed him.

"We did as you said. You told us we would be safe here. You told us if we moved here we would be left alone, and now you move us again?"

"Get outside, Levi." This time Rossett spoke softly.

"How many times? How many times will you lie to us? Move us? How many times?" The old man was shouting now.

"I'm just doing my job."

"Doing your job? You call this a job?" Cohen grabbed Rossett's arm and yanked him back toward the room.

Rossett head-butted the old man, who dropped to the floor, dazed but still conscious.

Behind them, Martha screamed as the young bobby dragged her from the bed. Other constables ran back to the house to assist their colleague, and quickly the room filled with shouting policemen, two of whom lifted Cohen and dragged him away. The old man looked confused for a moment and then his eyes found focus; he stared at Rossett as he was taken outside, a treacle-thick gobbet of blood hanging from his nose. His eyes fixed on Rossett's as he was pushed into the crowd and the waiting arms of his people. The blood dropped from his nose onto his long johns and the old man let it fall, red on gray.

It was Rossett who looked away first.

The rain started again as the wagons reversed around the corner. The older Jews were lifted by the younger ones up into the backs of the vehicles as two policemen stood either side and counted heads. Rossett stayed in the doorway and lit a cigarette, watching the houses opposite. He'd heard there had been shots fired at police during a clearance in Manchester a few weeks before. The Germans had come down hard on that street. The last thing Rossett wanted was for some locals to take umbrage while he had the two Germans watching.

All he noticed was a few curtains flicking open, then closing just as quickly. It seemed everyone was turning a blind eye and things were going to go quietly.

His forehead stung from the head butt and he gingerly touched it before sucking on the cigarette again.

The Jews were squeezed onto the back of the trucks, with canvas sheets eventually rolled down to cover the cargo from prying eyes, out of sight and out of mind.

Rossett waved four policemen across to him.

"You guard the back and front of the house, and don't let anyone in till I come back, understand?"

"Does that include the Germans, Sarge?"

"That includes Hitler; no one goes in there till I get back."

Two broke away to make their way around to the rear while the others stepped into the hallway out of the rain.

"Outside," said Rossett. "Nobody goes in, including you."

The bobbies stepped out and pulled what was left of the door closed behind them. As the trucks fired up, Rossett nodded to the uniformed sergeant.

"Get half of your lads in the empty wagon; follow us down to the rail yard. I'll need them to help load the train."

The sergeant nodded, looking almost shell-shocked, then took a deep breath and started issuing orders as Rossett walked back to his car. He'd almost made it when he heard Koehler call his name. When he turned, he saw the two Germans walking toward him.

"Well done, Sergeant. An excellent operation." Schmitt was smiling now. He held out his hand for Rossett to shake.

"It seemed to go well. We still have to load the trains, but I doubt they'll give us any problems."

"They will do as they are told. They understand when they are met with someone who is determined to do his job." Schmitt turned to Koehler. "I do enjoy early-morning sport. Thank you for the entertainment."

Koehler smiled and nodded to Rossett.

"Another satisfied customer."

"I'd best be going. Don't want to keep the trucks waiting too long."

"Of course, we don't want any of those Jews dying before we get them on the train!" Schmitt laughed a little too loudly at his own joke.

Rossett climbed into the Austin.

"I'll see you back at the office," he said to Koehler. "Unless you are coming down to the train?"

"No, you deal with it." Koehler turned from the car and headed to his Mercedes. Schmitt gave Rossett a wave and followed Koehler. It occurred to Rossett that Koehler never went to the station to see the Jews being loaded. Rossett watched the Germans get into the car and thought for a moment about how Koehler contrasted with Schmitt, who was now laughing and pointing at the truck. Koehler looked across to him and nodded his head. Rossett nodded back and watched them drive away.

"Were they happy with how things went?" Rossett jumped as the uniformed inspector leaned in through his window.

"Yes."

"Will you let them know what station we are from? It's nice to stay on Jerry's side, you understand?"

"Everything will be in my report."

"Anytime, Sergeant," said the inspector as he walked briskly toward the waiting area car, its engine already running, with a belch of smoke hanging behind it in the cold air.

Brewer lifted a hand to Rossett from the back as the area car pulled away from the curb. Rossett gunned the little Austin and fell in behind the trucks to make the journey across to Nine Elms goods yard.

THE GERMAN SENTRIES at the yard already had the barrier up as they approached. They waved the convoy straight through with a friendly, halfhearted salute and a shouted joke to the police hanging onto the back of the third truck. Although the rain had petered out to a drizzle, there was now a strong wind blowing across the tracks, and the wide-open spaces offered no shelter as the trucks bounced across the yard toward the waiting goods train.

Rossett always arranged for these operations to happen before the place came to life in the morning, a nightmare taking place while the rail workers had sweet dreams. He'd told the Ministry of Railways that he needed the yard in the early mornings so that it didn't interfere with their schedules, but in reality he knew it was because he didn't want too many judgmental eyes to see him pushing and prodding Jews into rail cars.

The freight train was already waiting for them when they arrived. It would have traveled all night, Glasgow to London, stopping along the way at Preston, Liverpool, and Birmingham to collect the Jews who were no longer useful. Rossett wondered when the trains would run out of cargo. He lit another cigarette and rubbed his forehead again, trying not to think about who would be chosen to fill the train the day it ran out of Jews.

He stayed in the Austin, about forty feet from the blackness of the freight car, watching as the trucks with the Jews backed up to the wooden ramp. Two railway workers quickly made themselves scarce as the police and HDT climbed down from their own transport and formed a human cordon to channel the Jews.

Rossett looked around the yard: no civilians in sight. He considered whether to pull on his hat but decided against it as a gust of wind shoved the little car and made it rock. Across the yard, the men waiting by the rear of the trucks glanced across for the okay to start work so they could get out of the rain as fast as possible.

Everyone wanted it to be over for their own reasons.

Rossett sighed, got out of the Austin, and made his way toward the waiting troops, who were squinting at him through the drizzle. As Rossett passed the other freight cars he could make out shouts and the banging of fists against the heavy timber doors. He'd once made the mistake of stopping and listening, a mistake he wouldn't make again.

"We okay to crack on, Sarge?" said the bobby nearest the canvas flap at the rear of one of the trucks.

"Who's counting?"

"I am, Sarge, and Kelly on the ramp," said another policeman, who held up his notebook.

Rossett nodded to the first policeman, who started to untie the ropes holding down the canvas. Once the flap was open and the tailgate dropped, the bobby stepped back, expecting the Jews to jump down.

They didn't.

Koehler had once said they were like "rats in a tipping barrel, creeping farther into the dark away from the light."

Apart from the wind and the flapping of the newly untied canvas, there was no other sound until Rossett took his cigarette out of his mouth and shouted, "Come on, we'll be here all day. Get them off!"

Almost immediately the men came to life and started to shout into the wagon. A couple of them jumped up onto the bed of the truck and disappeared into the darkness. Soon, the first of the Jews, men and women, many of them elderly, started to tumble down like leaves in autumn into the waiting arms of the HDT and police.

The wind whipped everyone in the yard, almost taking the sound of the count away with it.

"One . . . two . . . three . . ." as the first three shuffled along, confused and holding themselves with arms folded tightly, two old ladies and a teenage girl, their nightdresses providing little comfort in the rain and wind. Slowly the others started to jump down unaided, the younger ones helping their parents and grandparents. Some were crying, while others just looked around, sheepish and confused. "Fourteen, fifteen . . ." Nobody tried to make a dash for cover; nobody tried to fight back. They just did as they were told, the way they always did.

Rossett wondered if he would go so quietly. "Twenty-seven, twenty-eight . . ." He liked to think he would fight back, throw a punch or two or make a dash for it. Then again, maybe he'd just do as he was told as well.

He didn't know.

He hoped he'd never find out.

"Thirty-eight, thirty-nine . . ."

Along the track, Rossett could see the steam engine reversing to pick up the carriages. It would have been refilling with water on one of the sidings. Smoke and sparks belched from its chimney and the two red lights hanging at its rear looked like the devil's eyes closing in on a soul. He shuddered with the cold and turned back to the Jews. "Fifty-six, fifty-seven . . ." He glanced up to the freight car. The loaded Jews huddled away from the doors, some gathering straw and stuffing it into their clothing for warmth. Rossett wondered if they would get blankets at the port. He doubted some of the older ones would survive without them.

A German officer was walking toward them from the guards' van at the rear of the train, his leather trench coat glistening with rain. In his hands were a clipboard and torch. Rossett watched as the German glanced up at the locked cars as he passed, checking that no cargo was going to escape.

"Sixty-seven, sixty-eight . . ."

The rest of the team had no need to shout encouragement now; the Jews had got the message and were moving under their own steam, picking their way over the gravel, some in bare feet.

"Sergeant!" A lone shout. "Sergeant! Please! Sergeant Rossett! Please!"

Rossett looked over to the dwindling line of human cargo, unable to see who was shouting his name.

"Seventy!"

"Sergeant, please! I must speak to you, you must listen!"

Rossett craned his neck to look beyond the line of police, who had their backs to him.

"Seventy-two, seventy-three . . ."

"Sergeant Rossett, please! It is important information for you!"

The voice was near the freight car now. Rossett walked toward it, craning his neck to find the source.

"Seventy-nine, eighty."

"Sergeant, here!" Frantic now, almost a shriek. Rossett noticed a scuffle on the ramp and pushed his way through toward it.

"Get these people on the train, we have a timetable!" shouted the German officer. Rossett waded into the pushing group of Jews and police, cast a glance to the German officer, who was now only thirty or forty feet away, then felt a hand grab his collar, dragging him forward toward the darkness of the freight car.

He reached into the pocket of his raincoat for his sap as he grabbed the bony wrist of the hand that was doing the pulling.

"Please, Sergeant; please, I need to speak to you!" An old Jew owned the hand that was twisting and wrapping itself up in his raincoat. Rossett had the sap out, and he jabbed it into the old man's ribs, but still the hand held fast, clinging for dear life.

"Get on the train." Rossett was pushing the old man backward up the ramp, but in doing so he himself was boarding the train. Aware that with every step he was getting closer to its cargo, he lifted his sap so that the old man could see it. "Get on the train!"

The old man pulled him nearer, two hands on his lapels now, eyes bulging, and Rossett felt salty breath on his face. The Jew stepped on tiptoe to draw Rossett closer still. For a moment he thought the old man was about to kiss him.

"Sergeant, you must listen. My name is Galkoff. You must listen to me." Galkoff was whispering now, his lips brushing Rossett's ear. Rossett twisted his head but the lips stayed close. No matter which way he turned he felt the brush of stubble on his cheek, and for a thousandth of a second he thought about his own father and a rare kiss from a dying man on a dirty pillow years before.

"Eighty-four! That's the lot!" called a voice from the foot of the ramp.

"Please, it's so important. One moment. I have treasure . . . treasure for you," Galkoff whispered, looking down the ramp past him and then back up into Rossett's face.

Rossett finally managed to prise a finger off his lapel with his free hand.

"Get on the train."

"It's for you, all for you."

"Get on the train!" A shout this time.

"I know you, I've seen you come and go to the house many times. I know you are an honest man." Galkoff clamped his free hand onto the side of Rossett's face and stared deeply, with desperate, watery brown eyes. The old man released his lapel and looked back into the train, one hand still clutching Rossett's face, fingertips like ice picks sliding across his skin. "I knew you before all this. You came into my shop. I knew your family, your father, your mother. They were good people, honest people. As soon as I saw you I recognized you. I read about what you did in France. I was so proud of you fighting for us."

Rossett vaguely remembered the old man now from the shop on the corner when he was a child. Suddenly, the yard fell away from him and it was just him and the old man, looking into each other's eyes.

"I remember, but you have to get onto the train. I can't help you. It's my job to put you on the train."

The old man pulled him forward again; he gripped Rossett and pushed his mouth close to Rossett's ear.

"Behind the bookcase, third floor, front room. My treasure is behind the bookcase. It is payment for you to help me, to do a thing for me. You are a good man, you'll do it. I knew it the moment I saw you coming to the house, you'll do this thing for me." Whispering hot breath on a freezing cold ear caused Rossett to stiffen.

Just as suddenly as he had grabbed Rossett, the old man pushed him away and stepped back into the freight car as if falling from a cliff.

"Sergeant?" called the German from the bottom of the ramp. Rossett came to, the spell broken. He looked first at the German and then back into the gloom of the freight car. Ghostly faces with blackened eyes stared back, and he found himself taking a half step back, still looking for old Galkoff, who had disappeared into the darkness.

"I have a timetable!" called the German again.

Rossett finally turned and walked back down the ramp, glancing over his shoulder into the freight car, where eighty-four pairs of eyes watched him go. At the foot of the ramp, the German proffered the clipboard, which Rossett signed without checking. The two railwaymen abruptly raised the ramp and swung the freight door shut with the solid clang of a heavy iron hasp and the final screeching stuttering slide of a rusty bolt to hold it fast.

Rossett looked up at the locked door as the German pulled the clipboard from his hand. The train jolted as the distant engine took up the slack. From inside, Rossett heard some cries as the shock of the movement hit home.

Rossett felt as if he were in a dream. Galkoff's whispering so close to his ear had unsettled him. It was more real, less clockwork, more human. He felt that he could still hear the old man, feel his panicked breath on his cheek. Rossett touched his face where the old man's stubble had brushed and looked around to see if anyone else was affected by what had just happened.

They weren't.

Behind him the HDT and police were already boarding their trucks. He saw that the German officer was making his way back to the guards' train car. A whistle sounded somewhere, and the train suddenly jerked again, like a circus elephant against a chain, and then slowly, so slowly, the car in front of him started to move along the track.

He took another step back and looked from one end of the train to the other, from the engine to the guards' car at the rear, where the German was hopping up onto the ladder before it started to move too quickly. The train picked up speed and as the guards' car passed him, the German waved from the still-open door and shouted something about seeing Rossett next month.

Wind blew drizzle into his face, and he wiped it with the back of his hand, realizing he was still holding his sap. He watched the red lights at the back of the train move away for a moment and then turned toward his car. He put the sap back into his pocket, embarrassed that he'd almost used it on an old man, aware that the hand that was holding it was shaking a little.

He wanted a drink.

The car windows had misted, and he had to use the back of his hand to clear a four-inch-wide smear on the windshield. It distorted the view of the world outside, and the lamps of the yard became exaggerated stars. The train was already out of sight on its way to the docks. He thought about what Galkoff had said and shuddered again. The little car coughed into life as the troop trucks, their cabs shiny with rain, bounced past him across the rough freight yard to the exit.

Rossett lit another cigarette, suddenly realizing how many he smoked on mornings like this, and made a decision to try to ease up. He checked his watch. Seven thirty, bang on schedule, just as usual.

ON THE TRAIN, amid the crying and the clanging, Israel Galkoff leaned his head against the coarse wood of the doors and said a little prayer that his treasure would be safe; it was all he had.

His only hope.

CHAPTER 4

BY THE TIME Rossett got back to the house, light was breaking through the early morning cloud and the streets were starting to fill with commuters. The drive across town had taken longer than expected, but he was glad for the traffic; it had given him some time to settle his nerves. The encounter with the old man had shaken him, made that morning's work seem more personal.

He thought about the old man's shop, nondescript, just like all the other shops he had followed his mother in and out of when he was on his school holidays. He'd never given Galkoff a second thought back then. He wondered why he was such a threat to society now. The old man hadn't changed, thought Rossett as he sat at a traffic light and looked at the banner of the Führer shaking hands with King Edward that covered half of the building across the road.

"The old man hasn't changed, we have," he said to himself as the traffic light changed and he moved on.

When he arrived back at Caroline Street, the two bobbies at the front door of the house straightened up and took their hands out of their pockets when they saw him.

"Has anyone been in?" he asked as he slammed the door of the Austin.

"No, Sarge," said the younger one.

"You, come with me," said Rossett, pushing open the door. "What's your name?" he said over his shoulder as they marched up the stairs.

"Baker, Sarge."

"Is your notebook up to date, Baker?"

"Yes, Sarge."

"Good."

He'd normally have left the search of the house to the removal team that would turn up a few hours after the Jews had left. The team, usually led by a retired bobby or a German civil servant, would inventory the house, take anything valuable, then lock up the property until there were workers who needed accommodation. The landlord would receive a peppercorn rent and a warning about renting his houses to Jews in the future.

Often, the best-case scenario was that the building was owned by one of the Jews in the first place, in which case the property would have already been signed over to the state on the grounds that since the Jewish Acts in Parliament, Jews were no longer allowed to own property. Rossett knew it was an unfair system but excused it on the grounds that it stopped them sleeping rough and having to be cleared up if they died of the cold on the streets.

"Don't we normally wait for the removal lads, Sarge?" Baker said, taking off his helmet to prevent its hitting the low ceiling on the stairs.

"Not this morning. I want you to witness something."

"Witness something?"

"There are only two things that will get you sacked in this job, son: women and property. You need a witness when you handle either of them; never forget."

"Yes, Sarge," replied Baker, now a little nervous.

Rossett didn't know if anyone else had heard Galkoff talking about "treasure" when they had been on the ramp, but he didn't want to take the risk of word getting to the cleanup team and someone getting sticky fingers. He also didn't want anyone accusing him of taking whatever was behind the bookcase. Theft from the state carried a death penalty. Whatever was up there belonged to the state, and Rossett intended to see that the state got its due.

They entered the room, and Rossett noted the upturned chair and bedding thrown across the floor, a broken water jug lying on the bed, and the lock of the door splintered on the inside. The old man hadn't gone quietly.

Against the far wall stood a wooden bookcase. It was heavy and old and must have taken four men to carry it to the third floor. Its shelves were less than half full.

"They must have burnt the books to keep warm," Baker said, reading his mind and filling in the gaps.

Rossett nodded. It was a fair deduction except for one thing.

There wasn't a fireplace in the room.

"Give me a hand. They might have hidden something behind it."

They both took a hold on the same side, looking to lift one corner away from the wall and pivot it around.

"What if it's a booby trap, Sarge? I heard one house up north was rigged with explosives by a load of communist Jews."

"Just lift it."

The bookcase creaked but moved easily on the bare floorboards. Rossett realized the old man had planned it that way; he'd have known they'd be coming eventually, and had chosen the last room they'd get to so as to have time to hide his secrets from the initial search.

Behind the bookcase, Rossett could see a hole in the wall where a fireplace had once been. He lifted the bookcase farther out and then squeezed into the gap, bending from the waist and twisting himself to peer into the darkness.

"Fetch me a candle. I can't see a thing," he said, arm reaching behind him, fingers snapping.

Baker grabbed a candle from the floor next to the bed and lit it quickly. He passed it to Rossett, who, holding it next to his face, pushed farther into the gap. At the back of the surprisingly large void lay some sacking and a small brown suitcase, maybe eighteen inches long and nine high.

Rossett reached for the case and pulled it toward him, aware that he was getting soot on his raincoat. He was keen to get out of the space and started to back out, but then he stopped.

It was no good going to all this trouble and then only doing half the job.

He set the case to his side and cursed as he banged his head on a jagged brick before stretching into the gap again. Some old soot dropped from the chimney above and he rested his hand on it, feeling it crunch under his palm. He took hold of the sacking and pulled it toward him to look underneath.

Sooty, curly black hair and a pale white face emerged.

A child, a young boy, maybe seven years old, blinked at him.

The boy didn't move. He sat with his back to the wall, big brown eyes staring and lips clamped tight.

The only movement was the shadow cast by the flicker of the candle.

Eventually, Rossett spoke.

"Come here."

The child's eyes stayed fixed. Rossett knew the boy was willing him to go away, and Rossett wished that he could.

But he couldn't.

"Is that a kid?" Baker leaned over his shoulder, straining to see what was going on.

The little boy's wish wasn't going to come true; Rossett wasn't going away.

He'd been found.

CHAPTER 5

"**B**OY, COME." ROSSETT flicked an impatient finger toward the boy, who gave the slightest of jumps in response.

Rossett leaned in, grabbed the sacking, and pulled it clean away from the boy, who was wearing a duffel coat and Wellington boots that trapped his calves like flower stems in oversize flowerpots.

"Come on, now, out." Rossett grabbed a leg and the boy slithered back farther into the corner, eyes now shut, lips trembling, and hands pulling the coat up as far as it would go. Rossett was about to shout when Baker spoke softly behind him.

"Come on, sausage, we're the police. We won't hurt you."

The words hurt Rossett. The child opened his eyes and looked at the young bobby. "Come on, son, come out, please?"

Rossett realized he was crowding the space, and he nodded his head, motioning that he wanted to get out of the gap and into the room.

"Maybe he doesn't speak English, Sarge? Some of them refugees haven't had time to pick it up yet," said Baker once they had straightened up.

"My grandfather told me to wait for him." A tiny voice from the fireplace.

"We are the police, sunshine, you can trust us," replied Baker, bending forward to look into the gap again. The young bobby made Rossett feel impotent and unable to communicate, and he wiped his sooty hands together to clear off the dust. "Come on out and we'll clean you up and get you a cup of tea. How does that sound?"

"Is my grandfather there?" said the mouse, and the two policemen looked at each other, unable to lie to a child, but able to put him on a train to an uncertain future. "Can I see my grandfather?"

"He's gone ahead." Finally Rossett found his voice, but he was unable to look at the boy when he spoke.

"Gone where?"

"Ahead."

"Where?"

"Please, come out."

"I want my grandfather first."

Rossett turned to the window and looked out. In the street below he could see the inventory squad had arrived; they were unloading boxes from the back of the truck as they waited for their supervisor.

He turned to the young bobby and nodded toward the fireplace.

"Drag him out."

Baker nodded, got down on all fours, and disappeared into the gap. A moment later the child squealed as the bobby backed out dragging him by the leg above his Wellington. Rossett bent down to help pull the child, who was by now silent, farther out of the space and onto his feet.

Baker stood up and wiped down his uniform, then silently stood by the door, blocking any chance of a darting run by the child.

"What's your name?" Rossett asked, crouching down and wiping soot from the coat of the child, who didn't reply.

"Boy. What is your name?" This time more firmly.

The child stood, silent, head bowed, eyes closed, with the slightest tremble playing on his lips.

Rossett stood and turned to the tiny suitcase for clues, then turned back to the child again, leaning down.

"I knew your grandfather when I was your age," he said softly. "Me and my mother used to visit his shop." Rossett glanced at the bobby, who was diplomatically studying the palms of his hands and scratching at the soot. "He was a nice man. I liked him," Rossett whispered.

The child didn't look up, and Rossett sighed and wished he was better with children; it had been so long since he'd had to talk to a child, he'd forgotten how to.

He turned back to the case and tried the catch; it was locked.

"Do you have a key for this?" The child didn't respond, so Rossett fished in his coat and produced his penknife. It took him less than five seconds to release the flimsy lock. He lifted the lid and found a dirty shirt that had once been white, some undershirts and underpants, and a couple of pairs of well-darned socks.

At the bottom of the case were a few envelopes, written in an educated hand postmarked Amsterdam. Rossett took them out and opened one, glancing at the boy as he did so.

The boy stared back, indignant at the invasion of his privacy, his bottom lip jutting slightly.

Rossett unfolded one of the letters and turned it over, smelling it before reading the first page.

"My dearest, darling little Jacob," he said out loud. Without looking, he felt the boy stiffen. Another secret exposed, another layer peeled away.

He didn't read on. He placed the letters into his pocket, but as he was about to close the case, he noticed it felt heavier at one end. He rummaged through the clothes again until his hands brushed against something solid, chunky, and heavy. His hand closed around it, and, on pulling it free, he saw it was a sock with something stuffed inside. He tipped it out into the palm of his hand and a red suede pouch dropped out. He discarded the sock and, loosening the strings on the pouch, emptied some of its contents into the palm of his hand.

Gold sovereigns. The noise they made caused Baker to step forward from the door and look. He whistled lightly as he watched the shiny coins drop from Rossett's palm onto the folded clothes in the case.

"Cor blimey, must be a few bob there, Sarge." Rossett glanced back at Baker, who nodded and tilted his head toward the bounty. "We could have us a fine time with them lot."

Rossett picked up the coins and placed them back into the pouch. He fastened it tight and then stood, slipping the pouch into his pocket. He took the boy by the arm while picking up the small case with his other hand.

Suddenly back on duty.

"We could have a fine old time, Constable, but we aren't going to, because they aren't ours. Write up exactly what has happened here and then bring your notebook to me later so I can sign it and you can sign mine. I'm going to book this stuff into the found property system back at the nick."

"I was only joking, Sarge." Baker looked even younger than he was, exposed by the stickler everyone at the nick said Rossett was. "And what about the kid?"

"What about him?"

"Is he found property, too?"

Rossett looked at the young boy, who stared back, still angry over the letters.

"I suppose he is," said Rossett in a voice that sounded colder than he'd expected.

He pushed past Baker and led the boy down the stairs. At the front door he found the inventory team waiting for him. The other bobby he'd assigned to guard the front was blocking their entry. He glanced back at Rossett and then down to the boy.

"Who's this, then? Have you caught a tiddler?" The bobby ruffled Jacob's hair, but the child didn't respond.

"Let them in now, you're cleared to leave. Make sure you tell the lads around the back," replied Rossett. Looking outside to see who was leading the inventory team, his heart sank when he saw Gruber, the German civil servant who was often the lead man in these clearances.

Gruber was known for being a jobsworth. The story went he'd been banished from Berlin for a minor clerical error and that he was determined to never slip up again, in case his next posting took him closer to a front line and further from any chance of getting back to the Fatherland.

"Sergeant, we are running late, it is gone eight thirty o'clock!" the little German stuttered in broken English, as he folded the heavy ledger he was carrying and rushed toward the front door while pulling out a pocket watch and holding it up for Rossett to see. "My team have much of work to do today, this really won't do!" By now, Gruber was no longer looking at Rossett, but staring at the child.

Rossett noticed everyone was.

"I'm sorry, Herr Gruber, I had to make sure the house was completely clear, for your safety."

"What is this?" Gruber pointed at the child.

"He was hiding; it's nothing to worry about."

"Hiding? How many others are hiding?" Gruber stared past Rossett at the house and then back at the child.

"Nobody else is hiding, the house is clear now."

"The suitcase, is that the child's?" Gruber pointed again.

"It's just some spare clothes."

"It should be on the inventory. If it was in the house it should be on the inventory." Gruber held up the ledger as proof of his statement.

"It's just some clothes; it has no value."

"You found it in the house, it goes in the inventory. No exceptions," replied Gruber, holding out his hand for the case.

"It is my grandfather's case. He brought it with him when he came to this country." The boy spoke loudly, and both men turned to look at the waif with no small degree of surprise. "It is not yours, it is mine."

Gruber stared for a moment, dumbfounded, then held out his hand again.

"Sergeant, give me the case now."

Rossett sighed and held out the case to the German, who reached for it with a smile on his face. The boy suddenly pulled against Rossett and made a grab for the case.

"No! It is mine! No!"

Gruber leapt back as if a dog had suddenly snapped at him. He blushed, then stepped forward and struck the boy across the face in one fluid movement.

"*Juden shichzer!*" He reached for the case from an openmouthed Rossett, who still held the boy by the arm, and once again made to strike the boy with his open hand. Rossett turned slightly and pulled the boy behind him, shielding him from Gruber.

Rossett held up the case toward the German and glanced past him at the twelve-man inventory team, some of whom had taken a few paces forward, disturbed either by their boss's assaulting a child or maybe by Rossett's stopping him.

"Take the case, Herr Gruber. Of course, you are correct; it should go on the inventory." Rossett spoke quickly, trying to defuse the situation.

Gruber paused and looked at Rossett, slowly realizing that his behavior was drawing attention. He smoothed his jacket front and took the case.

"Thank you, Sergeant, we must do these things in the correct manner. It is important, always very important." The German took a step back, glancing at his team, most of whom turned away or looked at the floor. "My men should really get to work, if you are finished here?"

Rossett nodded and stepped aside, being careful to hold the boy away from the German in case the child saw fit to kick out.

Gruber entered the property and his men slowly followed him inside, some nodding to the boy, who once again looked downward. Rossett watched them file into the house, then led the boy to the Austin and sat him on the backseat before taking his place behind the wheel. He felt in his pocket for his notebook and realized he still had the sovereigns; he took the pouch out and thought about handing them to Gruber.

It would make his life easier to just get rid of them now. No chance of their going missing from the police safe if the German entered them into his inventory. A sharp tap on the window caused him to start, and for some reason he couldn't explain, his hand thrust the sovereigns out of sight into his coat. He looked across to the passenger window, where one of the inventory team was gesturing to him urgently to open the window.

Rossett leaned across and opened the door. As soon as there was space, the man thrust the case through the gap and onto the front seat.

"For the lad. Gruber won't notice. He tossed it onto a pile of stuff in the kitchen. Here, take it."

Before Rossett could speak, the door closed and the man was jogging back to the house. The boy leaned forward and took the case, pulling it over the seats and held it close to his chest.

Rossett turned to look at him, and the boy said,

"It was my father's. He gave it to me."

"If he gave it to you, it's yours now," Rossett replied, turning back to look out the windshield.

"Where are you taking me?"

"I don't know."

"I want to go with my grandfather."

"You can't."

"Why?"

"Because he is gone. Maybe you can catch up with him."

"Where has he gone?"

"I don't know."

"How do I know where I can catch up with him?"

"You don't."

"Who took him away?"

"I did."

"Where did you take him?"

"To catch a train."

"Where was the train going?"

"I don't know."

The boy sat silent for a while, confused by the conundrum of his missing grandfather.

Rossett started the car and crunched it into gear,

"Where are we going?" asked the boy, silent tears drowning his eyes.

"To the station."

"Where Grandfather got the train?" A little hope almost lost in his voice.

"Not that kind of station. A police station."

Rossett waited for the next question, but it didn't come, so he eased out the clutch and pulled away. The only sound from the back was the sniffle of tears, which embarrassed them both.

CHAPTER 6

ROSSETT PARKED THE Austin at the front of Wapping Police Station and looked up with some trepidation at the old building that faced onto the Thames. Since moving to Charing Cross he had been an infrequent visitor to his old nick. He retained a barely used office, and Brewer, his liaison inspector, was based there, but Rossett never felt welcome when he called.

He felt like an outsider, unwanted, an embarrassment. And, although he'd never say it out loud, that hurt him. He was banking on the Brits welcoming the child and treating him more fairly than the Germans in Charing Cross, with their sentries and swastikas.

Even he wouldn't subject the boy to that.

He stepped out onto the curb, then opened the rear door and dragged the child by the hand out of the backseat. He led him up the steps and into the busy inquiry office, where the sergeant on duty was arguing with an Irishman. Rossett stood waiting at the locked door that would grant him access into the police-staff-only area.

The sergeant on duty glanced across and then carried on with his argument, deliberately causing Rossett to wait, something Rossett noticed had started to happen more and more since he'd been working with the Germans. He sighed, allowed the sergeant his little victory for a moment or two, then impatiently rapped on the door with his free hand.

"Any chance someone can open this door, please?" shouted Rossett, interrupting the dispute, which had turned out to be about a stolen bicycle. The desk sergeant ambled across and disappeared momentarily, Rossett heard a click, and the door swung open.

"Apologies, Detective Sergeant, I never saw you hiding there." Rossett ignored the sergeant and pushed past. "New recruit to your department?" The inquiry sergeant scrubbed the boy's hair, but Jacob ignored him as he trailed behind Rossett.

The sergeant chuckled as he watched them pass and said to their retreating backs, "He'll fit right in with you, Rossett. He doesn't say much either."

On entering his office, Rossett took off his raincoat and inspected it for soot. It was showing the signs of age, and the marks he'd picked up in the fireplace merely blended in with already present scuffs and stains. He hung it on the back of his door, then reached into the pocket, removed the pouch of sovereigns, tossed the pouch into his desk drawer, and locked it.

He put his keys into his inside suit pocket, the one without the hole in it, and turned to face the boy, who was standing in the center of the office still looking down at the floor, suitcase clutched tight to his chest.

"Have you eaten?"

Jacob shook his head.

"Are you hungry?"

Jacob shook his head.

"When did you last eat?"

"Tuesday."

"Tuesday?" Rossett looked at his watch, even though it didn't have a date function, and then back at the boy. "You last ate two days ago?"

Jacob nodded.

"You must be starving."

Jacob just stared at the floor.

Rossett sat down behind his desk and studied the child. The old duffel coat he was wearing was slightly too big, but it was of good quality and probably bought for him to grow into. It was buttoned to the neck, and Rossett could see a bright green hand-knitted scarf peeking out from the collar. It was the kind of coat any boy in London would have worn to go to school, except for the fact that it had a crudely stitched star of David on its breast, almost hidden behind the clutched suitcase.

Jacob was wearing gray shorts that stopped short of the Wellingtons by four inches or so. Rossett guessed him to be under four feet tall and could see that he was well underweight for his height and age.

The boy's thick brown hair was shorn crudely at the back and sides, and his gray little face, all cheekbones and almond eyes, could almost have been that of an old man.

He made a sorry picture, and Rossett was aware that the boy smelled of damp.

"Look at me."

The boy looked up.

"How old are you?"

"I'm seven, nearly eight."

Rossett raised an eyebrow; he'd guessed the boy to be much younger.

"My grandfather says I will shoot up to be big and tall like my father soon."

"Where is your father?" Rossett asked, guessing he already knew the answer to the question.

"Men came one morning, men like you, and took him." The boy looked at the floor again.

"Look at me, boy."

Up came the little head again.

"Your mother, where is she?"

"She died."

"When?"

"Some time ago, I don't know, I was little." The boy bit his lip.

"You lived with your grandfather?"

"Yes."

The mix-up in tenses caused Rossett to take his turn at looking down. He guessed the boy's father had been a professional, maybe doctor or solicitor. They'd been the first to be cleared, especially if they had been young and fit. It occurred to him that it might not have been men "like"

Rossett; it might well have been Rossett himself who'd come calling that morning.

It puzzled him that the boy hadn't been on the inventory; the old man had hidden him well.

"Do you want something to eat?" Rossett broke the silence between them.

Jacob nodded. Rossett stood, took him by the arm, and led him through the station to the canteen.

As usual, space was cleared for him as he made his way through the nick. The only difference was that heads popped out of doorways once he had passed. People were curious to see the little boy with the star of David on his lapel clomping through the shiny-floored corridors in his oversized Wellingtons, holding the "Jew catcher's" hand.

They entered the canteen to find it half full of breakfasting coppers and civilians. It was noisy with chatter and the crash of cups and plates, and Rossett felt the boy shrink slightly in his grasp.

There were rows of long tables with a few smaller, square, wooden four-seater tables for sergeants and inspectors who didn't want to sit among the ranks.

Rossett normally sat alone at one of the square tables, facing the room so as to be able to see the comings and goings of the canteen. That would also give him some protection from the whispering that would take place behind his back. He sat the boy down at a small table and leaned down in front of him so as to speak face-to-face.

"I am going to the counter over there. Do not move from this seat. Do not think about running away. If you do, all of those policemen over there will catch you. And when they do, I will throw you in a dark cell with bad men until I can think of something really evil to do with you. Do you understand?"

The boy nodded and chewed his bottom lip.

"Say it; say 'I understand.'"

"I understand. I won't run away."

Rossett stared at the boy for a moment, ramming home the point, then nodded. He turned and walked to the nearby counter and ordered two teas and two breakfasts. While he waited he glanced across to the child, who, true to his word, was sitting still and staring intently at the tabletop, suitcase held like a shield across his chest. Rossett pondered what to do with him and silently cursed old Galkoff for putting him in this situation.

"Two teas." The lady behind the counter crashed the teas onto the worktop, managing to spill half of them in the process. Rossett nodded and made to pick them up. "If you want my advice, you give 'im some milk as well. Good for the little bones, see," she said, looking across to Jacob.

"I'll take some milk as well then."

The woman poured a glass and passed it across the counter.

"Some of 'em don't get enough now, what with it being rationed, bless 'em." Rossett offered some coins and she waved him away, saying, "I'll fetch the breakfast over when it's done, Sergeant." Rossett placed the money on the counter, ignoring her dismissal, then placed the drinks on a small tray and walked across to the boy.

He set the drinks down and slid the milk across first.

"Drink that, it's good for you."

The boy took the glass in both hands and drank the milk down quickly in almost one gulp. Rossett almost smiled when he saw the white mustache on the boy's top lip, but instead he slid a napkin across for him to wipe it away. The boy ignored the napkin. He licked his finger, wiped it across his top lip, then licked it clean.

"Do you want some more?"

The boy didn't reply, he merely looked down at the tabletop again, ashamed by his greed.

Rossett turned to glance around the canteen and saw the usual sudden swiveling of heads from people afraid to meet his gaze.

"Thank you."

Rossett turned to look at the boy.

"What?"

"Thank you for the milk."

"Uh, yes, well, it wasn't me; it was the lady behind the counter. She suggested it."

The boy nodded, face down to the table, the top of his head bobbing. Rossett turned back to the canteen again.

"Thank you for helping me." Rossett turned to look at the boy and this time found Jacob staring at him. Rossett nearly fell into his almond eyes.

"I . . . I'm . . . just doing my job."

The boy carried on staring until Rossett turned away. This time it was he who was avoiding someone's gaze in the canteen, a strange feeling and one that he didn't like.

The server arrived at the table with the breakfasts and another glass of milk.

"Here we go!" she said brightly. "Some growing-up juice and a lovely breakfast to warm you up!" She slid the plates off the tray and plonked the glass down in front of Jacob, who was shyly looking back down at the table. "Come on now, eat up! 'Ere, give me that case so the dog can see the rabbit!" She took the case from the boy, who gave it up more easily than he had done earlier that morning.

"Now then, would you like some hot buttered toast and—oh!" She stopped, frozen in midair as she was reaching for some butter to offer the boy. Rossett glanced at her and then back to the boy, confused by her shock.

"What is it?" he asked, looking down at the boy's plate and then his own.

"He's a Jew." This time she spoke quietly, conscious of the others in the canteen. "He shouldn't be here, Mr. Rossett. You of all people should know that." She looked around nervously and twisted the tea towel that was hooked into her apron.

"He's a child."

"I could get into so much trouble, Mr. Rossett. He'll have to go. I'm sorry." She paused. "I'm so sorry." This time she spoke to the boy, who looked from her to Rossett and then back again.

"Nobody is going to say anything about a child eating for ten minutes. Who are you going to get into trouble with?" Rossett leaned back in his chair, the frustration of an already stressful day becoming difficult to contain and his head starting to throb. He took out his cigarettes and slid them onto the table, a conscious statement declaring his intent to stay.

"Please, Mr. Rossett, I don't want to end up losing this job. People can cause such a fuss about these things; I have to be very careful now."

"Who is going to cause a problem for your serving food to a child? Who? Tell me who?" Rossett snatched the cigarette pack back up into his hands as he looked around the canteen, desperate for someone to point a finger at.

"You."

The accusation hung in the air between them; Rossett looked from the canteen lady to the boy, who was staring openmouthed right back at him.

"I wouldn't cause you a problem about something like this," he said quietly, confused.

The canteen lady twisted her apron some more and eventually shook her head and turned back to the counter.

Rossett watched her go and then turned to the boy, who was still staring back at him.

"Eat." Rossett gestured to the plate as he fumbled the cigarette packet open, his own appetite defeated by his twisted stomach and his banging head.

The boy's head dropped again, but Rossett was relieved to see him pick up some toast and slide a tomato onto it. Rossett turned away from the table and scanned the room again; this time a few dared to look him in the eye for a moment, so he turned back to the boy and lit a cigarette. He watched the boy for a while as he nibbled at the tomato and toast, and considered his options.

He needed to get rid of the child as soon as possible. There was no hope of catching the train. He wasn't even certain where it would be unloading. He'd always just assumed it was Dover, but even if he found that out for certain, he'd have to establish if there was some sort of holding camp or whether the boat was waiting and ready to sail straightaway.

He checked his watch: nine forty. Maybe he could drive the boy to Dover and reunite him with old Galkoff, but it didn't take him long to dismiss that option. It was a long journey that might prove fruitless. He drew deep on his cigarette, watching the boy, then imagined staring the old man in the face as he pushed the child toward him.

He shook his head and picked up his mug of tea, rubbing his forehead with the hand that held the cigarette.

I wonder when I became a coward? Rossett thought to himself as he watched the boy eat mushrooms one by one with his fork, chewing them carefully while staring straight down at the plate, as if he was scared to look away in case the food ran off.

"The boy shouldn't be eating that." A voice from behind. Rossett swiveled angrily in his chair to confront this latest busybody, only to find Koehler. The German stepped closer to the table, reached across, and picked up the boy's plate. Jacob looked up, watching it go.

"This is pig," Koehler held up a thin sausage with his fingers and studied it, wrinkling his nose. "Well, at least some of it is. The boy is Jewish; he shouldn't be eating this."

"I wasn't going to eat it. I was eating the other things, not the sausage," Jacob said, staring longingly at the plate and then at Koehler, who smiled, took a bite out of the sausage, and put the plate back down.

"Eat the egg," said Koehler softly, like a father, as he pulled a seat from an adjacent table and sat down opposite Rossett immediately to the boy's right. Rossett watched as Koehler dipped the sausage into the egg and took another bite. He then looked back at Rossett and shook his head.

"You've got yourself a problem, John." Koehler spoke quietly as he chewed.

"The boy was hidden. His grandfather told me where he was as he got onto the train. By the time I'd found him the train had gone. How did you . . . ?"

"Gruber telephoned me. That prick isn't going to let anything happen without letting me know," Koehler replied. He looked toward Rossett's uneaten breakfast and, taking the cue, Rossett slid the plate toward him. Koehler picked up the sausage and placed the plate between himself and the boy, gesturing for the boy to help himself.

"What are we going to do about you, little piggy?" Koehler turned to the boy. "What is your name?"

"Jacob," the boy replied brightly to his new friend, and Rossett blushed, realizing that he hadn't used the boy's name once.

"What are we going to do about Jacob?" Koehler took another bite of sausage and looked again at Rossett.

"I haven't decided; I thought maybe downstairs?" Rossett didn't want to mention the cells by name. He was certain Koehler would understand what he meant and would realize he didn't want to scare the child further.

Rossett took another drag on his cigarette and then tapped it against the ashtray, even though it didn't need it.

Koehler nodded. "It's an idea. There is another train due on Sunday; it wasn't scheduled for a collection, but it will be refueling. I can arrange for the boy to be on it."

"Will I get to see my grandfather then?" said Jacob, his mouth full, staring up at Koehler.

"Of course, you will," Koehler replied, lying smoothly without the slightest hint of deceit in his voice. "Sergeant Rossett will arrange everything for you. He can even drive you to the station if you would like?"

Jacob nodded, and Koehler looked across to Rossett. "It is the least the sergeant can do for you, isn't it?"

Rossett nodded dumbly at the boy before stubbing his cigarette out into the ashtray.

"Yes."

"You see, little piggy? Uncle John has solved all your problems!" Koehler spoke to Jacob but looked at Rossett. He dipped again at the egg and leaned forward, resting his elbow on the table and beckoning Rossett in closer. "Is everything all right, John?"

Rossett suddenly regretted stubbing out the cigarette and looked at it before shrugging.

"Yes."

"Are you sure? You look tired."

"I am tired."

"This is hard work we do; it can drain you if you're not careful."

Rossett nodded but didn't speak.

"If there was a problem you'd tell me, wouldn't you? As well as being your boss, I like to think we are friends. We are friends, aren't we?"

"Yes . . . we are."

Koehler stared at Rossett, letting the silence run long and do its job.

"I have dreams," Rossett heard himself saying.

"Dreams?" Koehler replied quietly.

"Nightmares."

"About what?"

Rossett shifted in his chair and pulled his tie slightly before picking up the cigarettes again. He noticed Jacob was watching him, slowly chewing, curious. Rossett pulled at his tie knot again, then opened the cigarettes and took one out.

"They are . . . they . . . they stop me sleeping."

Koehler nodded. "All soldiers have nightmares, John."

"I sometimes see faces, the faces of the people we send away." Rossett looked at Jacob and then back to Koehler, who leaned back in his chair and folded his arms. "They crowd me."

Koehler rubbed his mouth with one hand and frowned, looking for words, before leaning forward again.

"Our job is . . . difficult. What we do has to be done. We don't have to like it but we have to do it. Because, if we don't . . . well . . . I think you understand?" Koehler whispered and tilted his head at the end of the sentence, making sure Rossett realized what he was saying. "I don't want to treat these people like this; they aren't animals. But if we falter, if we lose our drive, others will take our place, and that won't be good for anyone involved. Not you, not me, and not the Jews." Koehler's voice was barely a breath.

Rossett nodded and put the unlit cigarette in his mouth.

"I understand." He said, making the cigarette bob.

"Good. Try not to think too much, John. It isn't good for you."

"No."

"Is there anything else?"

"No."

"Good. That is all arranged then." Koehler brightened and slapped his thighs, then stood up. He buttoned his coat while looking around the room. "Make sure you eat all of your breakfast, Jacob. I want that plate to be clean, yes?"

Jacob nodded and picked up some toast. Koehler smiled back at him and made to walk away from the table. As he passed Rossett, he paused and placed his hand on his shoulder, bowing slightly as he spoke softly.

"Oh, by the way, there was nothing else left in the house, was there?"

"No, just the boy." Rossett stared up at Koehler, who was still looking around the canteen. His heart pounded and he was certain the German must have felt its percussion through his shoulder.

"And his suitcase, of course."

"Yeah, the boy and his case, that was all."

"Gruber mentioned he had taken the case from the boy."

"He did."

"But Jacob has it here?" Koehler looked down at Rossett now, his hand still in place on his shoulder.

"The boy needed it. It has his clothes."

"Of course. Gruber is such a . . . what is the word?" Koehler carried on looking around the around the room as he searched for it. "Jobsworth. Gruber is such a jobsworth. Every detail has to be checked and double-checked."

Rossett nodded, unsure of what to say.

"Men like me and you fight to create empires. Men like Gruber, they make sure we keep them."

"Yes."

"Well, as long as there is nothing else you need to tell me?"

"No, there is nothing else."

"Good. I'll be on my way then." Koehler tapped Rossett on the shoulder and smiled at Jacob. "Good-bye, Jacob."

"Good-bye, sir."

"Good-bye, Sergeant."

"Bye."

Koehler walked away, his shoes clicking on the lino floor as he made his way through the benches on his way to the door. Rossett listened to the sound fade away and eventually realized he was holding his breath. He sighed, leaned back into the chair, and put his unlit cigarette into the pack again. He twisted and turned the packet in his hand on the table.

He blew out his cheeks and put the packet down again, drumming his fingers on it, thinking about the coins in his desk. The moment had passed for him to enter them into the property system. He'd had two chances to mention them to the Germans and both times he'd shied away from it, for reasons he wasn't entirely sure of himself.

I can book them as found property next week, he thought. I'll make up a story about their being found in a pub or something. It was flimsy, but it would ensure that they didn't have to stay in his desk for longer than was necessary.

Problem solved.

His stomach lurched and his fingers started to drum again as he remembered Baker, the young bobby he'd been with when he'd found the boy. He sighed out loud and rested his head in his hand. The boy stopped eating and looked at him.

"Are you all right?"

Rossett looked up at the little face through his fingers and nodded. "I've just remembered something I had to do."

"Was it important?"

"Very."

"Maybe we can do it now?"

"It's too late now."

"Will you get into trouble?"

This time Rossett didn't reply, he just stared at the boy and sighed once more.

"My grandfather says that if you do something wrong it is best to just be honest and tell someone what you have done. He says that if you are always honest, you will not be punished."

"What your grandfather tells you is true, most of the time."

"But not this time."

"No, not this time."

CHAPTER 7

BY THE TIME Jacob had finished eating, Rossett had smoked two more cigarettes and drunk another cup of tea. He had taken the boy by the hand and walked him through the station, aware that even more people were watching as they passed. Word must have got around that the boy was a Jew and had sat eating in the canteen with the men who were supposed to be making sure he wasn't seen again. Once Koehler had visited it would have flashed through the whole station like wildfire.

He'd originally planned to take the boy straight down to the jail but had decided to put it off for as long as possible. Rossett knew what it was like to sit on your own in a cell, how long it took for time to pass as you stared at the four walls. It was Thursday, so that meant Jacob would have three days of staring at those walls if all went according to plan. Rossett figured the longer he could put it off, the better it would be for the boy.

As he walked toward his office his heart sank to see his door was open. He knew he'd closed it, and the sudden thought that Koehler was in there and had opened the desk and found the coins filled him with a sickening dread. His step faltered, and Jacob glanced up as Rossett patted his jacket feeling for his desk keys. He felt them rattle but took little solace from the sound. How hard would it be to open the desk? He could do it with a spoon if he put his mind to it.

He guessed the German wouldn't be so subtle.

"Are you all right?"

"I'm fine," replied Rossett, disappointed that he'd given away his feelings so easily to the child again.

"Is it the thing you forgot to do?"

"Yes."

They entered his office and Rossett found Inspector Brewer seated at his desk. Rossett's eyes flicked to his drawer and saw it was closed. Brewer got to his feet as soon as Rossett entered and charged around the desk past Rossett to the door.

"What the hell do you think you are doing, Sergeant?"

"Sir?" Rossett watched as Brewer stuck his head out and checked the corridor before slamming the door shut and turning to face him.

"You know what." He pointed at Jacob. "This! What do you think you are playing at? Bringing a bloody Jew here?"

"I wasn't sure what else to do with him."

"Do what you always do, man! Stick him on the bloody train and wash your hands of him! Christ al-bloody-mighty, Rossett, this job is already sensitive enough without you bringing bloody Jews here!"

"The train had gone, sir." Rossett was uncomfortable with Jacob holding his hand; he gestured for the boy to take a seat in the corner on a small wooden chair.

"Don't make him bloody comfortable, man! Get him in the bloody cells! You've already fed and watered him from what I've heard."

"I need to arrange a cell for him, sir. I was going to call down to speak to the jail first, as a courtesy."

"A jail?" It was Jacob, his eyes confused, looking up at Rossett. "Are you putting me into prison? I haven't been naughty." The bottom lip trembled again.

"No—well, yes, but not like you think, it's just somewhere to sleep until—"

"I don't want to go to prison." Jacob's words tailed off, like feathers falling to the floor. Rossett put his hand onto the boy's shoulder and knelt in front of him.

"It will be okay. It's not really a prison, it's—"

"For Christ's sake, Rossett!" Brewer exploded. "Just bang him up and get on with your job!"

A shadow appeared through the frosted glass of the office door, followed by a polite tap. All in the room fell silent and looked nervously at the shadow, like three conspirators caught in a trap.

Eventually, Rossett stood and opened the door to find PC Baker. Rossett stared at the bobby, who stared back, notebook in hand.

"Sorry to bother you, Sarge." He glanced over Rossett's shoulder at Brewer, who was standing red-faced behind him. "I can come back later if needs be."

"No, erm . . ." Rossett searched for his name.

"Baker, Sarge."

"Of course, of course, Baker, what do you want?"

"My notebook, Sarge. You wanted to sign it, so as to confirm what we found when we searched—"

"Of course. Yes, give it here." Rossett spoke quickly, panicked, and snatched Baker's notebook out of his hand.

"Sergeant, can't this wait?" Brewer sputtered, barely able to contain himself, but anxious not to have a bobby gossiping about him and Rossett.

"I can come back, Sarge, if it suits?"

Rossett ignored them both, scanning the pages of densely written copperplate. He inwardly cursed Baker's thoroughness when he reached the part about the coins.

I witnessed Det Sgt Rossett remove some gold colored coins from a green pouch and let them fall into the case, the DS then collected the fallen money and placed it back into the pouch, which he then put in his coat. I do not know the exact amount of coins, which looked like golden sovereigns, but I would estimate that the pouch was five inches long and it appeared to be almost full. I did not see the coins again after the Sergeant took them.

Rossett read the notes again. On paper it looked as if he had pocketed the pouch. Had he been alone with Baker he would have taken some time to explain that this made him look bad and that maybe another paragraph should be added explaining that he'd asked Baker to make a detailed pocket notebook entry. He dared not mention this while Brewer was there; those coins were quickly becoming a curse, and he was aware that it was now three people he'd hidden them from.

It would have been easier to split them with Baker at the scene, thought Rossett as he fumbled for a pen.

It appeared being a bent copper was easier than being a straight one.

"That's fine, Baker." Rossett signed the notebook entry; his signature sealed his fate if anyone asked later where the coins had gone. He just had to hope that Baker would keep his nose out and not mention them to anyone. He passed the notebook back to Baker, who hesitated before leaving; he cast a glance at Jacob and then Brewer.

"I enjoyed working with you, Sarge," Baker said. "If there is ever anything else I can help you with, just say. It makes a change from walking the beat."

"I will, thank you." Rossett took hold of the door handle and gestured for Baker to leave. The bobby nodded, then turned, and as he passed, Rossett noticed him glance at Jacob and wink.

Rossett closed the door and turned to face the inspector, who appeared to have calmed slightly.

"Just get this whole thing sorted out, Rossett; I don't want any of this coming back to land on my toes. Do you understand?"

"It won't, sir. I've already spoken to Koehler. He—"

"Koehler knows?"

"He was just in the canteen, sir."

"I don't want to hear anymore. Just get rid of the Jew before anyone else becomes involved."

"I will, sir."

"We'll have bloody Hitler here next." Brewer stepped past him and opened the door; he turned to look at Jacob. "Your lot are more trouble than they're worth." Jacob didn't look up, so Brewer looked at Rossett.

"You've done a good job keeping me out of these matters in the past, Sergeant. Make sure you keep doing that, understand?"

"Sir."

Brewer left the room, and Rossett sat down on the edge of his desk.

"I don't want to go to prison," said Jacob, causing Rossett to look up. "I could have stayed in the fireplace."

"I know," replied Rossett, shaking his head, "but it's too late to put you back there now."

"Because of your job?"

"Yes."

Jacob played with his fingertips awhile and then looked up at Rossett.

"I have bad dreams too."

"What?" Rossett roused himself again.

"I have bad dreams, like you."

Rossett looked at the door and then back toward Jacob, unsure what he was supposed to say.

"I can't find my mother. I'm lost and I don't know where she is. I can hear voices, but I don't remember what she sounds like so I don't know if it is her."

"They're just dreams."

"That's what Grandfather says."

"He's right."

"It's just . . ."

"What?"

"When I wake up, I think for a moment she is still alive; and then I remember she isn't, and I'll never see her again."

CHAPTER 8

"**WHAT'S HE DONE?**" The custody sergeant leaned over his high counter and peered down at Jacob, who was craning his neck up to return the gaze.

"Nothing. I've told you, he hasn't done anything."

"Well, he's not going in my cells then."

"Bernie, please, I have to lodge him somewhere, and at least here I can keep an eye on him."

"If he hasn't done anything he isn't going in my cells."

"It's just till Sunday, Bernie. Come on, help out an old pal?"

Bernard Clark leaned back from the counter and crossed his arms over his fat stomach. Rossett didn't speak. He'd let the old man have his moment of power and hope the big old sergeant would give in and let Jacob be lodged in one of the two youth cells behind the counter.

"Why can't you take him home with you?"

"You know why."

"No, I don't."

"You do." Rossett didn't want to point out the obvious, although he couldn't understand whether that was for Jacob's benefit or his own.

"I don't."

Rossett leaned forward onto the counter and beckoned for the sergeant to come forward so he could whisper; his heart sank when Clark merely raised an eyebrow and cocked his head.

Rossett was regretting this idea more and more as time went on.

"Bernie, look, as a favor to an old mate, just let him sleep here a few days; I'll sort out his food and exercise. If you want, I'll take him out of a day and keep him in my office. Just let him stay here of a night; I can't have him all the time."

"Why can't he go home with you?"

Finally, Rossett's patience gave way. "Because he's a Jew." He immediately regretted what he'd said and quickly looked around him. A few heads of passing bobbies turned to look at him, and he, in turn, looked down to Jacob, who shamed him by staring back and tilting his head.

"If he is a Jew, why don't you ask your mates in the SS to let him stay in their cells over at Charing Cross?"

"They aren't my mates, and you know they aren't."

"Are you sure?" Clark eyed the tiny Nazi-party badge on Rossett's lapel. Rossett subconsciously reached his right hand up to touch it and then smoothed down his suit jacket front.

"You know it wouldn't be right sending him to Charing Cross, Bernie; it's no place for a child."

"You've sent enough people there, Rossett. One more won't make a difference. Besides, wherever he is being sent on Sunday will be worse, I'll wager." The custody sergeant picked up his mug again and this time risked a sip.

Rossett stared up at Clark and swallowed hard.

"I could make life very difficult for you, Bernie," he said, aware now that quite a few people had gathered to witness his humiliation. His cheeks burned, not with embarrassment but with anger. "You are making this hard for the child, not for me. I hope you are proud of yourself."

Clark stood up, collected a clipboard off his desk, and theatrically pulled a pen out of his tunic pocket before stepping down from behind the high counter. He walked around to stand side on to Rossett, who hadn't moved. Clark leaned in close to Rossett's ear and, for the first time during their exchange, lowered his voice so that only Rossett could hear him.

"I'm not making it hard for the child, mate." Then a little closer. "You are, you bastard."

Rossett turned his head to look at Clark; he'd known the man the best part of ten years. All that was forgotten right at that moment. None of it mattered.

He tried to think of a reply, looking into the face of Clark, who waited, expectantly, rocking on his toes.

Nothing came.

Clark shook his head and walked off to the cells to carry out his rounds, leaving Rossett and Jacob standing before an empty desk.

Rossett looked down at Jacob, who was also watching Clark walk away, his tiny suitcase resting at his feet. After a moment, Jacob turned to look up at Rossett.

"What did he mean, it'll be worse for me on Sunday?" said Jacob, with that furrowed brow again.

"Pick up your case and come with me," Rossett replied, already turning and leaving the jail.

CHAPTER 9

WHEN THE SS had arrived in London back at the start of the occupation, they had immediately chosen several stations that suited their purposes and evicted the local Met Police within hours. Over time they had fortified these stations, and some had become small self-contained garrisons and jails rolled into one.

Charing Cross was one such place. Situated on Agar Street, the station was ideal because of the narrowness of the road outside the front entrance, which allowed them to set up barriers and sentry points at either end. The small triangular courtyard at the rear of the station also ensured privacy for the loading and unloading of prisoners.

It was a perfect location for the SS and Gestapo HQ in London.

Most useful of all was the small cell complex situated in the basement of the building, far enough from prying eyes or ears to provide discretion, but close enough to central London for convenience.

The buildings that backed onto the courtyard had all been requisitioned as admin offices, and most of the back windows that overlooked the yard had been either blacked out or boarded up to ensure privacy.

Rumors of occasional volleys of gunfire coming from the yard on Sunday mornings were mostly dismissed as resistance propaganda by those whose wage packet carried the imprint of the Nazi eagle.

The times required the judicious use of the blind eye and the shut mouth.

Koehler had offices on the third floor of Charing Cross, and Rossett had had cause to visit on many occasions to attend briefings and meetings. "A little piece of Germany," Koehler had said as they walked out into Agar Street one morning, and Rossett had had to agree. As he had looked up at the red swastika banners that hung from the building's eaves to the ground-floor windows, with black-clad sentries springing to attention, rifle butts cracking on the pavement, and German staff cars blocking the narrow road, it felt closer to Berlin than Brixton.

Today, as he pulled up at the sentry point in the Austin, it felt more like Germany than ever. A military brass band had formed up outside the station entrance and the barrier guards were in full dress uniform, a contrast from their normal caps and battle dress. Rossett wound down his window and cursed as it reached halfway, then fell at an angle into the door panel, dislodged from its runner again.

The young SS man leaned down, smirked at the crooked window's position, then frowned at Rossett as he looked into the car. Rossett showed his warrant card and the sentry flicked a cursory eye at it, and then looked across at Jacob, who was craning to look at the band.

"What do you want?" He was asking Rossett but looking at Jacob.

"I need to see Major Koehler; it's about the boy."

"Today is a bad day. It's the anniversary of the Beer Hall Putsch, that's why the band's here. You'll have to park somewhere else and walk back if you want to go in." The German turned away in that time-honored fashion favored by guards who only dealt in black and white and brooked no questions.

Rossett swore, jabbed the little car into reverse, and backed out onto Chandos Place, looking for a space among the Mercedes staff cars that were parked all around. The Austin found a home, and after wrestling with his window, Rossett finally alighted. Taking Jacob by the hand, he walked back to the sentry post.

He waved his warrant card at the sentry, who merely stared at him as he ducked under the barrier and walked toward the front entrance to the HQ.

As they walked, the band struck up a tune he didn't recognize, and a group of uniformed and nonuniformed dignitaries walked out of the building and took up their places on the steps, blocking the entrance.

To avoid pushing through, Rossett decided to wait. He led the boy some distance from the door and found a place among the assembled office workers and SS men who had come out to listen to the band and the long speeches that Rossett guessed were bound to follow.

A group of secretaries parted to let them stand near the railings, away from the front of the crowd. Jacob leaned forward to look at the band, twisting on the end of Rossett's arm. The boy's head bobbed as he tried to see through the adults gathered around him. Eventually, one of the secretaries glanced down and then, smiling at Rossett, took the boy's hand and led him to the curbside so he could better see what was going on.

Rossett thought about protesting but instead took out another cigarette and cadged a light from a blonde who smiled and allowed her gaze to linger a little longer than was polite before looking downward with a flicker of eyelash. He drew on the cigarette and studied the blonde out of the corner of his eye. She looked familiar, and he remembered seeing her in Koehler's office. He wondered for a moment if he still was attractive to women. He was only thirty-five, still lean, a little over six foot, and his face, aside from an old scar under his left eye, uncreased.

It seldom occurred to him that he missed a woman's company; he had Mrs. Ward for his household needs, such as they were. There were times when he thought about another relationship, some nights, long nights, lonely nights of drinking, when he wished he had someone who loved him to tell him to stop.

But he didn't.

He just drank alone with his pain, his memories, and his loss.

He shivered and dragged on the cigarette, then took it out of his mouth and studied it. He noticed the yellowing of his fingers from the nicotine and wondered when that had started to happen.

The band was in full swing, or as close to swing as a brass band could get. He sighed and looked at his watch: almost midday. This was taking too long. He had work to do, a report to write regarding the morning's raid, then a meeting in the East End with a rabbi about some resettlement plans.

He didn't have time for this. He looked toward the band impatiently.

"We still have the speeches to come. You've picked a bad day." Rossett turned to find the blonde had made her way to stand closer to him, her voice husky after too many cigarettes, with the barest hint of a northern accent hovering around the edges. She smiled, having to shout over the noise of the band bouncing off the buildings opposite. "Unless you like brass bands and boring speeches, that is."

"I didn't know there was a parade on today. I would have waited," Rossett replied, ignoring her joke.

"Are you here to see Sturmbannführer Koehler?"

"I am." Rossett was unused to hearing Koehler given his full title. The German favored a less formal approach in conversation and was also fond of using the army rank of major instead of the slightly more ostentatious SS rank.

He'd once told Rossett his title "scared the English into silence," and Rossett had nodded, silently agreeing.

"I've seen you come and go a few times. I manage his outer office. You're Detective Sergeant Rossett, aren't you?" She smiled and Rossett found himself awkwardly smiling back, surprised that the girl was flirting with him and not really sure how to deal with it.

"I am."

"I'm Kate; we've spoken on the phone." Kate had grown tired of shouting and was leaning closer to Rossett, her hand touching his arm. Rossett looked down at her hand and then back into her eyes. She added, "I'm Major Koehler's personal secretary. You remember me?"

Rossett noticed one of the other secretaries turn and wink at Kate, who smiled back. He had a sudden feeling he was being ambushed. A man in a suit shushed Kate with a finger to his lips. Rossett felt a curious bubble of irritation at the man rise and then subside. Kate frowned, placed her hand on Rossett's shoulder, and stood on tiptoe as she spoke, lips close to his ear, pulling him toward her.

"I was wondering, maybe you could show me around London some-time? I don't get to see much of it, so much work and being a single girl working for Jerry and all." She dropped back and smiled, waiting for Rossett's reply.

Rossett had felt a butterfly flit across his stomach as her lips brushed his ear, and he looked down at the girl. It was the second time that day someone had been that close, and he knew which occasion he had pre-ferred.

"I, er . . ." was all he could manage initially, and Kate tilted her head as she waited for him to find his voice. "I suppose I could. I'm not really the best at . . ."

Kate smiled, deal done. She fished in her handbag and produced a card like a magician.

"My number." Rossett looked down at the card, unsure if he should take it. He looked up to see Kate frowning.

"If you don't want to?" This time she looked small and sad, and Ros-sett marveled at the woman's charms. "If there's someone else . . ."

"No, it'll be a pleasure," he replied, doubting any such meeting would ever take place but too much of a coward to say it out loud.

"Excellent!" She reached up inside Rossett's raincoat and placed the card in the outside breast pocket of his suit jacket, patting the pocket as she closed his raincoat. She smiled at him, her hand still resting intimately on his chest, then suddenly broke away and pointed to the curbside where Jacob was standing; the other secretary was crouching behind him, one hand on his shoulder, pointing to the band while she whispered in his ear. The little boy was smiling and Rossett noticed that the suitcase was swinging in time with the music.

"Your little boy is enjoying himself. Have you brought him to have a look around the HQ?"

Rossett didn't know what to say. He looked first at Kate and then back to Jacob. His eyes were then drawn to two men watching him, on the far side of the road.

Gestapo. He vaguely remembered them from a briefing a few months back. One of them had traveled with Koehler to a clearance job out in

Romford. They'd never spoken, but he suddenly had the feeling they were about to.

"He's not my little boy." Rossett turned to Kate. "I shouldn't have brought him. I'd better go. Can you tell Major Koehler I'll call him later today?"

"Of course, but you will call me as well, won't you?" She smiled and Rossett felt himself blush. He looked across the road and was dismayed to see the Gestapo walking toward him; they must have realized he was about to leave.

"Of course, soon."

"Do you promise?"

"Yes." Another glance to the Gestapo.

"What is your first name? Everyone just calls you Rossett; I don't know your first name."

"I have to go." Rossett looked at her blue eyes and found that was all he could say. He started to push his way forward to get to Jacob to take him back to the car, looking back to Kate with a smile of apology, already regretting leaving the conversation on such an awkward note. Kate looked confused, and she tilted her head and looked past his shoulder to where Jacob was standing. Rossett followed her gaze and saw the secretary and Jacob being spoken to by the Gestapo. Rossett approached them and produced his warrant card.

"Is there a problem?" he said as the first Gestapo officer looked at the card and then turned back to the secretary, dismissing him without a word.

"*Sie haben einen Jude hierher gebracht?*" "You've brought a Jew here?"

The secretary looked surprised and then a little frightened. Rossett leaned in to try to take Jacob.

"*Ich wusste nicht, daß er Jude war.*" The girl seemed panicked, and her hand withdrew from Jacob's shoulder in a flash, as if the boy was suddenly hot to the touch.

Rossett understood what she was saying in her clumsy English-accented German: "I didn't know he was a Jew."

The secret policeman pulled Jacob toward him and pointed at the star of David on his breast pocket.

"Sind Sie blind? Haben Sie nicht sehen?" "Are you blind? Did you not see?" The Gestapo man jabbed his finger into the star and Jacob looked scared, almost close to tears. The secretary looked across to Rossett and pointed.

"Er hat ihn gebracht, hat mit mir nichts zu tun!" "He brought him; it is nothing to do with me!" Rossett could barely understand her broken German.

The small crowd, who were watching the incident with more interest than they were giving the band, turned toward Rossett, who took another step forward to put his hand on Jacob's shoulder, pulling the boy toward him defensively. He showed his warrant card again with his other hand, like a matador attempting to distract a bull.

"Wer zum Teufel sind Sie?" "Who the devil are you?"

The other man pulled back at Jacob, yanking the child from Rossett's grasp. Jacob cried out and looked at Rossett with frightened eyes. Rossett found himself taking another step forward. He gripped the Gestapo officer's coat lapel and started to ease him back, with his fist pushing firmly into the other man's collarbone. Rossett's other hand twisted into Jacob's duffel coat hood, and he almost lifted the boy off his feet as he pulled him away from the Gestapo officer's grasp.

"He's with me, nothing to do with you. He's my prisoner," Rossett said flatly, sounding matter-of-fact even though his mind was racing.

The German tried to pull away from Rossett but was unable to. He yanked on Rossett's forearm but found it to be like an iron bar, unbending and ensuring that he couldn't reach the boy. The German then tried to reach with his right hand into his pocket. Rossett, seeing this, yanked down on the leather collar of the coat, forcing the German to fold sideways and fumble, off balance, reaching for Rossett's arm again. The second Gestapo officer tried to move around his colleague to reach Rossett but struggled to get past, mostly because of Rossett's pulling and twisting the first German as a shield, in much the same way a rugby player would use a defender to push his way through a maul.

"Lassen Sie mich los!" "Let go of me!" the German shouted as Rossett took a few more steps backward, trying to get through the crowd and back to the railings, Jacob still held in his other hand.

The people on the pavement seemed to part as he moved. Rossett heard raised voices and a woman's scream as he dragged the struggling Gestapo officer along. Rossett's face remained calm, a policeman's professionalism masking the creeping realization that he had hold of a Gestapo collar in front of SS headquarters.

This day was getting worse and worse, and Rossett wasn't expecting the situation to improve in the near future.

It didn't; the air swooshed out of his lungs as the German sentry he'd spoken to earlier smashed a rifle butt into his kidneys from behind. Rossett's brain started to shut down as he tried to turn to face the source of the blow to his back and also keep hold of the Gestapo man.

Bang!

The rifle butt slammed in again, and this time his legs crumpled and he sank to his knees. The Gestapo officer pulled free and produced a pistol from his pocket, which he leveled at Rossett's head. The thought crossed Rossett's mind for the briefest of moments that he was about to be shot as around him the crowd were yelping and pushing each other to get as far away as they could.

He realized he'd lost his grip on Jacob, and he searched, head spinning, tunnel vision setting in, trying to rise up from where he crouched on all fours on the pavement, trying to swallow down the pain in his kidneys, and, most important, trying not to get shot.

He looked back to the Gestapo man, who was regaining some composure now that he had a pistol in his hand.

"Nehmen Sie diesen Mann fest."

"I don't speak German." Rossett was blowing hard, the air slowly returning to his lungs. "I'm fucking English, you Kraut."

CHAPTER 10

THE INTERVIEW ROOM had hardly changed in the ten or twelve years since Rossett had last visited. The only thing different, as far as he could tell, was the shade of nicotine yellow the ceiling had turned. It wasn't lost on him that last time he had been there he'd been sitting on the other side of the table, where now an empty seat waited for whoever was going to ask him some questions.

Rossett imagined himself sitting there all those years ago, fresh faced, except for the bloodied dressing, and still in uniform. He'd arrested a man who'd stabbed a bookie on the Old Kent Road one night after a dispute about some winnings. He thought back to the chase that had taken place after he'd come across the two fighting. He'd had to run for almost a mile and a half through midnight streets before finally catching the bloke and disarming him, but not before he had his face sliced open by a well-handled shiv.

He touched his cheek and ran his finger along the scar, remembering how the girls in the dance halls used to love it, the air of danger and excitement it implied, the bad boy chasing them around the dance floor.

He thought about Lucy, his wife. He saw her eyes again, playfully smiling at him from across the dance floor the first time, holding his gaze and making his stomach flip and the scar redden even more as his cheeks flushed.

He wondered what Lucy would say to him now.

He wondered what that young bobby would say to him now.

Then he remembered that they were both dead.

The door opening dragged him back from the past and into the room. It was with no small amount of relief that he saw Koehler enter. The German was in full dress uniform, Rossett guessed for the parade; it struck him that he'd never seen Koehler in uniform before. Rossett sat back in the chair away from the table and stared at Koehler, who closed the door behind him and leaned against it, sticking his hands in his trouser pockets.

"What were you thinking?" Koehler spoke softly, shaking his head.

"He's just a child. I didn't want the Gestapo getting involved."

"He's just a Jew. You could have been shot."

"Those bastards would have thrown him in a cell."

"What did you bring him here for? To listen to the band?" Koehler tilted his head. Rossett sighed and ran his hand through his hair.

"Yeah, fair enough. You're right," he said by way of surrender. "I was stupid. I'm sorry."

Koehler stepped away from the door and took the seat opposite Rossett.

"Stupid Englishman, give me a cigarette."

Rossett fumbled in his coat, produced a pack, and slid them across with some matches. Koehler lit up and blew smoke out of his nose as he waved the match out. He slid the cigarettes back and stared at Rossett for a moment before speaking.

"I'll speak with Schmitt, explain about the good work you do for us."

"Schmitt?"

"You met him this morning; he's the new head of Gestapo. We'll put down this incident to a misunderstanding about a prisoner. I'll tell him you didn't know who they were and that you thought they were trying to take your prisoner away, to rescue him."

"Where is Jacob?"

"You need to stop worrying about the Jew and you need to listen to me. You have to remember, Rossett, that you have been chosen to do a very important job for the Reich. A job which you have been doing very well, until today, of course. I warn you, another day like today would go very badly for you. Upsetting the Gestapo never goes well for anybody. Do you understand?"

Rossett nodded.

"You will need to write a letter to apologize to Schmitt, and maybe one to the station commandant as well, just to smooth things over. He wasn't best pleased that the band stopped playing to watch you get dragged up the steps of the station, even if the rest of us were."

Rossett smiled, despite himself, and was relieved to see Koehler smile back.

"I'll write them as soon as I get back to the office."

"No, you take the rest of the afternoon off. In fact, take tomorrow, as well."

"I've too much to do. I can't."

"You can. You have to. It's an order. You're working too hard, Rossett. This is a tough job. For some people it's easier than others. But for you? Well, I think it's starting to catch up. You need a break. When did you last have some time off?"

Rossett shrugged his shoulders. It seemed that he worked every day and that he had been doing so for months. Maybe Koehler was right; maybe he did need a break. Rossett leaned forward and, placing his elbows on the table, rubbed his eyes with the palms of his hands. He suddenly felt very tired and needed a drink.

"Are you all right?"

Rossett nodded and placed his hands on the table palm down. "Before you came in I was thinking about when I was in uniform." He looked up at Koehler.

"In France?"

Rossett smiled and sadly shook his head.

"No, before that, when I first joined the police, before the war." He lowered his head at the memory and stared at the back of his hands again. "I just wanted to be a copper, lock up bad people. Ever since I was a little boy that's all I wanted to do. Maybe I should go back to it?"

Rossett looked up at Koehler, who silently shook his head.

"No, I thought not."

"None of us can go back to before the war, especially you. The world is a different place. You just need to make a space for yourself in it. Soon your work for us will be finished and we will look after you. Maybe a promotion, a nice job at Scotland Yard, maybe some sort of liaison role, propaganda. We'll look after you, remember the work you've done for us. You are our friend."

Rossett let out another sigh.

"What?" Koehler tilted his head and raised an eyebrow. "You can't change direction, you're too far down the line now."

"Like those trains we put the Jews on?"

Koehler didn't reply. He chose instead to look at the still-smoking cigarette butt on the floor, then ground it out with his polished boot before looking back to Rossett, who hadn't taken his eyes from the German.

"Where do they go to? Is it true what people say about the camps?" Rossett pushed, for maybe the first time. Koehler linked his fingers on the table like a bank manager who was about to give him some bad news, tilted his head again, and considered Rossett for a moment. The two men faced off across the table like chess players who had no board but had decided to play anyway.

"They go to Poland, most of them anyway."

"And what happens to them there?"

"What do you think happens to them?"

"Do they work?"

"Some of them."

"I hear rumors."

"Who from?"

"Different people. They say that the Jews are killed when they get to Europe. Is it true?"

"We aren't animals, John."

"I saw Germans killing unarmed people in France. It does happen."

"You of all people should know that was war. Now it is different."

Rossett sat silently looking at Koehler, who calmly stared back.

"Are we friends, Ernst?"

The German smiled, like a father to a child.

"I think so, yes. Why?"

"Would you tell me the truth?"

"Yes."

"I need to know if I am killing these people."

"You are putting them on trains, John, making sure things run smoothly, doing your job and following orders."

"If I put them on the train and the train takes them to their death, that means I am killing them, just the same as if I shot them myself, doesn't it?"

The German leaned across for another cigarette as Rossett spoke and then took his time lighting it, letting the silence and the smoke float to the ceiling before answering.

"You do a job for the Reich. If you did not do the job, someone else would do it. The job you do brings you a car, extra pay, and, most importantly, security in troubled times. You need to worry less about what you do, and just get on with doing it. They are only Jews, Rossett. Young or old, that is all they are. I've worked you too hard. I can see that now and I am sorry. You must take a few days off, I insist. Being around those people drains you. They suck the life out of you when they get under your skin, even the children. Some time off and we will start again on Monday, fresh and new. Yes?"

Rossett nodded silently, and Koehler stood and moved to the door, beckoning for him to follow.

"Come now, I will see you out, so you don't get into any more trouble."

Rossett picked up his cigarettes and stood wearily. He was tired. His head hung heavy and his back hurt from the rifle butt as he shrugged on his raincoat. He followed Koehler down the short corridor to the old custody desk, where Rossett had handed in his prisoner all those years ago. A couple of German soldiers were hanging around, and they sprang to attention and saluted as Koehler passed them. Rossett was aware that a few eyed him silently as he followed. He guessed news of his "Kraut" comment had gotten around the building, and he doubted it had gone down well. They walked past the cellblock, where a lone, overweight, and somewhat untidy guard was writing on a chalkboard. The guard stiffened and then fumbled with some keys to open the iron gate that led to the exit of the jail. As the guard nervously rattled the lock, Rossett glanced at the board and read down the list of names it held. At the bottom he saw:

Zelle 14: Galkoff: Jude (Koehler: Sonderzuge oder Ausführung)

Rossett heard the keys in the lock and the groan as the gate pulled open. Koehler thanked the guard and stepped through the gate while Rossett stared at the board, softly mouthing the words he'd read there.

"*Ausführung . . . ausführung . . .*" His mind searched for the meaning of the words next to Jacob's name.

"Rossett, come on, I have work to do."

Rossett finally passed through the gate and followed Koehler along another corridor to the stairs that led into the main building. As they climbed he repeated the word, silently this time, over and over. He could hear Koehler talking to him about a party function he had to attend that night, complaining about having to wear his uniform all day and then all night, but the German's small talk grew ever more distant as the words on the chalkboard fell into place.

They passed through another door and found themselves back in the main entrance of the old police station. It was busy with people coming and going, and the old inquiry desk was now manned by two Home Defense Troops and one female SS officer. Koehler led Rossett past the desk, and they stopped by the heavy doors that led back out onto the street—the doors that Rossett had been carried through an hour or so earlier.

Koehler held out his hand and Rossett took it to shake.

"Go home. Leave everything to me for a couple of days. Try to rest," Koehler said as he shook; Rossett felt the firm grip of the German and noted that it felt sincere, like his eye contact.

"The board, in the jail," Rossett heard himself asking,

"What board?"

"I saw Jacob's name, and next to it was written 'special train or execution,' with your name."

Koehler stopped shaking his hand but continued to hold it. The two men faced each other and Rossett saw a flash of something he hadn't seen before pass behind the eyes of the German. He felt Koehler's grip tighten and became suddenly aware that several of the cells below ground had been empty and that if he found himself in one, nobody would come looking for him.

"I just wondered what it meant, that's all."

Koehler's face softened. He released Rossett's hand, walked back to the desk, and spoke to the female. She rummaged under the counter and passed him a book, which he signed and then tore a page from. Koehler walked back to Rossett and passed him the piece of paper.

"This is for petrol; fill up that old car from the pump in the courtyard and then tomorrow take that landlady of yours with the comfortable arse down to that freezing beach you both like to sit at. Buy her some tea and ice cream and then take her into the sand and fuck her. It'll do the both of you good. Now get out of my sight, I don't want to see you till next week at the earliest."

Koehler turned smartly and walked off toward the main stairs that led to his office. Rossett stood in the foyer for a moment watching him go. He stuffed the chitty into his pocket and walked out into the street, which had returned to normality after the earlier parade.

He walked down the steps and past an old man with a dustcart who was coaxing a few cigarette butts down the gutter with a balding broom toward a half-blocked grate.

The old man obviously didn't care what would happen if the grate became fully blocked and had to be investigated. Nobody would point a finger in his direction when things went wrong.

Rossett wished he could say the same.

CHAPTER 11

ROSSETT SAT IN the car and stared at the petrol chitty Koehler had given him. There was no upper limit filled in, which meant the Austin was going to have a full tank for the first time in years. Maybe he would ask Mrs. Ward to take a run down to the beach; they could fill a flask and fetch that tartan rug she kept folded on the settee in the front parlor. He felt something stir inside for the first time in a long time and wondered whether Koehler had been right, whether maybe he had been working too hard, thinking too much.

He started the car and looked across to the open courtyard gates. He knew the petrol pump was located on the far side of the garages, which had once been Bow Street Runner stables back when the Met had been a private army guarding the streets from the muggers and murderers who lurked in the gaslit shadows.

He pulled across and the sentry approached his window. Rossett cursed when it dropped into the door again as he opened it.

"I've got a petrol requisition, I need to fill up."

The guard glanced down at Rossett's warrant card and the note he held in his other hand.

"You will have to come back later. The area commander's cars and escort are inside, and I can't let anybody in until they go. The yard should be open after eight."

The young German shrugged as he spoke. Rossett glanced past him and saw the three big Mercedeses and a troop truck parked, taking up half the yard.

"I'll be two minutes, I promise. This tank is tiny."

"I'm sorry, those are the orders."

The German stepped back to his hut, conversation over, and Rossett moved the little gear lever into reverse and cursed his luck.

"First time off in years and I still have to come back later," Rossett muttered under his breath, deciding to make use of the broken window's being down by sparking up another cigarette.

He opened the packet only to find it was empty. This day was getting better and better. He pulled out onto Charing Cross Road in search of a tobacconist and, spotting one, dodged the Austin across the street and bumped it up onto the curb facing into traffic.

There was a fog coming down, pushed by the cold November air. A few of the passing cars had their headlamps on and the afternoon felt damp, heavy with winter. Rossett ran his fingers through his hair and noticed it was wet to the touch. He longed for some warmth and made a mental note to get a good fire going in his room as soon as he got home, damn the coal ration. If he was going to have a holiday, he was going to spend it somewhere warm.

He wrestled the window back up and stepped out onto the pavement. Next to the tobacconist's, he noticed a small off-license window display that caught his eye. He stared at the bottles that lay in wooden boxes on beds of straw and thought about buying some Scotch and spending the evening warming his throat as he warmed his feet. Rossett stopped and tried to remember if the pleasure at the start of the bottle was worth the pain at the end. The pain that brought tears and the tap tap tap of his old service revolver against his temple as he screwed his eyes and tried to shut out the world and dam the tears that the Scotch shook free.

It wasn't, not tonight. He walked on to get the cigarettes.

The fog inside the tobacconist's shop was almost as thick as the fog outside. A small man with a waistcoat and a puffing pipe was stocking some shelves. He scuttled behind the counter on seeing Rossett and stood expectantly, hands clasped across his chest like an eager mouse relishing cheese.

"May I help you, sir?"

"Sixty Players."

The pipe dropped a fraction at the corner of his mouth like a railway signal at a passing train. The shopkeeper dropped the cigarettes onto the counter and reclasped his hands.

"Can I interest sir in a nice cigar for after dinner this evening?"

The pipe fluttered an expectant fraction and Rossett frowned. He was on holiday; maybe a cigar would be nice?

"What would you recommend?"

The pipe perked up and the little man lifted the counter flap and led Rossett by the elbow to the case he'd been stocking as Rossett had entered.

"We have a wide selection, sir, all excellent."

He stood back and studied Rossett like a tailor, then slid back the glass door and produced a box of Cubanas. With the solemnity of a bishop at a coronation, he held the box in front of Rossett and slowly opened the lid.

"I think sir will find these to his taste. One can still smell the sunshine on the box. A mild cigar, sir, a relaxing smoke perfect for that recline in an armchair after a tough day."

The edges of Rossett's mouth twitched.

The little man pulled four cigars from the box.

"Will sir be paying cash?"

Rossett nodded, feeling the weight of the day slip from his shoulders. The little man puffed on his pipe, sending smoke signals to the gods of a good sale, job well done.

Maybe this is why women buy hats? thought Rossett as he patted his pockets looking for his wallet in his raincoat, realizing he felt better for the time he'd spent in the shop. The little man dotted the invoice with a flourish and turned it to Rossett for him to see.

The pipe dropped again as the tobacconist looked up into Rossett's eyes.

"Sir?"

Rossett stared back blankly, the moment's contentedness suddenly crushed under the realization that he had left the pouch with the coins in his desk back at the station. His blood dropped from his face to his feet as something else hit home.

Koehler knew about his going to the beach with Mrs. Ward. He'd never told anyone he'd been to Southend with her, and yet the German knew.

That meant he'd been followed.

That meant they didn't trust him.

And if they didn't trust him before today, they certainly wouldn't trust him now; those coins in the desk could be an end to his warrant card and a start to his death warrant.

He needed to get them out of the station quick.

"Sir?"

Rossett drifted back to the shop like a man regaining consciousness. He looked at the shopkeeper as if seeing him for the first time. Willing his brain to say something, he realized his mouth had been hanging open, and he clenched his jaw and swallowed hard.

"I . . . I just remembered something, something important."

"These are such stressful times, I'm sure these fine cigars will lighten your burden this evening with maybe a brandy. Next door offer a fine—"

"How much is all this?"

The shopkeeper seemed disappointed that his run of form had failed him, and he placed his finger above the invoice total and smiled.

Rossett pulled a pound note from his wallet and then realized he would have to pull a couple more; he glanced at the shopkeeper and shook his head with disbelief at the expense of the cigars. The sales spell had been well and truly broken and the warm feeling long gone.

"Would sir be interested in opening an account?" The shopkeeper finally removed his pipe as he placed the change on the counter; Rossett noticed the two cracked yellow teeth the pipe had been resting against.

"No."

CHAPTER 12

NOT BEING TRUSTED was something Rossett knew all about. He understood suspicion. He worked for the Germans and wore a swastika on his lapel. Everywhere he went people eyed him, guarding their words as much as they would guard their ration book if he were a thief.

People assumed he was reading their minds, and sometimes he felt as if he was. He didn't trust the public, and the public didn't trust him. He'd gotten used to it, lived and breathed it, was comfortable with it and accepted it. He read their eyes, watched their hands, listened to their bodies as much as he listened to their voices. That was why he had been such a good thief taker before the war, and why he'd become such a good Jew taker after it.

Suspicion was his job.

It had never occurred to him that the Germans suspected him. He'd done everything they had asked, and he had, in return, never asked a question or ruffled a feather.

Until today.

He cursed himself inwardly and shook his head outwardly. That one question about where the trains went: had he asked it yesterday, he would have slapped his forehead and regretted it, then got on with his job, hoping that Koehler would let it slide from his memory as Rossett proved his worth.

But he hadn't asked it yesterday, he'd asked it today, and in that moment, as he'd patted his empty raincoat pocket and fired the tiny part of his brain that wondered where the pouch that had been there before had gone, he'd remembered Jacob, the pouch full of sovereigns, Koehler, the Gestapo, the shouting and the struggling as he'd been dragged into the cells. Most important, he remembered Koehler's statement about Mrs. Ward and Southend.

A woman whom Rossett had never mentioned or described, and a trip he had most definitely never told anyone about.

The Germans had followed him.

The Germans didn't trust him.

The Germans might still be following him.

And up until that morning he would never have cared if they were, because he had nothing to hide. But now a pouch full of sovereigns lay in his office like a body in a cellar. Waiting to be discovered to condemn a half-hanged man to the drop.

He had to get the sovereigns and he had to get them quick.

As he opened the door of the Austin and bent to get in, a hand grabbed his shoulder, and Rossett spun and twisted, tearing the hand from his coat and driving the wrist upward and away from its joint. His assailant's arm straightened, then flexed against its own elbow, and Rossett pushed it farther up and back as he faced the body that barely hung on to the other end. He cocked his right fist and was about to punch hard into the ribs of his attacker when he stopped.

A young uniformed policeman, eyes bulging and mouth open, stared back in shock.

Rossett released his grip and let the policeman's arm drop; passersby stopped and stared at Rossett. The bobby stepped back gasping, cradling his right arm.

"Bloody hell, Sarge. I was only saying hello!"

"You should know better than to grab a man when he isn't looking!" Rossett almost shouted, his cheeks flushing.

The passersby started to move again, and the young bobby regained some composure, straightened his helmet, and brushed his sleeve.

"I'm sorry, Sarge. You bloody well nearly ripped my arm off. Where did you learn that move?"

Rossett realized it was Baker, the young policeman from the search earlier that day. He looked up and down the road and wondered if that was too much of a coincidence, the old instincts jangling.

"What are you doing here?"

"It's my beat, Sarge. I saw the car parked the wrong way with no lights and half on the curb. With this fog coming in, I thought it might be a bit of process for me."

Rossett relaxed slightly, relieved to see that Baker was just a young bobby looking to placate his sergeant with a summons file for a motoring offense.

"When I got over and I saw the window half cocked, I realized it was yours. I was going to surprise you, for a lark. Sorry, Sarge."

Rossett smiled and shook his head.

"I'm sorry, Baker. You gave me a start, and old instincts kicked in. Is the arm okay?"

Baker gave a relieved smile and rubbed his shoulder.

"You near tore it off, Sarge, but it was a bit daft of me, my fault. Are you working on a case?"

"No, I'm buying cigarettes. I'm having a few days off so I thought I'd stock up. Sorry about the parking, a lot on my mind."

"How's that little boy?" Baker ignored the apology.

Rossett flushed again and opened the door of the Austin.

"He's fine."

"Poor little blighter, did he catch that train?"

"No."

"Oh, right, is he stopping at the station then? I'll drop by and see him, friendly face and all that."

"No, he's, er . . . he's over at Charing Cross."

Baker chewed his lip and nodded, realization dawning that the boy had been handed over to the Germans.

"How long for?"

"I don't know."

"I expect he'll be okay, they'll look after him . . . won't they, Sarge?"

"Yes, I'm sure they will."

"It's just you hear stories, about what goes on."

The men nodded to each other, embarrassed by the conversation but not sure how to end it.

"I'd best be going. Hope the arm is okay."

"It'll be fine, Sarge. Sorry for the fright."

Rossett nodded and got into the car as Baker stepped into the street to stop the oncoming traffic. The little Austin fired up and Rossett bounced off the curb and pulled forward into the gap Baker had made. He stopped by the officer, who stood, arm raised, holding back the tide.

"That was good work today, Baker, at the house. You did well."

"Thank you, Sarge. It was an honor to work with you."

"An honor?"

"Yes, Sarge, you're a bit of a legend to us young lads: war hero, top thief taker when you was a copper, 'straightest man in the Met,' my old sergeant calls you. It was a real honor for me."

Rossett nodded, gave a half smile, and tried to ignore the "when you was a copper" line as he drove away.

CHAPTER 13

ERNST KOEHLER SQUEEZED his toes, stretched his toes, and then squeezed his toes again. He leaned back in his chair, sighed a weary sigh, closed his eyes, and, for the first time that day, relaxed a little. After a moment he opened his eyes and stared at the boots that stood to attention on the desk in front of him.

The words of his old drill sergeant echoed across the years.

"A size too small will make you stand tall, gentlemen. Always wear dress boots that pinch."

Ernst squeezed his toes again and decided that the man was obviously an idiot or a sadist, or, God forbid, an idiot sadist.

The intercom on his desk buzzed.

"Herr Schmitt to see you, sir."

Koehler sighed and flopped back into his chair without answering; he banged himself on the forehead with the heel of his hand, then reached over to the intercom.

"Send him in, please."

A moment later the heavy oak door of his office swung open and the Gestapo man entered. Over his shoulder, Kate made the briefest of eye contact with Koehler, who smiled in reply.

"Could you have someone make us tea, please, Kate."

"Not for me," said Schmitt.

Schmitt took a seat without asking and waited for Kate to shut the door behind him. Koehler leaned back in his chair and smiled warmly, deciding to leave the boots on the table between them.

"So, Schmitt, what can I do for you?"

"I want to know why the Englishman has been released."

"Detective Sergeant Rossett?"

"Yes."

"I believed it was a simple misunderstanding; the sergeant thought your men were trying to take his prisoner from him."

"The 'prisoner' was already away from him, watching the fucking parade."

Koehler smiled at Schmitt's swearing, the only indication that he was angry about the incident. Other than that one word, the man was implacable, his voice monotone, his face expressionless, hands placed calmly upon the left leg that was crossed over his right.

"I think you'll find that the sergeant was in control of the situation." Koehler smiled. "There was little chance of the prisoner's escaping."

Schmitt leaned forward slightly, but as he was about to speak, the office door opened and Kate and a secretary carrying a tray entered. Schmitt leaned back in his seat and waited for the teacups and pot to be placed on the table. Nobody spoke, and Kate merely nodded to Koehler once the items were laid out.

"Thank you, Kate, that will be all."

The two women left the room, and Koehler picked up the pot and poured the tea. He slid a cup across the table to Schmitt, who uncrossed his legs and folded his arms.

"I didn't want tea."

"You really must try it. It's excellent, Earl Grey, the real thing from my private supply."

"I don't drink tea."

"Try it."

Schmitt pushed the cup back across the table toward Koehler, spilling some into the saucer.

Koehler raised his eyebrows, "Please Schmitt, it really is . . ."

"Can you take your boots off the table so I can see who I am talking to?" Schmitt snapped, his irritation plain to see, and Koehler smiled.

"Of course, forgive me; it is awfully rude. They pinch terribly and I was just glad to have them off after the parade." Koehler spoke but merely looked at the boots, leaving them where they stood.

"Why did you let the Englishman go?" Schmitt banged his fist upon the desk, then pointed at Koehler. "He assaulted a member of the Gestapo. He should be shot, not released! I demand to know why you let him go."

Koehler paused midsip and placed his cup back down on the saucer he was holding with his other hand.

"May I remind you I'm your superior. I would warn you to respect that." Koehler kept his voice calm, friendly in tone, certain he had just won round one.

Schmitt stared hard at Koehler, then leaned back in his chair and looked up at a painting of the Führer on the office wall. When he finally spoke, his voice was smooth as silk.

"Sir, may I remind you that one of my men was attacked by an Englishman outside the area HQ, in full sight of many witnesses, both German and English." Schmitt turned from the painting and looked at Koehler. "He was attacked by a man who was harboring a Jew, a Jew who had evaded an authorized eviction that very morning, a Jew you had eaten breakfast with the selfsame morning and yet decided not to detain, and, no less, a Jew who was tapping his foot to the fucking SS garrison band while the commander of occupied England stood not less than forty feet away."

This time the swear word wasn't said with anger; this time it slipped out like a snake's tongue, full of menace. Koehler looked at the teacup for a moment and then placed it carefully on the table, buying time. He was beginning to regret leaving the boots on the table but now didn't want to lose face by moving them. He shifted position in his chair to allow himself to maintain eye contact with Schmitt, who stared back, unblinking.

"As I said earlier, I believe the matter to be a misunderstanding. Detective Sergeant Rossett has told me that he will be apologizing to you and the area commander by letter as soon as he returns from his leave. I realize that this has caused you some embarrassment, and for that I am also sorry. But, you have to understand, Rossett fulfills an important role for us here in England, not just in London. The sergeant gives a certain . . . respectability to what my department is doing here." Koehler sipped some more tea, aware that he was walking in a verbal minefield and being careful as to where he placed his stockinged feet.

"So, just because Churchill told the old king to give him a medal, we allow him to punch Germans?"

"He didn't get a medal, Schmitt. He got the Victoria Cross, which is much more than a medal."

Schmitt waved his hand dismissively at Koehler.

"I don't buy this 'British Lion' bullshit. He hid in Dunkirk for a few weeks and then made a stand in some shithole in England, so what? We should have shot him when we caught him, not given him a fucking job."

Koehler smiled and took some more tea before speaking.

"He held up half a Panzer brigade on his own for almost a week, managed to get into a German port and capture a torpedo boat and its crew, then made them sail down the coast to pick up fifteen injured colleagues and sail across the channel. And if that wasn't enough, he brought the boat back across to France to pick up a dozen more and took them home as well. Churchill called him the British Lion for a reason, Schmitt, and if you had been in combat you'd know what that reason was."

The two men sat in silence. Schmitt bridled at the dig but decided not to dignify it by answering, while Koehler was reluctant to push the knife any farther home. After a moment, Koehler removed his boots from the desk and leaned forward, placing his elbows on its polished surface.

"Look, I'm genuinely sorry for what happened today. Rossett was wrong to do what he did and he knows it. I've been pushing him too hard; what happened is as much my fault as his. I can assure you no such thing will take place again. If you wish, I can tell people he is suspended while he takes a few days away from his desk. Would that help?"

Schmitt waved a hand of acceptance, some dignity restored. He turned his head to look back up at the Führer. Koehler thought that with his blond hair and blue eyes, the Gestapo man looked like he was posing for a propaganda picture.

"Sir, I apologize for my outburst. It was wrong of me to act in such a manner." Schmitt spoke to the painting as much as to Koehler. Eventually, he turned back to Koehler, who in turn waved his hand, dismissing the incident as already forgotten. "But . . ."

Koehler grimaced and suddenly wished he'd left the boots where they'd been.

"I feel that you may have missed my point. Some people in this building have suggested that you and the Englishman have got a little too close. It is suggested in certain quarters that your fondness for Earl Grey, Savile Row, brown shoes, and, if I may say, English secretaries, has clouded your judgment while you have been stationed in London. This may be one of the reasons for my posting here. To help you"—Schmitt looked around for the words before allowing his eyes to fall back on Koehler—"retain a sense of your role."

Schmitt smiled at Koehler, who curled his toes under the desk, then smiled back.

"I can assure you, my work here has been of the highest standard. The operation I am in charge of has been commended at the highest level for its efficiency."

"I'm merely relating what I have heard and what my, or rather our, superior officers have told me. I mention it just so you are aware of what people are saying. I wouldn't want you to become complacent in your relationships or, God forbid, your role."

"My relationship with the sergeant is far from complacent." Koehler opened a drawer on the desk and tossed a manila file onto the tabletop. On the top corner was a photo of Rossett. "Sergeant Rossett is as closely monitored as any other British member of this department. But what you have to understand is that we have to be delicate in our handling of the sergeant. This is a man of whom the Führer himself has spoken."

"Yes, yes. 'Give me a thousand men like the British Lion and we'd have crushed Russia by Christmas.' I read the newspapers. Your point is?" Schmitt sighed.

"My point is, this man is an important tool for the Fatherland, this man follows orders, this man does his duty, and most important, this man sets an example. When the British surrendered, did Rossett run off to Canada like Churchill and the king? No. They wanted him to go and he stayed. He laid down his arms and carried on his service to his country. When he was interned with the rest of the army, did he cause problems? No. When he was released he quietly rejoined the police and got on with the job he was doing before the war. Even after his wife and son were blown up by the resistance bomb at King's Cross, he didn't complain."

Koehler picked up the file and held it in his right hand, using it to point at Schmitt.

"I manage Rossett, I nurse him, I make his life as good as I can without his knowing it. And it isn't easy. He isn't the sort of man who will accept a big office and a cushy job. I can't bribe him with a new flat and a pay raise: he wouldn't take it. He's like a monk, Schmitt. He needs his hair shirt. It reminds him he is alive."

Schmitt shook his head, then stood up as Koehler put the file back into the open desk drawer.

"These are confusing times, Major."

Koehler closed the drawer and stared up at Schmitt while he made a silent decision.

"The Führer wants to give Rossett an Iron Cross when he comes to London next year."

"An Iron Cross?" Schmitt couldn't hide his amazement.

"For services to the Reich in relation to the Jewish question. It'll be a major propaganda benefit to the occupation. They are planning a whole series of articles on Rossett to be featured in the press, about his wife and son being killed by the resistance, his commitment to the cause, how much he loves the new Britain, all of that shit. He'll have to go on a tour around the country, fly the flag for us, meet the king, slap Mosley on the back and look like he is enjoying it while the newsreel and *Daily Mail* cameras follow him around."

"But . . . but he's not committed to the cause. He's just a flatfoot who thinks he is doing his job."

"We know that, Schmitt, but the British people don't. They will see a handsome war hero who has embraced the Reich shaking the hand of his grateful Führer. And today, for five minutes in a London street while a military band played out of tune, an idiot Gestapo officer and a snot-nosed Jewish kid nearly caused the lot of us to end up in a concentration camp."

"Does Rossett know any of this?"

"Of course he doesn't know. He'll know when I think the time is right. And he will do as he is told, just as he always does. The Führer thinks very highly of Detective Sergeant Rossett, and for as long as he does, we will too."

"So this idiot gets an Iron Cross while brave soldiers are dying on the Eastern Front? It's a disgrace."

"You may think that, Schmitt, but say it outside of this office and you'll be digging trenches with those brave fools in the ice. Do you understand?"

Schmitt swallowed hard and nodded silently. Koehler picked up his pen and opened a folder on his desk, and Schmitt took his cue to leave the office, exiting without another word.

ONCE OUTSIDE, SCHMITT picked his way through the outer office and the secretaries it contained. Kate gave him the smallest of smiles, which Schmitt returned with a scowl, muttering, "The British Lion my arse," as he pushed the outer door open and went off to ruin somebody else's day.

CHAPTER 14

THE BRITISH LION was hiding from a sixty-two-year-old cleaning lady by sitting in a toilet cubicle with his trousers around his ankles.

Rossett had arrived back at the Wapping station ten minutes before, slipping inside via the back door that opened onto the garage. He'd passed through the late afternoon's nearly deserted station like a wraith, most of its occupants having left for the day, and trotted up the stairs on his toes so as not to make a sound. He'd been pleased with his progress right up until he had exited the stairwell onto the floor that his office was on. It was then that he had seen Edna's backside, like some lumbering elephant backing toward him, swiping a mop this way and that like a trunk with every step. He'd ducked into the toilet to avoid her and the bone-crushing boredom that would come with the gossip the woman endlessly emitted whenever she had an audience.

It was only when he entered the toilets that he realized he was trapped. He couldn't risk going back outside where she might spot him. Just ignoring her wasn't an option either; Edna could block a corridor with a mop and bucket better than a fallen tree could block a country lane. The last thing Rossett wanted was to be stuck with her if Brewer turned up. He didn't want to meet his boss in case he'd heard about the trouble at Charing Cross. The thought of Brewer's raising his voice again made him shudder. Not through fear of the inspector, but fear that he might just snap and end up killing his boss with a mop.

Rossett opened a cubicle door and sat down. He stared at the toilet exit and heard the clang of the mop bucket as it moved ever closer, like some sort of galvanized glacier. He sighed, leaned back, pushed the cubicle door closed, and dropped his trousers, letting them sit around his ankles.

Even Edna wouldn't disturb a man at one with his toilet. Rossett remembered his father crossing the backyard with a copy of the *Daily Mirror*, heading for the privy. He smiled at the memory; it seemed as if he was watching someone else's life. He could see the kitchen table, hear his mother singing and watch his father through the distorted glass of the back window. Another life, another lifetime ago.

The toilet door opened and Rossett tensed. He looked at the back of his cubicle door as if he could see through it and coughed the universal cough of the engaged.

"You going to be long, Mister Rossett?" Edna called, her voice as shrill as a cockney mynah bird.

Rossett clenched his fist to his forehead and grimaced before answering in a voice that he hoped sounded more relaxed than he felt.

"Just a minute."

"Cor, you've had a day an' a half, ain't yer?" called Edna, foot jammed in the door and Woodbine bobbing. "I 'eard about you 'avin a little kiddy with you and then gettin' into a fight with some Germans. Is that true?"

Rossett closed his eyes and leaned back, disbelief flooding his battered brain.

"You don't 'alf like fightin' them Germans, don't you? I wonder sometimes why they give you a job in the first place, what with you killin' so many of 'em during the war. My 'Arry reckons it's so they can keep an eye on you, so you don't go round killin' another load of 'em. My 'Arry bagged a few in the first war, not as many as . . ."

Rossett stepped out and went through the motions of washing his hands. He'd flung the cubicle door open with such force that Edna broke off from her rambling and let the exit door close an inch or two before shouldering it open again.

"I was just saying, my 'Arry bagged a few, but not as many as you. Mind, he never got no medal for it, what with 'im deserting when 'e was on leave. I told 'im, I said, 'You get your arse back there and fight,' but . . ."

Rossett dried his hands and pulled the exit door, causing Edna to sway slightly as the weight lifted off her. Rossett stopped and stared at her for a moment before making a decision.

"Edna?"

"Yes, Mr. Rossett?"

"Do you ever shut up?"

Edna raised a hand to her mouth and stared at him for a moment before taking up the mop and turning toward the toilets. Rossett watched her go and for a moment considered apologizing but then decided against it. Upsetting her was a price worth paying for some peace and quiet.

He walked to his office, quickly closing the door behind him and sitting down at his desk. He listened for a moment and stared at the frosted glass of the door in case Edna found her voice again and burst in looking for a fight. Once he was certain he was going to be left alone, he unlocked the drawer and saw that the red velvet pouch was still there, just as he had left it.

He carefully held it over the drawer, so that he could drop it back inside if disturbed, opened it, and slid three fingers in, pulling out some of the coins.

Three bright gold sovereigns looked up at him, and they felt warm to the touch. The afternoon light was fading as the fog descended, so Rossett clicked on the small desk lamp and held the coins close to the bulb.

This pouch could change my life, he thought. There must be over a hundred of these things in here.

His office door opened, and Rossett simultaneously clenched his fist around the coins and dropped the pouch into the drawer as he looked up to see who was coming in without knocking.

Brewer stood in the doorway. He had his overcoat on and looked to be heading home.

"What are you doing here? I was told you'd gone on leave." Brewer looked around the small office as if seeing it for the first time.

"I had a few things to sort out before I went, couple of files to be signed off."

The two men looked at each other, unsure of what to say. Rossett felt uneasy, not because he was holding three gold sovereigns tightly in his fist either. There was something about Brewer that seemed strange; he hadn't expected Rossett to be there when he'd opened the door. That meant he was coming into the office for another reason. Rossett's nerves twitched again as he thought of the pouch that lay in the open drawer inches from his right hand. He willed himself not to look down at it or close the drawer.

"Is there something I can help you with, sir?"

Brewer looked unsure for moment. He looked out into the corridor and then back into the office, buying time, thought Rossett. Maybe he wasn't going home, maybe he had come back to the station to check on Rossett?

"Koehler called. He told me you had some bother up at Charing Cross. Is that right?"

"It's all sorted now."

"What happened?"

"A misunderstanding, nothing for you to worry about."

"He said you got rid of that Jew."

"He's heading out on the Sunday train, sir."

"Good, that could have been embarrassing." Brewer turned to walk away, then stopped and looked back at Rossett.

"What Sunday train?"

"Major Koehler said there was a train arranged?"

"Not as far as I'm aware. I have to sign off the schedules and I've not seen one." Brewer shrugged. "Anyway, not to worry. It's not our problem now."

Rossett felt his stomach shift and suddenly the coins felt heavy in his hand. It was his turn to look around the office.

"Are you sure you're all right, Rossett?"

"Yes, sir."

"You're clenching your fist so hard I can see the whites of your knuckles, man. You need to relax."

Rossett glanced down at his fist, then eased his hold on the coins but kept them in his hand. He forced himself to look back up at Brewer and smile.

"I'm okay, sir, I just need a bit of a holiday. Few days off will sort me out."

"Get along then. Leave what you have to do until you come back."

Brewer pushed the office door open and stepped back, flicking his head as an invitation for Rossett to leave.

"I'll only be a minute, sir, just a couple of signatures."

"Leave them. Come on, I'll walk you out."

Rossett felt his heart speeding up. He was certain Koehler had told Brewer to check his office. Had he also asked him to search it? He couldn't leave the coins there, just as he couldn't suddenly mention them out of the blue.

But Koehler didn't know about the coins. Maybe he was just being paranoid?

The coins seemed to heat up in his fist.

"Honestly, sir, I'll just be a minute."

Brewer was about to speak when Edna appeared at his shoulder. She glared at Rossett before jabbing the inspector in the ribs with the end of her mop.

"'E's a bleedin' disgrace to this station and you proper police! I've never bin so insulted. When my 'Arry finds out what 'e's said 'e'll be down 'ere to knock 'is bleedin' block off!"

Brewer tried to shield his ribs as the old cleaner jabbed him again. He turned to Edna, and as he did Rossett reached down, snatched the pouch out of the drawer, and slipped it into his raincoat pocket in one movement. Relief flooded through him and he almost cried out with delight.

Brewer grabbed the end of Edna's mop.

"Stop jabbing me, woman! What are you on about?"

"'Im!" She pulled the mop free and waved it toward Rossett, who was rising, hand emerging from his inside pocket. Rossett smiled warmly at Edna, further enraging her, so that she now wielded the mop pole like a musketeer's rapier in his general direction.

"Are you still going on?" said Rossett as he rose from behind his desk. Edna's eyes bulged and the mop pole froze for the briefest of moments before she prodded Brewer with it again.

"Did you 'ear that? He's a bleedin' disgrace! To think that tongue has spoken to the old king, Gawd bless 'im!"

Edna was shrieking now, and for a moment Rossett thought Brewer would produce his sap and set about the woman to quiet her down. Instead, Brewer eased himself back into Rossett's office, defending himself only with strategically placed elbows covering his tender ribs.

"Stop it! Calm down at once! If you don't stop shouting I'll have you ejected from the building!"

Using Brewer as a shield, Rossett stepped out of the office. A few heads had popped out of offices along the corridor, and he shrugged in reply to their puzzled glances. Behind him he heard Brewer trying to placate the cleaner as he backed out of the office. Rossett walked toward the exit, pleased that for the first time that day he wasn't the center of attention. He pushed open the door that led to the stairs and started to jog down them, toward the car, toward peace and quiet.

CHAPTER 15

ROSSETT WASN'T A fan of pubs. They reminded him of the times when he was a detective before the war. Long, smoky afternoons stretching into nights like a contented cat. Colleagues and criminals and a tone-deaf pianist playing a half-dead piano in the corner of the room.

Pubs reminded him of the happy times, when he had joined in with the songs, enjoyed the rowdy laughter that erupted from groups of good friends, watched lovers holding hands under the table, and always had a pint waiting for him before he'd got his coat off.

Rossett wasn't a fan, but he needed a drink, and he needed one badly.

Rossett knew that needing a drink and wanting a drink were two very different things. He knew that wanting a drink nudged your brain and cocked its head toward the bar with a cheeky smile and a wink, and if you were in the mood you joined it for a pint.

But needing a drink was an altogether different sort of character. Needing a drink squeezed your head and poked at your eyes; needing a drink scratched at your throat and choked your tongue till it felt swollen and flopped around your mouth like a dead carp in a bucket. Needing a drink was a demon that wouldn't leave you alone until you were lying on the floor, begging for mercy, tears flowing, grasping for something that had gone away.

Needing a drink was a bastard, but right now, Rossett needed a drink.

He stared at the pub. It was called the Harp, and although it was close to Wapping it didn't see many coppers pass through its doors. That was why Rossett drank there when he had this painful thirst. Nobody to see him falling down and suffering silent tears as he was propped in the corner by someone who felt pity for the drunk that he was.

He liked the Harp, with its leaded frosted windows and its averted gaze. It didn't talk about him the next morning because it didn't remember him.

He stared at the windows. The light-colored glass was lit from inside, and he could see the outlines of people, almost make out the pint glasses held in their hands, laughing and joking, calling to him. He looked down at his own hands and thought about Jacob. The boy had reached for them and held them that morning, clinging on for dear life, grasping tightly the hand of a man who had let him slip away.

He needed a drink.

He was going to have a drink.

Rossett got out of the car and crossed the pavement toward the pub. Breathing hard, he pushed open the door and immediately felt at home with the smoke and the sounds he'd hated moments before.

Just a couple, he told himself, until I get some petrol.

"What can I get you, love?" The barmaid smiled.

"Bitter and a Scotch."

"Ooh, you mean business."

"I'm not stopping long."

With big brown eyes she smiled at him, knowing he would be. She'd heard it all before, seen the look, the lick of the lips, the leer of the alcoholic hopping off the wagon that was taking him home.

Rossett already had some coins waiting on the bar before she finished pouring the pint, and by the time the whiskey turned up the pint was half gone.

"Tough day?"

"Yeah." Rossett looked around the pub with a half turn, scoping the room quickly and expertly.

"You work local?"

He took another drink and put the almost-empty pint glass back down on the bar before reaching for the Scotch.

"Another pint." He killed the conversation and then drank the Scotch in one swift drain of his glass. He shook his head as he felt the burn in his throat and chest. The barmaid returned and looked at the empty glass as she placed his pint on the bar.

"Another?"

Rossett nodded as the barmaid picked up the glass, her turn to shake her head.

He leaned his right elbow on the bar and took another look around the pub. He could feel the alcohol relaxing him, easing its way through his bloodstream like mercury. He exhaled deeply and took a more measured sip of his pint as the barmaid put the Scotch on the bar. He paid her without speaking and just nodded when she returned with his change.

The bar was half full, thick with smoke and noise. It hadn't changed in the year or so since he'd last been there. Most of the clientele were dockers, big burly hard-drinking men who started their days early and grafted hard for their money. The remainder were heavy drinkers who had slipped down the road, coming to rest in the bottom of a glass.

He sipped his pint and looked around for a table. The long narrow bar was filling up as people sought shelter from the night. Table space was at a premium, so if he wanted to sit down he was going have to share, and he wasn't in the mood for sharing. He was never in the mood for sharing.

He sipped his pint and turned back to the bar, where the big brown eyes were waiting.

"I'm glad to see you've slowed down a bit, I wasn't sure if I was going to be able to keep up."

Rossett nodded, regretting standing right next to the pumps. The barmaid finished pouring a pint and took it to a waiting customer up the other end of the bar as Rossett took out his cigarettes and lit one. He placed both elbows on the bar and stared at his pint for a moment, feeling the weight of the sovereigns pulling at his raincoat pocket and his conscience. He took a drag of the cigarette and washed down the smoke with the last of his bitter before waving his glass down the bar, hoping to catch those brown eyes.

He thought about Jacob and wondered if the child was okay.

"Bitter?"

Rossett looked up into those brown eyes again and nodded, thinking they reminded him of someone.

"I am, but can I have a drink as well?" The brown eyes smiled at his bad joke. "You must get sick of looking at miserable drunks," Rossett said, aware that the drink was making him talk, taking his edge off.

"I get sick of looking at any kind of drunk, but at least the miserable ones keep themselves to themselves."

"What's your name?"

"Barbara, what's yours?"

"Another Scotch, thanks."

Barbara smiled and waited for Rossett to pay for the foamy pint that she had placed in front of him. He fished out some coins.

"Have one yourself, Barbara, so I can say sorry for being a miserable rude drunk."

Barbara smiled and took the money to the till. She dropped some coins into her own glass and returned with the change and placed it next to Rossett's pint.

"Been a bad day for you then?"

"Very bad, very very bad, if I'm honest."

Rossett swirled the Scotch around its glass on the bar and then smiled at Barbara before picking it up and drinking half of it in one gulp. This time it didn't burn too much. This time it went down easy, and somewhere deep inside an alarm triggered in Rossett, telling him he was getting drunk.

He decided to ignore it.

"I'm sure it wasn't that bad."

"I let someone down, Barbara. I let them down badly."

"They'll understand. Can't you explain tomorrow?"

"No, because he is gone, gone for good, never to be seen again. He needed my help, and I let him down." As Rossett spoke he waved the glass in front of him.

"I'm sure it's not as bad as all that."

"It is."

"It's just the drink talking. You'll see, it'll be better in the morning after you've had a sleep."

"Lovely Barbara, you really have no idea, do you?"

Rossett finished the Scotch and tilted the empty glass toward her. He noticed her frown. She took the glass and poured another measure, taking the money from his change on the bar.

"You're going to get drunk."

"That's the plan."

"You should go home to your family."

"I should, but I can't, so I won't."

Rossett smiled sadly, and Barbara shook her head and made her way up the end of the bar. He watched her go and drank some more bitter; he'd scared her off, just as he always did when he was drunk. They liked him at first, but then his pain scared them away as it floated to the surface, buoyed up by the booze.

"I couldn't even look after a child," he said softly.

"Kids, eh? They drive you bloody mad if you let them."

Rossett turned and found a docker standing next to him at the bar. The big man was waiting to be served and had overheard him muttering.

"What?" Rossett stood up from leaning on the bar and stared at the docker, who smiled back.

"I was just saying, kids . . . they drive you bloody mental if you let 'em. My two lads are grown up now. But they still drive me barmy sometimes. I say to them, 'Why don't you piss off and get your own place?' But they never listen."

Rossett tilted his head and took a sip of his beer as Barbara smiled at the docker and took his empty glass to fetch another drink.

"How many you got?" The docker smiled at Rossett again.

"None."

"Count yourself lucky, mate. They bleed you dry."

"Do they?"

"Yeah, once you got 'em you can't get shot of 'em. Always looking for something. Lads are the worse, mind. My two never leave me alone. You, mate, are a very lucky man. If your missus ever wants kids you tell 'er what I said."

"My missus is dead."

The big man froze, not expecting the bluntness of Rossett's reply.

"Eh? Oh, I'm sorry, guv, I didn't know." He stared at Rossett, looking for a rescue from his embarrassment, but he didn't get one.

"So is my son. They were blown up, the pair of them. Bang . . . gone. Never seen again. They found bits, mind, but nothing you could look at and say 'that's them.' No face or anything, just bits and pieces lying round here and there . . . that's all."

The docker stared at Rossett, then looked around the bar for rescue. He didn't get one and turned back to Rossett.

"I don't know what to say, mate." He shook his head. "Bloody Germans."

"It wasn't Germans, *mate*. It was the English that did it. Pram full of explosives. BOOM!"

Rossett waved his hands in the air as he shouted "boom" and a few people in the bar looked around. The docker looked at Barbara and then back at Rossett. His mouth moved silently before he picked up his pint from the bar.

"I'm sorry, mate."

"Why don't you just piss off?" Rossett replied.

The docker nodded and turned to go.

"I'm sorry, mate."

Rossett didn't reply. He turned back to the bar, rested both elbows on it once more, and stared at his beer.

"I think you've had enough."

Rossett looked up to Barbara, who had made her way down the bar toward him. She was wringing a towel in her hands. Rossett reached into his pocket, produced his warrant card, and flicked it toward her before dropping it back into his pocket.

"I think you need to get me another Scotch."

It was getting dark.

CHAPTER 16

ROSSETT COULD FEEL the gloom surrounding him. He felt like a man climbing a mast on a sinking ship, barely able to keep ahead of the rising sea of depression. It always happened when he was deep in drink; it was why he hated boozing at home. He wanted to maintain a distance from his revolver and the chair by the window, where he'd sat too many times in the past, scared that that toothpick lamppost and the grime on the window would be the last thing he would ever see.

He wasn't sure how many drinks he'd had, but he knew he was drunk. He guessed he could still drive, although he would have to bank on the fog still being outside and slowing everyone else down enough for them to avoid him. He'd smoked half a pack of cigarettes, drunk a belly full of bitter, and spilt a fair few glasses of Scotch. He'd be sorry in the morning, but then, he was sorry every morning.

He stared at the inch of bitter left in the bottom of his glass and then looked around the bar, in full swing now, offices and businesses closing having brought in a few more on their way home. Someone burst out laughing a few feet away and he felt someone else push into his back as he tried to squeeze past. It was time to go and get the petrol from Charing Cross.

He swallowed the last of the bitter and slid the change off the bar into his pocket, brushing his hand against the pouch full of sovereigns, there again, there to remind him.

He took the change out of his pocket and tapped it on the bar. Barbara looked down from the other end, and he nodded to her and left it as a tip. She smiled but looked like she didn't mean it. He didn't smile back.

Rossett turned to leave and walked straight into the broad back of one of the dockers. It felt like he had hit a stone wall. He placed his hand on the man's shoulder and tried to push his way past. The docker didn't give way; he just turned slowly, pushing against Rossett's hand, scowling at him.

"You've just knocked my pint all over me."

Another night Rossett would have raised his hands and apologized. He might have even put his hand in his pocket and bought the man a pint.

But not tonight.

Tonight he stared at the docker and thanked God, because tonight, just when he needed it, tonight he was going to have a fight.

Rossett stared at the man, maybe in his late fifties, broad of shoulder and thick of back from hefting weights all his working life. He was holding his pint glass in his right hand and Rossett could see the stain of spilled beer across his chest. He smiled.

"So what?"

"So what?" The docker looked at Rossett, confused, and then at his friends, who, by now, were also staring at Rossett.

"So what if I spilled your pint?"

"So what?" the docker repeated, thrown that the conversation was not going as he expected.

Rossett stared at the docker for a moment and then subsided inside. The man wasn't a fighter; if he had been they would already be on the floor. The man was just having a pint on his way home from work. Rossett's anger ebbed like a wave on the shore, and he regretted the way he had reacted.

"I'm sorry." Rossett spoke softly, and the docker looked even more confused as he stepped to one side to allow Rossett to pass.

"Yeah, well, be more careful, all right?"

Rossett nodded and passed through the group and out the door, pausing on the pavement to take out another cigarette.

Maybe I'm not as drunk as I thought, he said to himself as he lit up, *or maybe I'm going soft in my old age?* He looked up and down the street. It was dark and the fog was down, thick and heavy and smelling of dirty riverbank and soot. He thought about leaving the Austin, then remembered he had to get the fuel before he went home and wondered if he should eat something before driving over to Charing Cross.

He heard the door swing open behind him as the sounds of the pub grew loud, then faded again, causing him to look back over his shoulder as he put his match to the cigarette.

The docker he'd knocked into was staring at him.

Rossett stared back. Maybe he'd got the man wrong: maybe he was a fighter after all, or maybe he had been whipped up by his friends and had had to come out to save face. Either way, the urge to fight had gone from Rossett, and he half smiled at the man and shook his head by way of apology.

"I think I've had too much, pal. I'm heading home."

The big man stared back, and Rossett noticed the balled fists and the swollen chest. He took a few steps away from the docker to get a reaction space and then turned side on as he spoke, taking the cigarette from his mouth as he did.

"I'm sorry about knocking into you. It's been a hell of a day. Let me buy you another drink?" Rossett pointed to his pocket but didn't put his hand in; he knew better than to be caught by an onrushing man while reaching for his wallet.

"Not so tough now, are you?" The docker lowered his chin as he spoke, fists still tight. He took a deep breath and a half step forward.

Rossett held out an open hand and took an equal step back toward the Austin, maintaining the distance between them.

"I don't want to fight."

"You should have thought of that."

"We're both drunk, just leave it."

Another half step forward, another half step back.

"You ain't acting hard now, are you?"

"Look, I don't know if your pals have wound you up, but just go back inside and tell them you chased me off and we can both leave it there, eh?"

The docker took two steps forward and Rossett took one back and raised both hands in front of him, careful to keep them open, palms out.

"I'm a policeman. Trust me, you don't want the trouble."

"I don't care if you're Sherlock fucking Holmes."

Another step forward.

Rossett planted his back foot and kept his hands outstretched. The docker raised his fists and lowered his head even more, and Rossett knew there was no going back now. They were going to fight.

Drunk or not, a clarity descended on him. He felt everything else slipping from view and only saw the big man in front of him. The sounds of distant traffic faded. Even the fog seemed to lift. Jacob drifted from the place at the back of his mind where he'd been all day, and even the weight of the sovereigns seemed to lighten. He could feel the pavement under his feet through his shoes, feel his toes curl to find purchase, and feel the adrenaline reach out from his core to fuel every part of his body.

Rossett knew one thing in life, one thing more than any other: he knew how to fight.

The docker stepped in again and this time Rossett took a half step forward, dropped his head, and slammed his open palms against the massive chest, sending the other man stumbling backward three or four steps. Rossett didn't advance; he just drew back his hands, right held open next to his cheek, left extended eighteen inches in front of his face, still holding the lit cigarette.

He didn't speak or move, he just waited.

He didn't wait long. The docker regained his balance, paused, then charged back across the ground he had just given. Rossett dipped his left shoulder and with a slight pivot on his toes slipped his right fist through the big man's hands and landed it square on his nose.

The docker's head recoiled and he stumbled back. Rossett withdrew one step back and a half to the left, both hands open, exactly where they had been before the rush, as he waited to see how the docker reacted.

A lot of men have never been punched square in the face. They might have had fights in the school yard or scuffles in a pub, but most have never felt the mind-numbing explosion of pain that comes with a good right fist square on the nose. They've never had their brain shut down for a second and then spark back to life with a white-hot flash of pain that makes their eyes water and their ears ring. Rossett had learned over the years that there are two types of men in a fight: those who you can stop with one good punch . . . and those that keep coming.

He stood, hands held high, and waited to see which one he was facing.

The docker reached a tentative hand to his nose and tilted his head forward to meet it. Rossett took another step to the left and waited and watched as the docker inspected his fingers for blood, finding none. He looked up at Rossett, confused by the speed of the punch and the pain that was making his eyes water.

Rossett considered stepping in and finishing the fight but decided to wait. He wanted to give his opponent the chance to go back into the pub, finish his drink, and lick his wounds as he told his pals he'd chased Rossett off with a kick up the arse.

Rossett didn't want to fight anymore.

Unfortunately, the docker did.

The big man grunted and raised his hands. Moving slower than he had before, he turned to face Rossett. Having learned his lesson from the charge he'd made before, he slowly took a step forward as Rossett took another to the left.

"I don't want to fight," Rossett said, aware now that words were useless but trying them anyway.

The docker tracked Rossett as he took another step to the left.

"Stand still." The docker finally spoke, his voice thick and nasal as he tried to catch his breath.

Rossett decided to finish it.

"Sounds like I've broken that nose, do you want me to straighten it for you?" Rossett said, and the big man snorted and charged forward again.

Rossett feinted left and took a half step to the right. The docker, who was by now used to turning left, followed the feint and caught a left hook from Rossett as he closed in. Once again the punch landed square on that broken nose. The docker's legs gave way as his brain shut down for the second time in a minute. He landed face first on the pavement after dropping like a dead weight. Rossett danced away, enjoying the punch he'd just thrown but casting a glance toward the pub in case reinforcements were coming out.

The docker lay on the wet cobbles for a moment, groaning; he slowly rolled onto his side and reached up to his face to check if it was still there. Rossett lowered his hands and watched. Fight over, adrenaline high, he realized he'd enjoyed the moment, then suddenly felt guilty as he looked at the man in front of him on the ground.

Rossett noticed the squashed cigarette still half held in his fist and flicked it away, then rubbed his hands together, feeling for the first time that the knuckles of his right were sore.

He crossed and offered his left hand. The docker stared in confusion for a moment, his senses still muddled, then recognized Rossett and waved him away,

"I'm all right."

"You're not. Come on, here." Rossett offered his hand again but the docker ignored it and somehow managed to push himself onto all fours. He knelt there for a moment, head bowed, and then looked up at Rossett, who offered his hand again. This time the docker took it.

Rossett heaved the big man to his feet and steadied him as he swayed, senses still scrambled. His nose was a mess, swollen and red with a deep cut at its bridge, blood and snot bubbling from one nostril. On his forehead, Rossett could see a swelling he guessed was a result of hitting it on the cobbles when he went down. The docker touched the lump, flinched, then touched his nose and looked at his fingertips, which now were dipped bloodred.

"I'm sorry." Rossett took out his handkerchief.

The docker took it and wiped his nose, pulling a face, and, as he did, a thick greasy bubble of snot and blood popped from his nostril and soaked the cloth, and his nose began to bleed hard as something unseen gave way. The docker swayed at the sight of the blood. Rossett took his arm, led him toward the Austin, and leaned him against its side.

"Hold the hankie against it and tilt your head. Should I go get one of your pals?"

The docker shook his head.

"I'm surprised they didn't come out to help you." Rossett glanced toward the pub, whose doors remained firmly closed.

"I fight my own battles," the docker replied, looking up into the night, bloodred hankie clutched to his face like an oxygen mask.

"Well, you look like you fought this one all right. Do you want me to help you back inside?"

The big man shook his head. He'd just been humiliated outside, he didn't want to be humiliated inside as well.

"I can't leave you here on your own. That bump looks nasty."

The docker touched the lump again. It had visibly swollen in the seconds since he'd last checked. He lowered the hankie and looked in it like someone panning for gold, then up at Rossett.

"I don't live far. I'll walk home," he lied badly, as another snotty bubble burst forth.

"Let me drive you?"

"I'll walk."

"You can't stand up, let alone walk. Look, I'm sorry, please let me drive you."

Rossett opened the door of the car and eased the big man toward the seat before he had a chance to resist. Still dazed, the docker gave way and almost fell into the car, allowing himself to be led like a child. Rossett slammed the door, causing the docker to flinch, and another fat gob of blood dripped out onto his top lip as Rossett ran around the car and jumped in. He glanced across at the docker, who was leaning back in the seat, hankie raised and eyes closed.

"Are you all right?"

The docker nodded slightly but didn't open his eyes.

"Where are we going?"

"Battersea."

Rossett started the car and edged his way out into the fog and toward the main road. The adrenaline was subsiding and he was suddenly aware that he was drunk, very drunk. The car's headlamps did little more than bounce back off the dirty yellow fog, and he was relieved to find he could just about make out the rear lights of the cars on the main road when he turned onto it. The two men overheated the interior of the car, and Rossett had to wipe at the window with the back of his hand as he drove. He risked the odd glance at his passenger, who remained silent. After a few minutes, he was relieved to see the docker tilt his head forward and inspect the handkerchief again.

"Has it stopped bleeding?"

"Just about. That was a corker of a punch you got me with."

"I'm sorry."

"Both of 'em nearly took my block off."

Rossett glanced across, and, in the half-light, he could see the mess he'd made of the other man's nose. He shook his head.

"You should get something cold on that."

The docker touched it again, like it was an unexploded bomb, and then smiled at Rossett.

"Jim Parker." He held out his bloody hand.

"Rossett."

They shook, and Parker touched the lump on his forehead.

"You knocked me out cold there, Mr. Rossett. I went down like a sack of spuds."

"Rossett will do."

"Don't you have a first name?"

"We can stop for ice if you want?"

Parker glanced at Rossett.

"I'll be all right, I reckon. Bit of swelling will teach me a lesson."

"I'm sorry about knocking your pint. I overreacted, it's been a bad day."

"It was me who overreacted. I shouldn't have followed you out, after you said sorry."

The two men nodded to each other, apologies accepted.

"Terrible night after a terrible day, eh?" Parker finally said.

"To be honest, I was drowning my sorrows in the pub. I didn't want to go home."

"Trouble with the missus?"

"No, work."

"Looks like I did you a favor following you out then?"

Rossett smiled.

"You did take my mind off things."

"You're welcome, chum," Parker replied, touching his nose and shaking his head, "although it would've been easier if you'd just told me. I would've just bought you a drink instead."

Both men smiled as Rossett wiped the windshield with the back of his hand again. They turned south and crossed the river heading for Battersea, and Parker pointed occasionally, giving directions as they neared his home. Eventually, they pulled up in a terraced street filled with dimly lit back-to-back, two-up-two-down houses.

Rossett stopped outside Parker's but didn't kill the engine. He turned and offered his hand to shake.

"No hard feelings?"

"Already forgotten, but I'll not shake your hand till we've had a drink together. Come inside and have a quick one before you go?"

"I can't."

"Come on, you said you didn't want to go home yet. Just a quickie?"

Rossett glanced at the house and pondered for a moment.

"I'm half drunk as it is, I should really be—"

"Come on, cup of tea then. My missus will have laid out some dinner by now. Besides, I might need you; she'll give me another hiding if I walk in like this. Come on, nice cup of tea?"

Rossett smiled and nodded.

"Just a cup of tea."

Both men got out of the car, and Rossett waited by the front door as Parker made his way toward him. The big man still looked unsteady and had to rest his hand on the car's hood as he stepped onto the curb.

"Stand by," said Parker as he opened the front door, which led directly into the parlor of the tiny house.

Rossett felt the heat of the coal fire that was crackling in the hearth as soon as he entered. The room was tidy and furnished in a manner that many would have called old-fashioned, but that Rossett would have called homely. Two comfy but threadbare armchairs framed the fireplace, and the thin woolen rug that lay at their feet was the only carpeting in the room. The solitary lightbulb burned under an orange tasseled shade that gave off a glow almost as warming as the fire, and a fat lazy cat glanced up from a tiny two-seater settee with slow blinks and a wide yawn.

Rossett liked the room. It felt like one fit for a family, like a room that had sheltered a lot of love.

"Is that you, Jim?" a woman shouted from the kitchen. "You're home early."

Parker cast a glance at Rossett and rolled his eyes.

"I've brought a visitor, love." Parker smiled at Rossett. "That's my Queenie."

Before he finished his sentence the woman appeared at the door that led to the kitchen. She was a similar age to Parker, maybe a few years younger. Her face wore the weight of a hard life, although it wasn't a hard face. She smiled at Rossett before turning to Parker and gasping.

"Oh my lor', Jim, what's happened to your face?" She stepped forward and reached for her husband.

Rossett frowned and regretted agreeing to go into the house.

"A gang of geezers tried to have me off. Good job Rossett here was passing by, else they would have done."

"What would they want with having you off?"

"Well, we had words, see. It wasn't nothing. Mr. Rossett stepped in to help. We saw 'em off though, didn't we?" Parker looked at Rossett for backup, and Rossett smiled thinly and nodded, aware, after being a copper for so long, that the best way to lie was not to say anything.

Queenie looked at Rossett, then her husband. Rossett knew immediately that she wasn't as daft as her husband hoped. She gave the slightest of shakes of her head and then led Parker to one of the armchairs and pushed him down. He sat, fitting the armchair like a glove.

"I'm all right, girl, just a bruise or two, that's all."

Queenie prodded the lump on his head, and Parker yelped and put his hands up to cover it.

"At your age, Jim Parker, fighting in the street?" She looked across to Rossett and nodded to the other armchair. "Sit."

Rossett found himself doing as he was told, and Parker smiled at him.

"I warned you."

Rossett was beginning to like these people.

"I'VE ONLY GOT a drop of rabbit stew, Mr. Rossett," Queenie called from the kitchen as Rossett balanced the teacup and saucer on his leg while holding a plate of biscuits in his other hand.

The fat cat was now sitting in front of him, back to the fire, eyeing him suspiciously.

"I really should be going."

"Nonsense, you can stay for a bite. You were good enough to bring my Jim home, least I can do is feed you."

Rossett looked around for somewhere to put the biscuits he'd been holding for the last five minutes without eating. He stood, stepped over the cat, and placed the plate down on a yellowing cotton tablecloth that half covered the dark brown wood.

On the table, next to some tired flowers, was a photo in a frame, of a young man in uniform. Rossett squinted at it, trying to make out the badge on the beret its subject was proudly wearing. He was holding the picture when Queenie walked in with some cutlery.

Rossett showed her the picture. "Your son?"

"My Arthur."

Rossett knew from her tone that Arthur wouldn't be joining them for supper that night, or any night ever again.

"The war?"

She nodded sadly, and Rossett put the picture back on the table carefully.

"Did you serve, Mr. Rossett?"

Rossett nodded without looking at her.

"Such a terrible waste."

She put the cutlery on the table and left the room. Rossett returned to his seat, took a sip of tea, and stared at the cat, which stared back at him, blinking slowly again, as if it missed Arthur, too.

Rossett heard the clump of big feet coming down the stairs and looked to the kitchen door as Jim entered. He'd washed his face and changed his shirt, but the dirty purple bruises under his eyes were darkening by the minute.

"I should be getting along."

"Don't be daft, she's warming that stew now. Here, have a tot."

Jim bent down to a small cabinet and produced a bottle of brandy. He crossed the room in two steps and poured a drop in Rossett's tea before Rossett had a chance to cover it.

"Nice for her to make a fuss every now and then."

Rossett sighed and glanced to the door as Queenie entered with a breadboard and loaf. She placed it on the table, moving the picture of Arthur back a few inches to make way.

"Mr. Rossett was asking about our Arthur, Jim," she said as she headed back out into the kitchen.

"My eldest." Jim remained standing, holding the bottle like a wine waiter looking for a glass. "Joined up before the war, Royal Engineers. The bastards got him on the road back to the beach; he was trying to blow a bridge to slow them down."

Rossett subconsciously moved his hand to his lapel, feeling for the swastika badge; it wasn't there, lost in the fight.

"Terrible days" was all he could think of to say as he took another sip of tea.

"Were you over there?"

Rossett nodded.

"Did you make it out or were you captured with the others in France?"

"I made it out, for what it was worth. I finally got captured outside London after the surrender."

The men looked at each other and paused in the way that everyone seemed to do since the war, unsure of what to say, unsure of where they stood, scared to criticize governments past or present for where it might lead.

They settled on a silent nod of understanding and left it there.

Queenie reentered and frowned when she saw the brandy.

"Didn't take you long?"

"Come on, girl, we've got company!" Jim waggled the bottle at her. She smiled back and rolled her eyes at Rossett before turning and leaving Jim balancing the plates.

Rossett smiled. He liked these people an awful lot.

CHAPTER 17

THE MEAL WAS excellent and Rossett was glad he'd stayed. It had been a long time since he'd eaten good home cooking and fresh-baked bread, and longer since he'd laughed at a table with people who loved each other and welcomed strangers in these troubled times.

The table was cleared, fire stoked, glasses filled, and he found himself having to worry only about keeping the cat that was sitting on his lap purring.

Rossett was contented for the first time in a long time.

Queenie came out of the kitchen and nudged her husband, who was sitting opposite Rossett staring into the fire.

"Mr. Rossett's glass."

Jim picked up the bottle from the floor near his feet and leaned across to pour, but this time Rossett was quicker and managed to move the glass just out of reach. The cat shifted slightly and flexed its claws as a reminder to him that it was comfortable and that if he moved again he would be sorry. Queenie drew one of the dining chairs up to the fire and sat between the two men, holding her own small drink on her knee.

In the corner of the room some band music was whispering out of the radio, and all three, plus the cat, listened to a song Rossett remembered as "Supposing," by Jay Wilbur and His Orchestra.

He'd danced to it once with his wife in a parlor just like this, cheek to cheek, with just a crackling fire and a crackling radio for company. They'd made love that night and then lain in front of that fire, letting it warm their bodies as a storm lashed the windows outside and drowned out the wireless.

They'd stared at each other, not speaking, inches from each other's face, looking into the depths of love as they stroked each other's hair.

Two people as close as two people could be.

"It's a beautiful song." Queenie dragged Rossett back into the present. He glanced at her and she smiled sadly at him, as if she'd heard his memories out loud.

"I once danced to that song," Rossett found himself saying.

"Happier times?"

"Happier times," replied Rossett as he rested his hand on the cat's head and stroked its cheek with his thumb. The cat shifted slightly and tilted its head to get the full effect.

"Do you have pets, Mr. Rossett?"

"No."

"We got him to keep the mice down, not that he does. He spends all day staring at me and then all night sitting on Jim's lap. I'd love to know what he is thinking."

"He'll be thinking how lucky he is to have ended up in this house with you two"—Rossett paused, then looked up from the cat to Queenie—"and he's not the only one."

Queenie smiled as they sat and listened to the dance band for a moment more. Rossett became aware that Jim was breathing deeply, and he looked across to see that the big man had closed his eyes and started to doze.

"It's all the early mornings. He drops off every night."

"I'd best be going."

"It's all right, I leave him there. He doesn't sleep very well in bed anymore, tossing and turning and mumbling away."

Rossett nodded and turned back to the fire.

"Do you sleep well, Mr. Rossett?"

Rossett turned back to Queenie, and the cat nudged his hand because he'd stopped stroking its cheek.

"No."

"Did you lose her during the war? I could see her in your face during that song, so very sad." Queenie stared at him, and he thought that she might cry, her own pain letting her know how much his hurt.

"After the war. It was a bomb, her and my son."

Queenie didn't speak; she left it up to Rossett to carry on if he wished. Eventually, he looked up from the cat and stared into her eyes.

"I was still in the camp, prisoner of war. I'd just started to get her letters through as everything settled down. A bundle arrived one day, and I sat and read them all at once. She'd been writing and writing. She didn't even know where I was and she just kept sending them to the High Command."

"She found you."

"Just as I lost her."

"One day I had her in my hands, my son had scribbled some lines, I could smell her on the paper, feel her fingers holding the sheets I was holding. I had a picture of my son and her, and I felt . . . I felt . . ." Rossett tilted his head, confused by his own words; he knew what he wanted to say but couldn't say it.

"You were falling in love again?"

"I hadn't fallen out of love. I still haven't."

Queenie touched his arm and Rossett turned back to the fire. His eyes felt heavy. He looked at his glass and then squeezed the bridge of his nose with his free hand, damming the weight that was building up behind his eyes.

"We've all lost so much," Queenie said, as much to herself as to Rossett. "I wonder when it'll start to get better, when we'll start to get things back. All of this . . . it all seems so pointless."

Rossett nodded.

"The priest told me, 'You just have to keep going, it's a sin to give up,'" Rossett said, his voice reedy now, emotion building.

"Is that why you stayed in the police?"

"I needed to do something. I . . . I couldn't be on my own."

Queenie touched his arm again, and this time left her hand resting on it.

"That's why I'm glad I had my Jim. I couldn't have coped on my own. You shouldn't be alone, you need someone. Would you find another lady?"

Rossett thought about Mrs. Ward, his landlady, and what Koehler had said about taking her to the beach. For the most fleeting of moments he considered a future with someone else before silently shaking his head.

"So you'll stay on your own forever?"

Rossett nodded.

"Oh, Mr. Rossett, that's such a waste."

Rossett turned to Queenie, opened his mouth to speak, and then stopped. He tilted his head, and suddenly silent tears ran down his cheeks like the first rains of autumn.

"I'm damaged, Queenie," he said softly, "broken, inside . . . I've done such terrible things . . . caused so much pain . . . I've killed so many people, I could never . . . I can't ever . . ."

Queenie held his hand, and Rossett looked back to the fire, wondering why the tears came so easily and so often.

"Mr. Rossett, you're not a bad man, I can tell that. You could never be," she whispered urgently.

Rossett couldn't bring himself to look into her face and instead looked down at her hand; paper-thin skin barely hid the blood that ran through her veins, her swollen knuckles smooth and white as they gripped onto him for all they were worth with a thin gold ring that hung on her finger like a band on a pigeon's leg.

"You're a good man," Queenie said again, as if she needed to hear it herself once more for confirmation.

He took a deep breath.

"Today I sent a little boy to a place where he could die, a little boy who hadn't done anyone any harm. A child, just like my own, a child who trusted me, needed me . . . and I gave him to people who would sooner stroke your cat than give that little boy water. I do that every day. Like a boiler man, I shovel them into hell like they are coal. I do that every day, because if I stop . . . if I think about it, about what I am doing and where I am, I want to blow my head off to escape the misery of what I've become."

They sat in silence, Queenie still holding his hand and Rossett still holding the cat until he spoke again.

"I'm falling, Queenie. I'm falling and no one can save me."

"Oh, my love, there is always someone, there is always someone who can pull you back. You just need to find that person. It's like you meeting Jim. You don't know what's around the corner. There will be someone to save you. You just haven't met them yet."

"There is no way back. I'm soaked in blood and it'll never wash off." Rossett twisted in his seat, and the cat flexed its claws again and lifted its head as he picked up his glass and finished his drink in one angry gulp.

"Things will change. You will change. You just need to find a reason."

"I've already changed. I'm a monster." Rossett could feel self-pity evolving into anger. He'd felt it before.

"I couldn't save my boy, I've had to accept it, Mr. Rossett, and you have to accept that you couldn't save your family; they're gone. You need to move forward, save someone else with your love, save yourself with your love. You've still got it in you."

The fire in the hearth crackled. Rossett stared deep into it as Queenie spoke, and something stirred, something good.

CHAPTER 18

ROSSETT WAS AWARE he'd gained purchase and was moving forward.

He felt he had purpose for the first time in years.

He couldn't save Queenie's boy, he couldn't save his own, he couldn't save the boys who had died around him in the fields of France and the south of England, and he couldn't save the German boys he had killed with his own hands.

But he could try to save one boy, one mother's son who deserved the chance of life and love.

He could snatch one life back from the devil and give the child hope. He owed it to Jacob and he owed it to himself.

He had to try.

He had to try, so that if one day, in another place, he had the chance to look into his own son's eyes, he wouldn't have to look away.

He had to try.

He didn't have a plan; he just knew he wasn't going to be stopped.

He'd held a gun to his own head when he was drunk many times before, but tonight he was going to hold one against someone else's.

He glanced at his watch in the half-light off the Strand—9:40 P.M. He would have preferred it to be later. The small hours of the morning would have been ideal. The time when jailers are sleepy and guards are thinking about the warm bed that lies a few hours distant would have been the best time to strike.

Beggars can't be choosers, he thought, unwilling to hold off from what he had to do—in case, as the alcohol evaporated out of his body, so would his resolve.

It didn't take long to make his way through the fog to Chandos Place. He was relieved to find it empty except for a couple of parked cars and a solitary sentry standing by the barrier stamping his feet, staving off the cold. Rossett drove up and, for once, the window did as it was told.

"I'm filling up my car from the petrol pumps in the yard." He waved Koehler's petrol chitty under the torch of the sentry, who glanced at it and then shone the light around the car and then at Rossett's warrant card.

"At this time of night?" The boy spoke with heavily accented English.

"I'm away on holiday. I tried this afternoon but the yard was full with the area commander's transport detail."

"I'm not sure." The sentry glanced into the darkened yard and adjusted his rifle on his shoulder.

"Please, if you could, I'd really appreciate it. I've a long drive tomorrow, so I really need that fuel." The guard stepped back from the car and looked to the yard again. Rossett felt his heart beat faster. Maybe his plan, such as it was, was already coming apart.

"No civilians are supposed to be in the yard after nine."

"I'm not a civilian, I'm a policeman, and the order is personally signed by Major Koehler." Rossett waved the paper again at the sentry, deciding that if the boy came close to the car he was going to hit him with the sap that lay ready between his legs.

The German paused, still some distance from the car, and Rossett weighed getting out to overpower him. He judged the gap between them, not wanting to alarm the boy by appearing too keen.

"Please, I need to get that fuel. Please." One last try.

"All right, but be quick. I don't want to get into any trouble."

Rossett smiled broadly and gave the thumbs-up as he slipped the car into gear.

"I'll be in and out in minutes; you won't even know I've been here."

The German looked like he was already regretting his decision, but he walked to the barrier, put his weight on the fat end, and eased it up. Rossett pulled into the yard to find that it was still crowded from that day's parade. Two big Mercedeses were parked next to the fuel pump, dwarfing the Austin as Rossett pulled up as close to the pump as he could.

He slipped his sap back into his raincoat, dashed around the car, and quickly started to fill it with fuel. As he waited for the pump, he glanced around, checking for anyone watching, and was glad to see the yard was deserted.

The parked vehicles threw dark shadows, and the light from the yard lamps had to fight its way through the fog, as if God were lighting the world with a solitary match.

Perfect for what Rossett had in mind.

He looked to where the sentry would be standing, some seventy feet away, and was reassured that he couldn't see him through the fog.

"If you can't see them, they can't see you," his old instructors had said, and they were nearly always right.

He finished filling the car and took out the fuel hose, but instead of placing it back in the pump he took out a pack of cigarettes and jammed it behind the handle, opening the lever just enough for a steady trickle of fuel to drizzle out of the nozzle. He placed the pump onto the cobbles and glanced across to the sentry once more before creeping around to the Mercedeses. He bent down and took out his penknife, carefully piercing two tires on each car, just enough so that he could hear the steady hiss of air escaping, not loudly enough to attract attention but deeply enough to ensure the tires would be flat in a couple of minutes.

He left the cars and jogged across the yard to the heavy blue wooden door that led into the station; he pulled it and was relieved to see that it had been left unlocked. The Germans, like the English before them, relied on the security of a bored guard standing one hundred feet away and the question of who exactly would want to break into a police station.

The door opened onto the back stairwell; it had been the route by which English bobbies had brought prisoners through to the vans that would take them to a court of justice and twelve good men and true. Now, Rossett could only imagine what fate awaited escorted prisoners at the top of the steps; he was certain whatever it was, it wasn't justice.

He went quickly down the one flight of stairs that led to the back gate of the cell complex. At the bottom he found the familiar iron-barred black gate with its sturdy frame. Next to the gate, on the outside, was a bell push that allowed visitors to alert the custody desk that someone was there. Rossett pressed the bell, holding it for five seconds, knowing that the shrill ring, which he could hear in the distance, would have scared the life out of whoever was sitting behind the desk.

He released the bell push for a second, then leaned on it again. It wasn't long before he heard the clump of boots coming down the corridor toward him. After a second, the fat German jailer he had seen earlier hove into view around the corner; he didn't look happy.

"*Was ist's? Bin doch nicht taub!*" "What? I'm not deaf!"

As he'd guessed, the German wasn't happy. Rossett smiled and shrugged by way of reply.

"I'm sorry, I don't speak German," he lied, and the German stopped at the gate and scowled at him.

"I am not deaf! You must not ring the bell like that!"

"I'm sorry, I didn't know if anyone was there."

"Of course, there is someone here! What do you want?"

Rossett smiled again. "I need to come in; I have to speak to a prisoner."

"You can't. Rules. We don't allow anyone in after eight unless it is on the express orders of the commandant."

The German was already turning away as he spoke.

"This is on the orders of the commandant. One of the prisoners needs to be spoken to urgently. It's vital that I speak to him now. Just a couple of questions and then I'll be gone, two minutes at the most."

The jailer paused, then turned back to the gate. He held out his hand and tilted his head while resting the other on his hip.

"I need a written order. Do you have one?"

Rossett nodded and reached into his raincoat pocket. He took out his hand and, opening it, revealed five of the gold sovereigns. He held them just the other side of the gate, so that the jailer could see them through the bars.

"Just two questions, that's all."

The jailer stared at the coins and then at Rossett, who was banking on the fat man's greed extending to more than just strudel.

The jailer rubbed his chin and rested his other hand on his belt, tucking his thumb into the tight leather.

"Two questions?"

"That's all. I can speak to him through the flap; you don't even have to open the door."

"My boss is here." The German took a step toward the gate and played with the chain that hung from his pocket, the chain that Rossett knew held the keys to the complex.

"He won't even know I've been here."

"I'm not sure . . ."

Rossett flicked his head, beckoning the German to come close so he could whisper. The fat man took a step toward the gate, so that his face was twelve inches from the bars, as Rossett did the same.

"There are more of these, thousands. One of the Jews has hidden them and we don't know where. I need to speak to him. This'll be great for all of us."

"All of us?"

"Me, you, Koehler, your boss as well, if you want. Just open the gate. I'll be two minutes."

The fat man licked his lips and glanced back down the corridor before turning back to Rossett, who, like a cobra striking, leaned his right arm through the bars, grabbed the back of the jailer's neck, and pulled him forward, slamming his forehead onto the bars of the gate, which clanged like an alarm.

The jailer's head hit hard, but the blow didn't knock him out. He managed to grab the gate with one hand and with all his might pushed back as the trickle of blood from his forehead ran down into his confused, blinking eyes. Rossett allowed him a couple of inches before pulling with the German's movement, grasping his collar and jerking him away from the bars. The fat man almost overbalanced backward, and Rossett, sensing this, waited a microsecond for the jailer to lean forward again. As soon as he did, Rossett used his momentum and pulled full force on the back of his neck, causing the German's head to hit against the cold steel one more time.

Something cracked inside the jailer's skull, so loudly that Rossett heard the bone splinter over the clang of the metal gate and the noise of the sovereigns falling to the floor. The German's legs gave way. Rossett reached through with his other hand, grabbed his tunic, and lowered him to the ground, where he lay glassy eyed, not quite dead, but on his way.

Grabbing the chain from the trouser pocket, Rossett snapped the keys free, then rattled through eight keys before finding one that looked likely to work. He tried it in the lock and cursed when it wouldn't turn.

The German on the floor made a gurgling sound, and Rossett looked down to see that clear fluid was leaking from his nose and onto the linoleum floor. The German's eyes were moving side to side, as if watching a tennis match but not quite seeing the ball.

Rossett tried another key, but that one didn't work either.

"Which fucking key is it, you fat bastard?" he said to the German, who mumbled, then shut his eyes.

Rossett fumbled again and finally the lock turned. He pushed hard against the gate to slide the German out of the way. This time, he didn't mumble.

There was no going back now.

CHAPTER 19

ROSSETT WALKED, SCANNING the locked cell doors. He was dismayed to see that the Germans didn't use the small chalkboards to note who was in which cell. He'd been hoping he wouldn't have to approach the desk at the center of the complex, and that he would be able to find Jacob and get him away without meeting anyone else.

He checked cell 14, the one Jacob had been allocated that afternoon. The cell was empty, door open, beds bare.

He stood in the doorway and wondered if he was already too late. Maybe the boy had gone, been tossed into the system or, even worse, tossed into a pit. But then reason returned. The hour was late and the jailer was fat. It would be easier to keep the prisoners in cells together than dotted around the complex. It meant less walking when checking them. Only the ones who were to be questioned would be kept separate.

Not knowing where Jacob was made his task much more difficult. Now he had to overcome whatever the German equivalent of the custody sergeant was, and that wouldn't be easy, especially if a German custody sergeant was as obstinate as an English one.

As he approached the custody desk, he tried to appear confident, which was made easier by the fact that there was only one man there, and that the man was tucking into a massive sandwich with a plate of cake waiting as the next course.

Rationing hasn't reached the Reich, thought Rossett as he smiled broadly and nodded toward the cake.

"I've come at the right time!" Rossett noticed another, half-eaten sandwich in front of the empty seat to the custody officer's right. His friend from the gate wouldn't be finishing that tonight.

The custody officer glanced over Rossett's shoulder, looking for his assistant, and lowered his food. He didn't reply right away, chewing the thick crusty bread, but looked quizzically at Rossett, wanting an explanation for the disturbance of his supper.

"I need to speak to that Jewish boy," Rossett said, reaching into his pockets as if searching for the written order. "I've an order here somewhere, just a couple of questions."

"Where is Muller?" A few crumbs came out of the packed mouth along with the question.

"He's talking to my driver outside. I think they know each other," Rossett lied smoothly, still looking through his pockets.

The custody officer stood up and brushed some crumbs off his tunic, frowning at the inconvenience. He started to pull his key chain out of his own pocket and consulted a clipboard that hung on a hook behind his chair, turning his back on Rossett as he did.

"Will you need an interview room, or will . . ." He turned back to see that Rossett, still smiling warmly, had stepped behind the desk and was only a couple of feet away.

Rossett had picked up a bread knife, intending to reach the German before he turned around. Once the custody officer saw him, Rossett moved quickly, spinning the knife in his left hand and keeping it low as he drove it in hard, feeling its serrated edge slide home, scraping on a rib as it went.

The German grabbed at Rossett's arm and tried to reach for the knife, which was already out and about to plunge into his body again. The two men fell to the floor, and Rossett drove his forearm up under the German's chin and across his throat. Pushing up onto his toes to use his full body weight to hold the German down, he stabbed the knife home again. This time he felt a rib snap as the knife plunged in to its hilt. Rossett twisted it, feeling the blade resist and then spin freely inside the chest cavity.

Spittle and blood frothed from the German's lips as he gasped for air to fill his punctured lungs. Rossett pressed again with his forearm, face inches from the German, who was trying to shout but unable to make a noise.

Rossett pushed again at the knife, trying to end the struggle, but the German thrashed again and managed to grab a handful of Rossett's raincoat and pull. Strength flagging, but not spirit, he tried to punch with his free hand as Rossett stabbed again, feeling flecks of frothy blood blow onto his face from the German's mouth.

The German didn't want to die, and Rossett marveled at the strength he was still showing, even as his life faded away. The final push of the knife seemed to hit something critical, and the German suddenly let go of Rossett and exhaled deeply. More blood bubbled from his mouth, and his eyes looked upward toward his forehead, confused, as if feeling something inside he couldn't understand.

Rossett pushed onto his neck again, and this time the German didn't push back; he croaked a last breath, sighing as he went, sounding disappointed to be dying.

Rossett rolled off and knelt next to the body. He realized he was panting. He tried to control his breathing, and to not look at the man who lay before him, leaking blood on the floorboards.

Blood soaked Rossett's hand, and it took him a moment to realize some of it was his own; his hand must have slid down the handle of the knife when it was wet with the German's blood. He'd sliced his palm, and as soon as he looked closely at it, it began to hurt. The wound wasn't deep, but it opened as he flexed his fist, releasing more blood.

"Shit," he said out loud, looking for something to wrap the cut with as he stood up. He found a tea towel next to the cake and wound it tightly, clenching his fist to hold it in place. His fingers held it tight, and he took some solace from the fact that he didn't appear to have severed any ligaments or tendons.

He stepped over the German and checked the board, looking for Jacob's name.

Cell 6. He'd walked past it on his way to the desk.

If you'd used the cell chalkboards you'd be eating cake right now instead of staining the floorboards, thought Rossett as he pulled out the keys he'd taken from his first victim. He knew the biggest would be the cell door key; it always was, making it easy for the jailer to find on the big loop.

He dashed around to cell 6, opening the lock and pulling back the iron door. The cell was in darkness. About nine feet square, it held two iron bunk beds on either side of the room, and the light from the corridor lit a vivid rectangle on the floor. A thick smell of urine and body odor hung in the air, and Rossett squinted from both that and the lack of light.

"Jacob?" Rossett called to the bunks, remaining by the door not wanting to be jumped by a prisoner who thought he was a German.

"Yes?" came a small voice from the bottom left-hand bunk. Rossett reached into the gloom and pulled back the sheet. Jacob lay in the bed, clothed, alongside a man in his thirties, who had an arm around the boy, both of them blinking up into the light.

Rossett stared at the other man for the briefest of moments, then grabbed Jacob and pulled him from the bed and onto the floor. Gripping the top bunk, Rossett swung a leg into the bottom bunk and kicked the man hard in the face, once, twice, three times with the heel of his shoe.

Other men in the cell half rose from their beds but didn't intervene.

"You bastard!" Rossett kicked again. "He's a fucking child!"

"No!" Jacob scrabbled to his feet and pulled on Rossett's raincoat, desperately trying to stop him from kicking into the bunk. "No! Please, he's my friend!"

Rossett stopped kicking and looked down at Jacob, who was crying. "What?"

"I was scared," the boy sobbed. "He let me sleep with him . . . I'm sorry, I was scared."

The little voice trailed off as the sobs grew louder. Rossett looked into the bottom bunk. The man was bleeding from the nose and mouth, holding his hands up to prevent further attack and nodding furiously at Rossett. Behind him, Rossett heard the other bunk bed squeak. He turned and saw the two occupants had got up, unsure of what was going on.

Rossett grabbed Jacob off the floor and pushed him toward the door as he threw the cell keys at one of the men.

"Release everyone and get out."

"Who the hell are you?" The man on the bunk wiped his face as he blinked up toward Rossett, lips thick with blood.

"I'm the British fucking Lion."

CHAPTER 20

ROSSETT DRAGGED JACOB around to the metal gate where he had dispatched the jailer. The little boy had fallen silent again and was struggling to keep up. At times, he dangled and slid as Rossett jerked him along like a reluctant puppy. Behind them, the sounds of clanging cell doors could be heard as the breakout got under way, making Rossett quicken his step even more. They passed the jailer's body on the floor and slipped through the metal gate. Rossett tried to take the stairs a few at a time before Jacob finally slipped from his grasp and fell. He turned, hoisted the boy up in his arms, and went on. Jacob lay silently over Rossett's shoulder, a passenger of fate once again.

At the top of the stairs, Rossett slowly opened the heavy wooden door an inch, first listening and then risking a peek. In the yard, he could just make out the outline of the sentry, who was standing by the Austin.

Rossett cursed. He'd taken too long and the German must have smelled the petrol he'd intended as a diversion in case of emergency. The sentry seemed to sense someone was watching and glanced over to the door, which Rossett leaned back from and closed softly, suddenly aware that the forty-watt bulb above his head had beamed like a lighthouse across the foggy yard.

He put Jacob down and held his finger to the boy's lips, making eye contact and nodding his head. Jacob returned the nod and stood mute and unmoving. Rossett noticed the boy wasn't wearing shoes and that he had two skinny white toes peeking through a woolen sock like worms hanging out of a tiny tent.

Behind them, Rossett heard low voices, the prisoners slowly making their way up the stairs, unsure of what waited for them at the top.

They don't know what to do, either, he thought as he weighed his options and wiped his hand across his face.

Eventually, the man he'd assaulted moments earlier and a few others appeared below him at the foot of the final flight of stairs. Rossett turned and motioned for them to stop.

They did. Rossett looked down at Jacob and then around the empty landing. He took a deep breath, leaned against the door, swung it open, and walked outside.

He was beginning to regret planning rescue operations when he was drunk.

The sentry had slowly been making his way toward the door, and he was now holding his rifle in both hands, Rossett's only solace that it wasn't pointed at him, yet.

"I cut my bloody hand." Rossett held up his hand, with his tea towel bandage now red with blood, and forced a weak smile.

"There is fuel all over the yard." The sentry looked at the hand as Rossett walked toward him.

"I thought I'd be back before it leaked. I didn't realize how bad this cut was." This time Rossett lowered his hand and offered it toward the German to inspect. They were now only fifteen feet apart and Rossett continued to close the gap as he spoke.

"You shouldn't have left your car."

"Blood everywhere. Do you have a bandage? They loaned me this old tea towel in the jail, but it's bleeding something rotten."

The young German seemed to relax slightly and half turned toward the sentry post

"We have a small kit in the hut I could—"

Rossett hit him hard side on, and they both fell to the ground as the sentry's rifle clattered onto the cobbles next to them. Rossett had been hoping to take him from behind, but he suspected the half turn was the best opportunity he'd be given, and he'd taken it on instinct. As he struggled to cover the German's mouth, he regretted having left the bread knife sticking out of the chest of the jailer; it would have helped him subdue the young sentry, who was slipping and sliding in his grasp like an eel soaked in butter.

They rolled about the wet cobbles and Rossett smelled the petrol on the ground as he tried to find some purchase. The sentry swung a few punches, but they bounced off the top of Rossett's head, which was buried, defensively, in the German's shoulder and face. Rossett slowly, with a dreadful certainty, started to get the upper hand and tightened his hold on the German's face and throat. He hadn't managed to cut off the air yet, mostly because of the thick tea towel on his hand, but he could feel the sentry tiring. They rolled again and Rossett heard a mushy thud, then felt the German suddenly go limp.

He lay still under the sentry, holding on tight, unsure if it was a ploy by the German to buy an advantage, when suddenly he felt hands pulling him up. He raised his head and saw the prisoner he'd attacked earlier in Jacob's cell holding the sentry's rifle. Two other prisoners helped an unsteady and suddenly very tired Rossett to his feet.

"Thought you could do with a hand." The prisoner smiled through a fat lip and gestured that he had hit the German with the butt of the rifle.

Rossett breathed deeply and nodded.

"The boy?"

"My name is Leigh, James Leigh."

"Where's the boy?" Rossett ignored him and looked around the yard at the prisoners, who were moving out of the building cautiously. Many of them squatted in the shadows and looked toward Leigh, waiting. It struck him that they were disciplined and that Leigh appeared to be in charge.

The sentry groaned, and both Rossett and Leigh looked down at him.

"Must be losing my touch. Thought he was dead." Leigh smiled at Rossett.

"Where is the boy?" This time Rossett stared at Leigh coldly as he spoke, and the other man smiled and nodded to someone behind Rossett, who turned and saw Jacob emerge from the small group of men who were standing behind him.

Jacob stood in front of Rossett, arms folded across his chest and one foot on top of the other, taking up as little space in the world as he could. Rossett nodded to Leigh, grabbed Jacob by the shoulder, and guided him toward the car. He opened the door and pushed Jacob onto the backseat, then glanced back at the other men, who were slowly emerging from the jail doorway like nervous fox cubs from a lair.

"Give me the rifle," Rossett whispered and held out his hand to Leigh, who smiled and shook his head.

"I don't think so."

"Give it to me."

"I'll be needing it, old man. Sorry."

Leigh smiled again and theatrically worked the bolt on the rifle to drive a round home before turning and waving the others away from the door, urging them to take off into the night. A few dashed to the big Mercedeses and climbed in, while others skirted around the yard and headed for the sentry point, all of them moving silently. Rossett watched as the men moved around the yard. There was no panic; these men seemed to know what to do and were doing it carefully. Rossett counted at least ten of them and decided they were ex-military.

He now regretted having slashed the tires on the two big cars and considered warning them, but decided against it.

They weren't his problem. His only concern was the boy.

"I can't let you loose on your own with a rifle. Give it to me," Rossett whispered again, this time more urgently. He was aware of the absurdity of the situation; he'd just sprung a criminal from jail, but as a policeman, he was damned if he was going to arm the man as well.

"You aren't setting me loose on my own." Leigh smiled warmly. "I'm coming with you, chum."

Rossett shook his head, lowered himself into the Austin, and reached for the starter. Before he touched it, he heard the soft click of a safety catch, and he glanced up to see Leigh walking toward him, rifle leveled at his head.

Leigh leaned down to the door, smiled again, then said to Jacob, "Slide across, old chum. Uncle Jim is coming with you and your friend for a ride."

CHAPTER 21

ROSSETT STARTED THE car, eyes on the mirror.

"There is no reason to hold a gun to my head. I've just broken you out of prison," he said as they drove slowly across the yard to the sentry point. One of the released prisoners raised the barrier and glanced up and down the street before beckoning them forward.

"Stop."

Rossett did as he was told.

The man leaned down to Rossett's window, which dutifully dropped into the door as Rossett tried to lower it. Leigh leaned forward and beckoned the prisoner who was now acting as sentry over.

"Tell the ones who know it to make their way to the warehouse and the rest lie low. I don't want anyone making contact with their controller for at least seven days, understood?"

"Yes, sir."

"Those who aren't attached to us, let them know who we are and how they can contact us, then bugger off out of here."

The man nodded and stepped back from the car. Rossett half expected him to salute, but he merely waved them through and disappeared back into the fog. Rossett felt the prod of the rifle again and he gunned the engine, turned on his lights, and headed out onto the road. In his mirror, he saw the two big Mercedeses waddle out of the yard and shook his head.

"What?" From the back.

"Your friends won't get far in those staff cars."

"They know what they're doing."

"Is that how they ended up in jail?"

"Just keep driving."

"Where am I going?"

"Where were you taking the boy?"

Rossett glanced in the mirror and then back at the road.

"You did have a plan, didn't you?"

"Not as such."

The shadow in the back shook his head, and Rossett regretted confessing his lack of preparedness.

"Head for Wapping."

"Wapping," Rossett repeated flatly.

"And put that bloody window up, we're freezing in the back here."

"I can't. It's broken."

Rossett heard a chuckle and found himself squeezing the steering wheel tighter.

"It seems you are better at putting people into prison than you are at getting them out."

Rossett didn't reply.

A fine drizzle was rinsing away the fog, and the streets shone as if they were covered in sooty varnish. Rossett kept to the speed limit and stuck to the main roads as they headed across the city. He knew to steer clear of the German quarter, aware that he could still use the main roads there, but conscious that there might be routine roadblocks and checkpoints. Whether those roadblocks would extend out across the city as a whole depended on how soon the bodies at the jail were found.

They'd driven in silence for ten minutes when Leigh finally said, "I can see your mind working, Rossett."

"How do you know my name?"

"You told me who you were, old man, just after you kicked my face into the back of my head."

Rossett looked in the mirror again.

"Wish you'd finished the job now?"

"Yes."

"I should feel quite honored being chauffeured by the British Lion. It's a shame this car stinks of Nazi, though. Sort of takes the fun out of it."

Rossett felt something rising in his chest; he swallowed hard and managed to push it down again.

"Who are you?"

"I've told you, old man. James Leigh."

Leigh spoke with apparent disinterest, looking out the window at the passing buildings. If it weren't for the occasional dig of the rifle muzzle into the back of his seat, Rossett would have thought the other man was just enjoying a late-night drive. He gave off an air of casual arrogance, the one favored by some of the English officer class. Rossett had seen it many times. In some, it was genuine, the result of having been brought up by nannies and having people fetch and carry for them. In others, it seemed to hide the coldness that had built an empire and streaked many a bayonet with blood. Rossett wasn't fooled by the posh voice. He knew the man in the back of the car was a cobra. A cobra bred on the playing fields of Eton, but a cobra no less, to be treated with care and held at arm's length, preferably by the throat.

"And who is James Leigh?"

"Let's just say we are on opposite sides of this war."

"The war's over."

"Is it? Some of us are still fighting, dear boy. Some of us didn't give up."

"So you're resistance?"

"You really are a detective, aren't you?" Leigh mocked Rossett and smiled at him in the mirror. The occasional streetlamp strobed across his face, and in the flash flicker of darkness the smile disappeared. "Just keep driving, British Lion. We can finish the chat when we get to Wapping."

CHAPTER 22

KOEHLER WAS RIDING a bicycle along a narrow track lined with trees. It looked like Bavaria, and he could hear a woman laughing but couldn't quite see her. It sounded like his wife, Lotte, as if she was nearby, maybe on another bicycle just behind him. He looked up into the trees at the shafts of sunlight that warmed his face, and he was happy, really happy, laughing with someone he loved, and for a moment he felt like he was going to soar off the ground and up into the trees to swoop and roll with the birds that were singing above his head.

And then the phone rang.

He rolled and pressed his face into the pillow as it rang again, clenching his fists and his eyelids, desperate to hold onto his dream. But it was gone and he was back in bed with a phone that wouldn't stop.

He groaned and picked up the receiver, face still pressed into the pillow.

"What?"

"Apologies for the call, sir. We have a problem at Charing Cross."

Koehler didn't recognize the voice and he squinted at the clock next to his bed: 11:15. He'd barely been asleep. He tried to remember his dream again, but it was gone.

Like the life he'd been enjoying in it.

"What problem?"

"A breakout and a fire."

Koehler was awake now. He pushed himself up onto one elbow and rolled onto his side.

"How many?"

"Eight prisoners, sir, the resistance operatives who were due to go to Paris on Monday, all gone, sir."

"Oh God, no." Koehler rolled out of the bed and sat naked with his head in his hand. He pressed the earpiece of the receiver into his forehead, then put it back to his ear. "What about the fire?"

"It appears they created a diversion of some sort, sir, two jailers dead and one sentry. Couple of trucks burnt, but the building is undamaged."

"Who is this?"

"Staff Sergeant Werner, sir."

Koehler could almost hear the man springing to attention at the other end of the phone.

"Have you notified anyone else of this, Werner?"

"The army and the local police, sir, as soon as I found out. I've broken out the guard, but to be honest, I'm not sure it'll do much good; I think they are long gone."

Koehler vaguely remembered Werner from the occasional inspections he'd been roped into performing: efficient, unobtrusive, his men well drilled, no more, no less. The man seemed old school and assured. The only thing that made him stand out was the Knight's Cross with oak leaves he wore at his neck, an old hero who was still fighting for the Fatherland.

"Who is the duty officer, Werner?"

"Lieutenant Brandt, sir."

"Is he any good, Sergeant?"

There was the slightest of hesitations before Werner answered, "He is the duty officer, sir."

"I didn't ask you that, Werner."

"He is very young, sir."

"Jesus Christ." Koehler rubbed his eyes. "Make sure you are with him when I get there. No matter what he says, make sure you are with him. Understood?"

"Yes, sir. Sorry for waking you, sir."

"Don't be. I would have had you shot if you hadn't."

Koehler put down the phone and clicked on the bedside lamp, which threw a twenty-watt shadow as far up to the high ceiling as it could manage.

"What is it?" Kate spoke behind him, in smooth German.

"You'd better go," Koehler replied in English, already crossing the room to collect his uniform from the back of the chair where it was draped. Behind him, Kate slipped out of the sheets and picked up her clothes from the floor.

"Have I got time to wash, or do you want me to walk out naked?"

"No and no."

Kate stopped and looked at Koehler. Stung by his abruptness, she paused, then turned her back and started to dress. The silence dropped around the room and caused Koehler to look up as he pulled on his trousers. He glanced across to Kate and for the first time noticed how thin she looked. Her ribs pushed against her skin when she bent forward to collect her clothes. He sighed, stopped dressing, and crossed the room to her.

"I'm sorry, that was rude. Forgive me. You can wash after I've gone. Just make sure you lock the door as you leave."

Kate stopped and turned. In the dim light of the lamp she looked beautiful, naked and unashamed as she stared at Koehler, her blond hair hanging across her face. Koehler felt an urge to scrape it away from her eyes and tuck it behind her ear.

"Thank you," she whispered.

Koehler kissed her forehead and felt a stir as she smoothed her hands across his chest; he tilted his face forward, wearily, and rested his lips against the top of her head.

"Do I matter to you?" Kate spoke softly and Koehler felt her lips moving on his chest.

"Yes, of course."

"I'm not just some girl from the typing pool you fuck?"

"No, you matter to me."

"Do you love me?"

"I have to go. There has been a breakout at Charing Cross. The resistance we rounded up last week: all of them are gone."

"Do you love me?"

"I have to go."

Kate lifted her head from his chest, and this time Koehler did brush away the loose hair. He smiled, and Kate chewed her lip and then smiled back, without confidence. As if the smile was a signal for him to carry on getting dressed, he let go of her and quickly gathered his things. It was only as he finally pulled on his tunic and hastily rubbed his boot toes against the back of his legs that he noticed that she was still standing, naked, watching him.

"Make sure you lock the door when you go. Leave the key with the guard downstairs."

Kate nodded, and Koehler picked up his cap from the table next to the door, placed it on his head, and turned to her. The Nazi at the door made Kate suddenly feel very naked, and she held her dress up to her breasts to cover them. Koehler nodded, as if he understood, then opened the door. He paused, looking back at her.

"I like you very much, Kate. You make . . ." He looked at the floor as if the words could be found there, then back at her. "You make my time here . . ." He paused again, not wanting to trap himself in a lie. "Better. You make my time here better."

"Thank you," Kate said. Koehler nodded and left the room, closing the door softly behind him.

Kate stood still for moment and thought she might cry. Instead, she sighed, sat down on the bed, and rested her head in her hands before scraping her hair back and pinning it up away from her face. She looked back toward the door, picked up the telephone from the nightstand, and dialed.

The phone rang only once before it was answered by an English voice.

"Yes?"

Kate flinched at the harsh voice. "It's Kate. I'm in Koehler's room."

"You shouldn't ring me on that line. What do you want?"

"There has been an escape from Charing Cross. Koehler has just left to go there."

"Who has escaped?"

"The resistance. All of them, I think."

"All of them?"

"I think so. Koehler was shocked when he took the call. This isn't good for me; it puts me in a bad situation."

"It puts all of us in a bad situation, but especially Herr Koehler," the man replied.

"What should I do?"

"Do nothing."

Kate heard the click of the other phone disconnecting. She sat staring at the receiver in her hand, then gently placed it back into the cradle.

"Do nothing," she said to the empty room. "If only it were that easy."

CHAPTER 23

WHEN KOEHLER ARRIVED at Charing Cross he was dismayed to see several trucks unloading bleary-eyed troops onto the pavement. NCOs dashed around shouting and pointing while junior officers stood clustered, waiting for meaningful instructions from someone who knew what he was doing.

Koehler told his driver to stop before turning into the yard, got out of the car, and stared at the chaos.

So much for German efficiency, he thought as he watched the scene. Through the crowd, he saw Werner and waved for the senior NCO to join him.

Werner arrived with a crash of stamping boots and a salute. Koehler lazily saluted back and then gestured with the same hand toward the crowds of men.

"What's going on, Werner?"

"Lieutenant Brandt thought it best to call out the local garrisons, sir, to track down the escapees," Werner replied flatly.

"Where is Brandt?"

"He's in the jail, sir. He's . . ."

"He's what?"

"Flustered, sir. I told him you wanted him here, but I think he felt it best to keep things moving."

Koehler looked at the old soldier and then shook his head.

"Where did it all go wrong, Werner? What happened to the finest army in the world?"

Werner didn't reply, and Koehler took out a cigarette and lit it, watching the crowds of soldiers form up into ranks, rain reflecting off their helmets and boots.

"Have the men mount the trucks again, then join us in the jail."

Werner saluted and Koehler walked through the yard past the still-smoking frames of the trucks until he noticed two soldiers standing guard over the body of the sentry. The two soldiers sprang to attention, and Koehler leaned into the shadows to look at the young man, who sat with eyes open and dried blood covering his face. His tunic was unfastened and his guts sat in his lap, raw and exposed, where they had been placed by whoever had sliced him open and by gravity. It looked like the boy had tried to push them back into his body before he died, as his hands were still clutching at the bloody mess.

Rain was falling heavier now and spotting the blood on the boy's face, causing it to look like red tears flowing down his cheeks. Koehler shook his head.

"Jesus." He looked at the two young men who stood over their dead colleague like bookends. "Cover him up with something. Don't let anyone else see him like that."

He entered the jail and walked down the steps and through the gate, where the custody assistant lay facedown and dead. Another German soldier snapped to attention next to the corpse, and Koehler noticed that the man was standing in the blood on the floor. He saluted and passed. No point in looking any closer than he had; he'd seen enough corpses to last a lifetime. Instead, he made his way to the custody desk.

As he approached, he heard someone talking loudly and excitedly.

"We need to get boots on the streets, as many people as possible fanning out looking. Get me more troops!"

Koehler turned the final corner and saw a young lieutenant on the phone. Around him stood three junior NCOs, who noticed Koehler first and sprang to attention. Koehler could have sworn he sensed relief on their faces that someone else had finally turned up to take command, but he decided maybe that was just his imagination or his ego talking.

"Don't have more troops come here," Koehler said quietly but firmly.

As he mounted the steps up to the custody desk, he looked down and was amazed to see the body of the senior jailer still lying on the floor, a knife poking out of his side.

The lieutenant turned at the interruption and immediately snapped to attention when he saw Koehler; comically, he held the phone to his head as if he were saluting with it.

"Are you Brandt?"

"Yes, Herr Major!" Brandt stiff-armed a Nazi salute, which Koehler returned. It suddenly struck him how often soldiers tended to salute when things were falling down around them.

"What is this man doing here on the floor?"

"I thought you would want to see him, sir!"

"Well, I've seen him. Now get all the bodies moved to the morgue."

Brandt turned to the NCOs and gestured to the body on the floor impatiently.

"Get this moved! Now!"

Koehler rubbed his face and turned to Brandt.

"Lieutenant?"

"Yes, sir!"

"Could you please stop shouting?"

"I'm sorry, sir." Brandt took a half step back from Koehler, who took the seat that had been occupied by the jailer before he had died. The cake was still on the desk in front of him, and Koehler absentmindedly prodded it with a fork. He noticed it was slightly stale and wondered how long it had been waiting to be eaten before he had got there.

The NCOs were making heavy work of moving the body until Werner appeared and whispered a few instructions, getting the job done. Just Koehler, Brandt, Werner, and the pool of blood were left at the desk.

"How long is it since the escape?" Koehler asked.

"We think it is about one hour, sir!" Brandt shouted, then flinched before adding quietly, "The sentry was discovered at eleven ten by a routine patrol of the perimeter. The guards noticed nobody was manning the yard post, so they entered to look for him. He was found barely alive."

"They patrol the perimeter in fifteen-minute spells, sir." Werner filled in the information for Brandt, who looked at the sergeant before nodding.

"Every fifteen minutes," Brandt repeated for no reason.

"So, the breakout happened around eleven?" Koehler looked at his watch. "Almost an hour ago."

Koehler stabbed the fork into the cake, leaned back in the chair, and looked at the ceiling. "Shouldn't we start the search, sir?" Brandt broke the silence.

"Where should we tell them to start, Lieutenant?"

"I . . . er . . . I don't know, sir."

"No, you wouldn't, because they could be anywhere by now." Koehler felt his blood rise for the first time in a long time and he slowly lowered his gaze from the ceiling to the young officer who stood in front of him.

"I did my best, sir."

"I hope your mother can knit, Brandt, because your best has probably consigned us to the Eastern Front just in time for Christmas."

Brandt broke from his stiff-necked attention for the first time. He shuffled his feet and looked at the floor like a schoolboy who had broken a teacher's window. Koehler looked at the young man and shook his head.

"Get the men outside to form up some roadblocks around the city for now, keep them there for a few hours, and then stand them down. At least then we can tell Berlin we tried to recapture the prisoners."

"Good to see you have things so thoroughly under control, Major."

Koehler looked up to see Schmitt staring at him through the still-locked iron gate that led into the station.

"Would you let the Gestapo in please, Werner?" Koehler said, his voice as flat as his morale.

"I don't mind waiting. It's quite refreshing seeing you behind bars." Schmitt smiled at his joke and Koehler saw that there were another two Gestapo chuckling behind him.

Werner crossed to the gate and after a couple of tries found the correct key and opened it.

Schmitt entered and looked around the custody area.

"Where are the bodies?" Schmitt addressed Brandt, who, for a moment, looked like he was about to cry. Instead, he turned to Koehler and gestured with a nod.

"He said to move them."

Koehler raised an eyebrow and made a mental note about his junior before saying one word.

"He?"

Brandt blushed and rephrased his statement.

"Major Koehler said the bodies should be moved."

Schmitt smiled again and stepped up onto the dais. He looked at the blood on the floor, then at Koehler.

"Oh dear, some people might think you are trying to hide the evidence, Major. How am I supposed to investigate the escape if the evidence has been cleaned up?"

Schmitt dragged the toe of his shoe through the blood as if he were painting with his foot, and Koehler sighed loudly.

"It isn't your job to investigate the escape; it's mine. This is an SS matter, not a Gestapo one."

"I thought you could do with some help. As soon as I heard what had happened I rushed over to see what I could do."

Schmitt smiled at Koehler with crooked teeth, and, for the briefest of moments, Koehler thought about making them even more crooked. Instead, he asked, "How did you hear about the escape?"

"News travels fast, Herr Koehler, a bit like your prisoners. Have you found them yet?"

"We are still establishing how they escaped."

"Ah. That's a no, then?" Schmitt smiled as he spoke, happy at his own little joke, and Koehler looked past him at the two Gestapo who were standing behind him. They were enjoying the moment and looked like snakes trying to smile.

Koehler pulled the fork from the cake again and tapped it on the counter, knocking a few crumbs onto the polished wood.

"Brandt, do we know how the prisoners got out?" He decided to ignore Schmitt and establish some facts. As he spoke he stared at the fork and the crumbs.

"Erm . . . to be honest, sir, not yet. Maybe they overpowered the jailer and escaped that way?"

Koehler looked at the blood on the floor and immediately regretted having moved the bodies; he involuntarily glanced at Schmitt, hoping he hadn't noticed that regret on his face, before turning back to Brandt.

"How many escaped?"

"Eight prisoners, sir, the ones who were due to go to Paris. Apparently, they had been brought here from outlying stations so that they were together for the transit on Sunday." Brandt pointed to several files on the desk, proud that he had done something right at last in getting the prisoner information together.

"Who knew they were being moved here?" Koehler suddenly sat up in the chair and stopped tapping the fork.

"I don't know. They were resistance, so that would be a Gestapo matter, I suppose?" Brandt sounded apologetic as he spoke, nervous at upsetting his new friend, Schmitt. Schmitt, in turn, looked at the young officer and then at his own men, who still stood silently by the gate, smiles gone and waxy faces reestablished, showing nothing and giving nothing away, the classic look of the secret policeman.

"Who organized the transfer of the prisoners here?" Schmitt preempted Koehler's question by asking his men first. They replied with shrugs and uneasily took their hands out of their pockets.

"Do you have a leak in your office, Herr Schmitt? Maybe I should call Berlin to organize an investigation?"

"There is no leak in my office. Besides, I've only just arrived in London." Schmitt snapped his head around toward Koehler as he spoke, already covering himself from blame as best he could.

"Well, it is a coincidence that as eight resistance are brought to Charing Cross for the first time, they somehow manage to escape one of the securest buildings in London, don't you think?" Koehler added a quizzical lilt to his voice and looked again at the cake fork before turning to Schmitt, the balance of power shifting his way again.

"Nobody from my department would have spoken; it is impossible any leak came from the Gestapo. It could have been anyone—the transport department, the custody department, a civilian cleaner, even the building security!" Schmitt pointed at Brandt, who quickly shook his head and looked at Werner, who remained impassive.

An old soldier who had heard officers looking to lay blame many times before knew better than to give them a moving target.

"I had no idea of the importance of the prisoners. None of us did! I would have ensured we had more men on guard duty had someone informed me! Nobody in this building would have known except the custody staff, and half of them are dead!" Brandt's voice sounded a tiny bit desperate, as if he were calling for his career to come back like a lost dog.

"How many men were on guard duty, Lieutenant?" Schmitt gave the impression that he had found his victim, and the more evidence he could raise, the more secure his own position became.

"Sir! There was a party for the anniversary of the Putsch; I gave many of the men leave to attend. Had I been informed of the importance of . . ." Brandt trailed off as Koehler raised his hand to silence him.

"This isn't finding the prisoners. We need to get patrols to their last known addresses and round up anyone who knows them." He spoke to Werner. "We need someone to go through these files and get all the necessary information and then pull together some snatch squads. Notify the Met Police, as well . . ."

Suddenly it was Koehler's turn to trail off as he spoke. The sentence dangled in midair as he slowly turned his head, mouth open, midword. He suddenly stood up from his seat and gestured to the two Gestapo men to get out of the way of the custody board where the prisoners' names were chalked.

"Oh, God," he whispered, then stepped down to make his way along the corridor to the gate that led to the yard, followed by the others, who trooped after him casting confused glances at each other. The jailer's body had gone, but the blood and gore remained. Koehler looked at the mess on the floor, then stepped closer to the gate and studied it. He pushed it closed and looked again, then turned to look down the corridor to where the small procession had followed him.

Schmitt broke the silence.

"What is it?"

"They didn't break out. Someone broke in."

"But nobody knew the resistance were here, sir!" Brandt said, holding out his hands to Koehler, desperate to be believed.

"Whoever broke in wasn't coming for the resistance. He was coming for someone else."

"Who? There was nobody else here who would warrant this sort of operation." Schmitt spoke to Koehler but looked at Brandt, who shrugged a reply and in turn looked at Werner.

Who managed to ignore them all.

"It was the Jew," Koehler said softly as he leaned against the wall, closed his eyes, and then slowly sank to his haunches.

Schmitt watched Koehler in amazement and then, openmouthed, turned to Brandt.

"What Jew?"

"I don't know, sir."

"The fucking Jew Rossett brought today; he's gone, as well, isn't he?" Koehler spoke from down by the floor.

Brandt looked at Werner, who nodded silently back before staring straight ahead again.

"The boy?" Schmitt spoke to Koehler, who remained crouched, back to the wall, forearms on his knees and head leaned forward, looking exhausted, like a recovering long-distance runner.

"Yes, the boy."

"Are you saying Rossett did this?" Schmitt looked from Koehler to Brandt.

"Yes," Koehler replied.

"But why? I don't understand. Surely this was the resistance?"

"The resistance didn't know who was being held here. It was Rossett. Trust me, I'm correct," said Koehler, lifting his head back and resting it against the cold wall of the jail. He looked up at Schmitt by turning his eyes only.

"But how did Rossett know they were here?" Schmitt looked from Koehler to Brandt, who looked like he was about to cry again, so overpowering was his confusion.

"He didn't. Don't you see, man? Rossett wasn't interested in the resistance; he was after the boy. With the resistance, he just got lucky. Rossett would have released them as a diversion. Jesus Christ . . ." Koehler's voice trailed off and he hung his head again before taking a deep breath and rising to his feet, sliding his back up the wall. "Don't you see? He would have come here after everyone else was gone. He had a pass to get into the yard past the sentry."

"What pass? How do you know?" Schmitt looked again at Brandt for answers, but the young officer just gulped and shook his head.

"I gave him a requisition for fuel. He must have shown it to the sentry to get into the yard, and, once inside the perimeter, he would have tried to talk his way in here. Judging from the skin and blood on the gate, I'm not so sure he managed it. I think he slammed the guard's head into the gate and then used the keys to get in. He will have made his way around to the desk and overpowered the duty sergeant."

"That easily?" Brandt leaned forward to inspect the gate as he spoke, noticing for the first time the blood and scraps of skin stuck to the black iron.

"Fat old men eating cake and a green soldier on a soft posting in England? How hard could it have been?"

Schmitt looked at the gate, then back at Koehler.

"You gave him the means to get in? This is your fault."

"It doesn't matter whose fault it is. Unless we get this matter resolved quickly, we are all, each and every one of us, as the English are so fond of saying, in the shit."

CHAPTER 24

ROSSETT STOOD IN the darkness and willed his eyes to adjust to the black that surrounded him.

They didn't.

He breathed.

The black seemed to just get blacker. It felt like he was standing in space. He had no depth, no sliver of light to focus on, just cold, dark, inky black, and it was starting to cause him to panic.

He breathed again, quicker this time, snatched breath that didn't quite fill his lungs.

The cold, wet wall he could feel with his hands appeared to be covered in moss, and somewhere in the darkness he could hear water dripping. He'd walked forward fifteen paces before hitting a wall, and then twenty in the other direction before he hit another. He hadn't found the source of the drip, drip, drip of water on stone, as the sound had neither faded nor grown louder as he'd moved. It had just seemed to follow him, drip, drip, dripping its way into his imagination.

He'd been in a place like this before, as deep, as dark, as damp, and as dangerous as this place, and that place had sucked the air from his lungs as well, just as its memory was doing now.

He tilted his head back and sucked in more air.

His heart pounded and he leaned his head forward again, resting it lightly on the cold stone.

He wiped his fingertips against the wall and then sniffed them. They smelled of damp and dirt, like the moss he could feel growing from the broken brick, looking for light just like him.

Drip, drip, drip.

Rossett was starting to panic.

He turned his head, tilted it, and felt another flicker of fear, like the first few sparks catching at kindling.

He ran through what had happened since he'd left Charing Cross, then winced at the memory of being outwitted by Leigh. He should have just taken Jacob and run when he had the chance. Instead he'd thought he was releasing a few petty criminals or maybe low-level resistance, but the way Leigh carried himself, the way he'd behaved with the others and with Rossett, made him realize he'd released a nightmare onto the streets, which in turn had locked him up in the cellar of a dock in Wapping.

Rossett breathed deeply again and listened to his heart banging in time with the drip, drip, drip.

Relax, breathe, don't panic.

He'd had better days, and he was getting the feeling that this one was only going to get worse.

He lifted his head; the cold stone had calmed him. He felt his way slowly around the wall with his hands until they were resting on timber instead of stone. Gingerly, he probed the door for weakness, but felt only solid iron hinges and timber and no handle.

He felt a chill ripple through him like a stone cast into a pond, and he pulled his coat tight by jabbing his hands in his pockets and folding them across his front. He could have murdered for a cigarette.

They'd taken everything from him except the clothes he stood in: his warrant card, his wallet, everything, including the sovereigns.

Rossett wanted to sit down but resisted the urge. It was going to be a long night, and shivering on a damp floor wouldn't help matters. He decided to try to keep moving and stuck out one hand as he counted off some paces forward again, into the darkness.

"Try to keep still, you're going to trip right over me." The voice came from down below near to the floor, and Rossett froze midstep. Eyes wide in the darkness, he turned his head this way and that trying to locate the source of the voice.

"Who's that?" Rossett replied, hoping his voice didn't give away the shock he felt at hearing someone else in the room.

"Just one of the rats," the voice said, chuckling, and Rossett took a step backward and held his hands up in front of himself in a futile gesture of defense.

"Who is it?" This time Rossett heard the panic, felt it tumble from his lips, and he hated himself for the weakness.

"All right, chum, calm down, 'ang on while I get this lit . . ." Rossett heard a rattle and then saw what seemed like a supernova of light five feet in front of him and near to the floor.

The match flared, then settled as it found a lantern, and a weak amber glow filled the room. An old man lay on the floor next to the light, on some wooden planks covered with dirty straw under a few empty coal sacks.

The scene, lit by the lantern, gave off a desperate air of someone locked away for a long time with just drips and rats for company.

The old man seemed to touch the match to his lips before he puffed it out with the slightest of wheezy breaths, then pushed his hand across his face, pushing dirty lank gray hair from his eyes and up back onto his head.

Rossett noted how dirty the man was. He must have been in the room for a long time. For the briefest of moments, Rossett wondered if he was going to end up looking like the specimen on the floor and he looked to the door for confirmation.

In the light of the lamp, the door looked more solid than it had seemed in the darkness, and, on looking around the rest of the room, he saw his suspicions confirmed, that there was only one way in, and getting out appeared to be a tall order.

The man on the floor hadn't spoken while Rossett carried out his survey, and when Rossett looked back to him he merely smiled and shook his head.

"You ain't gettin' out, mate, not unless they let you, and I wouldn't be buildin' your 'opes up either. I've been here for a couple of weeks now, maybe longer."

Rossett didn't reply. He crossed the room, picked up the lantern, then walked the perimeter studying the wall. He'd guessed the size correctly; the light from the lamp barely made it from one side to the other. The old man had set up his bed about two-thirds of the way across from the far wall, Rossett guessed to get away from the damp that was leaching through the old stonework and pooling in places near the foot of the wall. He crossed to one of the pools and put his fingers in it, then tasted the cold gritty water.

"We're in a cellar, chum, below the water, I reckon. It dries out sometimes, always bloody cold though. They bring in a stove when it gets really bad, but even that ain't much good. There's underground streams and rivers round 'ere ain't been seen for centuries. We could be next to one of them. Sometimes I can just hear it rushin', I think." The old man seemed to realize something. He looked up at Rossett and smiled. "But that could be me mind going. You never know, do you?"

"Who are you?" Rossett finally spoke, his voice soft now, panic gone and a cool calculation restored by the lamp.

"George Chivers, and you are?" The old man stayed on the floor but proffered a hand to shake, which Rossett ignored.

"Why are you here?"

"Ah well, chum, that's a long story."

"Tell it quickly," Rossett replied, cutting off the old man, who smiled and shook his head.

"In a 'urry, are you?"

"Tell it quickly."

"It's a misunderstandin'. Seems I've upset our mates upstairs and they think I've got something they need."

"Is that it?"

"And I think they're tryin' to raise a bob or two, for the cause."

"What cause?"

"To kick the bleedin' Germans out of Blighty! Where've you been, sunshine?"

Rossett stepped back from Chivers and looked around the room again. In the corner he saw a few small upturned wooden fruit-packing boxes. He picked one up, placed it near to the door, and sat down, retaining control of the lamp by placing it at his feet.

Chivers watched for a moment and then rummaged in his pockets under the sack, bringing out a small pouch of tobacco, with which he commenced to create a damp, twig-sized cigarette. He stayed on the floor, propped on one elbow, finally looking up at Rossett as he licked the cigarette paper and rolled it between his fingers. The paper looked dirty and gray, same as the man who was holding it, but Rossett licked his lips at the thought of having a smoke. He nodded toward it and half managed a smile through his burgeoning hangover.

"Any chance I can have a drag of that?" Rossett gestured toward the cigarette. Chivers clutched it to his chest and shook his head.

"No bleedin' way; get your own." Chivers rolled the cigarette in between his fingers and then pulled a match out of the box that lay next to him. He lit the cigarette and savored it like fine wine, closing his eyes and holding on to the taste as long as he could. If it hadn't been for the hacking cough that broke his concentration, Rossett doubted the old man would ever have breathed out again.

Eventually, he surfaced, and the coughing, which sounded like wet mud being churned in his chest, subsided. Chivers glanced up from the floor with blinking eyes and offered the cigarette to Rossett by nodding and holding it up in his direction.

"'Ere . . . 'ave it" was all he managed to say, his breath short as he tried to fight off the cough that lingered not far away.

Rossett stood and took the cigarette. Close up, he realized just how ill the man looked. The gray skin wasn't just the result of dirt. The man had the sort of coloring an undertaker would spend a week trying to get rid of. He smelled of damp and his hand shook slightly as he passed the cigarette to Rossett, who looked at the toothpick of tobacco, then took a drag.

He offered the cigarette back to Chivers, who shook his head and slowly started to rise from his bed. Rossett returned to the orange box and watched as Chivers crossed the room to urinate into a tiny grille set into the floor in the far corner.

The man was little more than a skeleton dressed in dirty rags. Rossett wondered if the same fate awaited him. Chivers picked up a metal mug that had been lying next to his bed and held it up.

"Tea?"

Rossett shook his head.

"Can't say I blames you." Chivers looked down into the mug, then fished something out before taking a sip. "Been 'ere almost as long as I have." The old man scratched himself with bony fingers. He looked at Rossett for a moment, then picked up another orange box and sat opposite him.

"Seein' as you woke me up, maybe you can tell me 'oo you are?"

Rossett took another drag of the stale cigarette and for a moment thought about snuffing it out with his foot, then thought better and nipped off the burning end before slipping it into his pocket. He might need it later.

"Maybe you should explain what you are doing here for a start?" Rossett replied, still looking for some explanation for his current situation.

"I'm 'ere because them bastards won't let me go!" Chivers laughed as he spoke, then started to cough again, hunching over and spilling his cold tea.

Rossett waited for the coughing to subside and sat quietly watching the old man wipe his mouth with a rag that might once have been a scarf.

"There must be a reason why they put you down here."

Chivers smiled, showing teeth that were almost as moss covered as the walls, and slowly shook his head.

"'Ow do I know you ain't one of 'em come to ask me questions?"

"Because I'm banged up here with you?"

"Bah! They've tried this before, stuck a young lad in with me one night tryin' to get me to talk. I told 'im to piss off, same as I'll tell you. Piss off."

Chivers stood up from the crate and turned away, as if he had somewhere to go and was ending a business meeting. Rossett watched him stand and then cross the room to lean against the wall where he had urinated earlier. After a moment, the old man coughed and spat a solid chunk of phlegm into the grate with startling precision before turning to face Rossett again. His cheeks looked hollow in the shadows and his eyes like potholes to hell.

"You can piss off, all you Churchill-loving monarchists. Nobody's going to win this war 'cept us. And I ain't 'elping a bunch of cowards 'iding in Canada while good communists battle 'alfway across Europe to save Britain. Government in exile? Don't make me bleedin' larf. Government in fucking 'iding, that's what they are . . . cowards, the lot of 'em."

Chivers spat again.

Rossett shook his head and regretted putting out the cigarette.

"I'm glad you got that off your chest," he said, leaning forward to rest his elbows on his knees and easing the strain of sitting on the box.

"It 'ad to be said," Chivers replied.

"I was talking about the phlegm."

Chivers stared at him across the room for a moment before starting to laugh and crossing back to his box. He sat down before the coughing started again, milder this time, but still loud enough to startle a donkey.

Rossett looked at the broken old man and felt another shiver of his potential fate.

The two men sat for a while, with just the mysterious drip drip drip to break the silence until Rossett stood and prowled the room again. He stopped over the grid in the floor and leaned low to look into it. It was about nine inches wide and smelled foul, a makeshift toilet that wouldn't flush. He considered lifting the cast-iron grate but decided against it; he wouldn't fit through it, and even if he could have, he doubted that he would want to.

"They give me a bucket of water most days to wash in and then pour down it. I don't know 'ow it'll cope with two of us. It'll be fair foul, I'd imagine."

Rossett turned to look at Chivers from the grate.

"When do they bring the water?"

"How the bleedin' 'ell should I know? They just do. Door opens, I get me tea, some grub, and the bucket. Sometimes I get some baccy and a drop of oil for the lamp, other times, like I said, when it's very cold they put in a stove to dry meself and get some warmth in me bones."

Rossett looked at the door, willing it to open. He decided that would be his best chance of escape. The room's only weakness would be the humans who came in.

As if reading his mind, Chivers smiled and said, "They make me stand in the corner before that all 'appens. They bang on the door and shout for me to get there. I reckons they can see me, 'cos if I don't move they don't come in. They just leave me for a while, and it's a long time made longer when you ain't got some grub and water, so I do as I'm told. Even when they come in, they 'ave guns, so don't you be thinkin' 'bout jumping anyone, else you'll get me killed."

Rossett crossed back to his box and sat down again, glad to be away from the smell of the grid, even if it was only to experience the smell of Chivers.

He stared at the old man and said, "Why haven't they just killed you? What's the point of going to all this trouble?"

The old man smiled again and pointed a finger at Rossett before cackling, "As if you didn't know. I'm not daft, you know?"

Rossett shook his head and leaned back on his box, allowing his back to rest against the damp wall and closing his eyes for a moment.

"Humor me. Tell me, why haven't they . . . we . . . killed you?"

Chivers shook his head and smiled again.

"I'll tell you what you already know, just for conversation like. You lot won't kill me 'cos I knows where the guns are." The old man sat back proudly, crossed his arms, and tapped his left foot, enjoying the conversation, as if he were in a pub bantering with his old friends.

"What guns?"

"You know what guns. You know what guns I mean all right."

"Humor me."

"Our guns, the communist guns and explosives. You want me to tell you? Well, you can piss off, 'cos I ain't going to." Chivers tapped his hands on his knees as if he were playing imaginary drums, then fished in his pockets again for his tobacco, chuckling to himself while shaking his head.

Rossett watched the old man and briefly wondered if Chivers had been on his own for too long and had gone mad. He leaned forward and spoke softly. "I thought you said I was the resistance?"

Chivers opened the pouch and placed the cigarette makings carefully on his lap before looking back up at Rossett and speaking slowly, as if explaining to a child.

"You are . . . but we are the proper resistance, we're the communists. We are the ones fightin'. You lot are the bleedin' government-in-'iding lot, and you want our guns because you lot are runnin' out of 'em. Bleedin' Yanks turned their backs on you now Roosevelt is dead. Churchill has run out of chums, 'asn't 'e? The fat bastard."

"So you've got the guns?"

"Yeah, we've got the bleedin' guns. Comrades in Russia are making them and risking their lives getting them 'ere for us even though they need them for their own struggle back east."

"And you know where they are hidden?"

Chivers looked up from rolling his cigarette and winked a watery eye at Rossett, who, in turn, found himself half smiling back, bemused to find himself taking a liking to the old man.

"Too right, sunshine, I got 'em 'idden after we got 'em off the ship. Nobody knows where they are 'cept me, and if you think I'm tellin' you where they're at, you can piss right off, 'cos knowin' where those guns are is keepin' me alive."

Chivers gave Rossett a toothy smile and folded his arms triumphantly. Rossett shook his head and looked back toward the door. He'd had a long day, eventful to say the least. What had started out as a routine roundup had turned into one disaster after another, and he suddenly felt tired beyond belief.

He looked at the boards and sacks that made up Chivers's bed and decided he needed to sleep. Chivers, as if reading his mind, unfolded his arms and moved toward the bed defensively.

"You ain't 'avin' my bed." He quickly sat down on the boards, like a child protecting his favorite toy.

"I don't want it."

Rossett stood and checked the orange boxes. They were wide enough to sleep on if he laid them end to end. They wouldn't be comfortable, but they would be drier than the hard floor, and with fewer fleas than Chivers's dirty sacks.

He laid them out, watched by Chivers, who was now lying down. After a moment or two, Rossett finally lay down and pulled his coat around his chest, exhaustion caving in his head like the heaviest of hammers.

"Why are you stuck down 'ere?" Chivers said across the room and through the gloom.

"I made a mistake."

"What kind of mistake? It must've been a bad one to get you stuck in 'ere."

"It was the worst mistake a man could make."

"Go on?"

"I started thinking again."

CHAPTER 25

ROSSETT HADN'T HEARD a key in the door or the sliding of a lock. The first he knew of anything was when the boot hit hard into his left temple. Reflexes had done most of the work for him, and he'd half turned his head and rolled off the boxes onto the damp floor. He was almost at a crouch when someone else slammed something into his kidneys from behind, and the best he could manage in reply was a halfhearted shrug before the pain shorted out his brain and he fell to the floor completely.

Whoever was attacking him was carrying battery-powered torches, and they seemed to flick around him like spotlights as the kicks rained down. He covered his head as best he could and tried to turn this way and that in an attempt to put his own legs between him and the hobnailed boots that seemed to be coming from all directions.

The weird thing, he thought, was the silence. Whoever was upon him hadn't spoken a word, and neither had he. This was a disciplined attack.

After what seemed an age, but was probably only a minute, the attack stopped. Rossett lay still on the floor, covering his head, carrying out a mental audit of his body.

He was sore, but no major damage seemed to have been done. Either his attackers were amateurs or they were experts who hadn't wanted him incapacitated.

He guessed they were experts who didn't want to have to carry him to the interrogation he knew was coming next.

Rossett was an old hand at this sort of thing; he knew the drill. He didn't lift up his head. He could hear the deep breathing of his attackers, and he imagined them standing above him waiting for him to look up so they could start again.

He wasn't that stupid. He could wait.

Unfortunately, Chivers couldn't.

"Cowards! Three onto one fella!" Chivers shouted from his bed. Rossett inwardly sighed as the kicks started again, this time with less fury, but the pain was greater as they hit home on flesh that was starting to bruise from the first assault.

Rossett tried to stay focused, to find a pattern in the kicks to enable him to twist into them, but there wasn't one. Each man was waiting his turn to land the perfect blow. Rossett was tiring and his back screamed in pain as he rolled around like an upside-down tortoise. Finally, he broke the silence of the attack by shouting out, more in frustration than anger.

It surprised him that his shouting halted the attack, and he wished he'd done it earlier.

The cell fell silent again. A second passed until he heard more footsteps entering. He raised an elbow to allow himself to peek an eye out of his protective cocoon of wrapped arms and saw a pair of polished shoes next to the heavy docker's boots in the doorway.

Whoever was in charge had arrived. Rossett tried to look out into the hallway beyond the feet. He'd been hooded when they brought him in, and he needed to get an idea of what lay beyond if he was going to find a way out.

He didn't get long to carry out his survey. Somebody emptied a bucket of freezing water over his head, so cold it caused him to gasp and arch his body backward. Immediately, the kicking started again, this time for only a few seconds, before he was dragged to his feet, still gasping from the dowsing and the beating.

Someone pulled back his arms and Rossett shook his head trying to clear the water from his vision. He expected a punch in the face or stomach, but it didn't come. Whoever was holding him from behind had him pinned well, so that his arms couldn't move an inch.

He hung his head and tried to suck in some air. His body ached, but he didn't think any ribs were broken. He felt his left eye swelling after the initial kick, but even that was superficial. He didn't think he was bleeding; the only wetness was the ice-cold water that was running down his back.

The torches shone into his face, and Rossett knew what they were doing, disorienting him. He'd been through this before, years ago, in another place, worse than this. He knew what came next, interrogation, and he was ready. He hoped they would take him out of the cell to do it. He guessed they would. It would be part of the game, keep him guessing. He knew the rules: he'd played this game many times before, on both teams.

A face appeared in front of him, close up, with foul breath.

"Time to 'ave a little chat, chum." The face broke into a smile and then a laugh.

Rossett head-butted it, feeling teeth bite into his forehead. Suddenly the room exploded into action again, and in a moment he was on the floor once more, kicks and, this time, punches slamming home. He heard Chivers shouting for them to stop just before he passed out, a sense of cold satisfaction passing through his brain. He'd lost the fight but won round one; they'd lost discipline and he had outwitted them.

CHAPTER 26

HE CAME TO as they dragged the hood off his head, which lolled, too heavy for his neck, off to the side. He struggled to focus as the two men who'd carried him in left the room and slammed the door shut behind them. After a moment, clarity returned and he realized he was sitting on a metal chair, in a room lit by a solitary electric bulb that hung from the ceiling. He noticed that the bulb wasn't heavy enough for the thick cable it was attached to and that it sat at a slight angle, defying gravity.

He shook his head, then regretted the action as the room swam and his forehead ached.

The chair he was sitting on was in the middle of the room, and he could feel handcuffs pinning his wrists behind his back. He didn't try to stand up, guessing that his hands were threaded through the chair frame. He looked at the door, this one just a domestic wooden one. Across the room there was a boarded-up window. At least, this time he was certain he was above ground. No point putting a window in to look at a sewer.

The room was square, brick walls with a brick ceiling and a flagstone floor, probably in the same warehouse as the dark cellar where he'd just been.

As he looked around, Rossett's head throbbed. They'd given him a good beating. He flexed his face and it felt numb. He squinted and tried to wiggle his nose, which didn't feel broken although it was blocked. He guessed it had bled, and when he looked down at his raincoat his guess was confirmed. A fat, damp streak of thick black blood was down the front of the coat, with some on his suit and shirt. It must have been leaking out while he was knocked out and sitting in the chair.

He traced his tongue across his teeth feeling for a gap. There wasn't one, although he did find a sore spot that must have been a split in his lip.

Those fellas had given him a good beating.

He tried to guess how long he had been out for, but realized he didn't have any reference other than the pain in his wrists from the cuffs he'd been straining against, which wasn't too bad, so he hadn't been out long.

He looked back at the door and wondered if they were watching him. He tried to hop the chair around a little bit to see if there was anything on the wall behind him, but gave up when his ribs cried out for him to stop.

Maybe a few were cracked, after all?

He sighed and breathed in deeply, feeling the pain rise up from his right side. Yes, at least one was cracked. It felt like a knife was being twisted, and he sighed and hung his head. Maybe he hadn't won the first round, after all.

The sound of the door opening caused him to lift his head again.

A docker entered the room carrying a small wooden table. He glanced at Rossett but didn't speak, merely set the table down in front of Rossett and then walked around the chair and tugged on the handcuffs, checking that they were still tight.

He walked out of the room and closed the door, leaving Rossett to study the table in front of him. It was made of rough wood, bare except for a steel U-bolt that had been placed through the center, almost like a four-seater café table, marked with stains he didn't like the look of.

Rossett sat in silence for a while, staring at the table, trying to imagine what was going to happen next. He guessed they were making him wait in an effort to confuse him, to unsettle him, to weaken him.

The only reason they would be going through this process was to question him, and that was the puzzle. What would they ask him? They must have known he was just a low-ranking copper. What could he offer them other than information they probably already knew?

Whatever they wanted to know, Rossett was sure of one thing: he wouldn't be leaving the warehouse alive if they had their way. They would view him as a collaborator, and that was a death sentence unless he could escape or convince them otherwise. He looked around the room again and realized he didn't hold out much hope of either.

The door opened and three of the dockers walked in. Rossett recognized one of them as the one he'd head-butted. The man had a split in his top lip about half an inch long, and Rossett thought he spotted a gap behind it where a tooth had once been.

He expected another beating, but the men merely stared at him for a moment until one of them produced a Browning pistol from his pocket, cocked it, and rested it against Rossett's bruised left temple.

"Don't try anything else or I'll kill you. Understood?"

Rossett nodded silently as the pressure of the pistol increased fractionally against his head.

The other two men walked behind him, and Rossett stared at the table as he felt the handcuffs being unfastened. His right wrist remained shackled, and he meekly allowed it to be pulled around in front of him and secured to the U-bolt that was fastened through the table.

He held his other wrist behind his back, aware of the gun and not wanting to do anything unless he was told. Once the handcuff was clicked shut around the bolt, the pressure of the muzzle decreased and the three men stepped back toward the door. Rossett allowed his free hand to drop to his side in an effort to let the blood flow again. The small room was suddenly claustrophobic as Rossett felt the eyes of the dockers bore into him.

He slowly lifted his gaze to the men, who stared blankly back. Even the one with the split lip seemed disinterested. They were obviously waiting for someone or something. Rossett felt uneasy. The men he had taken for rough dockers now had the appearance of disciplined guards. He risked another look, then lifted his hand to his handcuffed wrist and rubbed it.

"I'm sorry about the lip," he said to the guard with the split lip, who simply ignored him, staring straight ahead. "Do any of you want to tell me what is going on?" Again, none of the men looked at him, so Rossett sat back in his chair and stared at them.

For a moment, he considered picking up his chair and throwing it, but he decided he didn't want another kicking, and even though the table wasn't that big, it was too unwieldy to serve as a weapon. The room fell silent except for the nasal breathing of the man with the split lip. Rossett gingerly touched his nose looking for a break, but all he found was dried blood and soreness. For a moment, he thought one of the men smirked, so he smirked back.

A good five minutes of silence passed before the door opened again and Leigh entered, smoking a cigarette and carrying a mug of tea, which he placed in front of Rossett.

"Cup of char, old man. No sugar, I'm afraid," Leigh said warmly and smiled as he slid the mug across.

It was the first time Rossett had seen the resistance man since he'd been dragged out of the Austin and had a bag shoved over his head when they arrived at the docks.

Rossett picked up the tea with his free hand and took a drink, happy to take whatever he was offered as a means to sustain him.

"Not worried we've drugged it?"

"It wouldn't matter if you had. I've got nothing to hide, and if you were going to kill me you already would have," Rossett replied, still holding the mug close to his face.

Leigh smiled and remained standing as one of the guards briefly left the room and then returned carrying another chair, which he set down on the other side of the table from Rossett.

This is it, thought Rossett. This is where they torture me. He took another drink in an effort to ready himself.

Leigh still didn't sit; he simply took out some cigarettes and placed them on the table with a lighter.

"Help yourself."

Rossett looked at the smokes and then back at Leigh.

"I know what you are doing."

"I'm not doing anything, old man, I'm not that sophisticated. If

I had my way you'd be dead in the river by now. I'm just following orders."

Leigh smoked his cigarette in an effete manner, wafting it in front of his face as he spoke, his other hand resting on his hip.

Rossett took it all in.

"So you're not the boss? Who is?"

"You'll find out soon enough, old man. Patience. Just drink your tea, there's a good fellow."

Rossett glanced at the three dockers, who stood impassively, unmoving behind Leigh. They were definitely military men, disciplined, and Rossett wondered if they were some of the commandos he'd heard rumors about. Wild men dropped in from Canada, operating independently and causing havoc wherever they could.

Some people saw them as heroes, but Rossett had also heard stories of entire villages being executed after raids on local garrisons of Germans. Innocent people just trying to get by, innocent people dragged into a futile fight with the Germans and then executed while the ones who caused the trouble got away scot-free.

Suddenly the tea tasted bitter, and he put the cup down.

"Are you lot commandos?" he asked, but got no reply. They just stared straight ahead, only Leigh giving the merest of hints by raising an eyebrow. "I've heard your lot have caused hundreds of civilians to be executed with your little games."

One of the dockers glanced at Rossett, then resumed staring at the far wall.

"I thought so. Cowards, the lot of you. Hit and run and let others bear the consequences. Too scared to stand and fight. Was it you lot who bombed King's Cross? Murdered women and children? Blundering around with rucksacks full of explosives in the hope of killing someone who mattered?"

"We're fucking freedom fighters, mate," blurted one of the dockers, breaking ranks before Leigh could silence him.

Rossett flexed on the handcuff, causing it to crack loudly against the U-bolt.

"My fucking wife and son, you bastard, my fucking wife and son!"

Rossett rose out of the chair as far as the handcuff would allow, and the two dockers took half a pace forward toward him. Leigh didn't move except to raise his hand to stop the dockers from advancing any farther.

"Sergeant, please, sit down, have a cigarette, and calm yourself." Leigh gestured to the seat and nodded sympathetically at Rossett. "Please, take a seat."

Rossett looked first at Leigh and then at the dockers before slowly sinking back down to his seat. He reached for the cigarettes without taking his eyes off the dockers, took one out, and lit it.

"How do you sleep?" Rossett finally asked Leigh.

"I might ask you the same. They call you the Jew catcher, don't they?"

"I don't kill women and children."

"Don't you, dear boy? Hmm, interesting." Leigh stared at Rossett over his cigarette, his casual words barely making up for the dead eyes that fixed Rossett's. "That's not what I heard."

Rossett flicked his cigarette straight into Leigh's face, causing the other man to flinch and turn away. Rossett started to rise from his chair again, but before he could reach over the table, the dockers had descended on him and pushed him facedown onto the wood, restraining him with such force that Rossett was certain his arms were about to break.

"Gentlemen, please!" Leigh called over the din of the struggle. "Please, at ease, come on, at ease."

Rossett felt the weight lifting from his back and arms, and he looked up from the tabletop at Leigh.

"Sergeant, can we be civilized for a moment?" Leigh asked, and Rossett found himself nodding in agreement.

Leigh waved his hands to the dockers and they finally stood back from Rossett, who raised his head off the table, wiped his mouth, and inspected his fingers for blood. He glanced at the dockers and then looked back at Leigh.

"Three of you with a handcuffed man?" Rossett spat onto the floor and then wiped his mouth and checked his fingers again. "Take these cuffs off and I'll break your fucking necks."

"Don't rise to the bait, gentlemen; the sergeant is trying to provoke a reaction." Leigh turned to Rossett and smiled again. "Do be quiet, old man, there's a good fellow."

"Fuck off, you ponce," Rossett replied. "I've seen your kind when I was doing some proper fighting, all airs and graces on the surface, but as soon as it gets nasty you're nowhere to be found. There were enough of you lot in France, and you all made sure you got home before me and my mates."

Leigh theatrically rolled his eyes.

"Now, now, there is no call for that, is there?" was all he said before taking another drag on the cigarette.

Rossett could see that, although Leigh was affecting the casual air, his words had stung him. He was about to launch another volley when the door opened again and an older man entered, dressed in black tie, almost as if he'd come from a night at the opera. The new man carried a brown leather bag that had the look of a doctor's case in one hand and a handkerchief in his other.

He nodded and then sat in the waiting chair opposite Rossett. He placed the case on his lap, popped open the catches on the top, and peered into it, only once looking up at Rossett and nodding before returning to his search.

Rossett wondered what the man was looking for, and briefly imagined some extreme torture device, but all that emerged was a thermos flask and a brown paper folder containing some files and documents.

The man nodded to Rossett as he placed the bag on the floor and then opened the thermos. Into the metal cup that acted as a lid, he poured a misty hot liquid that sat steaming on the table.

"Do we need all these men in here, Leigh?" The man's voice sounded heavy, much heavier than Rossett thought it should. Leigh nodded and two of the men left the room, leaving just one, who resumed his position by the wall.

"You will call me Windsor," the man said to Rossett as if addressing a child. Rossett didn't reply. "It isn't my real name, before you ask." He wiped his nose with the handkerchief and opened the folder in front of him.

"I wasn't going to ask," Rossett said quietly, but Windsor ignored him and carried on.

"You are John Henry Rossett, ex–Coldstream Guards, where you attained the rank of sergeant. Military medal, Distinguished Service Cross, and the Victoria Cross. I should salute you, or rather your medal, but I'm afraid I could never salute a traitor to the king." Windsor read from the file, only looking up at the end of his statement. "You joined the Guards in 1939 at the outbreak of war, leaving the Metropolitan Police to do so. You served with the BEF in Belgium and then France and finally England during the invasion. You were taken prisoner of war in 1941 and interned in France for three years before being released to take up your old job with the Met. You were married and had one son. Both your son and wife were killed in the King's Cross explosion of 1942."

Windsor studied the papers, flicking back and forth between the sheets before glancing up.

"Did you get to meet your son? I'm looking at the dates here, and it seems . . ."

Rossett didn't reply.

"Hmm, unfortunate." Windsor studied him for a moment, then returned to the papers. "On your release, you returned to Wapping to work as a Police Sergeant, from which you were seconded to the Office of Jewish Affairs. You joined the Nazi Party in early 1945 and you hold an honorary rank in that organization."

Windsor looked up again, then wiped his nose once more.

"Is anything I've said thus far inaccurate, Sergeant?"

Rossett still didn't reply. He just took a sip of tea from the mug he was still holding. Windsor sniffed and wiped his nose again before taking a sip of his own drink.

"Hot lemon, best thing for a cold," he said to Rossett as he placed the tin cup back on the table. "Damned London is always so damp this time of the year, gets me every time."

Windsor wiped his nose again and then studied the files in silence before looking up. "It says here that the Germans think very highly of you, Rossett. They see you as being loyal to the cause."

Rossett lit a cigarette.

"Seems they are intending giving you an Iron Cross. Congratulations." Windsor didn't smile as he spoke. He was matter-of-fact, like a civil servant relaying facts about a planning matter. Rossett found it disconcerting and spoke for the first time, then cursed himself for breaking his silence.

"First I've heard."

"Yes, well, it was to be a surprise that your friend Koehler has arranged. I expect he thinks it'll be good for propaganda, you getting a medal from the king and then one from the Führer. It'll look good in the *Daily Mail*, you setting an example."

Rossett took a drag of the cigarette and swallowed the smoke, breathing it out through his bloodied nose with a whistle. He stared at Windsor a moment, then shrugged.

"What's this about?"

"All in good time. Now, let me see . . ." Windsor ran his finger along the pages before glancing up again. "It says here you have personally supervised the removal of over six thousand Jews from London in the last two years or so and have helped facilitate the removal of many more around the country by assisting other forces in the setting up of their own Jewish offices. It appears you are a very thorough man, Sergeant Rossett, no stone unturned."

"I'm just doing my job."

"Doing it rather well?"

Rossett shrugged and felt his cheeks burn. When the facts were read so coldly they made hard listening.

"Where do you think these Jews are going?" Windsor picked up his cup again. "Have you ever asked?"

Rossett shook his head.

"Best not to, eh?" Windsor took a sip and placed the cup down on the table before turning another page and leaning forward to study the text.

"I've a copy of your bank statement here. You don't appear to be well rewarded for your dirty deeds."

Rossett looked down at the document and was surprised to see it was an up-to-date statement of his account. His surprise must have registered on his face, because he noticed Leigh chuckle behind his boss and wink.

Windsor looked up from the papers.

"Many of your colleagues get a bounty from the Nazis for carrying out such an unsavory role, yet you don't. Why is that?"

Rossett shrugged again.

"Is it because you enjoy what you do?"

"I just do my job."

"Do you not like Jews?"

"I just do my job. I do as I'm told."

"Do you not like them?" Windsor asked again, this time placing the papers down. "I'm curious, because I can't imagine sending that many people to their deaths without hating them."

"I don't send them to their deaths. They go to France."

Windsor smiled and shook his head.

"You don't actually believe that, do you? That they just go to France to live happily ever after?"

"I just do my job."

"They are murdered, all of them. Shot, stabbed, gassed, or starved, but all of them—men, women and children—die."

Windsor stared at Rossett, who swallowed and then shook his head.

"That's all bollocks, propaganda spread by you lot."

"I don't think so, and I don't think you believe that either, not when you really think about it," said Windsor softly.

"What would be the point? What would be the point of just killing them? Tell me."

Windsor reached down to the case and produced another file, which he placed on the table and then opened before spinning the contents around so that they faced Rossett. Rossett saw some grainy photographs. One showed a pit full of bodies, all skin and bone, gray and dead.

At the top of the pit stood a line of waiting ghosts, heads bowed, waiting to fall forward after the volley of bullets that would come from the guns trained on them from behind.

Rossett squinted at the photo and then leaned back as far as the handcuff would allow.

"Propaganda. I've seen it before. The government in exile churns that stuff out all the time. I've heard they use actors and try to stir things up here with them. That's all bollocks, I just do my job and pay no attention, simple as that."

Windsor nodded, picked up the photo, and placed it with several others, most showing similar scenes of grim, gray despair and death. He left the folder on the table next to Rossett's shackled hand and Rossett frowned as his eyes roamed across the pictures.

"Are you sure, Sergeant?"

"Of course. Who would just stand there waiting to be shot like that?"

"The same people who quietly walk onto the trains at Nine Elms, that's who."

Rossett thought about the shuffling early-morning loads he'd seen leave so many times. It was true that not many of them ever struggled or tried to fight back. He could think of barely a handful who had ever tried to run away. He'd assumed it was because they trusted him when he told them they were going to work on farms in France. Why wouldn't they? He believed it himself.

He looked at Windsor, who had also sat back from the table and was holding the tin cup under his nose, breathing in the steam off the hot lemon, eyes staring at Rossett through the haze.

"What confuses me, Sergeant Rossett, is why today is different, why today, of all days, you decided to stop doing your job."

Rossett glanced at Leigh and then back at Windsor.

"I don't understand."

"Every day, you get up and do your job for Jerry. You don't ask questions, you don't cause problems; you just go and do what you do. We know this. We've watched you. We've even thought about killing you to stop you, and we would have if the powers that be hadn't thought it would be bad propaganda seeing off the brave British Lion. So we've let you get on with it, let you do your dirty deeds for the Germans. And you've done it bloody well, right up until today, and quite frankly, I want to know what's happened today for you to say enough is enough, to throw it all away to rescue one Jewish boy. I want to know why."

Rossett thought for a moment and nodded toward Leigh, who had lit another cigarette. He replied, "I was using the kid as an excuse to spring the resistance lads who were at Charing Cross. I couldn't let his lot be shot, could I?"

"Nice try, Sergeant." Leigh raised an eyebrow and smiled.

"Come along, Sergeant, please don't waste my time."

Rossett looked from Leigh to Windsor and then back again. He traced his finger through some spilt tea and then sighed deeply. "I felt bad about the boy, all right?" Rossett looked up at Windsor.

"Really? How very noble." Windsor smiled at Rossett and then steepled his fingers and rested his chin on them. "It's just that I wondered . . ." Windsor suddenly reached down again into the case, and Rossett wondered what mystery he would pull out next. He was dismayed to see it was Jacob's pouch, the one with the sovereigns.

"I wonder if your newly found conscience was pricked by these?" Windsor emptied some of the coins onto the table, then placed the pouch down next to them.

"It wasn't the money. Why would I have gone back when I already had it in my pocket?" Rossett replied, shaking his head and looking first at Windsor and then up at Leigh.

Windsor smiled, reached into his pocket, and produced another handkerchief, this one clean.

"I think, perhaps, you were going back for this, or rather its friends, the ones the boy has told you about." Windsor placed the handkerchief on the table and slowly unfolded it to reveal a small cut diamond, shining in the bare light of the weak bulb. The size of a little fingernail, it glistened and seemed to light the room itself.

Windsor traced his index finger around the diamond, causing it to roll on the cloth and catch the light, then looked at Rossett.

"I think the boy is the key to more of these, and you went back to get that key. You haven't found your conscience; you've merely found your price. When I asked the boy about the diamond he told me you knew where the rest of them are buried, that he'd told you his part of the secret and you knew where the rest of these things are hidden."

Rossett stared at the diamond. He'd never seen anything like it before in his life. For some reason, his mind flashed back to his wife and a promise he'd made a million years before, on the night he had asked her to marry him: *"One day I'll buy you a beautiful ring."* He'd meant it. She'd laughed, but to him it was vow, a vow he hadn't fulfilled.

She'd died before he could buy her the ring, and he suddenly felt ashamed. With his free hand, he wiped his forehead, feeling the gash in his palm stinging and suddenly glad of the pain. He then sat back from the table as far as he could, as if to distance himself from the diamond and the photographs of the dead and the dying.

His head throbbed both from the beating and the pressure he was under, and he closed his eyes a moment to rest his senses.

"I didn't know anything about any diamond." Barely whispering, the fight gone out of him.

Windsor smiled and shook his head.

"Sergeant, please, let's not play games."

Rossett shook his head slightly and spoke softly again.

"I didn't know about the diamond, ask the boy. I don't know how all this has come about. I don't know anything about any diamonds."

"You had it in your pocket, with the coins. Did you not know about them either?"

"I hadn't really looked. I didn't know it was there." Rossett knew the truth sounded unlikely even as he said it, but he said it anyway, eyes still closed.

Windsor looked at the file as Rossett spoke, then absentmindedly picked up the diamond and folded it back into the handkerchief before slipping it into his pocket. He sighed and chewed his bottom lip, looking at Rossett's lowered head before speaking again.

"John, it won't serve you to lie to us. We've already spoken to the boy.

He has told us you're going to get the rest of the diamonds. I know you are lying."

The use of his first name caused Rossett to lift his head and open his eyes; he heard it so little nowadays, it almost felt like Windsor was talking to someone else.

Windsor tilted his head sympathetically and continued, as if talking to a child, "You aren't leaving here. You do know that, don't you? We'll find out soon enough where the diamonds are. We can trace your movements today, speak to people you've spoken to. We will find out your plan. One way or another. Even if it means spending some time interrogating the boy—thoroughly—we'll find out."

The final part of the sentence hung in the air.

Windsor finally closed the file on the desk.

"John?" he continued as he stood from the table, his voice louder now, more certain. "Make no mistake, you are going to die here, in this place. It can either be a good death—you'll be remembered as a patriot, I'll see to that—or it can be a bad death, a difficult death, a long death. Do you understand?"

Rossett looked at Leigh, who folded his arms grimly as Windsor spoke.

"Don't make this difficult, John. We will find what we are looking for whether you tell us or not. There is an easy way and a hard way. Please . . . I implore you, choose the easy way."

Windsor crossed to the door, which Leigh opened for him. He left the room without a backward glance.

Leigh paused, then smiled at Rossett.

"I'll not be long. Don't go anywhere, will you?" Leigh left the room and closed the door behind him. Rossett looked at the guard and then lowered his head onto the tabletop to think. His forehead rested on the wood that had been warmed by his arms and he closed his eyes to shut out the world, but thoughts bounced around like wasps in a nest and he couldn't focus.

It was going to be a long night.

CHAPTER 27

JACOB WAS COLD. The smelly old blanket the man had given him was too thin, and, when he pulled it to cover his shoulders, his feet popped out the other end and his bare legs got goose bumps. He opened one eye and looked at the men playing cards across the room. They looked rough and he didn't like them.

One of them glanced over, and Jacob shut his eyes quickly and pretended to be asleep. He lay still before he slowly opened his eyes again, so slowly at first that he was looking through his long eyelashes like a tiger through the long grass in Africa, like the one his mother had shown him in a book.

He thought about his mother, and about how she had once gently stroked her fingertip across his eyelashes and teased him.

"My beautiful man has the eyelashes of a beautiful woman!" she had said before suddenly tickling his belly.

He missed his mother.

The men across the room started to laugh, but not in the same way as his mother had. When they laughed loudly they sounded angry, so he closed his eyes again and wished they would go away.

Jacob *really* didn't like the men.

He rolled over to face the wall. Maybe he'd see grandfather tomorrow.

He hoped Grandfather was all right. He'd done and said everything the old man had told him.

He remembered the words exactly. *"When somebody asks, you tell them what?"* The old man had sat on the end of his bed and made Jacob stand with his back to the fireplace, repeating the words.

"I tell them there is more treasure, but I don't have it."

"And then what do you say?"

"I tell them the name."

"And what is the name?"

"Rossett."

"And then what do you say?"

"I tell them it is a puzzle and that I must go with them."

"And then what?"

"I never tell them the rest until it is time."

Jacob smiled as he remembered his grandfather's face. The old man had wrinkled his nose, smiled, and then thrown his arms wide as Jacob ran toward him.

"Good boy. You must never forget this, you must always remember and practice the puzzle in your mind so you will remember . . . yes?"

Jacob had nodded as he had buried his head in his grandfather's shoulder, smelling the worn warm cardigan.

Lying on the bed right now, he imagined he could smell his grandfather again, pretended his grandfather was still with him, keeping him safe.

"My treasure," his grandfather had said as he held him close. *"My beautiful, beautiful treasure."*

CHAPTER 28

"**C**AN I HAVE a drink?" Rossett said, his voice heavy and defeated.

The guard on the opposite side of the room shook his head and remained standing, stiff as a board, arms behind his back and eyes raised, looking at a space on the wall opposite, above Rossett's head.

"I'm parched. Come on, chum, just a little water? I've a hangover from hell and you fellas gave me a good kicking. I just need a drink, please?"

Rossett picked the empty mug off the table and proffered it, but this time the guard didn't even shake his head; he merely ignored Rossett, who held the mug up for a moment longer, maybe ten inches off the tabletop, before smashing it down in frustration.

The ceramic mug shattered when it hit the table, and shards flew in all directions. The guard flinched and looked at Rossett but didn't move from his position, merely shaking his head a fraction and resuming his vigil on the spot on the wall.

Rossett sighed and wiped his arm across the table to clear off the fragments of broken mug before leaning back in his seat.

"One cup of fucking water? That's all I want."

Rossett jerked his handcuffed wrist, and the heavy wooden table jolted. The U-bolt his wrist was handcuffed to rose an inch or two before dropping back down, safe and secure.

"I'll shove this fucking table down your throat." He slammed the table again, this time harder. It lifted an inch off the floor and banged back down.

The guard finally looked at Rossett wearily.

"Look, do us both a favor and be quiet, eh? We've got a long night, and you've got bigger problems than trying to get my goat, so shut up."

Rossett shook his head and leaned forward again.

"Shit house" was all he said before he gripped the leg of the heavy chair under him and in one movement swept it up and tossed it across the room at the guard, who easily fended it off by raising his own leg and trapping it with his foot. Rossett was crouched over the table, standing as straight as his handcuffed wrist would allow. The table was too heavy to use as a weapon, but he gestured with his free hand for the guard to come in and *have a go.*

The guard sighed wearily and pushed the chair back toward Rossett, stopping when he was about two feet from Rossett's reach and sliding the chair closer with his foot.

"You ain't gonna wind me up, so sit down and maybe I can get you that drink if you beh—"

Before the guard finished his sentence, Rossett gobbed a dirty ball of bloody phlegm and spat it across the distance between them.

The guard turned his face, but the spit landed with a thick splat against the side of his head. He touched his ear and, feeling the mess there, grimaced as he flicked it away.

"You dirty bastard" was all he said. He launched himself across the gap as the one-armed Rossett took a half step back and kicked with his right foot toward the guard's advancing left knee.

The kick landed perfectly and Rossett thanked the gods, as that had been his only chance.

The guard stumbled forward and Rossett trapped the man's head tightly under his free left arm. Pushing forward and down with all his might, not allowing the guard to straighten up, he managed to force the guard, facedown, almost onto the tabletop.

Close to his handcuffed wrist.

He squeezed, tighter than he had ever squeezed before. He knew he couldn't strangle the guard from this position, but he could keep him from crying out. The guard pushed against Rossett's arm, trying to maneuver it over his ears, and Rossett squeezed harder and looked down to the reddening head of the guard as it lay between Rossett's chest and the table.

Rossett took a deep breath and jerked the guard a couple of inches closer to his handcuffed wrist, which was straining like a guard dog on a leash, trying to get into the fight.

He drove his knee into the guard's side and jerked him again. Now the guard was weakening. Fighting for breath, he moved a few inches, pulling at the arm around his neck, and Rossett had his chance.

Using the broken ceramic handle of the mug he'd held in his manacled hand since smashing it, he traced its sharp edge along the guard's neck, beneath the ear that he'd just gobbed on. Rossett closed his eyes and heard a muffled yelp as the shard broke the skin and dug into the tissue beneath.

As he expected, the guard found new strength as he felt the blood trickle out, and Rossett gripped even harder, feeling the skin split and catch, inch by inch, as he pulled the handle across the throat, pushing it deeper, searching.

The guard thrashed at Rossett's back with fists that were trying to find his head. Rossett ignored the blows as he dug with the shard, searching until finally he found the point he'd been looking for. His hand suddenly became hot and wet with the gush of a burst jugular. The guard frantically grabbed at Rossett, and one hand scratched on the table. There was another muffled cry, softer this time.

"Sssssh" was all Rossett could think of saying as the guard flapped an ever-weakening hand against his back. Rossett waited for the flapping to stop, and as it eased he thought about how many people he had felt pass to the other side in his hands.

Finally, the guard stopped moving.

Rossett twisted the shard deep into the wound to check if the man was still alive.

He wasn't.

Rossett relaxed his grip and slowly let the body slide to the floor. He knelt next to the guard and quickly patted him down. He found nothing except a pocketknife, some small change, matches, and an empty wallet. Rossett placed the booty on the table and then, with his free hand, he pulled his raincoat belt out from behind him where he had fastened it between the two loops when he had bought the coat.

He hated the flapping intrusion of a loose belt, and it was a tradition that he always tied it behind him before he wore a coat for the first time.

Those who might have wondered why he never threw it away would have had their question answered as he took the belt in his teeth and opened the pocketknife quickly with his bloody hands.

He glanced toward the door as he worked. He placed the belt on the tabletop and managed to cut off the end opposite the buckle. Then, holding it up as if it was a dead snake, he shook the belt and dragged it through his teeth for a moment until out of the end dropped a bright and shiny handcuff key, never used but salted away for a worst-case scenario.

Rossett nearly cried out with joy when the key rattled onto the table, and he quickly uncuffed himself, rubbed his wrist, and surveyed the room once more. He was free of the table but not yet free of the room.

He pressed his ear to the door and listened: nothing. He knew there was at least one guard out there, and surmised that if the door was sturdy enough to prevent noise from getting out, it could just as easily stop noise from getting in. For all he knew there were twenty of them sitting waiting for him. Rossett turned the handle slowly and then tried to ease the door open.

It didn't budge. Locked.

He crossed to the boarded-up window and looked through the cracks. It was dark outside and there was glass in the window, but other than that, it offered no clues.

He squeezed his fingers behind the old timber of the bottom board. At first, he could barely get his fingertips into the gap, but by rocking them back and forth, he slowly managed to get three fingers of each hand behind the wood.

He gripped it, noticed he'd opened the cut on his palm again, and then rocked the plank back and forth against the nails that held it in place. It creaked and groaned, and Rossett looked back to the door, stopping to see if anyone had heard it from outside.

Nobody stirred, but as a precaution, Rossett took out the pocketknife and opened the blade. If anyone came in to stop him, he would kill him or die trying.

He pulled on the board again, this time concentrating with one hand at one end. The nails gave, a quarter of an inch, then a little more with each twist. Once he freed one end, he eased the board back and it gave way at the other end, the leverage making the task easier.

He held the plank, about four feet long by six inches wide, in his hand and crouched down to look through the dirty window. He still couldn't see anything outside, and set to work on the next one after placing the first at his feet.

This time the board came easily. Gripping tightly with both hands, in no time he'd removed four boards and exposed the lock of the sash window.

It was painted shut, and Rossett cursed under his breath as he jabbed and scraped at the old paint with the pocketknife. His fingers ached as he pulled at the iron lock until at last it gave, and he set to work on the paint-fastened frame. Picking and scraping seemed to take an age, and each rattle of the window frame sounded like cannon shell landing in the small room.

His heart raced, and, as time passed, he became more and more certain someone was going to enter the room to relieve his now drained and very dead guard.

Rossett decided that if he was disturbed, he would just jump through the window. Regardless of what lay on the other side, whatever it was, it had to be better than Leigh and the handcuffs.

Once again, not much of a plan, but the best he could come up with.

He finished chipping the paint and then, with all his remaining strength, he pushed, until finally the window gave in and moved. The swollen wood had the resistance of a glacier as inch by inch it unevenly made its way up in the frame.

When he had exposed a gap big enough for his head, Rossett smiled as he felt the cold night air on his face, but his smile faded when he saw the hard concrete quayside four stories below.

"Fuck," he said to the pigeon-shit-stained windowsill before pulling his head back in again.

He stood back from the window and completed a half turn, looking around the room, almost hoping that it had changed in the moment he'd had his head outside.

It had to have been just five minutes since he'd killed the guard, but it felt like five hours, and he suddenly felt exhausted. He leaned his hands against the window frame and bowed his head.

He took a deep breath and sighed. There was no giving up, there was never any giving up, it wasn't allowed.

He gripped the frame, and instead of pushing, he rested his face against the remaining boards and pulled. The window rose slowly, inch by inch, side-to-side applied pressure walking it up the frame until there was a gap big enough for him to fit through.

Rossett didn't bother looking out this time. It didn't matter what he saw, he was going through it.

He crossed the room and dragged the guard to behind the door, gently resting the body where it would block the door from opening. He placed the chair and table quietly in a similar manner and then put the guard's belongings, plus the handcuffs and key, in his pockets.

His ribs were starting to ache again as the adrenaline of the fight wore off. He rubbed his side and arched his back, and, body aching, he crossed back to the window.

At the window, Rossett bent over and stuck his head and shoulders out before completing a half turn, so that he was sitting, legs still in the room, upper torso in the cold night air, on the window ledge.

There was no going back as he shuffled out of the window, looking up into the gloom like a rock climber seeking a crevice to hold.

He grabbed the top of the sash window he'd just opened and lifted his right foot up and out onto the ledge. He left leg was still hooked inside, and he used this as a brace to allow him to lean back farther, looking up and then left and right.

To his right, there were more windows, the same size and shape as the one he had climbed out of. The brickwork was old and the building seemed to stretch as far as sixty feet till it reached the corner.

To his left, there was only one more window before the corner of the building. Between the windows was a gap of about five feet: too far to jump.

He leaned back, using the window frame as a brace, and looked up, trying to ignore the pain from his ribs. Maybe two feet above his window was what appeared to be a brick ledge that jutted out about twelve inches. Rossett guessed it was the gulley for the roof, but from his position, he couldn't be sure. For all he knew, if he reached the ledge it might not be the roof at all; it might just lead to more smooth brick, and he'd be stuck.

He looked down, never the best option for someone as nervous about heights as he now found he was.

Beneath him were the warehouse walls, which seemed to go on forever until they reached another window, possibly ten feet below. Rossett imagined himself dropping to the window and trying to hold on with his fingertips, then realized that would be suicide and dismissed the thought.

He looked around again and caught sight of a broken drainpipe that was snaking around from the overhang like a bent straw. Rossett wondered whether he could reach the pipe if he stood on the window ledge.

The pipe looked as if it was pinned to the building by a cast-iron bracket that had a small bush growing out of it, not exactly the securest anchor in a storm but an anchor all the same.

Rossett looked at the window ledge again and tried to weigh the odds of survival.

Somewhere out on the Thames, a foghorn sounded, and Rossett

rested his face against the window and closed his eyes. The glass was cold, so cold it hurt his cheek, and the cold soaked through to his teeth, setting them on edge.

He nodded to himself. Now was as good a time to die as any; at least this way it would be quick.

Another foghorn answered the first, and Rossett took his cue and pulled his leg out of the room. He half crouched as his whole body finally made it outside. The window wasn't tall enough for him to fully stand up in, so he had to use his right hand to brace against the upper wall that surrounded the frame. He looked down again and tried to guess if he could jump the width of the quay and make it into the oil-slick-black water that was lazily slapping the dock wall below. He couldn't. It was too far, even for a running jump, let alone a crouching one from a window ledge.

The quay was designed for wagons to unload directly onto ships; it must have been thirty feet wide. It looked like a canyon in the misty gloom and briefly mesmerized Rossett, who had to force himself to look away and back up toward his only chance of salvation.

Come on, Rossett, move, he directed himself, as he started to gingerly shuffle his way along the brick ledge. He glanced at his feet a few times and finally settled with his left foot half on and half off the ledge, his right pushed tight next to it, calves aching.

Gripping the bottom of the upper brickwork as tightly as he could with his right hand, he slowly straightened himself into a position as close to standing as he could manage.

With his left hand he reached toward the drainpipe, only to find that he fell short by an inch or two.

"Fuck," he muttered through gritted teeth as he tried to adjust his right hand on the bricks as best as he could without actually letting go.

He paused and took a breath, looking around him for something else to hold on to. For a moment, he considered climbing back into the room, and then decided that even if he wanted to, he probably couldn't. It would mean leaning out and letting his braced right arm come free. There would be only one winner in that eventuality, gravity, so he decided against it and looked up again at the drainpipe.

"The fucking thing doesn't look like it'll take my weight anyway," he said out loud, as he reached once more with his left arm, every tendon stretched so tight that his ears sang with the strain.

Just a little more . . .

His fingers caught hold of the three-inch pipe.

It felt cold and rough in his hand as he tugged it to test its strength. Surprisingly, it didn't budge. He guessed that where it extended around the ledge it was secured by more pipework and brackets. Maybe things were looking up.

He stretched as far up the pipe as he could manage, letting his fingers walk up bit by bit, before taking a deep breath and stepping off the ledge.

It seemed to take an age before he managed to grip the pipe with his right hand, and his whole body tensed as the pain in his ribs stabbed at him. His desperate right hand caught just below his left, and he hung like a bell ringer frozen in time for a second or two as he waited for the pipe to give . . .

It didn't.

He gritted his teeth and grunted through them, and the pain, as he flexed his biceps and managed to lift his body an inch or two higher before releasing his right hand and quickly lifting it over his left, his toe-caps scuffing on the bricks as they tried to find a hold. He flexed again, managing to get left over right.

He was moving in the right direction.

This continued four or five times, rhythmically, flex grunt grab, flex grunt grab, as he made his way inch by inch up the pipe.

He could feel the blood pumping through his upper body and his sinews stretching.

He'd climbed plenty of ropes in the army, but never with broken ribs, and never with a wet pipe that was too wide to be gripped easily. His hands ached as they'd never ached before. Little by little he made his way up until finally, his groan was interrupted by an answering groan from the pipe.

Rossett froze as the pipe shifted. From above, some flakes of old metal and grit fell, landing on his upturned face and forcing him to blink his eyes. He hung, not moving, not wanting to stress the old brackets more than they already were. He felt the pipe move again, and he risked ducking his head under his arm to see if he could reach the ledge again.

He couldn't.

He was maybe twenty inches from the bend in the pipe, and he felt like his arms were going to pop out of their sockets.

As he flexed and pulled, the pipe jerked and more dirt fell down, this time going into his eyes. He felt his feet scrabbling against the bricks again, even though he didn't think his brain had told them to.

Maybe they didn't want to die, either?

He didn't dare move, but the pipe did, a few inches this time. He twisted his head from side to side, looking for a handhold in the brickwork, but there was none to be had. The pipe moved again and suddenly everything seemed quiet as he watched the pipe snake over the ledge, a rigid rope emerging from a cliff face out into the dark.

Rossett thought about Windsor and Leigh. He thought about his wife and young John Henry, and how he missed them. He thought about Jews and Germans and the choices he'd made; he thought about all the dead men, those he'd killed, those he'd helped kill, and those he had held in his hands, comforting them as they went. He thought about Mrs. Ward and a lonely beach, he thought about diamonds and death, and then, finally, he thought about Jacob and how he'd let the little boy down again.

Somewhere on the river another foghorn sounded.

Then John Henry Rossett fell.

CHAPTER 29

ROSSETT SLAMMED THROUGH the wooden cargo doors and into the cellar like a bomb. The rotten wood seemed to explode around him when he hit, and the three-foot-square cotton bales below felt tougher than the wood that had been above.

He landed on his back and the air concussed out of his lungs as he sank into the bales that had broken his fall. He stared through the broken wooden cellar doors and up into the night sky where he had just been. He tried to reinflate his lungs, but they felt as flat as pancakes, and all he managed was a whistling wheeze.

His whole body seemed numb for a moment, and he wondered if he'd broken his back. Slowly he managed to turn his head to look around the dark space in which he'd landed. Then he focused on his right hand, watching as it rose off the cotton bale and slowly flexed.

He tried to breathe again, and this time a tiny gasp of air made it into his lungs. In the back of his mind, he thanked God for not being so cruel as to let him survive the fall only to die of asphyxiation, as he rolled onto his side and started to cough life back into his battered body.

He lay gasping for a moment before rolling back to look up at the broken hatch doors once again, marveling at his luck. The doors were maybe eight feet square; he'd barely fit through them, let alone noticed them when he'd looked down from the window. The overhang of the window ledge plus the night's shadows had hidden them from his view. He was glad they had, because if he'd tried to aim for them, he doubted he would have managed to hit them. He realized that the doors were there to allow the unloading of carts into the dock cellars. He remembered them from better times, dotted at intervals around all the warehouses in the area.

The doors were well out of reach above him. If he was going to get out, that wasn't the way he was going.

Slowly Rossett eased himself off the bales and onto his feet, climbing down three or four of the stacked bales to reach the floor, his body aching from the effort. Halfway down the pyramid of cotton he found the length of drainpipe he'd been clinging onto before the fall. He picked it up and hefted it. It was an unwieldy weapon, but a weapon all the same.

At the bottom of the stack he bent forward and rested his hands on his knees, breathing deeply before looking back up to the shattered doors above and shaking his head. He stood up straight, brushed off the dust that he'd disturbed when he'd landed on the bales, flexed his back, and started to look for a way out.

It struck him that he was out of the interrogation room but still stuck in the building, and he wondered if anyone had heard him fall.

He reached the wall and found it damp to the touch, familiar stone in the darkness. Rossett took out the box of matches he'd taken from the guard and struck one. Holding it up to light his way, he saw a sliding cast-iron door set into the wall opposite him and made his way across to it.

He dropped the match and carried on forward in darkness before finally reaching the doorway. He gripped the edge of the door and was relieved to feel it slide. The heavy fire door moved on its well-greased rollers almost silently. He opened it just far enough to pop his head out and found an empty corridor that seemed to run the length of the building.

The corridor was lit by a yellowing glass lamp set into the far wall. It was half covered in moss and barely lit the entry to another passage that turned off to the left.

Farther under the building.

If he was going to get out, he was going to have to go into the lion's den first.

Rossett squeezed through the doorway and walked toward the light, straining to hear if anyone was coming as he made his way along the damp corridor. He guessed that it wouldn't be long before someone found the dead guard upstairs, and it would take them even less time to figure out which way he'd left the room. They'd search high and low for him, literally. He didn't have long to get out.

He reached the corner and stopped. Leaning against the wall and crouching slightly, he eased half of his head around the corner to peek into the next tunnel. On a chair fifteen feet away sat a docker, snoozing, arms folded, chin resting on his chest. Rossett could just hear the man's even breathing.

If it weren't for the old Webley pistol the man cradled in one hand, half tucked into a warm armpit, he would have been just like the tens of other watchmen who were dotted around the docks that night.

Rossett looked at the door the guard was sitting outside. It looked like the one he and Chivers had been behind, except on this side there was a handle.

Without thinking, he raised the cast-iron pipe and charged across the fifteen feet as quietly as he could. When he was a few feet short of his target, some deep-seated instinct caused the guard to open his eyes and look up at the onrushing Rossett.

Rossett looked back into the guard's disbelieving eyes. The man tried to unfold his arms and raise them in time to protect himself and free the Webley, but the pipe came down with a dull whack, hard on the top of his head.

Rossett raised the pipe to hit him again, but the guard merely slid off the chair, either unconscious or dead. The pistol clattered onto the floor, and Rossett picked it up, eyes on the fallen man. He shook the pistol next to his ear and then opened the breech to find four rounds and two empty chambers. Rossett nudged the guard with his toe, then stepped over him and carried on down the corridor before stopping and staring back at the door. He sighed, shook his head, then put the pipe carefully on the floor, returned to the guard, searched through his pockets. A few coins, an empty wallet, and a set of keys on a chain. Rossett reached around the guard, the age-old trick of the policeman's search, checking the small of the back, where he found a long thin knife in a leather sheath stuck under the guard's thick leather belt. Rossett pulled the knife and the sheaf free and then half drew the knife. It was finely balanced and glistened in the gloom of the hallway. It seemed to give off its own light as he turned it in his hands, and he slipped it into his own waistband, feeling the man's warmth against his back from the blade.

He stared at the man for a second, then flicked through the keys on the chain looking for one to open the door. He got lucky first time, turned the key in the heavy door, and pushed it open.

"Chivers?" he called softly into the darkness. "Chivers? You there?"

"'Oo's asking?"

"Who do you fucking think? Come on, you're getting out."

Rossett didn't wait for Chivers to follow; he left the open door and made his way farther along the corridor. Every twenty or so feet, there was another door, same as the one he'd opened for Chivers. The lack of guards led Rossett to believe these rooms were empty, or possibly being used for their original storage purposes. Either way, he didn't have time to search them. He looked over his shoulder as he went and saw Chivers walking some thirty feet behind him, clinging to the shadows and his suspicions.

Rossett stopped and gestured for the old man to catch up. Chivers took his time, looking around at the doors as he went.

"What the bleedin' hell is goin' on?" Chivers whispered when he finally caught up to Rossett, glancing at the pistol in the other man's hand.

"We're getting out of here. Do you know the way?"

"You came back for me?"

"Not exactly. Look, do you know the way out?" Rossett watched the corridor, anxious to keep moving. Chivers remained a short distance away, looking even older and grayer than he had done in the cell earlier. It struck Rossett that the old man didn't trust him and was suspicious of what was going on. "Okay, I ended up back in the cellar after falling from the upstairs window. I came across your door. I thought you might be able to help me get out."

Chivers didn't reply. He looked again at the gun and then back at the guard on the floor.

"Is this a trick?" the old man asked, still looking back to where he'd come from.

"Why don't you ask him?" Rossett replied as he walked off to find his own way out.

CHAPTER 30

JACOB HAD FINALLY drifted into a light sleep. He knew he was dreaming but almost felt that he could open his eyes and see his grandfather smiling and warming some bread in front of the fireplace.

He felt the heat of the fire and squeezed tighter next to his grandfather on the old bed they shared; he loved the old man and wanted to be as close as possible.

Close in his dreams, at least.

The old man disappeared, scared off by all the shouting that started in the room behind Jacob as he lay facing the wall. He squeezed his eyes shut as he listened to the men swearing and the scraping of chairs. He tensed his whole body and waited for someone to grab him, but they didn't. They just ran out of the room, and Jacob lay silently listening to the boots clattering and getting farther away.

He didn't know where or why they were going, but he was glad they had gone.

He waited, then turned his head and looked over his shoulder. The room was empty behind him and he rolled off the bed, wrapping the flimsy blanket around his shoulders both for warmth and in a pathetic attempt at protection before creeping to the table. He looked at the half-open door through which the men had gone, then turned to see what food they had left.

There was some bread, cheese, and cold tea. He snatched up the bread and cheese and shoved it in his mouth, then slurped the tea out of the huge enamel mug, sloshing some onto his clothes and the table as he held it with both hands.

Jacob wiped his mouth on his sleeve, padded toward the door, and looked outside. The corridor was empty, but he could hear people shouting somewhere in the building.

He looked back into the room, at the second door on the opposite wall, chewed on his lip for a moment, then crept over to it and put his hand on the knob.

He was going to find his grandfather.

CHAPTER 31

ROSSETT AND CHIVERS climbed the stairs at the end of the corridor. The Webley led the way, with Rossett following close behind. Chivers mumbled something about going back for the lamp, but Rossett raised a hand to silence him and stopped moving up. He tilted his head like a dog in the night and listened to far-off voices and the clattering of boots on hard flagstones.

"Shit," said Chivers under his breath as he moved up a step closer to Rossett and peeked around his hip.

Rossett ignored him and continued up the stairs toward the wooden door a few feet farther on, moving slightly quicker than he had before.

Into the fight, never away from it.

They arrived at the door and Rossett rested his ear against it, hand on the doorknob. Beyond it he could hear nothing, and he wondered if his captors had moved on with their search.

Chivers whispered his suspicion. "Maybe they think you made it out?"

Rossett felt someone turning the knob from the other side, and both men took a step back and stared as it slowly rotated. Rossett raised the Webley and simultaneously reached under his coat for the knife, just in case the .455 wasn't enough for what lay beyond.

The door opened a fraction, and Rossett cocked the pistol and prepared to kill one more time. His brow furrowed and he kicked the door open to surprise whoever was on the other side.

Jacob stared up at the gun and then gave a soft cry, raising his fists in front of his chest as his body tensed. His chin dropped and he shut his eyes.

In the hundredth of a second that his trigger finger tensed, Rossett's eyes screamed at his brain to not shoot, and his brain held fire. He looked down at Jacob, who in turn slowly raised his head, as if finishing a silent prayer.

"You came for me?" Jacob said softly, and tears welled as he became the littlest boy Rossett had ever seen. For a moment, Jacob seemed frozen in time, unsure of what to do next, but as the first tear slid down his face, the little boy ran to Rossett and held him tightly around the waist.

"You came for me," Jacob said again, this time with more certainty, as Rossett reached down and stroked the boy's hair.

"Come with me, boy," Rossett replied, prising free one of the child's hands and dragging him behind him as he crossed the room.

"'Oo's this?" said Chivers, now suddenly aware that he was a little bit farther away from the protecting Webley. Rossett didn't reply.

He stopped at the door that still hung open, where the guards had evidently gone, before he looked around the room.

Now there wasn't any other way for the three of them to go: they had to follow the guards. Rossett just hoped the guards didn't decide to come back as they went forward.

He felt Jacob's hand squeeze his own, and he looked down at the boy.

"Thank you," Jacob said, cheeks glistening with tears. "My grandfather said you would look after me."

Rossett looked at Jacob and then reached down and stroked the boy's cheek with the palm of his bloodied hand. The words hurt more than his broken rib, so much so that he briefly considered telling the boy he hadn't been coming for him, that he'd merely been looking to save his own skin.

He decided the boy had been hurt enough in one day. Unable to look at the young, innocent eyes, he turned away and peered back through the doorway to where the men had run, resigned to play the hero for a few more minutes, at least.

The space he was looking into was cavernous and full of packing cases, and, like every other room in the building he'd been in, it was poorly lit. From where they stood, he couldn't see the exit, so, leading Jacob and Chivers slowly forward, he worked his way around the cases to look for one. The building seemed quiet, and Rossett supposed that the earlier panic of the guards had subsided.

The room was actually some sort of loading bay. Rossett saw his Austin parked near the far wall, next to a slightly newer and larger but just as battered Morris. Between him and the cars stood a Bedford truck and about thirty feet of open ground.

The way out of the building to his left was a large sliding wooden door that filled the outer wall. In it was cut a small wicket gate that was half open, tempting them outside.

Rossett turned to the others and held his finger to his lips, motioning for them to stay put. He tried to open his hand to allow Jacob to let go, but the boy held on tightly, shaking his head.

Rossett glanced back to the door and then carefully prised himself free of Jacob's grip, passing Jacob's hand to Chivers, who started at it blankly.

"What?"

"Take his hand."

"Why?"

"Just do it." Chivers shrugged and took hold of the hand. Jacob's eyes pleaded with Rossett, but he turned away and crept toward the gate. He stopped next to the hinge side and flattened his back against the twenty-foot-high, thickly painted black wooden doors. His position allowed him to look through the outward-opening gate into the street beyond.

Rossett realized he was on the opposite side of the building from where he had fallen. This exit led out into the maze of warehouses and thin streets that laced the docks like veins, allowing goods to flow out from the heart of the quays and into the city, then onward to the rest of the country.

He glanced back to Chivers and Jacob, and was relieved to see they had slunk back into the shadows. He placed his hand on the gate, keeping his back to the door, and gently eased it open a few more inches so he could see farther into the street. As the door moved, he heard voices outside.

"He'll still be in the building. You make sure nobody comes out. Captain Leigh has phoned for a few others to come down to help with the search. I'm going down to tell Taylor in the basement to keep his eyes open."

Rossett didn't hear a reply; he was too busy moving back into the darkness and drawing the knife out of his waistband.

A man stepped through the gate and walked quickly toward the room that led to the stairs. Rossett let him take four or five steps before coming up behind him and striking him across the back of the head with the Webley. The man didn't drop immediately; he managed another two steps before finally staggering drunkenly to the side and dropping face-down onto the floor, his Thompson clattering onto the concrete and into the gloom.

The noise it made was as loud as if it had fired, and Rossett was already turning to the gate, Webley outstretched, as the sound echoed back off the far wall. Rossett crouched next to the unconscious man. Pistol trained on the open door, he reached and felt around for the Thompson.

His fingertips found the barrel and he dragged it toward him, then picked it up and held it with one hand, pointing both weapons at the exit. He risked a look over his shoulder and flicked his head toward the cars before turning back to the gate.

Behind him Jacob and Chivers ran as quickly and as quietly as they could manage to the Morris. Jacob, recognizing Rossett's old Austin, pulled Chivers on, silently pointing the way. He climbed into the back while Chivers looked for some keys.

"Pssst!" Chivers stage-whispered from the open door of the car. "Where's the bleedin' keys?"

Rossett looked across and then back to the door; he was beginning to regret releasing the old man. He moved slowly toward the gate at a crouch, the Webley now in his pocket and the Thompson cocked and ready.

He stopped short of the light the streetlamp was casting inside and listened as best he could over the sounds of Chivers cursing as he tried to find some keys or a way of starting the car.

Somewhere over his shoulder, he heard the Austin's hood creak and then tensed as he saw a Webley snake around the doorframe from outside. Whoever was holding it moved with less care than he should have.

Rossett moved silently to his right and reached his free hand toward the emerging pistol. Had he wanted to, he could have fired the Thompson at the wooden door, probably killing whoever was holding the gun before he even had a chance to look inside, but he didn't want to bring the entire search party down on his position, and he wasn't even sure how many rounds the machine gun held, if any.

As soon as he saw the wrist holding the gun he grabbed it. Covering the hammer with the web between his thumb and index finger to prevent its firing, he dragged the arm toward him. The body on the other end of the arm soon followed, suddenly stopping when it saw the barrel of the Thompson staring back.

"Let go of the pistol," Rossett said to the silhouetted man, who complied, half in and half out of the doorway. Behind him, Rossett heard the Austin fire up and Chivers give a little cheer. He gestured for the man in the doorway to step inside and face the wall; the silhouette shook its head.

"What? And let you shoot me?"

"If you don't do as I say, you die; if you do, you don't," replied Rossett, taking a step back and gesturing with his head again.

The man stepped in and half turned, trying to keep his eyes on Rossett and to present as small a target as possible. Rossett recognized him in the half-light as the one he'd head-butted in the cellar earlier. He saw how the thick black scab on his lip had hardened as the night had worn on, and wondered if he looked as battered himself.

"In the corner," Rossett gestured, this time with the Thompson. As the guard turned to look, Rossett hit him hard on the back of the skull with the butt of the Thompson and watched as he fell onto the dark floor facefirst and out cold.

Rossett bent down and gave the man a quick search. In a coat pocket he found his own warrant card and lighter. Whoever this bloke was, he'd obviously been the first to search Rossett after he'd been knocked out and had kept some of his property on him. Rossett was glad to return the favor. He found a few shells for the pistol, which he pocketed, and another long knife, which he threw into the street outside as far as he could.

Behind him, the Austin revved, impatient to go, so Rossett crossed to the gate and listened before popping his head out into the night. The street was deserted, so he turned back to the car and gave a thumbs-up before closing the gate and pulling on the large wooden sliding door of the bay.

The door groaned and jerked its way open. Rossett had to push and pull one-handed because he was holding the Thompson, and his ribs cried out with the effort.

He cleared enough room for the Austin, which pulled forward onto the street, and Rossett crossed the bay and slashed the tires of the other car and truck.

He turned back to the Austin, whose brake lights shone dimly, lighting the warehouse and the packing cases. A mix of red and black shadows, the warehouse looked like hell's storeroom, and Rossett was glad to be leaving it behind.

He crossed at a run, and just as he reached the Austin, which by now was puffing exhaust out of its little pipe, he heard the engine gun and watched as it pulled out into the street and away.

Away from him.

Rossett ran a few steps behind the car and was tempted to level the machine gun when he heard the rattle of gunfire behind him.

He kept running, not after the car this time, but to the far side of the street and the shadows that lay there. Head down, he was vaguely aware of the Austin weaving away as fast as its little engine would allow. He dared a quick glance and saw a ghostly face staring at him from the rear window: Jacob, losing him again.

He ducked into an alley just as the brickwork around him exploded in a thousand tiny flecks of dust and debris. Whoever was firing the Thompson behind him had set it to auto and fired high in a long, drifting burst.

Rossett splashed along the alley as fast as he could. He saw a few positions that would have afforded him cover but ignored them. He didn't want to get into a gunfight, he wanted to get away.

Ahead, the alley ended in a T junction, offering him a choice of left or right. He chose right, toward the direction the Austin had traveled.

Before he reached the junction, he heard shouts behind him followed by shots. The shots were more carefully aimed this time, and Rossett felt a blast of air as one passed too close for comfort. He ducked into the right alleyway and skidded to a halt. The alley stretched with no breaks for more than a hundred feet. Even at a sprint he wouldn't make it before someone came round behind him and took careful aim.

He turned back to the junction before crouching down and easing the gun around the corner. There was no light at his end of the alley, so he knew his assailants wouldn't be able to see him. He flicked his head out and saw two men moving toward him, silhouetted by the lights of the street behind them, both hugging the walls and gates, crouching down to make themselves smaller targets.

These fellas aren't idiots, thought Rossett. They could have done me a favor by just keeping on running. He guessed they knew these alleyways well. They would have known he wouldn't have sprinted on for fear of being shot. He looked back over his shoulder along the alley and wondered if he should start running, but finally decided to engage the enemy.

Keep attacking, keep going forward.

His thumb flicked the fire rate switch to auto. Then he stood up, took a deep breath, stepped out into the alley, and swept it with bullets.

One of the men cried out, and Rossett ducked to the left-hand side of the alley as he fired. He rested his back against the wall, pulled out the magazine of the still-smoking Thompson, and inspected it.

Empty.

Rossett stuck his head around the corner again. This time he saw four silhouettes, moving slowly, each hugging the wall or each other for cover. One appeared to be holding his arm; at least the magazine hadn't been wasted.

He leaned back against the wall and drew the Webley, letting the Thompson drop to the ground. He glanced around the corner again and saw that the clatter of the Thompson falling had caused his four assailants to duck down behind some rubbish bins; it bought him some time, so he opened the Webley and loaded two more shells into the empty chambers.

"Rossett?" A voice came round the corner. It sounded like Leigh, but hoarse, stressed.

Rossett realized the one he'd shot had been his tormentor in chief, and he smiled in satisfaction.

"John?" This time Leigh sounded calmer, trying to regain his composure, as if he'd not expected to sound so frayed when he'd shouted, and Rossett guessed the man was cursing that he'd shown weakness, both to Rossett and to his men.

Rossett didn't reply. Why should he? He didn't want to give away his position, and there was nothing to negotiate. He wasn't going to surrender, and he guessed neither were they.

He heard an old metal bin lid fall to the ground and risked another peek, checking that they weren't sneaking up on him. He could make out the four men crouched, almost comically, behind a row of bins they'd dragged across the alley. Rossett wondered if the bins were empty and whether they'd be thick enough to stop a round from the Webley. He crouched down to take another look.

"Rossett, we know you are stuck there. To the left is a dead end, and you'll not climb over those walls, old man. And be careful, I'm warning you not to try dodging back; we're dug in, and these Thompsons will cut you to pieces."

Rossett leaned back and looked to his left, the alley stretching for maybe thirty or forty yards into the darkness, a dark tunnel of doom. He couldn't make out the end, but he was aware of the walls on either side, at least eight feet high, covering the backs of the adjacent warehouses.

Some had barbed wire on top, while others just had worn, rounded brick that would be difficult to climb over at best, impossible at worst. He couldn't make out any available cover except a few narrow gaps set into the wall for gates, and those gates were heavy steel.

These warehouse owners wanted to protect their stocks.

Rossett felt like a rat in a maze.

He leaned his back to the cold brickwork and breathed out, looking up into the night sky, his breath blowing white as it escaped into the heavens.

The sky had cleared and a light breeze had picked up, blowing the last of the fog back to the river.

Not a bad night to die, he thought as he squeezed the grip of the Webley and tapped the barrel against his leg, still looking at the stars and puffing out his cheeks.

"Come on, old man, say something! We need to talk! Maybe we can work something out."

It struck Rossett that the reason they weren't advancing was that they didn't want to hurt him, at least not badly.

They thought he knew where the diamonds were. He smiled. At last, he had a card to play.

"Go and get that arm seen to while you still can!" Rossett called out before crouching and firing off one solitary round at the center of one of the bins.

The Webley boomed in the alleyway as Rossett dodged back behind the wall, which exploded around him as someone let go in return with a Thompson. He raised his arm to protect his face from the shards of flying brick, but almost as soon as it had started the firing stopped with a barked order from Leigh.

They wanted him alive; that was their weakness.

Rossett took a breath and ran across to the right of the alleyway at full pelt. He waited for a burst of gunfire, but the only thing that the four resistance men fired off was curses.

He kept on running as he heard the clatter of bins being knocked over behind him. His footsteps echoed off the narrow alley walls, clear and crisp except when they splashed through dirty puddles that kicked water up his legs and over his shoes. He was almost blind in the darkness. Like a bat, he tried to see with the sounds his shoes made, squinting his eyes, trying to make sense out of the gloom.

Behind him, to further confuse his senses, he heard his pursuers sprinting almost as fast. He felt like a fox pursued by hounds, a fox with a Webley .455.

He trailed his arm and half turned his torso, slowing only slightly, and fired off one shot down the alley. It was high and wide but seemed to do what he needed. He heard the men cursing and ducking even as he turned and carried on with a renewed burst of speed.

He was running so fast he nearly slammed into the wall at the bottom of the alley as it made a sharp right. His shoulder clipped the wall and spun him, and Rossett sprawled onto the wet flagstones before rolling, scrambling to his feet, and running on.

His chest was heaving and his ribs ached. His raincoat flapped around him and he felt he was slowing with every step. He could see the end of the alleyway now, maybe fifty feet ahead. Beyond it lay a cast-iron streetlamp that was leaking milky white light like melting ice cream onto the wet flagstones.

Rossett ran on, heading for the light. He couldn't hear the men behind him now, and he wondered if they had broken off the chase so as not to get too far from their base. Surely, someone had heard the gunfire and had called the police or, even worse, the Germans.

The resistance wouldn't want to be too far from safety with illegal Thompsons, and they would be reluctant to chase him halfway across the city carrying on the gunfight. Maybe he'd escaped, after all?

He burst from the end of the alleyway like a bullet from a gun.

The street was empty. Rossett looked left and right as he crossed, slowing slightly, to the other side of the road. He saw warehouses on the alley side opposite and thin three-story tenement houses, none of which showed any light through their dirty windows.

Rossett ran on, crossing cobbles now that hurt his feet. He was slowing down, from both fatigue and awareness that he wasn't being chased anymore. He tried to let his breath catch up to his legs and shoved the Webley back into his coat pocket, keeping hold of the butt. He eventually stopped on the corner of a main road he didn't recognize, looking around for a street sign as he caught his breath.

He sighed when he saw one: The Highway. He knew where he was; he was taking some control again.

The road looked pretty deserted in both directions as Rossett leaned back into the shadows, breathing hard and rubbing his ribs, which now felt as if they were poking out through his coat.

Somewhere in the distance he heard the noises of the early-morning city, and he looked down at his appearance with dismay. His coat was covered in a mix of blood, mud, dirty water, and sweat.

He knew there was a hospital nearby, and hospitals and docks meant the streets were soon going to be full of people on their way to work. He needed to think quickly.

He studied the palms of his hands in the half-light and crouched down to a puddle to rinse them, then wiped his face in an attempt to get rid of some of the blood that had leaked from his nose.

He suspected he'd made himself look even worse and wiped his sleeve across forehead and face.

A losing battle.

He heard the clip-clop of hooves and stepped back as a milkman and cart trotted around the corner two streets up. A long milk round fortunately lay in the other direction, and Rossett breathed a sigh of relief.

He needed to clean himself up if he wasn't going to attract attention; he needed a wash and some clothes.

He looked left and right and decided to move away from the milkman to begin his search. As he crossed the road he saw car headlamps switch on, maybe three hundred yards away in the direction the milkman had traveled, and Rossett quickened his step.

The car drove slowly at first. Rossett slipped his hand into his coat pocket, gripping the Webley as he heard the engine drawing nearer.

It may just be an early-morning riser on his way to work, he told himself, conscious of the fact that few, if any, residents in this area would have the means to buy a car. He risked a look over his shoulder and wondered if it was a police patrol, briefly considering flagging it down. After all, he was still a copper. How would a late-night patrol know about what had happened? Maybe he could make up a story about being mugged?

All these possibilities flitted through his mind, but he knew they were outweighed by the facts: he had a Webley in his pocket and had left bodies all over London that night, and there was bound to be a report of shots being fired in the area.

Koehler wasn't a fool. He'd soon figure out what had happened, assuming he hadn't already.

Rossett was on the run, and the car behind him was speeding up.

CHAPTER 32

"**WOULD YOU LIKE** another cup of tea, sir?"

Koehler shook his head and forced a smile as he passed the heavy mug back to the young WPC who had been hovering around him for the last hour. She looked slightly hurt at his rejection; she turned and said the same thing to Schmitt, who impatiently waved his hand for her to get away from him. Koehler suddenly felt sorry for the girl and gently tapped her arm.

"Actually, another cup would be nice, thank you."

The WPC smiled before casting a sideways look at Schmitt, who carried on ignoring her.

"These English with their tea," Schmitt said in German to no one in particular. "It's just milky piss."

Koehler wondered if he should reply, then decided it was best to just continue staring out across the Metropolitan Police's communications room at Scotland Yard. Both he and Schmitt were in the Gestapo liaison booth, a small glass room high above the banks of telephonists and radio operators, next to the Met's own supervisor's booth. They had kicked the night-shift liaison officer out on their arrival.

Through the glass to his right Koehler had noticed the night-shift chief inspector sneaking sly glances at his two high-ranking German visitors. In fact, Koehler had noticed how every police officer in the room seemed to be looking at them without actually looking. He wasn't enjoying the experience and slumped even deeper into the shiny black leather office chair that had been wheeled in especially for him.

He looked across at Schmitt, who seemed impervious to the atmosphere in the room.

"I'm not sure this was a good idea," Koehler finally said, in English, to Schmitt, who was writing something into his notepad.

Schmitt looked up from his pad and raised an eyebrow before answering in German, "What else was there for us to do?"

"I don't feel like we are doing anything." Koehler shrugged as he spoke, a man of action stuck staring at a room full of people working.

"We have men rounding up known associates, not that we'll have any joy with them. By nine o'clock this morning, Charing Cross will be full of people who claim not to know anything and not to have seen anything. And that will just be the German guards. Trust me, this is the best place to be. If there is one thing every stereotype tells us, it is that if anything out of the ordinary happens, the English tell a policeman."

Before Schmitt finished speaking he started writing in his notebook again, leaning forward so as to prevent Koehler from seeing exactly what information he was making note of.

The WPC came in with Koehler's tea and smiled in a manner that made Koehler wonder if she was flirting with him. He found himself smoothing the front of his uniform.

"Thank you."

"You're welcome, sir," she replied, with another smile that made Koehler smooth his hair after she had gone. He took out a cigarette and lit it, blowing the first plume of smoke into the air above Schmitt, who looked up and then shook his head.

"Must you?"

"I must." Koehler took another drag and stared at Schmitt, who had already returned to writing in the notebook. "What are you writing?"

Schmitt sighed, then put his pen down, folding the notebook over it.

"My notes about tonight. I would have thought you should do the same."

"What's the point? We are both in the shit," Koehler replied, speaking in German this time, aware that the chief inspector in the next booth was only a thin sheet of glass away, and looking in his direction.

"The point?"

"If we don't find the resistance prisoners, we are in the shit; if we do, we aren't. Well, we are, but it won't be as deep. As for Rossett? Well, if he turns up, he has some serious questions to answer."

"Questions? I think he has more than questions to worry about if, as you say, he is the cause of all this."

Schmitt stared at Koehler, who shook his head before picking up the mug of tea that was steaming in front of him on the desk.

The two men sat in silence, staring out through the windows of the booth.

"What did you do before all this, Schmitt?" Schmitt looked across, surprised at the question. He hesitated.

"I . . . I worked for the party, after I left university. I thought about maybe going into politics, but ended up being a policeman. It took me some time, but eventually I realized I could do more good for the Fatherland in the Gestapo. Why?"

"I was a teacher," Koehler said wistfully, still speaking into the mug, holding it close to his lips with both hands as he looked out across the banks of policemen and -women below. "I taught history in Munich. I loved it." Koehler trailed off.

Schmitt stared at Koehler for a moment, then glanced past him at the chief inspector, who was staring back through the glass with a telephone held to his ear. The inspector suddenly stood up and pointed to the telephone in the German booth, and Schmitt snatched it up as he continued to stare at Koehler.

"Yes?"

"Reports of shots near St. Katharine Docks. We've had several people call, sir. You asked to be notified if anything unusual—"

Schmitt put his hand over the receiver and elbowed Koehler, causing him to spill some tea onto his leg.

"Shots have been heard near St. Katharine Docks. What do you think?"

Koehler grabbed the phone from Schmitt.

"Get everything you have over there, English, German, everything! I want roadblocks so tight not even a pigeon can get out. Now!"

Koehler slammed the phone down and picked up his cap.

"Do you think it's them?" Schmitt was folding up his notebook and getting to his feet, eyes fixed on Koehler.

"We've more chance of catching them out there than we have in here. Besides, I don't think I can drink any more of that tea."

CHAPTER 33

ROSSETT STARTED TO run again in an attempt to get across the road before the car behind him got too close.

He wasn't fast enough. He heard the engine revving and the crash of a gear change. They were coming after him. Rossett looked along the street for cover and then decided enough was enough. He stopped running, pulled the Webley out of his pocket, turned, and took aim.

He thumbed the hammer on the big gun and sighted at the oncoming car, which was maybe fifty feet away, engine racing in too high a gear for the speed that it was traveling.

Rossett let it close on him, aiming fractionally above the left-hand headlamp where he knew the driver was sitting; he took a deep breath to steady his hand, the cold calmness of the reaper coming down around him once more on that long night.

The car slewed to the right, thin tires sliding on wet cobbles before it stopped some thirty feet from Rossett, who lifted the muzzle of the gun slightly.

It took a moment before he realized it was his car.

"Don't bleedin' shoot! It's us!"

Rossett recognized Chivers's voice as he eased the hammer on the Webley with his thumb, lowering the pistol as he walked toward the car. The passenger door opened and Jacob got out, nervously holding his coat closed with two tiny fists.

Rossett drew closer and had an urge to take hold of the boy and hug him, but he merely said, "Get in the back."

Chivers was still in the driver's seat, and as Rossett reached the passenger door he looked around the street. He noticed a woman's face at an upstairs window. Opposite where the car had stopped a small general store was coming to life, and Rossett saw the shadow of a shopkeeper behind the closed sign, watching him.

Rossett got into the car.

"Drive."

Chivers ground a gear and over-revved the engine. The car lurched a few stuttering feet, then stalled.

Rossett looked at the old man, who cursed and fiddled with the broken ignition barrel that hung halfway out of the dashboard.

"Couldn't you get a better bleedin' police car?" Chivers said, squinting at the wires and touching them together like a Stone Age man looking for a spark.

Rossett glanced over his shoulder at Jacob, who was sitting silently on the backseat. The boy looked like he was made of porcelain; he was pure white and unmoving. His eyes held Rossett's stare.

The car coughed to life, and Rossett held out his right hand in a calming motion to Chivers.

"Just relax, take it slow."

Chivers nodded, looking out of the windshield grimly as he over-revved the little car again. This time it pulled away, slowly but steadily. Chivers made his way to the right side of the road and looked across and grinned at Rossett, who nodded back, doing his best to ignore the crunch from the gear box.

"Thought we'd lost you," Chivers said first to Rossett and then to the mirror, looking at Jacob. "Didn't we?"

Jacob didn't respond.

"I thought you'd left me."

"I saw them bastards coming with the machine guns. They'd have cut us to ribbons. Sorry, chum."

Rossett looked at Chivers and decided not to challenge him.

"I understand."

"Little fella 'ere was screaming that we 'ad to go back for you. I couldn't shut 'im up, couldn't make 'im understand I wasn't leavin' yer."

Rossett twisted and looked at Jacob, who smiled back at him.

He nodded thanks to Chivers but didn't speak. Chivers looked at him out of the corner of his eye and then quickly looked away.

"Where are we going?" Chivers ground another gear as he asked the question, his whole upper body twisting as he pushed the lever home.

"Head for Tower Bridge. We need to get south of the river, away from here. Drive slowly and take it easy," replied Rossett as he looked over his shoulder again, checking that they weren't being followed.

"I might take it easier if you put that pistol away."

Rossett looked down at the gun, then pulled his coat from underneath him and put the pistol half into his pocket, out of sight but still close at hand.

"Where do you live?" Rossett asked Chivers, still looking out the back window.

"Why?"

"I need somewhere to clean up."

"Miles away."

"Where?"

"Far away, that's where, and you ain't bleedin' going there. Soon as I'm a couple of miles from 'ere, we're splitting up, chum. Thanks and all that, but I don't need to take a copper back home, especially one with a Jew kid."

"Pull over."

"I was going to do a few more miles—"

"Pull over and stop the car now." Rossett was looking out the window at the street ahead, and he reached for the steering wheel.

"All right! Bleedin' 'ell, don't get shirty."

Chivers pulled the car to the curb and reached for the door handle, but Rossett gripped his arm.

"Wait."

"Wait? I thought—"

"Look." Rossett pointed ahead. About a third of a mile down the long, straight road, there were two trucks parked at an angle to the curb. Almost as soon as Chivers leaned forward to squint at the trucks, the flash of a flare, the kind the police used for directing traffic when the smog was really heavy, sparked to life in the distance.

"What is it?" Chivers leaned even farther forward, so far that his breath fogged the windshield.

"A roadblock. Turn around."

The little Austin crunched a gear, then Chivers pulled a U-turn and started to head back the way they had come.

"What if we run into Leigh and his mob?"

"We won't."

Rossett looked over his shoulder at the flares in the distance, and then down at Jacob, who stared back, calm and trusting, pale in the streetlamps.

He couldn't bring himself to look at the boy for long.

"We need somewhere to wait this out, somewhere where we can get this car off the street."

Ahead in the distance, Rossett saw the flash of another flare. Chivers read his mind and took a sharp left turn down a side street.

"Wherever we're going, chum, you need to think quick, because they ain't lookin' for me. I can get out of 'ere anytime I like."

"They're looking for whoever has been firing those shots. If you don't live or work around here, you'll be going with them."

They drove along the narrow cobbled street, which was starting to shade light blue as the sun came up behind the wet gray clouds. They were approaching a low railway tunnel as Rossett looked left and right before suddenly gripping Chivers's arm.

"Stop!"

Chivers almost cried out and jabbed the brakes so hard that both Rossett and Jacob jerked forward. Rossett didn't speak; he climbed out of the car and jogged under the tunnel, searching off to his right, gun in hand, then disappeared from view.

Chivers selected first gear and briefly thought about driving away, but then remembered how loudly Jacob had screamed before and waited instead, chewing his bottom lip and glancing in his mirror.

A moment later, Rossett reappeared, attracting Chivers's attention with a low whistle. He beckoned him forward and gestured for him to turn a sharp right after the bridge. Chivers did as he was told and found himself in a narrow alley that ran adjacent to the raised railway line. Alongside the alley were open arches for the bridge that supported the trains. Rossett appeared at Chivers's window and tapped on it.

The window dropped into the door as soon as Chivers touched the handle, causing the old man to jump with fright.

"Stick the car under this arch quickly; we haven't got much time."

Chivers maneuvered the car under the arch, and before he had time to kill the engine Rossett dragged open the passenger door and pulled Jacob out.

Rossett took Jacob's hand and set off at a pace, in the opposite direction from where they had come from. The boy trailed behind him, while Chivers splashed through the puddles bringing up the rear.

It was only when they reached the end of the alley that Jacob realized where they were.

Rossett had brought him home.

CHAPTER 34

ROSSETT RAN, HOLDING the Webley against his leg. He felt Jacob speed up as they reached the end of the alley, so much so that when he stopped, the boy whipped around him and almost broke away from his grasp.

He crouched down and pulled Jacob in close.

"Wait here."

The boy shook his head. Rossett let go of his hand and gripped his shoulder, pushing him down as he did so, willing the child to take root.

"You must wait. I'm going to check if it's okay."

Jacob shook his head again.

"I want to come."

"You must wait and be quiet, very quiet. I'll come back for you. I'm only going over there." Rossett gestured with the pistol to the alleyway opposite. "You'll be able to watch me from here." He tilted his head looking for a sign of agreement, and when it didn't come, he looked up at Chivers, who had joined them, out of breath and struggling not to cough.

The old man took hold of Jacob by the upper arm and nodded to Rossett, who, in turn, nodded to Jacob and held his index finger to his lips.

"Sssh," he said, before turning and looking out across the street.

Dawn hadn't quite broken and Caroline Street was empty. It struck Rossett that he'd been in the same place doing the same thing almost exactly twenty-four hours earlier, looking at the dirty brown house, which had then been full of cowering Jews hunted by the Nazis. Now the house was empty, and it was he who was cowering while being hunted.

He stared at the house, with its darkened windows and drooping curtains hanging like old boxers' eyelids, and wondered if it was fate that had brought him full circle.

Then he remembered that he didn't believe in fate, he only believed in himself.

Rossett took a deep breath and jogged across the road, again holding the Webley against his leg. He stopped when he reached the other side and glanced back at Jacob and Chivers, the boy staring at him as Chivers looked around furtively. Rossett gestured for them to follow, and as they did, he looked up and down the road to check that it was still clear.

In the distance, Rossett heard faraway traffic and the rattle of milk bottles on front doorsteps, and as Jacob approached he instinctively reached out and took the boy's hand. He was pleased to see nobody had bothered to replace the officers he'd left standing outside the house the day before, who had by now long gone off duty. The only sign that the Jews had been evicted was a notice pasted to the front door at an awkward angle like a hastily slapped-on postage stamp.

Rossett couldn't read it from where he was, but he knew exactly what it said: ENTRANCE TO UNAUTHORIZED PERSONS STRICTLY FORBIDDEN, BY ORDER OF THE MINISTRY OF JEWISH AFFAIRS.

He wondered who had pasted it up, aware that it was normally his job after the inventory had been completed and the property emptied.

A calling card left on so many empty houses he'd lost count.

"Where are we going?" Chivers whispered behind him.

"Follow me," Rossett replied, heading down the side alley until he reached the rear of the house. The yard gate was unlocked and the three of them slipped in quietly. The back door had the same notice stuck to it as the front, and Rossett noticed Chivers reading it as he jammed a piece of old timber against the back of the yard gate to slow down anyone who might follow.

He moved past the old man and spun the Webley in his hand before using the butt to smash a small pane of glass in the back door. He reached through to turn the lock, pushed open the door, and surveyed the houses that overlooked them at the back; all seemed quiet. Somewhere in the distance he heard the milkman again. He looked at the houses opposite once more and then went inside.

Rossett, Jacob, and Chivers entered the grimy kitchen, which smelled of cabbage and sour milk. The bare floorboards creaked as he walked through the house, and he had to reach down and put a hand on Jacob's chest to keep him from pushing past him and up the stairs once they reached the hallway.

Rossett listened. All he could hear was the drip of a lonely tap somewhere in the house, and he glanced at his companions as they looked upward too.

The sky was brightening outside and some light was elbowing its way past the small window in the top of the front door, allowing Rossett to see the dust and grime he'd not noticed that morning. Wallpaper was peeling away from the tops of the walls; it looked like blistered, moldy skin where the damp had discolored it and gravity had taken hold.

Rossett looked up the stairs and decided the best place to be was above street-level windows that might attract nosy neighbors. He was aware that the price for privacy was being trapped on an upper floor with nowhere else to go should someone else come into the house. He decided a back room overlooking the low roof of the slightly extended kitchen might give them an option of escape—not much of an option, but an option at least. They could drop the ten feet to the ground from the kitchen roof, assuming the yard was empty and provided an escape route.

He would have to hope that the posters on the front and back doors kept prying eyes away, and if they didn't? Well, he would cross that bridge when he came to it.

He started up the narrow staircase in the lead until Jacob finally broke away from Chivers's grip, pushed past him, and ran up ahead.

"Grandfather! Grandfather!" the boy's voice echoed around the old house, and Rossett stopped to watch the child bounce up the stairs. Rossett looked back at Chivers and then followed slowly, suddenly tired and aware that he'd barely slept in two days. His body ached, he was hungry, and he needed a drink. He glanced back at Chivers and saw that the old man also looked exhausted, taking each stair by pushing down on one leg and pulling on the worn banister as he climbed.

"You all right?" asked Rossett.

"Have you looked in the mirror lately?" Chivers replied.

They reached the third-floor landing, and Rossett led the way to the front bedroom, the place where he had first found Jacob. The door was half closed, and, as he pushed it open, he saw the boy sitting on the bed, crying.

Rossett didn't know what to do, so he did nothing; he just stood in the doorway, blocking Chivers from following him and watching as Jacob softly sobbed, sitting upright, hands folded neatly in his lap, looking at the floor.

After a moment, Rossett felt a slight push in the small of his back and he turned to look at Chivers, who nodded his head toward the boy.

"Do something. Don't just leave him."

Rossett entered the room, reluctant and unsure. He sat on the bed next to Jacob and hovered his hand an inch above the center of the boy's shoulder blades.

"There, there," he said awkwardly.

Jacob shook his head.

"Don't cry." Rossett looked up at Chivers as he spoke, feeling awkward, words clumsy and fumbled.

"I thought my grandfather would be here. I thought you'd brought me back to him."

Rossett looked down at the boy and then at the fireplace where he'd first found him.

"I'm sorry," was all he could think of saying as he finally rested his hand on the boy's back and rubbed it lightly.

Jacob let go with a desperate choking sob and seemed to fold under the weight of Rossett's touch, a little boy lost and alone and unable to keep it all in. His tiny body shook, and Rossett watched as the pale, thin fists balled tight in frustration and pushed up and into his eyes in an attempt to stop the tears that wouldn't be stopped.

Rossett knew how those tears could burn. He felt them now, too, brewing where his soul used to be, deep down, pressure building on his heart, making it feel as if it might break.

He took the boy in his arms and held him close, trying to stop the pain.

CHAPTER 35

K **OEHLER WAS IRRITATED.** Irritated by the weather: it hadn't stopped raining for two hours.

Irritated by the condensation on the windows of the car.

Irritated by the two children who had been sitting on the curb watching him for half an hour.

And most of all, irritated by the occasional tuneless hum Schmitt kept emitting every five minutes, for no other reason that Koehler could see than to irritate him.

They'd been sitting in a roadblock for nearly two hours after driving around the St. Katharine Docks area checking the lay of the land. The local police had been efficient in shutting down the area, and now, supported by some German troops and a larger number of HDT men, the traffic was slowly being allowed to leave the cordon.

Koehler estimated they had locked down about two square miles of London, a considerable achievement, but he still knew that at some point that day, unless they got some major results, he was in line for a dressing-down he wouldn't be forgetting for a long time, if at all.

He rolled his head to relieve some of the tension in his neck and stared out the front windshield at the line of traffic that was creeping forward, one car, one truck, one bus at a time to freedom. He wondered if Rossett or the escaped resistance men were watching and laughing at his attempts to round them up.

Schmitt started to hum again.

Koehler looked at the back of the Gestapo man's head and considered pulling his pistol and blowing his brains out.

"Schmitt?" he finally said.

"Yes?"

"Would you stop that?"

"Stop what?"

"The humming, would you please stop the humming you keep doing?"

"What humming?"

"You keep humming a tune. You've been doing it for two hours now. Please stop."

As Koehler spoke, he stared, chin in hand, through the smeared condensation at the two urchins sitting, feet in the gutter, staring back.

"I don't think I've been humming," said Schmitt, twisting in the front seat to look at Koehler in the back, his leather trench coat squeaking on the seat as he did so.

"You have." Koehler continued to stare at the children, losing the battle both inside and outside the car.

"Have I been humming?" Schmitt turned to the Gestapo driver, who looked in the mirror and then at his boss.

"I didn't notice, sir."

"See? I've not been humming."

Koehler sighed and looked at his watch. Nearly midday.

He wiped the window again and looked at the two gargoyles through the smudged water. After a moment, he fished in his pocket, took out some loose change, thumbed through it, then tapped the driver on the shoulder and passed him tuppence.

"Here, get rid of those children."

The driver took the money, grabbed his black trilby from off the dashboard, and got out. Koehler watched as he walked around the front of the car, putting the money in his pocket, toward the children, who turned to look up as he approached.

The driver aimed a kick at the nearest one and then shouted something in broken English. The boys scrambled away and ran off, shouting something about Hitler as they did.

Koehler shook his head in disbelief as the driver walked around the car and got back in, smoothing his blond hair as he placed his hat back on the dash.

"What was that?" Koehler asked.

"Sir?" The driver looked in the mirror, confused.

"The money. It was for the children, not you." Koehler's voice betrayed his confusion, and the driver stared back, equally confused.

"I thought . . . I'm sorry, sir, I didn't realize."

Schmitt looked at his driver and shook his head.

"You thought the major was giving you a tip to get rid of the children?"

"I . . . I . . . I didn't . . ."

"Jesus Christ," Koehler said, raising his hand to cut the driver off. "Just be quiet, please, the pair of you. Just be quiet and remember . . . I have a gun."

The car held its uneasy truce for a few minutes until Schmitt spoke.

"Is he waving at us?"

Koehler lifted his hand out of chin and looked up through the windshield toward the checkpoint. At the back of a bus a soldier was holding up his hand and pointing to them, and after a moment an HDT member came jogging up to the front passenger window, which Schmitt rolled down.

"Yes?"

"Sir, there is someone on the bus for you," the Englishman said in halting German, then stepped back and saluted before pointing to the bus.

Schmitt looked over his shoulder.

"He said—"

"I heard," Koehler replied, already opening the door, glad of the distraction.

Schmitt and Koehler walked toward the bus through the crowds of grumbling commuters who were being held up by the roadblock and being held back by the troops and police. Koehler boarded first, and a nervous-looking conductor on the platform at the back pulled his cap off his head and muttered a halfhearted "Heil Hitler" while looking at the ground.

Koehler ignored him and looked down the bottom deck, at the one German soldier who was standing in the aisle, a submachine gun slung over his shoulder. The soldier fired off a rather more enthusiastic "Heil Hitler!" and sprang to attention before announcing that his colleagues were waiting for Koehler upstairs.

Koehler climbed the stairs and, at the top, found a German with an unslung machine gun who saluted smartly and nodded his head down the bus. Koehler entered the top deck, followed by Schmitt, and made his way down the center aisle.

The top deck was heavy with cigarette smoke and, aside from the rumble of the engine below, utterly silent. Koehler glanced at the faces around him, although few met his gaze.

"I apologize for the delay, ladies and gentlemen. We'll have you moving as soon as possible," Koehler announced in impeccable English as he reached the HDT man, who was holding an identity card in his hands.

"Heil Hitler!" the HDT soldier shouted so loud it caused Koehler to jump. "We've found this geezer, sir. He seems shifty to me, thought you should take a gander."

Koehler took the identity papers from the soldier and studied the picture, then the man to whom it belonged.

The photo and papers looked in order, although the address the man was living at was given as Dartford, southeast of their location but not beyond the realm of possibility for him to be traveling on the bus. It was only when Koehler compared the photo on the card with the man once more that he saw the cause for concern.

The man had a fresh black eye, a massive lump clearly visible behind his left ear, and dried blood on his top lip and shirt. Koehler smiled.

"Rough night, Mr. . . ." Koehler read the papers and then looked down again. "Mr. Hunter?"

The man glanced up to and then away from Koehler.

"I fell over at work yesterday."

"Where do you work?"

"I'm a docker."

"It says here you are a laborer." Koehler studied the ID card and showed it to the man.

"I labor at the docks."

Koehler passed the card to Schmitt and walked away.

"Bring him," he said as he reached the top of the stairs.

He knew a liar when he heard one.

CHAPTER 36

AS KOEHLER STEPPED off the bus, a German sergeant came across at a jog.

"Sir, the police have found a body and shell casings. It looks as though there has been some sort of gunfight near a warehouse not far away."

"Do they know who it is who was shot?"

"That's just it, sir. He wasn't shot. Apparently, he had his throat slashed."

Koehler turned to Schmitt and the English prisoner.

"Take him back to Charing Cross. I'll go to the warehouse and join you there later."

The sergeant drove Koehler to the warehouse. It was only five minutes away from the roadblock, and the street outside was full of police and a wagon unloading some HDT men. Koehler told the sergeant to wait and made his way toward a uniformed police inspector who was talking to some constables outside the warehouse's sliding doors.

As Koehler approached, he saw the glint of brass spent cartridges in the gutter and leaned down to pick one up. He was studying it as the inspector walked over and saluted.

"Can I help you?"

"Ernst Koehler, major, SS," Koehler replied, still studying the cartridge.

"Ah, sorry, sir. I'm Brady, inspector over at Wapping." Brady flicked a casual salute, which Koehler ignored. Brady watched Koehler a moment before speaking again. "I'm not sure, sir, but I think they are out of a Thompson."

"You do?" Koehler replied, still looking at the shell casing.

"Yes. I, er . . . I fired a fair few in the war myself, and these look familiar."

Koehler nodded. He studied the casing and smelled it before looking up and down the road.

"Do we know what they were shooting at?"

"There are bullet holes in the wall next to the alley over there, and, by the looks of it, although it is only a guess, I'd say they sprayed at someone running across the road."

"Why do you say that?" Koehler looked at the inspector, taking notice of the medal ribbons on his tunic for the first time.

"If you look at the cobbles, sir, and the way the trail of bullets runs down the wall, I think it was long burst." The inspector mimed firing a machine gun as he spoke, drawing it across the road and toward the alley. "I think they were shooting at someone who ran across the road from the doorway there to the alleyway over there."

"Did they hit them?" Koehler followed the silent trace of imaginary bullets and looked toward the alleyway, where he could see fresh brick exposed by ragged bullet holes.

"There is some blood in the alley, but I think that belonged to the shooter, not the shot at."

"Why?"

"I found a small pool behind some bins, but it is this side of the bins. I'm only guessing again, sir, but I'd wager whoever was shot at was chased into the alley where he made some sort of stand, forcing the people chasing to take cover. There are more casings in the alley, plus we found an empty magazine on the floor."

"Do you think the person being chased is still around?"

"I doubt he would have managed to break into any of these buildings. Most of them are pretty secure to prevent theft. My men have had a good look around and we've not found sign of forced entry. My bet is that he got away. The alleyway opens out into another street, and beyond that, he could have gone anywhere."

Koehler stared at the alley for a moment, then nodded his head before turning to look at the warehouse behind him.

"They said you had found a body. Do we know who it is?"

The inspector produced an ID card and passed it to Koehler.

"Upstairs, sir. Whoever it was met an awful end. He had his throat cut with a broken mug. There was still a piece in his neck when we found him."

Koehler looked at the inspector and then back at the card.

"Do you know him?"

"No, sir, never seen him before, but . . ."

Koehler looked up.

"But what?"

"Well, sir, all this is just guesswork on my part."

"Go on."

"I don't think these people were local villains, sir. I've worked here for a long time, and I know what it's like, the black market and all. But this—this is strange, sir. I think we've stumbled onto something completely different."

"Why?"

"Well, there appear to be cells in the basement of this building, and the room where we found the dead man, it looks like it was some sort of interrogation room. It had a table with a bolt through it plus a reinforced door with a half-boarded-up window. Also, in the room outside, there are bunk beds, almost like a barrack room."

"What do you think it was, Inspector? What do you think happened here?"

"I think this was a resistance center, and they had a prisoner here who broke out."

Koehler studied the inspector for a moment and then looked back down at the ID card, flicking it in his fingers before looking back up.

"Find out who owns this building and who it was rented to. Search it from top to bottom for any clues as to who was here last night. When you've done that, ring me at Charing Cross."

The inspector saluted, and both men turned and headed in opposite directions. After a few paces, Koehler stopped, turned, and called out to the inspector, who was walking back into the warehouse.

"Brady?" The inspector stopped and turned back to Koehler. "Have you ever been over to Charing Cross?"

"No, sir. Why?"

"We might have an opening available rather soon. Remind me when you call. We need to meet up for a cup of tea sometime soon."

CHAPTER 37

"**D**IAMONDS?" **KATE SUDDENLY** realized she'd spoken too loudly and quickly looked around the tearoom before leaning in close to James Sterling.

"Good lord, Kate, could you say it a tiny bit louder?"

Kate's cheeks reddened, and she took a sip of tea before collecting herself and leaning in close again.

"Rossett has diamonds?"

"He knows where they are, at the very least, and we need them." Sterling opened a silver cigarette case and offered it to Kate, who shook her head, before he took one out for himself and lit it. He leaned back from the table and took a drag, then blew the smoke extravagantly into the air.

Kate waited for her uncle to complete his survey of the room, watching as he foppishly drummed his fingers on the table while looking at the nearby diners. She wasn't fooled by the casual nature of his glances. She knew Sterling would be scrutinizing every face, ensuring that there was nobody close whom he didn't recognize. She was used to this charade; she'd met him there once a week, every week, for the last two years. Same table, same old ladies dotted around.

Sterling acted like an indulgent uncle whenever she arrived. Often they would discuss nothing but fashion or gossip about film stars, but other times she would slip him important information about what was happening at the ministry. What her bosses, and her lovers, were scheming. In turn, Sterling would nod, never make notes, and let slip details that she would then pass back to the selfsame German lovers.

She was a double agent. The problem was, she'd been one for so long, she didn't know whose side she was on anymore.

Sterling took another drag and then leaned in close, as if he were about to tell her a secret about one of the girls in the typing pool. Kate leaned forward to listen, smiling and nodding, playing the part.

"It appears that Rossett struck gold when he found the little Jew boy. The child had pockets full of gold and a diamond."

Kate's eyes widened.

"I spoke to the boy, and he told me that Rossett was going to take him to get the rest of the diamonds when he broke him out of the jail," Sterling said.

"So, does Rossett know where they are?"

"I think the boy, or whoever is the guardian, has told him, as payment for getting him out."

"Where are they from, these diamonds?"

"You know what those Jewish Johnnies are like. They'd have hidden all sorts of things once they knew Jerry was rounding them up. I'd imagine the boy's parents have hidden them somewhere, and the one the boy had was some sort of down payment. What you told me about the boy being stuck in Charing Cross suggests that Rossett cocked up somewhere down the line and needed to break him out. It was just lucky for us he decided to break out our chaps while he was in there."

"Where are our men?" Kate asked absentmindedly, stirring a sugar cube into her tea.

Sterling smiled and stubbed the cigarette out, even though it was only half smoked.

"Here and there, safe enough. Most of them had only been in the country for a week or two when the Germans picked them up. How they found out about them so quickly, God only knows." Sterling looked up from the ashtray as he spoke, right at Kate.

She sipped her tea but didn't flinch under the old man's eyes. She'd played this game too long to let a look of guilt betray her. She put her cup down and picked one of the sandwiches off the plate in front of her. She remembered how her uncle James had fixed her with the same look when she was a child. She hadn't looked away then, and she wouldn't look away now. "So what now?" Kate asked.

"Well, that's where you come in, my dear. We need those diamonds; we need them very much. The money from Canada is starting to dry up as the Americans lose interest in a British resistance. The bloody Yanks are forging ties with the Germans over trade, and we are becoming an inconvenience. Every time the Germans find an American gun, it leaves Uncle Sam with a lot of explaining to do. Plus, so I hear, things aren't going well for the government in exile in Canada. Clement bloody Attlee wants to link up with the commies and Churchill won't hear of it. They're more interested in fighting each other than the Germans, which means our only way of getting weapons is via the Irish, and they, naturally, aren't too keen."

"Naturally."

"Indeed. We need those diamonds, Kate, and I hate to admit it, but your German friends have more chance of finding Rossett, and the diamonds, than we do."

Kate bit a tiny piece of sandwich as Sterling casually watched two uniformed German officers take a table on the far side of the room. One looked across and raised a hand, and Sterling waved back with his handkerchief, relaxed, ever the English civil servant, upper-class establishment all the way.

"How do we know the Germans are looking for him? They may not even know he took the boy out of Charing Cross."

"Koehler's not a fool. He'll have put two and two together." Sterling fingered a sandwich and frowned as he spoke, folding the bread back down and leaving it on the plate.

"If he hasn't? I can't tell him, it would be too dangerous," she said.

"Don't you worry, they'll be looking for Rossett soon enough. I've seen to that."

"So, you need me to let you know what the Germans know?"

"I do. Dear girl, I want you to work your charms on those chaps of yours to find out exactly what is going on, everything they know, as soon as they know it. We need to get to Rossett and his little Jew before the Germans, and you are going to do whatever they want to make sure we do."

"Anything?"

"Yes, anything. Remember, this is for your country."

Kate didn't reply, but her face must have given away her thoughts, because her uncle reached across the table and touched her hand.

"What you do is very important, Kate. We appreciate your hard work."

"I wonder sometimes . . ."

"What?" Sterling squeezed her hand.

"I'm not happy, doing what I do."

"My dear, none of us are happy, but this is a war."

"It isn't. We lost the war, Uncle James, look around you." Kate gestured and accidentally caught the eye of one of the German officers, who smiled at her.

She smiled back.

"We lost the country, but we still have the real king, we still have some of our empire, and we still have our government in Canada. They are still fighting." Sterling was barely whispering now.

"I don't see them fighting now, at least not here."

Sterling lifted his teacup with his free hand and took a sip, then placed it carefully down.

"A war is fought on many fronts and in many ways. People like me and you have to trust those above us to make the right decisions while we follow our orders. I admit, things can sometimes seem bad, but you have to remember, we aren't just fighting for ourselves, we are fighting for the generations that will follow. America shan't stand by forever. They'll soon see that fascism needs to be stopped, not embraced. And when they do, you will see, our weapons supply will start up again and all over Europe people will start fighting back. I promise you."

Kate frowned. "What if they don't? What will we do then?"

"We will keep fighting regardless. Me, you, and anyone else who will follow, we will keep fighting." Sterling squeezed her hand tighter still. He was smiling, looking away from the table, and she turned to follow his gaze.

The older of the two German officers approached the table and held out a hand to Sterling, who stood up and took it.

"Sir James, what a pleasure to meet you here."

"General Kruger, how wonderful to see you." Sterling bowed his head. "Have you met my niece?"

Kruger bowed and wetly kissed Kate's hand in an ostentatious show of chivalry.

"The general is awfully high up in the German-British combined command, my dear. Maybe he can entertain you for a while; I really must dash."

Kate beamed a smile at the general, who, in return, bashfully held out his hands and then took the spare seat nearest to Kate at the table. Sterling stood.

"Until next week?"

"Until next week, Uncle," she replied, hating herself a tiny bit more as each week went by.

CHAPTER 38

KOEHLER MADE IT back to Charing Cross police station about an hour after he had left Schmitt with the prisoner.

Once inside, he headed straight down to the interrogation rooms and, nodding to the guard standing outside, walked straight into the long thin room where twenty-odd hours earlier he'd sat with Rossett after he had been detained outside the station.

Less than a day and so much had changed.

He found Schmitt and another younger, heavyset Gestapo man seated, drinking coffee, while Hunter, the man off the bus, sat staring at the table, hands neatly folded in front of him.

Schmitt rose to meet Koehler, drawing him aside and whispering, "We've taken his fingerprints and someone is checking out his identity, but I've not started questioning him yet. I was waiting for you."

Koehler nodded, dragged Schmitt's chair around the table until it was positioned next to the prisoner, and sat down. He took out his cigarettes, lit one, and placed the others on the table in front of the prisoner.

"Take one." He nodded to the cigarettes.

"No, thank you, I don't smoke," Hunter replied.

"Oh, I'm sorry," replied Koehler, wafting the smoke away from the prisoner extravagantly. "Excuse me."

Hunter shook his head a little and returned to looking at his hands.

"Is there anything I can get you? A drink, maybe?"

"No, thank you."

"Are you sure?"

"I'm fine, thank you."

"If I were you, I'd have a drink while it is on offer."

Hunter shook his head again, and Koehler shrugged his shoulders before leaning in very close to him, his lips close to the man's ear.

"You see, these two gentlemen at the other end of the table are going to torture you, so, while you can, I'd recommend you eat and drink and make merry—well, as merry as possible under the circumstances."

The prisoner looked up at Schmitt and then at Koehler before returning his gaze to his hands.

"I haven't done anything. I was on my way to look for work. I don't know why I'm here."

Koehler took a drag of his cigarette and then reached across so that he could whisper. As he drew close, smoke escaped from his mouth and nose, like a dragon at rest.

"You are here because you are lying. Now, we know you were in the warehouse last night, we know there was a gunfight, and I know Sergeant Rossett did that to your face. You aren't going home, my friend. You are in hell." Koehler tilted his head, trying to meet the eyes of the prisoner, who carried on staring at the table. "Four feet away are two men who are going to torment you terribly. If I am honest, I think the whole affair will be a dreadful waste of time. Because I know you are just a foot soldier, doing your best for your country. I know you don't know much of the bigger picture, and I know that torturing you won't do any of us much good—especially you. The best we will get is some names of your commanders, and, more than likely, the names they've told you are false anyway, so the whole thing will be pointless. Why not tell me what you know, and spare yourself the harm that is going to come your way?"

"I was just on my way to work . . ."

Koehler leaned back in his chair, dismissing the rest of Hunter's statement, and took another drag before folding his arms and studying the prisoner. He sighed and looked at Schmitt, and then back to Hunter, before shrugging.

"Well, my friend, I tried." Koehler sighed, took another drag on the cigarette, then stubbed it out on the back of Hunter's hand.

CHAPTER 39

ROSSETT WOKE UP with a start, sucking in air and half arching his back. He gasped again, blinking up at the stained gray ceiling that stared back. He breathed deeply and wondered when the last time was that he hadn't been snatched from sleep by the panic of nightmares.

There was a hazy sunshine coming through the dirty gray net curtain that hung halfheartedly across the window, and it warmed his face, causing him to shiver when he realized how cold the rest of his body was.

He shifted to look down at Jacob, who lay on the bed next to him. The boy's head rested in the crook of Rossett's arm, so that he was unable to move it.

He stared at Jacob for a moment or two and realized he didn't remember falling asleep. He twisted to look out the window and estimated the time to be about midday, maybe a little later. Deep inside him, his stomach gave a little rumble of hunger.

He lifted his free arm and looked at where his watch had been, then remembered that one of the resistance had taken it when they first took him into the warehouse, along with his wallet and warrant card. That was before they had hooded him and dragged him to the cell.

It had been a long night, a very long night.

He looked at Jacob again and then wondered where Chivers was. Slowly, half an inch at a time, he eased his arm from under Jacob's head and slid out from under the boy until he was sitting on the edge of the bed, rubbing his forehead. Jacob was lying on his side, breathing deeply in sleep, face soft and smooth with the merest flicker of an eyelid betraying his dreams. Rossett raised his hand to the boy's head and almost touched it to smooth his hair, but then pulled away and continued to stare for a moment, strangely sad and not wanting to wake him. He folded the blanket they had been lying on over the boy and then stood and stretched, checking to see which parts of his body hurt the most.

All of it seemed to ache equally.

He crept out of the room and onto the landing, looking into a couple of the rooms before finding Chivers in the front bedroom, sitting in a threadbare armchair with a blanket over him, eyes closed, slack-jawed, breathing slowly and noisily.

Rossett crossed to the bay window, which gave a wide view of the street. He looked through the net curtains, careful not to disturb them. Outside, he could see normal life, normal people doing normal things.

He envied them.

A woman was scrubbing her step in the winter sun; another was carrying a basket of shopping, balanced awkwardly on her thigh and in the crook of her arm, the weight causing a crook in the body as she waddled home.

"'Ell of a day," Chivers said behind him, and Rossett turned from the window.

"I thought you were asleep."

"I was. But I've been checking every now and then. There was a Mercedes drove down before, but I think they were just cutting through. We're safe 'ere for now."

Rossett nodded and turned back to the window.

"You got any plans?" Chivers asked from behind him.

"I have to get the boy to safety."

"Easier said than done."

Rossett nodded, but didn't speak.

"'Ell of a responsibility, a young kid, especially a Jewish one."

"Yes."

The old man shifted in his chair and then smoothed down the old woolen blanket. Rossett turned from the window and stared at Chivers for a moment before he spoke again.

"I got him into this. I have to get him out."

"'Is grandfather, the one he was looking for, did you . . . ?" Chivers trailed off, unsure of what to say.

"Yes, I put him, and everyone else who lived here, on the train. He'd hidden the boy, and then sent me back here to find him and . . ."

"And?"

Rossett stared at Chivers, unsure if he should tell the whole story, unsure of whether the old man could be trusted with the secret of the treasure. He turned back to the window and rested his forehead against the cold glass. It felt good, and he closed his eyes a moment, then opened them again to watch some children run out of a house opposite and chase each other, darting around lampposts on and off the curb, chasing each other like leaves in the wind.

Faint laughter floated in through the window and scratched at the silence in the room.

"And?" Chivers tried again. "Look, chum, maybe I can 'elp you with the little fella, but you've got to be straight with me."

"Jacob had gold sovereigns with him, and . . . a diamond," Rossett finally said and almost immediately regretted it. He felt unburdened by the truth but unnerved by Chivers's reaction.

"Diamond?"

"Yes."

"So that's why you're 'elping 'im?"

"No. I didn't know he had it, not until I was being interrogated." Rossett absentmindedly wiped a hand across the dried blood on his coat. "The resistance, they found it. I didn't know he had it, I just thought he had some money to pay to someone to get him out of the country, or . . . to bribe me."

"Bribe you not to kill 'im?"

"I wasn't going to kill him."

"Maybe not with your own 'ands."

"I wouldn't kill him, he's a child."

Chivers chuckled and Rossett frowned at the old man before turning back to look at the children playing outside.

"Do you believe that the Germans kill them?" Rossett finally spoke, still facing the window.

"You've 'eard the Free BBC news, ain't you?"

"It's propaganda, half of it."

"Even if 'arf of what they say is 'appening in Europe is, it would be bad enough. All this talk the Krauts give us about Jewish camps full of happy Jews singin' songs and workin' for the Reich . . . well, it's all bollocks, ain't it? Nobody believes it, do they? Not really."

Rossett turned to face Chivers.

"Why would they kill them? It doesn't make sense."

"They kill 'em, my son, because they fuckin' hate 'em, that's why."

Rossett shook his head and went back to the window.

Chivers left him for a while with his thoughts before finally speaking again. "You can buy a lot of boat tickets with a diamond and sovereigns. Did you manage to get 'em back before we broke out?"

Rossett shook his head.

"Windsor, the man who interrogated me, said I knew where the others were. He said Jacob had told him I would be able to find them, and they wanted me to tell them where they were hidden."

"Do you know where they are?"

"No. I didn't even know the boy had one, let alone where the others are or even if there are any others. I have no idea why Jacob would say that."

"Because my grandfather said I should tell you the secret."

Both men turned to the door, where Jacob stood, blanket across his shoulders, thin and pale, dark smudges under his eyes and thick black hair.

"What secret?" Chivers asked the boy, and Jacob looked at him and then Rossett, who nodded that he should tell.

"The secret of the treasure."

CHAPTER 40

JACOB WAS SITTING on a wooden milking stool, back to the wall, faded wallpaper flowers surrounding him like pink fairies you couldn't quite focus on. Rossett had found an old dining chair and he was facing Jacob while Chivers remained seated in the armchair, coughing occasionally with the wet phlegm rattle that he had brought with him from the cellar.

"My grandfather told me that you would come back for me. He told me to stay in the fireplace until I heard you and then I was to call your name, so you could free me. But I didn't have to call your name. You just came and got me."

"'Ow did he know you'd go back to the 'ouse?" Chivers looked at Rossett.

"He would have known I'd have to go back to complete the inventory. Even if when he grabbed me at the train I hadn't listened, he would have known I'd come back eventually. The old man understood how things worked; he'd been watching it happen long enough. I suppose it was a gamble of sorts, but not much of one."

"Whenever you came to the house, as you left he would always make me look at you."

Rossett vaguely recalled now the little boy on the stairs, or a face at a window as he had displaced the Jews, time after time, herding more and more of them to smaller and smaller houses. He suddenly felt embarrassed that the boy had witnessed the work he'd carried out. He looked at the floor for a moment before Jacob spoke again.

"Grandfather said you were a good man just doing a bad job."

Rossett stood up from his chair and crossed back to the window. He leaned on the frame and took a deep breath.

"I knew your grandfather when I was your age. My mother used to visit his shop. Old Man Galkoff, we used to call him, except he wasn't that old. He used to give us sweets, the kids in the area. We all liked him."

"The diamonds?" Chivers said, then shrugged a "What?" when Rossett looked at him and shook his head.

Jacob looked at Chivers, then back to Rossett, who nodded. "What about the diamonds, Jacob?"

Jacob stood up and dropped the blanket, then took off his duffel coat and turned it inside out, holding it up in front of him. Like a conjurer the boy pulled at the lining and pinched at a seam before he loosened a thread and ripped an inch of cotton from the coat.

He fished in the lining and pulled out a folded piece of greaseproof paper, about one inch long and three wide. He smoothed the paper carefully and then gave it to Rossett before returning to the milking stool and sitting back down, coat over his knees and blanket returned to his shoulders.

Rossett unfolded the sheet. Inside he found a scrap of lined paper with some careful copperplate writing in black fountain pen:

> *Sergeant, if it is you reading this, I trust that Jacob will be*
> *before you, awaiting your decision . . .*

Rossett looked up from the note to Jacob and felt the old man's presence in the room with them.

> *. . . I beg you to think carefully, and to take time to look at the*
> *boy before you set your mind on the path you are about to take.*
> *I know these are hard times, harder for some than others, and*
> *I know you are a man who carries a weight of what has gone*

before on your shoulders, much as I carry the weight of what is yet to befall me and those I hold dear. When we have spoken in the past I have seen your pain, at what you have witnessed, what you have suffered, and the suffering you inflict upon others.

I know you are a good man, despite the evil that you do. I know you once loved, and that you lost that love. So I give you my treasure to protect, in the hope that you find your love again.

And keep it safe.
Jacob Galkoff

Rossett stared at the note and then turned it over in his hands before reading it again. He looked up at Jacob, who stared back, and then back at the note once more.

"Well?" Chivers couldn't contain himself any longer and held out a hand to read the note.

Rossett looked at the outstretched hand and then shook his head, before folding the note and keeping it tight in his hand.

"There is nothing there about diamonds."

"Let me read it." Chivers's hand beckoned again, but Rossett ignored him.

"There is nothing about diamonds," Rossett said again.

"What about treasure?"

"The treasure is here, in the room with us."

Rossett looked at Chivers and shook his head. The old man tilted his in reply, not sure whether he believed what he was hearing.

"Are you 'olding out on me?" Chivers finally said, the words accusing, hanging in the air like buzzards.

"No," Rossett replied, a cloud passing behind his eyes in such a way as to make Chivers lower his hand.

"The boy is the treasure?" Chivers spoke softly and Rossett nodded.

Chivers looked at Jacob and slowly leaned back in the chair; eventually, he chuckled and half coughed before smiling.

"What are you going to do?"

"I'm going to do what I started out to do, get him to safety."

"But . . . but what about the diamonds?" Chivers couldn't hide the disappointment in his voice.

"The diamonds aren't important, neither are the sovereigns. I wasn't helping him to get rich."

"Are you sure?"

Rossett stared at Chivers and remembered how heavy the sovereigns had felt in his pocket, and how he had felt when he'd first seen them.

"The diamonds and the money aren't important."

Chivers smirked.

"They might not be important now, but they bleedin' well will be when you try to get 'im out the country. Tickets don't come free, mate."

"I'll think of something."

"Diamonds, eh?" Chivers shook his head and then wiped his nose with the blanket, his sniffing the only sound in the room. "No wonder Sterling was so interested in you."

Rossett looked up, puzzled.

"Sterling. Didn't he interrogate you?"

"I had someone called Windsor."

"That's him, posh bloke, moans about the weather?"

Rossett nodded.

"He's the head of the royalist mob in London and the south, Sir James Sterling. Works at the Foreign Office, old mate of Churchill's."

"How has he kept his job?"

"Well, turns out 'e's also an old friend of Prime Minister Mosley. 'E walked with the Blackshirts before the war; he's 'arf Nazi, 'arf royalist, although 'e'd never admit it. Thing about Sterling is 'e's a survivor. There aren't many who know about 'is double life, and if you want to stay alive you'll keep quiet about it. When Mosley was put into power by the Krauts, first thing 'e did was get all 'is old Nazi mates gathered round 'im. Not the thugs though—oh no, 'e got the likes of the newspaper owners, all them lords and dukes, all them ones who gave 'im money and quiet support, he got 'em all round 'im and 'e gave 'em jobs. And Sterling, he was one of 'em. Apparently they knew each other from the Great War and 'ad kept in touch."

"So Mosley gave Sterling a job?"

"Nah, 'e just let 'im keep the one he 'ad. Easier that way."

"How do you know this? How do you know Sterling?"

"'E interrogated me, as well. Thing is, 'e doesn't know I knew 'im before the war. When us reds and them fascists were fighting all the city, I saw 'im at the odd rally. Once he gave a speech, load of old shite about empires and working with the Germans against communism."

"I don't understand how he could be a fascist and a royalist." Rossett shook his head.

"All them posh blokes are fascists deep down. They liked the idea of people like us not asking questions, and they certainly didn't like uppity Jewish communists rocking the boat. Mosley and 'is lads appealed to 'em. 'Ad Hitler been a posh geezer who promised to bow to the old king, they would have welcomed 'im ashore at Dover. As it was, 'e 'ad 'is own king who was prepared to bow to Hitler instead. The aristocracy, or those ones who bothered to 'ang around, see a king in Buck House and one of them in Downing Street and they think all's well with the world, service as usual."

Rossett shook his head at the old man's logic, pondering that he now knew Sterling's name and then wondering what to do with that information. Now wasn't the time to expose Sterling. How could he prove what Chivers had said? And besides, his knowledge might one day prove to be a useful bargaining chip, assuming he lived long enough to exploit it.

"We need to go and visit my mother," Jacob finally said, and both Rossett and Chivers turned to look at him.

Rossett frowned and tried to remember if he'd seen a mention of the boy's mother on any manifests before that week. There was only one Galkoff he could remember listed, the grandfather, and there were definitely no women of an age that Jacob's mother would have been.

Most men and women under the age of fifty had been rounded up first, so that they could be sent for work parties on the continent. Rossett would have known if there were any other than the handful who stayed in London for reserved occupations, he was certain.

"Where is she?" he asked.

"Willesden Cemetery," Jacob replied.

"Why?"

"Because she is dead." A child's logic.

CHAPTER 41

"**D**IAMONDS?" **KOEHLER STARED** at Kate before slowly lowering his pen onto the incident report he was writing of the events of the night before.

She nodded, walked around the desk, and sat on it, inches from Koehler, who leaned back in his chair, forced to look up at her. Kate smiled and crossed her legs, leaning forward and resting her elbow on her silk-covered knee.

"That's what the resistance say. Apparently, the boy Rossett sprang from jail had a pocketful of them, plus some gold."

Koehler leaned farther back in his chair, averting his eyes from the tops of Kate's stockings, and shook his head.

"It doesn't make sense."

"What doesn't?"

"If the boy had diamonds, they would have been found when he was searched, before they put him in the cell. It just isn't possible."

"Maybe he hid them?"

Koehler held up a hand to silence her, and Kate pouted and sat up straight on the desk, shifting herself so as to ease her skirt down to a respectable level. Koehler stood up and walked to the tall window that looked out onto the busy road, lost in thought.

"Rossett would have already had the diamonds. Why risk coming back for the boy?" He was talking to himself, so Kate didn't answer.

She glanced down at the incident report on the desk and then back to
Koehler before turning the report so that she could read it.

Koehler turned, noting that she was reading the report but deciding
to ignore it.

"Unless . . ."

"Unless what?" Kate replied.

"Unless the boy knows where more are hidden."

Kate silently rejoiced that Koehler had figured out the next step for
himself. It saved her from revealing that the resistance knew there were
more. She never gave away more information than she had to.

The less they thought she knew, the less of a threat she was to them.

"My contact told me there was an old man with him when Rossett
escaped, a communist they'd been questioning."

"What about?"

"I don't know, it's politics. You know they spend almost as much time
fighting each other as they do us."

Koehler turned back to the window, letting the "us" hang in the air,
making Kate feel self-conscious.

"This old man, do you know him?" Koehler finally asked.

"No, he's just a foot soldier. His name is George Chivers. It looks like
he just got lucky when Rossett broke him out."

"Chivers?" Koehler half turned to face her.

She nodded and smiled, then slid off the table and crossed to him.
Resting her hands on his chest and standing close, bodies touching, she
looked up into his eyes. "You think there are more diamonds?"

Koehler studied her for a moment, grasped her upper arms, then
took a pace back, putting space between them.

"I need you to discover everything you can about everyone in that
Jew house. I want every file looked at and then looked at again; I want
them cross-referenced with the Jewish census we took two years ago.
We need to find out who that boy is and where he is from. Get someone
to turn Rossett's office and his lodgings upside down, and bring every
scrap of paper over here immediately. And do it quietly. Nobody beyond
our team is to know yet. Damage limitation, all right?"

Kate nodded and lowered her hands. They parted, and she crossed to the large wooden double doors, pausing before she left the room to look at Koehler, who was dragging his coat across his shoulders already preparing to leave.

"Where are you going?" she asked.

"I'm going to the boy's house. There may be something there that can tell us where to look next."

"DIAMONDS?" SCHMITT LEANED in close to Hunter's bloodied face, a long drool of blood and spit hanging from his lips and coming to rest on his chest.

Hunter nodded his head, barely able to move a fraction, in the affirmative.

"How do you know?"

"I . . . I saw them . . ."

Schmitt stepped back from the meat hook on which Hunter was suspended. He wiped his face with a hand that was soaked in blood and studied Hunter, who hung by his handcuffed wrists, feet inches from the floor, stripped naked, beaten and abused to within an inch of his life.

The resistance man had been hung over the precipice of death and dragged back several times in the few hours that he had been in the cellar of Charing Cross. Schmitt and his assistant had worked quickly. Schmitt had wanted an edge over Koehler, and now he thought he had one.

He picked up a small jug off the floor, dipped it into a large bucket, and tossed ice water into the face of Hunter, who writhed in his handcuffs with shock.

"Where are they?" Schmitt spoke mildly. He turned to the table and put down the jug before picking up a scalpel from a leather roll that contained an array of glinting stainless steel tools.

"I don't know. Windsor said Rossett knew," Hunter replied, his voice a mere whisper of exhaled breath.

Schmitt moved beside Hunter, his face close to the injured man's armpit. He rested the scalpel against Hunter's chest. The touch of the cold steel caused Hunter to open his swollen eyes and look down. He squirmed when he saw it, straining to lift himself up and away, and failing miserably.

"The man you know as Windsor said that Rossett knows where the diamonds are?"

"He said the boy told him that Rossett knew." Hunter's breath was coming quickly now. He was clearly panicked by the scalpel, his imagination doing the torturer's job.

Schmitt turned to his assistant, who was washing off a wooden baton in the ice water, businesslike, paying little heed to the conversation that was happening a few feet away.

"And Rossett escaped from the warehouse with the boy and an old communist called Chivers?" Schmitt whispered.

"Yeah, I swear."

Schmitt pondered the information, reaching up to put his hand on Hunter's cramping shoulders as he did, patting the man lightly on the back.

"And that's all you know?"

"Yes, I was just a guard, I swear." Hunter opened his eyes to look at Schmitt, desperate to be believed. "Don't hurt me again . . . please don't hurt me."

Schmitt nodded, gently touched Hunter's face, then swiped the scalpel and cut off his nipple.

They heard the scream two floors up.

CHAPTER 42

THE LATE-AFTERNOON SUN was hiding behind the houses opposite the kitchen, where Chivers was searching for food in the cupboards. In the half-light, the old man had emptied nearly every one and found only pots, pans, dust, and four scabrous potatoes that sat in a chipped ceramic bowl like castaways in a sinking lifeboat.

"There 'as to be more than four old spuds, there 'as to be!" he said.

Jacob stood meekly staring at the potatoes, hands resting on the countertop, like a choirboy about to pray. Chivers emerged from the cupboard and looked at him.

"You must have 'id the food somewhere?"

Jacob shook his head.

"There must be a tin of bully beef or rice puddin', at least?"

Jacob shook his head.

"All you ate was old spuds?"

Jacob nodded his head before saying, "Sometimes we had cabbage."

"You 'ad gold and diamonds and all you was eating was taters and cabbage?"

"We couldn't eat the gold."

Chivers stared at the boy, shook his head, then held out his hand.

"Pull me up, boy."

Jacob took the old man's hand and, leaning back, dragged Chivers to his feet as the old man groaned. Once upright, Chivers inspected the potatoes, picking them up one after the other and then putting them back into the bowl. He sighed when the last one went down, rested his hands on the countertop, and looked at Jacob.

"Well, that's Christmas dinner sorted, but I don't know what we're gonna do for New Year."

Jacob didn't understand the joke, so he decided to stare at the potatoes while Chivers ruffled his hair.

Rossett entered the kitchen, stripped to the waist, hair wet, and pulling at some buttons on a striped shirt that had a worn collar and a faded dark stain on the breast.

Jacob looked at Rossett and saw the scars for the first time, thick and angry like tiger stripes, that covered his chest and leaked down onto his stomach and around to his back. Next to them were new injuries, inflicted the night before, the worst a dirty brown bruise that covered his left side. The little boy stared for too long, and Rossett smiled to hide his embarrassment.

"Bloody 'ell," Chivers said, looking at Rossett's torso, " 'ow'd you get those?"

Rossett finally managed to get the last button open on the shirt and he pulled it around his shoulders, wincing as it went.

"What have we got to eat?"

"Four taters and a dead mouse. Seems these people lived on fresh air."

Rossett looked at the potatoes and then at Jacob.

"Where did you get your food? Who did the shopping?"

"We couldn't shop. We weren't allowed to."

"Who said?"

Jacob looked at the floor.

"You did."

Rossett reeled and shook his head. His mouth moved, but no words came out; there was nothing he could say.

Chivers left the kitchen, followed by Jacob. Rossett crossed to the window and looked at the houses opposite, which were silhouetted now against a clear blue sky by the low sun.

He leaned against the old enamel basin and turned on the solitary tap, which coughed and eventually spat out some water. He rinsed his face, then drank from his hand.

After a moment's reflection, he walked into the back room to find Jacob and Chivers sitting on an old settee that had more stuffing outside the threadbare arms than in. Chivers scratched at his chest and frowned.

"I think I've got fleas from bein' 'ere," Chivers said.

"I'm going to finish getting dressed and then we'll leave," he said. "Chivers, go get the car, and bring it to the end of the alley."

"Where are we goin'?" Chivers looked up.

"You are going home. I'm going to get Jacob sorted."

"Oh no, oh no no no." Chivers pulled himself out of the armchair, stood in front of Rossett, and pointed at Jacob. "I ain't leavin' 'im till I know 'e's safe."

"He's safe with me."

"Yeah, for now. 'Ow do I know once you get your 'ands on the diamonds you ain't goin' to be off leavin' 'im?"

"I'm not. Besides, there may not be any diamonds."

"I'm comin' with you."

Rossett stared at Chivers. He knew that one swipe of his hand would knock the old man out cold and give them enough time to walk away, leaving him long behind, but he also knew the old man had resistance contacts, and those contacts could allay the suspicion Rossett would arouse by trying to get the boy out of the country.

Diamonds or not, he needed Chivers.

"Okay, go get the car. We'll go together."

"No funny business?"

"We'll go together."

Chivers nodded slowly, then looked down at Jacob.

"Come on, son. Let's go get the car."

Rossett turned as they left the room and started to tuck the shirt into his pants and pull his suspenders over his shoulders. Suddenly he froze.

"Chivers!"

"What?" Chivers was half out the back door when Rossett ran into the kitchen.

Their eyes met and Rossett raised a finger.

"We go together. From now we go everywhere together, the three of us. Okay?"

Chivers shrugged, took hold of Jacob's hand, and led him back through the kitchen toward the rear sitting room.

As he passed Rossett, he said, "Goin' to be like that, eh?"

"Yes, it's going to be like that." Rossett forced himself to smile at Jacob, who stared back at him blankly, not giving anything away, as usual.

"I'm going to get my coat and then we can get going, okay?"

Chivers sat down and shrugged.

"You stick near me, boy, you understand?" Chivers leaned close to Jacob, looking to the door as he did so.

"My grandfather said I should stay with the sergeant."

"You pay no 'eed to what 'e said; 'e ain't 'ere now, is 'e?"

"No."

"No, 'e ain't, because that sergeant got rid of 'im, that's why."

Jacob considered what the old man had said.

"But the sergeant is a policeman. You should always do what a policeman tells you."

"Not this one. 'E's a bad man. You just stay with me, all right?" Chivers took Jacob's hand as he spoke and the little boy frowned, looking at Chivers's swollen knuckles and liver spots, aware of how cold the old man felt. He was nothing like his grandfather, who was always warm, even when there was ice on the windows.

Jacob nodded and slid his hand away from Chivers.

"We're partners, you and me, boy, partners all the way."

CHAPTER 43

KOEHLER HAD DRIVEN himself, stopping off at his flat to get changed out of the damned uniform that had chafed his neck all afternoon.

He had parked at the end of Caroline Street and walked slowly along it, looking at the houses that were crammed in, like soldiers on parade, shoulder to shoulder.

He stopped and lit a cigarette, pausing to watch the children playing on the far side of the road with some rope hanging from the streetlamp. One of the children was watching him suspiciously, and Koehler smiled at the shoeless boy, who stared back, hands in his short pant pockets, shirt half out.

Unimpressed.

Koehler crossed the road and approached the kids, who, one by one, became aware of the tall blond man walking toward them.

"Children, may I speak to you, please?"

The children stopped playing and all stood, tightly clustered around the lamppost, different heights and ages but the same mucky faces and suspicious stares.

Koehler suddenly realized how quiet the street had become. He took the cigarette out of his mouth and cupped it in his hand at his side, so as not to set a bad example.

"Do any of you know the little Jewish boy who lived there?" Koehler pointed to the Jews' house, gray and dead except for the fresh poster and padlock on the door.

The children all shook their heads and Koehler noticed one looked close to tears. He smiled again and crouched down.

"Are you sure? Nobody is in trouble if you did, I just need to know."

"We never played with no kid, mister. He never come out the house," said the tallest of the children, a beanpole, buck-toothed, bowlegged urchin.

"But you saw him?"

"We never played with him, honest!" a little girl shouted, then looked at the tall boy for confirmation, nodding her head to push home the point.

"I know, but you saw him?"

The tall boy nodded, and then others, on seeing him do so, joined in with exaggerated head bobbing.

"He watches us out the window." The tall boy pointed, and Koehler turned his head to look at the house.

"Which one?"

"That one, we'd see his face watching."

"Watching!" the little girl chorused, causing Koehler to smile at her.

"But you never spoke to him?"

"No, he was a dirty Jew. We don't speak to no dirty Jews," another little boy chimed in, growing in confidence with the tall man and his posh voice and funny accent.

Koehler smiled at the group and then stood up, resuming his position as an adult over the tiny flock. He fished in his pocket for some change.

"You did very good not to talk to the dirty Jews. Here, here is some money for being so good. Now run along."

Koehler passed the coins to the tall boy and flicked his head, a clear instruction not to hang around. The tall boy took the money and ran off, followed by the other kids. The little girl stopped after a few paces and turned to Koehler, then shouted at the top of her lungs in a high-pitched shriek, "Dirty Jews, dirty Jews, we don't like the dirty Jews!"

ROSSETT PULLED THE thick black woolen coat on and shrugged his shoulders a few times in a futile attempt to get it to fit more comfortably over his shoulders. It was too tight and dug into his armpits. He tried stretching it by pulling the sleeves while staring at himself in a dusty mirror hanging by a rusted chain on the wall. He'd searched every room in the house before he'd found something that even came close to his size among the rags left by the inventory team up in the attic.

He picked at the thread of the star of David that was sewn onto the left breast, dirty and yellow, like a slovenly sheriff's badge, then rummaged in the pockets and found some mothballs and a seashell. He tossed the mothballs and studied the shell for a moment, wondering how it had got there, before dropping it on the floor.

He took his belongings from his bloodied raincoat, putting them, one by one, in different pockets, keeping the knife and the Webley till last.

He checked the knife in its scabbard before sliding it into the waistband of his trousers, then unlocked the Webley, checked the chamber, and put it into his left-hand coat pocket. The last of the spare shells went into the right pocket. The handcuffs and key he slipped into his suit jacket before he tried stretching the coat again.

It seemed to fit worse by the second, as though it were shrinking onto him, constricting him.

He was staring at his raincoat, absentmindedly pulling at the star of David, deciding whether he should take his raincoat with him, when he heard a little girl shouting in the street.

He tilted his head, trying to make out the words, and then went back to looking at the raincoat. A moment later something flickered in his subconscious and he became aware of the silence that had now descended.

The children weren't playing outside anymore.

Rossett quickly squeezed down the attic stairs and into the front bedroom, crossing to the window at a half run. He stood first to one side and then the other, craning to get as good a view as possible up the street in both directions without presenting himself at the window.

He saw the children running on the far side of the road, away from the lamppost where they had been minutes earlier. He looked down to the street in front of the house.

Nothing.

He looked back to the kids and stepped back from the window.

Something wasn't right.

He put his hand in his pocket, took hold of the Webley, chewed his lip, and for the first time that day pulled aside the net curtains and pressed his face to the glass to look through the window.

Below him, looking up, was Ernst Koehler.

Rossett pulled back from the window as if he had been struck by lightning. His heart jumped so abruptly, he could feel it slamming his chest.

In less than a tenth of a second he was on his way out of the room toward the stairs.

CHAPTER 44

KOEHLER HAD DECIDED to finish his cigarette on the pavement, and was thumbing through the large ring of keys he'd picked up from his office for the padlocks of the emptied Jewish dwellings when something told him to look up at the front of the house.

Such was his shock at seeing the face above him that the cigarette fell from his mouth and the keys from his hands.

He didn't pause to pick up either.

Koehler drew his Walther and launched himself at the front door in a flash. His shoulder slammed into the solid wood and he felt it lurch against the screws and padlock that had been used to secure it overnight in its frame, but not give way. He looked at the keys and then took a step back before firing two rounds at the iron lock.

He slammed into the door again, and this time it swung open under his weight, crashing into the hallway as far as its hinges would allow, then swinging back halfway toward him.

He crouched down in the doorway, using the frame to shield his body and training his pistol at the top of the darkening stairs.

It was then that Jacob and Chivers burst out of the back room to face him.

Koehler swung the gun toward the old man and the boy, and his finger twitched on the trigger before he saw that they were unarmed.

"No!" cried Chivers, raising his arms, the boy frozen in front of him, eyes wide, face pale, and mouth open in shock.

"Don't move! Don't fucking move!" Koehler screamed at Chivers, eyes flicking to the stairs and then back to the old man.

"Don't shoot!" Chivers shouted back, his arms rising almost straight up in the air. He glanced up to the top of the stairs, and Koehler allowed his gun to follow the old man's tell.

Rossett exploded round the bend at the top of the stairs, the big Webley leading the way, barely managing to stop himself from tumbling down them with the force of his movement. Instead, he hit the wall and skidded to a halt.

He crouched with his gun out in front of him, aimed squarely at Koehler. Koehler shrank slightly farther back outside so that barely half his face plus his gun arm were visible.

All four assessed the situation silently, like poker players, each waiting for someone to blink.

Chivers went first.

"Get back in the room, boy," he said softly to Jacob.

"Do ... not ... fucking ... move," Koehler hissed, his eyes on Rossett but his gun now on Jacob.

"Koehler." Rossett said one word, enough to convey his intentions.

"Don't move, boy," Koehler, said quietly, this time his eyes on Jacob, who balled his fists in fear, drawing them into his stomach and trembling slightly.

But not leaving the spot he stood in.

Koehler looked back up to Rossett, and then shifted his weight slightly, affording himself some comfort.

"Is this the old communist?" Koehler finally said.

Rossett didn't reply, just continued to stare down the sight of the Webley, weighing whether he could hit Koehler before the German got a shot off at Jacob.

Koehler licked his lips and then tried again.

"Chivers? Is that your name, old man?"

Chivers looked up to his left, slightly lowering his hands. Unable to see Rossett because of the steepness of the stairs and the shape of the hall, he returned to looking at Koehler.

"I don't know what you're talking about. Me and the boy was looking for coal, that's all. We didn't know he was up there," Chivers said, a little too quickly, embarrassed that it was all he could think of to say.

Rossett shifted his weight and shrugged the coat again. Moving forward slightly, he found that he could rest the Webley on the banister.

Koehler looked up again at him.

"Don't, John. I'll kill the boy. If you so much as breathe, I'll kill him."

Rossett swallowed, nodded, relaxed his arm as he raised the barrel of the gun a tiny fraction to make it look less of a threat. He lifted his empty right hand, aware that it wasn't the first time in the past twenty-four hours that someone who wanted him dead had used his first name.

"Okay, Ernst, just . . . just take a minute, yes?"

Koehler nodded, relaxing slightly but maintaining his cover.

"The neighbors will have sent for the police, John, when they heard the shots."

"The police aren't that popular round here."

Koehler smiled at Rossett from around the doorframe.

"You'll be telling me the Germans aren't, either."

"The other resistance men will be here soon," Rossett said.

"Are you telling me you've called for reinforcements?"

"I might have."

"Yes, you might." Koehler shifted his weight again, considering the outcome of a vanload of British resistance showing up.

"We're in a pickle, Ernst."

"So what do we do, John?"

"If I shoot, you shoot. If you shoot, I shoot."

"And we all fall down? That's how the nursery rhyme goes, isn't it?"

"Something like that."

The two men stared at each other for moment.

"We're friends, John, do you remember?"

"You once told me war does terrible things to men, do you remember that?"

"We aren't at war anymore. You lost, it's over."

Rossett slowly and very carefully eased himself out of his crouch and stood up, still holding out his empty right hand while pointing the Webley with his left. Koehler watched him stand and then noticed the coat.

The yellow star of David was half hanging off, and Rossett felt Koehler's eyes fall upon it. He subconsciously reached for it and gently tugged it, not wanting to rip the coat.

"You should leave it on. It suits you," Koehler said gently.

Rossett took a slow, cautious step down the stairs, then another. Koehler watched and waited to see what would transpire.

"You could just let us walk out, Ernst," Rossett said.

Koehler moved a few millimeters farther behind the doorframe.

"And let you have all the diamonds, John?"

"You know about the diamonds?"

"I know the lot."

"I could do you a deal to let us go?"

"Or I could shoot you," Koehler replied, deadpan.

"I thought we'd discounted that option."

Behind him, Koehler heard an engine in the street. He took the quickest of glances and saw two men in work clothes climbing out of a car some hundred feet away. One looked back at him and craned his neck to see what was going on, gesturing to his partner to look, as well.

They weren't police.

When Koehler turned his head back to the hallway, he saw that Rossett had taken three more steps down the stairs, and Koehler found himself having to lean back farther, pulling his arm with him to maintain safe cover. In doing so, he lost sight of Chivers and Jacob and had to adjust his aim to Rossett.

He blinked and Rossett stood now at the bottom of the stairs, gun still leveled, right palm still soothingly outstretched.

Koehler realized he was losing momentum in the situation and tried to find a better position. Behind him he could hear voices, still distant, but closer than the two men had been before.

He considered looking, but decided Rossett was too close to risk it.

He was off balance, both physically and mentally, aware of threats both in front of him and behind and unable to deal with both at once. He felt like a chess player on the back foot and watching the game slip away.

"Is that my people, Ernst?" Rossett said quietly. At the bottom of the stairs now, he took a half step to the left and a half pace back, slowly, as if he were trying creep past a sleeping bear.

Koehler didn't reply. He heard the voices call out something, then another voice, this time female, all out of sight behind him.

"I'll not shoot, Ernst, we'll just leave." Rossett moved gradually toward Chivers, down the hall to the rear, covering both him and Jacob with his body as Koehler eased forward again, still looking down the sight of his Walther.

Chivers, in jerky slow motion, lowered his hands and pulled Jacob back a step or two into the kitchen. Rossett followed, taking slow backward footsteps.

"Rossett," Koehler said, but then realized he didn't know what else to say, and watched as the three of them grew smaller in his sights.

"We'll go, Ernst. Nobody will know you saw us." Rossett was by now well into the kitchen.

"John?" Koehler spoke again, this time softly, as if to a lover leaving for the last time.

"Watch your back, Ernst."

Chivers had the yard door open. He took a step back and down. Once outside, he tugged Jacob hard, spinning the boy out of the line of fire and toward the back gate that led to the alley.

Koehler grimaced; he put pressure on the trigger to pull it, then eased off again, cursing himself for letting the situation get away from him so.

"'Ere!"

The voice behind him was harsh, threatening; he had to face that threat. Koehler slid back around the doorframe, away from Rossett, and turned to look at the two men, who were now less than ten feet away. They froze when they saw the gun in Koehler's hand as he swung it to bear on them.

"Stop!" Koehler shouted, his voice sounding different as it echoed off the wide street.

One of the men dropped a crowbar, and the other threw his hands out to protect himself from the gun, even though it was well out of reach.

"Don't shoot!" Crowbar shouted, arms going up.

Koehler yelled, "Who the fuck are you?"

"Landlord! I'm the landlord. I'm rent collecting. I thought you was breaking in!" cried the other man, hands still held out, eyes half closed with a knee raised.

"Fuck!" Koehler shouted as he turned and charged into the house.

CHAPTER 45

K **OEHLER CHARGED THROUGH** the house like a rampaging bull, head down, making for the backyard as fast as he could.

Once he reached the back gate he didn't hesitate, but plowed straight out into the alley at the rear, where he skidded to a halt. He looked left, then right, gun up, unsure. The alley was deserted of people but littered with bins and rubbish; it stretched maybe one hundred feet in either direction: to the left, a main road, to the right, the quieter end of the street, then another alley that ran parallel to the railway.

He took a few paces toward the railway, then stopped.

I'd go where it was busy, he thought. I'd blend in.

He turned and started to run to the main road.

He had managed only four or five steps when Rossett appeared at the top of the alley ahead of him, leaning around the wall, gun in hand, aiming straight at him. Koehler dove behind some bins, barely hitting the ground before he heard the boom of the Webley.

He was half lying in a puddle, and he felt the cold brown water soaking his trousers.

The Webley boomed again, slamming straight through the metal bin, inches above Koehler's head, which was pressed down hard on the flagstone paving. Koehler opened his eyes and lifted his head half an inch to take the pressure off his cheek. He listened for footsteps but heard nothing other than a distant rumble of traffic and the frantic beating of his heart.

He tried to think.

He'd been under fire before. Some people had called him a hero, he'd saved lives and he'd taken lives, but never like this. In the past he hadn't had time to think; in the past he'd operated on instinct, reflex, and wits.

No time to think how stupid the brave sometimes were.

Now, he had time to think.

And he was scared.

He turned his head and looked at the Walther, a useless lump of metal gripped by a frightened man hiding behind a bin.

He shivered as the water leached farther up his legs, then breathed deeply.

One breath.

Exhale.

Another breath.

Exhale.

Deep breath.

Pause.

He rolled over and away from the bin, arms outstretched, Walther pointing down the alley at the corner, as if he had spun out the end of an unrolled carpet.

There was nobody there.

Just the odd passing car, glimpsed and then gone.

Koehler quickly got to his feet and, hugging the wall, moved toward the end of the alley. Arms outstretched, he half crouched, half jogged forward.

When he reached the main road he leapt out, looking left and then right.

Rossett, Chivers, and Jacob were gone.

And so was his car.

"DID YOU HIT him?" Chivers was shouting as he accelerated the Mercedes and pushed his way into the late-afternoon traffic.

Rossett didn't reply. He was twisted in his seat, still holding the

Webley, which filled the car with the sickly smell of cordite. Behind them someone beeped a horn as Chivers squeezed into a tiny gap, reckless in his attempts to put distance between them and the German.

Rossett looked at Jacob, who was sitting in the middle of the big backseat, hands on his lap. The boy looked serene, almost too serene. Rossett had seen that look before on men who retreated into themselves just before their minds gave way.

"You all right?" he asked, smiling as he did, trying to reassure.

Jacob nodded but didn't look at him. Rossett continued to stare for a moment before he swiveled in his seat to face forward.

"You did good back there." Chivers glanced at Rossett as he spoke.

"What about you? All right?" Rossett said.

"I'll live. Where are we going now?"

"We need to get rid of this car." Rossett opened the Webley, fished out the two spent cartridges, and loaded two more. He looked at his two remaining spare shells.

Chivers glanced down at the gun and then at Rossett, easing off the accelerator.

"I know where we can get rid of the car, and I can get you some bullets, too."

They slowed to a stop at a traffic light. Rossett felt self-conscious in the Mercedes and pulled at the star of David again. This time he succeeded in yanking it off the coat, ripping the material slightly so that a small flash of gray inner lining could be seen against the black wool.

"Is it far?" Rossett replied, fingering the hole he had just made in the coat.

Chivers shook his head and pulled away as the light turned green.

"It's a place we use."

"We?"

"Yeah, we." As Chivers spoke he looked at Rossett. "I'm trusting you, do you understand?"

"Yes."

They drove for about fifteen minutes in silence, heading east, away from the center of London in the slowly building traffic of late afternoon, until Chivers steered the car to the curb in front of a parade of small shops.

"Wait 'ere."

Chivers got out of the car before Rossett could protest. Chivers walked into a butcher's shop and spoke to the butcher, then Chivers and the butcher rounded the counter and disappeared into the back of the shop.

"Come here," Rossett said to Jacob. The boy obediently climbed over the back of the front seat and squeezed close to Rossett, who slid his arm over the boy's shoulder as he continued to scan the area, the Webley in his free hand resting in his lap.

People seemed to pay them no heed while they waited, but Rossett wasn't fooled by the lack of interest. He knew, in that Mercedes, they stood out like a sore thumb among the working-class streets of the East End. Just because he couldn't see people staring didn't mean they weren't.

After a few minutes he thumbed the hammer of the Webley for no reason other than his own nerves. The click of the hammer made Jacob stiffen next to him, and Rossett squeezed the boy a little around the shoulders.

"It's all right," he said soothingly, even though he didn't believe it.

It seemed an age before Chivers reemerged from the butcher's and climbed back into the Mercedes. He tossed some sandwiches wrapped in paper to Jacob as he started the car, and the boy stared at the package on his lap as if it were toxic.

"Eat them," Chivers said, looking over his shoulder for a gap in traffic. "They're good." He clutched his own half-eaten sandwich in his free hand.

Jacob looked at Rossett, who nodded, and the boy unfolded the paper and picked up the bread.

"Beef drippin', put 'airs on yer chest." Chivers smiled at Jacob, who stared back before taking a bite and chewing it slowly.

After a moment, Jacob nudged Rossett and held out the sandwich.

"Are you hungry?"

"It's for you."

"I can share."

"I'm all right."

The boy looked down at the sandwich and took another bite before carefully folding the paper back around the bread and stuffing it into his pocket.

"You might be hungry later," he said to Rossett, who looked away because he thought he might cry.

A few minutes passed as they steered their way off the main road and into a maze of back streets filled with houses, occasional bomb sites, and tall, narrow warehouses and workshops.

Eventually, Chivers said, "You'll need to put the gun away."

"Why?"

"We're picking someone up."

"I'm not a threat."

"You are to them. Please, put it away." Chivers looked at Rossett, who in turn released the hammer and slipped the pistol into his coat pocket.

They turned a corner and Chivers slowed the car down to a walking pace as they drove along a narrow cobbled street of two-up, two-down terraced houses. The street was deserted, and as the evening drew in, one side was dark and in shade while the other clung onto the sunset rays.

Ahead, on Rossett's side of the car, two men appeared on the corner of the street. Flat cap pulled down, the big younger man wore an old battered peacoat over a dark blue bib and brace. The arms of the coat were slightly too short, and he was puffing on a roll-up cigarette that looked like a paper toothpick in his oversized hands. The older man had a full-length black woolen coat that stopped only a few inches from the ground. His hands were in his pockets and he was holding the coat closed, half hiding his face behind his upturned high collar. He reminded Rossett of a picture he had once seen of Dracula, and he had a sudden urge to tell Chivers to drive on.

Chivers eased past the pair six or eight feet before he stopped. As he did so, they both leaned forward to study the occupants of the car before separating and approaching it. Rossett turned his head to watch the men, one on either side of the car. They climbed into the backseat, Dracula behind Rossett.

The car started to move again.

"How's it been, George?" Dracula broke the silence. He was well spoken, which surprised Rossett.

"It's not been good, I've had it 'ard."

"We 'eard," Peacoat piped up in rough cockney. Rossett turned to look at him, noticing for the first time the Browning pistol the man was holding.

The pistol that was aimed at Rossett from the rear seat.

"Sterling was after us to buy you back; he said he'd do us a deal for you."

"I hope you told him to get knotted?"

"You stayed in there, didn't you?" Dracula replied, and Chivers smiled and nodded.

"Where are we going?" Rossett asked.

"Don't worry, copper, you're all right. Safe as 'ouses," said Peacoat, less than reassuringly.

Rossett stared at him, and the man smiled back and gave a little waggle of the pistol. Dracula reached across, gently putting his hand on the gun and pushing it down so that Peacoat had it rested on his leg, still pointing at Rossett, but fractionally less threatening.

"Just until we get acquainted properly, Mr. Rossett. I'm sure you understand."

Rossett nodded at Dracula, then looked at Chivers, who gave him a half smile that was meant to be reassuring.

It wasn't.

SCHMITT SELF-CONSCIOUSLY FACED the wall as Koehler took off his trousers and pulled on the clean pair Schmitt had brought him. Schmitt thought the wall smelled of Jews, and he felt slightly ill and wished that he'd waited outside.

He hated these fleabitten hovels. He felt they said everything that needed to be said about the Jews.

If they can live like this, they must be animals, he thought.

"What else did the prisoner tell you?" Koehler finally said, and Schmitt turned to face him, expecting him to be fully dressed now. He averted his eyes when he saw that Koehler was still buttoning his fly.

"Nothing else, really, just that this character they call Windsor believes Rossett and the Jew have some diamonds and that they are going to pick them up before fleeing the country." Schmitt glanced back to Koehler and was relieved to see that the other man had finally finished dressing. "Oh, and they have an old communist with them, someone called . . . erm . . ."

"Chivers?"

"That's it, Chivers. Apparently, Windsor had this Chivers held for questioning. Did Rossett say anything to you about the diamonds?"

"We didn't really have much of a discussion. Things were a little tense," Koehler replied.

"Do you think Rossett has them?"

"No. I think he is looking for them, the same as we are."

Schmitt considered this for a moment. He pulled back the net curtain to inspect the street outside, then let it go and checked his fingertips.

"I didn't think Rossett was the sort of man who would be interested in getting rich. He struck me as someone who believed in the cause."

Koehler shook his head and sat down to fasten his shoelaces.

"You really have no idea about Rossett at all, do you?" Koehler said as he tied his laces.

"I know he has worked for us without a problem until these diamonds came on the scene."

Koehler finished tying his laces and looked at his colleague.

"Rossett doesn't 'believe.' Rossett just does whatever job he is told to do. If someone in charge tells Rossett to kill Germans, he kills Germans. If someone in charge tells Rossett to round up Jews, he rounds up Jews. Jesus Christ, if you told Rossett to paint London yellow, he'd do it without question. The man doesn't think, he just does whatever he is told to do, he's a machine."

"Until yesterday?"

"Until yesterday."

"Well what happened yesterday?"

"He woke up."

"So what do we do?"

"I'm afraid we put him back to sleep." Koehler replied, staring at Schmitt, dead eyed. "Permanently."

"We have to find him first."

"We'll find him."

"What about the diamonds?"

"We take them out of his dead hands."

"And then?"

"Then? Well, we will cross that bridge when we come to it, don't you think?" Koehler left the question hanging and Schmitt considered an answer but didn't speak. He just nodded and returned to looking at his fingertips for signs of dirt.

CHAPTER 46

C HIVERS PULLED THE Mercedes up outside a timber yard surrounded by a high brick wall. Peacoat jumped out, unlocked the gates, pushed the far one open, and dragged the near one out of the way as the Mercedes drove into the yard, out of sight of the road.

Rossett got out and checked his surroundings, reaching for Jacob's hand as he did so. The yard was surrounded on three sides by bomb sites and derelict warehouses. It looked as though before the war the yard had been a loading bay for the warehouses, but now it was all that was left of whatever businesses had been here.

Peacoat was pulling the gates closed and locking them again, and Rossett realized they had chosen the spot well, as it provided excellent cover for any sort of clandestine operation. There was little passing traffic, and he imagined few people would ever need to visit the area unless they were there to do business with the yard.

He glanced around. The yard was filled with reclaimed timber, stacked according to size in long rows, some of which were almost ten feet high and sixty feet long. Chivers had parked the car between two of these rows, and at the end of it, Rossett could see a brick-walled office that backed onto one of the outer walls.

Dracula got out of the other side of the car and smiled at Rossett.

"Once a policeman always a policeman, Sergeant Rossett?"

"Just having a look around."

Dracula smiled and beckoned Rossett to follow him toward the office. Chivers got out of the car, winked at Rossett, and waited for him to walk ahead.

The clear evening was rapidly becoming a cold one, and when Chivers coughed again the old man's breath condensed in the air and the cloud extended a long way before it disappeared into the sky. Rossett shivered in the thin woolen coat and squeezed Jacob's hand as he walked behind Dracula.

"Are you cold?"

"No," the boy replied, but Rossett didn't believe him.

Dracula stopped at the office door and produced some keys; he looked back at Rossett as he unlocked the door and smiled again.

"Would you be so kind to give my associate your gun, Sergeant?"

"No," Rossett replied, unthreatening but unflinching.

"It's merely to set my mind at rest. I know you are a man of considerable talents when it comes to violence."

Rossett glanced at Chivers, who shrugged back at him.

"Give me the gun." Peacoat stepped forward and Rossett looked at the Browning that the other man was holding less than twelve inches from his damaged ribs.

Rossett half turned to Peacoat.

"Here." Rossett lifted his left hand, showing he intended to reach into his pocket slowly and carefully. "Just mind that Browning in my busted ribs."

Peacoat smiled, and Rossett looked down at his pocket to get the gun. His left hand moved slowly and deliberately, and his right, like a conjurer's, whipped back and across the Browning, pushing it away. Peacoat twitched in surprise and looked down at the rattlesnake right that was now holding the Browning and twisting it down from his grasp.

It was then, just as Peacoat's head turned, that Rossett punched him in the throat.

Peacoat's legs collapsed under him and he crumpled to the ground, blindly grasping at his throat as he tried to find his breath.

Rossett turned to Dracula, who stared at Peacoat and then at the Browning in Rossett's hand.

"As I said, you have considerable talents." Dracula spoke slowly.

Rossett put the Browning into his right pocket and nodded to the office door.

"Shall we?"

"Why not?" Dracula smiled in return and walked into the office as Rossett took hold of Jacob's hand again and followed him.

Dracula flicked the light switch and walked around the wooden desk that sat in the middle of the room. He gestured to the chair on the other side of the desk, but Rossett chose to stand by the window that looked out onto the yard. He nodded to the chair and Jacob reluctantly let go of his hand and took the seat instead while Rossett stared out the window, watching Chivers help Peacoat into a sitting position outside.

"Don't worry about him, Sergeant, he'll be okay."

"I'm not," Rossett replied, still watching outside.

"Can I offer you a drink?"

Rossett turned to look at Dracula, who had removed his coat and was standing by a filing cabinet in the corner. He shook his head and watched, one hand on the Webley in his pocket, as the other man opened the top drawer and took out a bottle of Scotch and two glasses, then closed the drawer and took a seat behind the desk.

Rossett kept his hand in his pocket and looked back outside, to where Peacoat was now on his feet. The big man was still holding his throat and in visible discomfort, but Rossett could see he was fuming from the way he kept pointing to the office and shaking his head.

Rossett wondered if he should just kill him, then wondered when even thinking such a thing had become normal for him.

"Mr. Chivers told me that you need our help."

"I need a car." Still looking out the window.

"And?"

"Maybe some money. I don't have any."

"Maybe?"

Rossett didn't like the way this was going.

"What's your name?" Rossett asked.

"My name isn't important."

"You know mine."

"Everyone in our line of business knows your name, Sergeant."

"Timber merchant?"

Dracula shrugged and smiled at Rossett, and then glanced to the door as Chivers walked in.

"You've upset him outside." Chivers said to Rossett as he tapped Jacob on the shoulder and moved the boy off the chair to take his place.

"Would you like a drink, George?"

"Cor, not 'arf." Chivers rubbed his hands together in anticipation and Dracula poured him a drink. He picked it up and drank half of it in one gulp, grimacing and twisting his head as the Scotch went down and clenching a fist to his chest.

"The sergeant was telling me what he needs, George."

"Can we sort him out?" Chivers's voice was raw from the whiskey.

"I'm sure we can come to an arrangement of some sort."

Rossett had been waiting for this. Communists or not, these men were the same as everyone else: they wanted some of the diamonds, if not all of them.

"I would have thought I'd earned a car, at least. If it wasn't for me, he'd still be rotting in that cellar."

"Yes, well . . ." Dracula half nodded and swirled the Scotch in his glass, then leaned back in his seat. Rossett glanced out the window and saw that Peacoat had gone. He moved away from the window into the corner opposite the door. If the big man had found another weapon, Rossett didn't want to present himself as a target through a window. He decided that if the man came through the door with a gun, he was going to kill him before he had a chance to use it.

"Sergeant Rossett, I'll make you a deal. You can have a car, plus forty pounds right now. In return, I ask for half the diamonds and gold you find. You will take Mr. Flynn with you as security on the deal, pending settlement," Dracula said, looking out the window himself.

"Mr. Flynn?"

"My associate outside."

"No. I go with Chivers, nobody else."

Chivers looked up at Rossett and then back to Dracula, nodding in agreement at the suggestion.

"I'll go with 'im; it'll be better all round that way."

"No, George, I'm afraid not." Dracula leaned forward and pulled open a drawer on his desk. "You aren't going anywhere."

Rossett almost felt the Browning coming out of the desk before he saw it. He watched as Dracula drew back the hammer on the automatic before it was clear of the drawer. Rossett fired his Webley through his coat pocket, hitting Dracula in the center of his chest and knocking him over backward before the other man had a chance to level the gun at Chivers. Dracula fell out of sight onto the floor behind the desk.

Rossett's ears were ringing after the boom of the Webley, and he pulled the gun out of his pocket and looked first out the window and then around the other side of the desk where Dracula was lying on his back, still half in his chair where it had fallen back under him, his arms spread like a fallen angel, dead eyes staring up.

Chivers was silently moving his mouth in shock, unable to believe what had just happened. Jacob was crouching, covering his face, in the corner.

"Chivers!" Rossett shouted, and the old man raised his head. "Get Jacob."

Chivers looked back to where Dracula had been, then slowly his eyes found Jacob in the corner.

Rossett looked out to the rapidly darkening yard. Somewhere outside, Flynn would be wondering what was going on.

"There'll be some money in the cabinet," Chivers said from the corner of the room, where he was holding Jacob, shielding the boy's eyes from the spreading pool of blood that was creeping under the desk toward them.

Rossett crossed the room quickly, pulled open the top drawer of the filing cabinet, and found a small cashbox.

The box wasn't locked. He found about three pounds in change, pocketed the money, and dropped the box onto the floor.

"What about a car? Do they have transport here?"

"A van, they've got a van. The keys will be in the desk."

Rossett ripped open the desk drawers, glancing up and out the window as he did so and then back to the drawer. He found some keys and put them in his pocket. Kneeling next to Dracula, he went through his coat and found a wallet, which he stuffed in his pocket, then took the man's wristwatch and slipped it on.

It fleetingly crossed Rossett's mind that stealing from the dead was becoming the norm, but he forced the thought from his mind so that he could concentrate on the matter in hand.

He ejected the magazine from the Browning in the dead man's hand and pocketed it, then stood up and crossed to the door, switching off the light.

He looked out across the yard, but couldn't see Flynn or the van.

"Where do they keep the van?"

"Parked down one of the lanes between the timber."

"Which one?"

"How the bleedin' 'ell do I know? I've not been 'ere for weeks."

Rossett looked out into the yard again and then back at Chivers. "I'll go get the van. Wait here."

"Be careful. He'll have a gun by now, and it'll be a big one."

"A machine gun?" Rossett asked.

"At least. This is where they hide 'em, in the stacks of timber; 'e'll 'ave been diggin' one out while we was talkin'."

Rossett nodded and looked outside again.

"Stay here."

Rossett crouched as he ran outside. Head down, he made for the nearest stack of wood and slammed into it, gasping as he jarred his ribs. He swept the lines of timber high and low opposite him with the Webley, but could see no sign of Flynn. He checked that the keys in his pocket were there and then started to move along the aisle toward the center of the yard.

The timber aisles were about eight feet wide. Rossett guessed they were that way to allow the van to reverse into any of them from the cleared square at the center of the yard. It would make unloading the van easier, plus it would save carrying the timber farther than was necessary. He decided that from the center square, he'd be able to see along most of the lanes at once, and from there he'd find the van.

Then it occurred to him that Flynn would be thinking the same thing, and he adapted his plan accordingly.

He wouldn't be hunted by Flynn.

He would hunt Flynn.

And then he would kill him.

Rossett looked up at the stacks around him. Selecting one that was made up of thick, dark, square, solid roof joists, he started to climb the twelve feet to the top.

After a few seconds, he was high enough to look over the yard. By now evening had crossed that blurred line into night, and the sky was nearly completely dark. In the little light that was left, he saw Flynn, some fifty feet away, about three aisles over, crouching on top of another pile of timber like a dangerous gargoyle.

The big man was looking down into the center of the yard, his head twitching this way and that. Rossett lowered himself from the stack quietly and looked back toward the office. He couldn't see Chivers or Jacob, but he gave them a thumbs-up anyway before creeping along the aisle to allow himself a closer shot at Flynn.

Near the end of the lane, he guessed he was about thirty feet away, close enough to take the big man down with the Webley, and still behind him so as to guarantee surprise. Rossett reached up to the top of an eight-foot pile of relatively new wood and slowly pulled himself up to look over.

Flynn was staring back. The look of surprise on his face was almost as expressive as the one Rossett could feel on his own.

Rossett dropped down immediately, just as Flynn let rip with a short burst from the machine gun he was holding and the timber above Rossett's head rained splinters. Rossett ran along the line of timber back

toward the office as the yard fell silent. Chivers appeared at the office
door.

"Give me a gun. I can help," Chivers whispered.

Rossett ignored him and dodged down the side of the office to the
yard wall. He looked up at the top, which was ten feet above him and
crested with some rusted and dangling barbed wire. Rossett took out
the Browning and stuffed it into his waistband. He threw the wallet to
Chivers with the van keys, removed his coat and hung it over his shoulder, then started to climb up onto the office roof via the window ledge.

Before he reached the roof he looked back to check that he was
below the height of the timber, then threw the coat up onto the black tar
that covered the flat roof. He waited a moment, took a deep breath, and
followed the coat. Lying flat, he spun quickly to face out onto the yard,
the Webley scanning it carefully. At ten feet, the roof height was almost
the same as most of the lines of timber he could see before him, and he
squinted through the dusk for sight of Flynn.

"Stay down low, below the window."

"Where the bleedin' 'ell are you goin'?" Rossett heard Chivers hiss
from inside the shed.

"I'm going to skirt the yard around the outside to come back in
behind him," Rossett hissed back. He threw the coat over the barbed
wire and dropped over the wall into the street outside.

Once down from the wall, Rossett ripped the coat down and ran
along the street, turning a right angle at the end of the wall and skirting the yard until he reached the gate they had passed through in the
Mercedes.

He flicked the coat around the gatepost, like a matador goading a
reluctant bull, and when no shots rang out he sneaked a peek and then
pulled his head back quickly. He waited a moment and then looked
again, crouching this time, in case Flynn had seen him and drawn a
bead.

There was no sign of Flynn, so Rossett checked the padlock on the
gate and now regretted having tossed the keys to Chivers. He regretted

it even more when he heard the machine gun firing on the other side of the yard.

Near the office.

Rossett fired the Webley at the padlock, blowing it apart, then kicked the gates open.

He started to run toward the office, drawing the Browning as he went, a gun in each hand.

He heard more shots, and despite the heavy pistols he felt helpless, a failure, a long way from Jacob, unable to help him, failing again.

He was shouting when he rounded the corner of the final timber aisle nearest to the office, trying to draw Flynn to him and away from the office. Running with both guns cocked at arm's length, he saw out of the corner of his eye an empty machine gun magazine on the ground.

In the door of the office, someone was slumped and clutching his chest, but it wasn't until he was close that he recognized Flynn.

The big man was bleeding out, staring at the hole in his chest as blood seeped through his fingers, a steady flow of life that pumped slightly more each time he moved the hand, trying to find a way to cover it completely. Confused, Flynn looked up at Rossett, then showed him his bloody hand before putting it back on his chest.

Rossett looked for the machine gun and, seeing it lying on the ground, kicked it away. He pointed the Webley at Flynn's head and looked into the office through the shattered window.

Still in the corner, Jacob in his arms, was Chivers, surrounded by broken glass, some falling from his shoulders like snow. He looked up at Rossett and then held up Dracula's Browning.

"You forgot, there was one in the pipe. The big daft bastard just ran into it," Chivers said softly, stroking the back of Jacob's head as he did so. Rossett glanced back at Flynn, who was now leaking frothy blood out of his lips.

"Is he dead?" Chivers asked.

"No, but he soon will be. We need to get out of here."

Chivers stood up and, with a grunt, lifted Jacob to his shoulder, holding the boy's face close so he wouldn't see Flynn. He stepped over the dying man and out into the yard without looking down.

Rossett crouched down and searched through Flynn's pockets for money. Flynn watched him as he did so and then silently shook his head, pleading with his eyes.

"I can't help you," said Rossett as he produced a pack of cigarettes and a box of matches from out of the peacoat. "It's time to die."

CHAPTER 47

WE CAN'T KEEP moving like this; we stand out a mile." As Chivers drove, Rossett was looking through the personal papers in Dracula's wallet.

"So what do we do?" Chivers leaned forward and wiped the inside of the van's dirty windshield with the back of his hand to clear a smudged rectangle free of condensation before crunching another gear. "We need to be off the road soon. When traffic starts to die down Jerry'll be more likely to stop us."

"I need clothes, and I have some money at my lodgings."

"They'll be watchin' your place."

"Maybe we can go to yours?" Rossett looked up from the wallet at Chivers. "You and Jacob can wait there while I check my place out."

"Sterling knows where I live. It'll be crawlin' with people looking for me. The royalists and us, we sort of operate an uneasy partnership."

"Very uneasy, from what I've seen so far."

"We normally stay out of their way if they stay out of ours."

"Unless they're kidnapping you?"

"They want our guns. They're gettin' desperate."

"Your family, will they be okay?"

Chivers shook his head.

"I lied. I don't have anyone, I just didn't want you knowing where I lived."

Rossett nodded silently. Modern Britain, where nobody trusted anybody else.

"I understand," he finally said, resuming his search of the wallet. After a moment, he tossed it out the window of the moving van, then wound the window squeakily up. Next to him on the bench seat, Jacob shifted and pushed in closer for warmth. Rossett obliged him by lifting his arm and allowing the boy to settle under his wing, like a duckling seeking comfort.

They drove in silence for a while, aimlessly drifting across the city like the Thames as Rossett pondered his options. He was aware they had been on the run for nearly twenty-four hours, yet they'd barely traveled six miles from where they'd been held by Sterling and his men.

He knew London was a good place to hide, but it was also like a spiderweb: if they kept moving someone was going to pick up their vibration and come looking for them. The clock was ticking on their options, and Rossett still didn't have any sort of plan. He'd been banking on the communists to help them, but that door had been slammed shut as soon as he'd pulled the trigger and shot Dracula.

Rossett watched Chivers for a moment, the old man's face lit by the oncoming traffic that was winding its way through the evening darkness.

"Why did he want you dead?"

"What?" Chivers turned to look at Rossett and then back to the road.

"Dracula, why did he want you dead?"

"Who?"

"The man at the yard."

"Oh, him," Chivers replied glumly.

The van stopped at a light and Chivers's face glowed red in its reflection.

"Why did he want you dead?" Rossett pressed again.

"I don't know." Chivers looked across again, this time holding Rossett's gaze. "Maybe 'e thought I talked to Sterling?"

The old man's face turned yellow, then green, but the van didn't move. Behind them someone beeped a horn, and Chivers moved into gear and set off again.

"He must have known you never talked. If you had, the royalists would have come and taken the guns."

"Maybe 'e couldn't risk it? I don't know. We never got a chance to ask 'im, did we? What with you bleedin' shootin' 'im an' all," Chivers replied.

Rossett went back to looking out the misted-up windows. Unable to see clearly where he was going in more ways than one, he wiped at the moisture and streaked it, making it worse.

"Head to the cemetery."

"At this time of night?" Chivers asked, wiping his side of the window again.

"We need to get moving. It isn't good that we don't have a plan, and nighttime will be the best time to get in and out of a Jewish cemetery."

"Maybe. I suppose they don't get many visitors there nowadays."

"Will you be able to find your mother's grave?" Rossett looked down at Jacob, who sleepily nodded in reply. "Are you sure? It will be very dark."

"Grandfather made me learn the way. I know where she is."

"Do you know what's there?" Chivers asked.

"What you want," Jacob replied matter-of factly before nestling again, his head resting against Rossett.

Rossett squeezed his arm around the boy's shoulders to reassure him.

"So we go to Willesden?" Chivers asked, and Rossett nodded in reply.

They had driven a few miles across the city in slowly thinning traffic before Chivers spoke again.

"I'm famished. Can we eat something?"

Snatched from his own thoughts by Chivers's voice and by Jacob's stirring under his arm, Rossett stretched his legs into the foot well of the van, taking a moment to think before he spoke.

"Okay, it would be good to get something warm inside us. I don't know when we'll be able to eat again."

"I know a little fish-and-chip shop up 'ere, not far."

"All right."

Jacob moaned softly in his sleep. Rossett looked down at the boy and wondered what his dreams were like.

He hoped the boy still slept in a warm, loving place and not the real world.

The van started to slow down as they passed a parade of shops, all in darkness except one, the fish-and-chip shop, splashing bright white light out over the wet winter pavement outside.

As they passed, Rossett leaned forward to get a better look. The shop was empty except for two people, a man and a woman, behind the counter. Both of them stared out of the window like shop dummies and neither appeared to be anything but ordinary.

"Do you know these people?" he asked Chivers.

"Not really, I've only been 'ere a couple of times over the years."

"They aren't connected to you?"

"No." Chivers looked quizzically at Rossett as the van slowed to walking pace and then bumped up onto the curb to park, some fifty feet up the road from the fish-and-chip shop.

"Are you sure?"

Chivers yanked the hand brake and switched off the engine before twisting in his seat to look at Rossett.

"I'm just bleedin' 'ungry, all right?"

Rossett looked at the old man, whose face was dark in the shadows of the night and the cab. Occasional cars passed along the road, but other than that the street was quiet.

It was normal, a place for normal people to live their lives in peace.

Rossett envied them.

He slipped his arm out from around Jacob, and the boy sleepily rubbed at his eyes with his right fist. Rossett checked the back window of the van and then the wing mirror. He looked again at Chivers, then opened the door and stepped out onto the pavement, stretching as he did so. He used the stretch to turn his body and scan the street on both sides and into the distance.

His ribs ached, his neck ached, his back ached.

He felt old, and he felt cold, but he also felt hungry.

"Well?" Chivers looked across the front seat toward Rossett.

"Two fish and chips and whatever you want." Rossett pulled some money out of his pocket and leaned into the van to Chivers. The old man reached across to take the money, which Rossett dropped into his palm. Before Chivers could pull away, Rossett gripped his hand, holding it so tight Chivers could move neither forward nor back.

"Just buy the food and leave, okay?"

Chivers tried not to cry out under the tight grip. Through thin lips he asked, "Do you want to go?"

"Just buy the food and leave," Rossett said, releasing the old man's hand.

Chivers shook his head, got out of the van, and slammed the door, causing Jacob to jump and finally open his eyes. Chivers cast a sullen look at Rossett over his shoulder before he started walking. After a few paces, he stopped and turned to face Rossett, who was still standing on the pavement watching him.

"You'd better start trusting me."

Rossett didn't reply. He just shoved his hands into the dirty black woolen coat, pulled it around him, and watched Chivers turn and take a few more steps before stopping again. The old man seemed to think a moment, looking off to the parade of shops. Then, having made a decision, he turned and walked back to face Rossett, close up, toe to toe.

"I'm your only friend, chum. You're stuck out 'ere with no one and nothing. Yeah, all right, you saved my life back at the yard, although we'll never know if 'e was goin' to shoot me or not, and you got me out of the warehouse with Sterling. I appreciate all that. But, and it's a big but, you'd . . . better . . . start . . . trustin' . . . me." Chivers poked a finger in Rossett's chest as he spoke to drive home the words. "Because you are up shit creek without a paddle, and you need as many friends as you can get. And, as far as I can see, you ain't got none but me and that kid, so you'd better start trustin' us. All right?"

Chivers finished speaking and stuck his chin out at Rossett, defiant and proud. Rossett looked at the old man a moment, then away at the houses that flanked either side of the road.

"Point taken. I trust you."

Chivers nodded, shrank back an inch, straightened his jacket, and flexed his scrawny neck.

"Right, then." His old smile returned. "Do you want salt and vinegar?"

Rossett smiled as he reached for the door handle of the van and pulled it open.

CHIVERS WALKED BRISKLY to the chip shop, casually glancing in the darkened windows of the other businesses as he did so. As he opened the door, a bell rang above his head, and the smell of fat, vinegar, and salt mixed with the heat of the burners washed over him and pinched the top of his nose.

"Yes, my darling?" asked the woman behind the counter, red cheeked and greasy skinned, dragged from her stupor by the presence of a customer. Next to her the man in the white apron started to stir at the boiling fat with a steel spatula, in turn smiling at Chivers.

"I need to use your phone. It's urgent, a matter of state security." Chivers was already lifting the flap and was halfway around the counter as he spoke. "And do me three fish and chips, plenty o' salt and vinegar."

KATE SLAMMED THE receiver down and ran into Koehler's office, not bothering to knock as she flung open the door.

"I've just had a call. Rossett is heading to a Jewish cemetery in Willesden!"

Koehler swung his feet off his desk, where they had been as he drank the small glass of brandy he'd allowed himself as a buffer against the stress of the day.

"Who says?"

"Some old man called Chivers. He just said he was with Rossett and the Jewish boy, and they would be at the cemetery soon."

"Did he say why?" called Schmitt from behind the door, where he had been sitting in an old brown leather armchair, an untouched brandy balanced awkwardly on his knee.

Kate put her hand to her mouth and looked at Koehler, embarrassed that she had spoken without first checking if it was okay. Koehler anxiously waved his hand.

"Speak."

"He didn't, sir; he just said where they were going and then hung up. I'm sorry."

Schmitt stood up.

"We need men down there now! Break out the guard, ring the police!"

Koehler nodded to Kate and waved her away as he picked up his phone receiver.

"We can't charge down there as if we are invading Poland, Schmitt. We need to be subtle. If Rossett realizes we are coming, he will disappear like a startled rabbit. Besides, we don't know what he is there for."

"The diamonds, it must be the diamonds."

"Possibly." Koehler dialed and put the phone to his ear. "Werner, is that you?"

Down in the bowels of the building, the old soldier sat upright in his tiny NCO's duty office, folding a newspaper and picking up a pen as he held the phone to his ear.

"This is he."

"It is Koehler. How many men do you have on duty tonight?"

"Thirty, sir. I thought it prudent after—"

"Get twelve of your best in three cars—your best, mind, armed and at the front of the building now."

Koehler slammed down the phone and drank his brandy in one gulp before standing up.

"The chase is back on, Schmitt! We might save our careers, after all!"

Schmitt stood and grabbed his coat from the stand, then tossed Koehler's across to him. Kate watched the two men sprint through the outer office and sat silently for a moment watching the door as it swung shut behind them. After a brief pause, she turned to the night-shift secretary.

"If they're off, I might as well head home."

The other girl smiled and returned to her magazine, and Kate collected her things and headed out the door.

The chase was most definitely on.

CHAPTER 48

JACOB FELT LIKE his stomach would pop. He couldn't remember the last time he had eaten so much. When Chivers had given him the food to hold he didn't know whether it was okay for him to eat or even how to eat it. Finally, the smell filling the van's cab teased him so much, a basic instinct had taken over, and he ripped into the paper and attacked the food. The smell had almost made him delirious and he had dug in and burned his fingers on the hot, greasy chips.

Chivers looked down at him and winked in the half-light.

"Good nosh, eh?" the old man said, his mouth full.

Jacob nodded. The warmth in his belly was lifting his spirits. He smiled up at Chivers, and Chivers smiled back. Jacob looked out through the windshield at the small street in which they were parked. It was full of houses, and he recognized it from when he and his grandfather had visited his mother.

It looked different at night. The houses looked warm inside, welcoming, the opposite of the graveyard they overlooked. Jacob tried to imagine what it would be like to live in one with a mother and father and maybe a brother and a sister.

He wondered if the people inside were listening to music on the radio. He thought about his mother playing the piano when he was very small.

She sang like an angel. He couldn't remember her face, but he could hear her voice. She was the best singer in the world, he thought, and now, as Grandfather always told him, she was an angel, watching over him.

He thanked her silently for the meal he was eating, and wished he could share it with her.

He saw Rossett walking down the street toward them and picked up the sergeant's fish and chips off the seat, so that he could eat them while they were still hot.

ROSSETT GOT INTO the van, and Jacob smiled and offered the package.

"I kept them warm for you."

Rossett thanked him and unwrapped the food. Fresh steam belched into the van, and the windows started to fog all over again. Rossett put some chips in his mouth and then pulled his coat cuff over his hand and wiped at the cold glass of the windshield to clear a portal.

"Did you 'ave a look?" Chivers asked around a mouthful of fish.

"There's a lodge at the entrance with a light on, but the gates are locked. The wall is easy enough to get over, though. We'll make our way around from there."

"Makes sense."

"You stay in the van and wait by the wall."

Chivers glanced across at Rossett.

"Don't you want me to come in with you?"

"It's six feet high. I don't mind lifting him over, but I'm not lifting you. You can keep the van running, just in case."

Chivers didn't argue. He just ripped some newspaper off and wiped his mouth, then sighed loudly.

"What do we do after this?" he asked.

"After the cemetery?"

"No, after all of this. Are you going with the boy?"

Rossett took some fish and looked down at Jacob, who was looking up at him.

"I don't know."

Jacob looked down at his food again.

"Won't be much for you 'ere 'cept a firing squad, mate, and that's if you're lucky. I don't think you've got much choice. If we can get 'im on a boat to Ireland or the U.S., I think you'll 'ave to go with 'im."

Rossett pondered for a moment as he ate. He hadn't considered that there might be something else for him. He'd just assumed that his path was charted, work then death. He didn't have anyone or anything to look forward to. No love, no sense of loyalty. He just worked. He'd always assumed that his dreams had died in the bomb blast that had taken his wife and son. Glancing at Jacob, he wondered, did he have a chance of new dreams in new places?

"I don't know what will happen. We'll wait and see," he finally said, more to himself than to anyone else in the van.

"Well, maybe you should start thinking?"

"What about you?"

Chivers shifted in his seat, as if the question had made him uncomfortable.

"I'm a ducker and a diver, I'll be okay."

"Maybe we can all go?"

"Me? In America or Canada? They don't take kindly to old communists over there, chum."

"Koehler knows your name. You can't stay here."

"Does 'e? 'E might think 'e does, but all 'e knows is one name I use." Chivers smiled at Rossett and tapped the side of his nose with a greasy finger. "London is a big place; there are plenty of battles to be fought. Besides, the movement needs someone to take over, seeing as you killed its bleedin' CO."

"What about Sterling?"

"What about 'im? I've got the guns, plus I've got enough men and explosives to wipe 'is lot off the map. 'E'll be more worried than me." Chivers shifted in his seat, as if to hide his doubt.

"Shouldn't you be attacking the Germans?" Rossett said, looking out the window at the houses around them.

"All in good time. Just wait, all in good time. I've got to sort out 'oo's the top dog first. Don't you worry about me. I've got plenty of tricks up my sleeve."

"Will you be able to get the boy onto a boat?" Rossett asked.

"I've an idea. There are plenty of good men 'oo will 'elp the cause."

"For a few diamonds?"

"Everybody 'as to eat, even communists," Chivers replied, looking at Rossett. "Even ex-policemen."

Rossett nodded and folded the paper over the chips.

"We'd better get moving."

Chivers nodded, started the van, and slowly drove down the street, keeping the lights off.

As they passed the high iron gates that led into the cemetery, Chivers looked at the Gothic caretaker's lodge behind them.

"You wouldn't catch me livin' there."

"There's worse this side of the wall," replied Rossett. He checked the rounds in the Webley and clicked it shut, then looked at Chivers.

"Yeah, a lot worse," Chivers muttered.

They drove for half a minute before Rossett spoke again.

"Here will do."

Chivers bumped the van onto the curb, with the cemetery wall on his side of the van. The road was narrower here, but Rossett had chosen the place well. Opposite where they were parked was a bomb site, barren and surrounded by an old wire fence that sagged under its own weight. An old battered, pre-war Leyland truck was parked on the site, and next to it, another builder's van in slightly better condition. If anyone passed, Chivers's van wouldn't look out of place, almost as if a contractor had arrived too late to park it on the bomb site and had left it on the road until morning.

"If you hear a shot," Rossett said, "drive to the end of the road and turn right, follow the cemetery wall until you reach the far corner, and wait there as long as you can." He made a quick scan of the street, then opened the van door and got out. "Come on, boy. Take me to your mother."

THE JOURNEY ACROSS London had been hectic, to say the least. The young soldier driving had done his best to follow the shouted instructions from the map reader in the rear, but the big Mercedes wasn't built for the narrow streets.

They'd bounced off so many curbs that Koehler struggled to keep the brandy down.

"We are nearly there, sir, less than half a kilometer," the map reader said.

Koehler looked over his shoulder out the rear window, past the three young men on the backseat. The map reader extinguished his torch and ducked down in the middle so Koehler could see past him.

"Stop," Koehler instructed, and the staff car glided to a halt in the middle of the road, blocking it completely.

Werner got out of the front seat of the second car and jogged up to Koehler's window, an MP40 slung across his chest, every inch the old soldier.

"We're nearly there," said Koehler. "Tell the other car to take up position on the far side of the cemetery but not to go in. I don't want chopping down by some idiot's crossfire."

"Yes, sir."

"You and your men come with us. Once in the graveyard, we'll fan out and move slowly until we can see Rossett and the boy. Tell your men stealth is the key. Nobody does anything until I say so, is that understood?"

"Perfectly, sir." Werner saluted and doubled back to the other cars to pass on the information.

Koehler turned in his seat to face the men in his car. It occurred to him that none of them was over the age of twenty, and he doubted if any of them had actually seen combat.

"Did you hear that?" They all nodded. "This is a dangerous man, very dangerous. I want you all to be careful, yes?"

There was a mass of bobbing heads in response. Koehler realized it was a long time since he'd led an operation of this sort. He lifted his machine pistol from the footwell and nodded to the driver to proceed.

"Slowly . . . go."

CHAPTER 49

"**L IE FLAT SO** nobody can see you," Rossett instructed as he lifted Jacob. The boy did exactly as he was told, hugging the top of the wall and resting his cheek on the cold stone. He waited as Rossett lifted himself, with the merest of grunts, up and over, dropping quietly onto the other side. He then grabbed Jacob, helped him down, and crouched with the boy.

All was dark, and all was quiet in the cemetery.

Perfect.

Rossett wanted to move quickly, but the pitch-black graveyard was littered with flat stones set in grass and shin-high tombs that were going to make progress painful if they proceeded at much more than a creep.

The streetlamps in the road behind him played havoc with his night vision, too bright to allow his eyes to adjust and too faint to cast anything more than blurred shadows ahead.

He felt Jacob reaching for the hand in which he held the Webley, so he shifted slightly and offered his other hand for comfort.

"Where do we need to go?" he whispered.

"I only know the way from the gate," Jacob replied, his voice wavering.

Rossett considered saying something to lift the boy's spirits, but he couldn't think of anything. Instead, he squeezed his hand and slowly, following the wall, they made their way toward the lodge by the main gate.

The lodge stood silent, a brown limestone sentinel guarding the dead. Upstairs, Rossett could see one dim light through a curtain, and he watched it closely for any sign of movement.

He jumped inwardly when he heard a dog barking a few streets away, and he glanced down in the darkness to Jacob, who was a shadow at his side.

"You all right?" he whispered.

Jacob didn't reply, and Rossett hoped the boy was nodding.

They reached the low wall that surrounded the lodge, acting as a cursory boundary between it and the cemetery. The dog had stopped barking, and somewhere, Rossett heard the sounds of distant car engines. He glanced back in the direction they had come and saw that all appeared well.

"Here?"

"The path, by the gate, I count," Jacob whispered.

Rossett saw the boy's white hand pointing to the gate like a ghost.

"Be very quiet."

"I will."

Rossett led the way around the side of the house, moving slowly and silently. They reached the path that led from the gate into the cemetery and Rossett stopped again, looking up at the front of the lodge.

It was totally dark.

In front, parked on the path, was an old car that looked as if it hadn't moved in years, sitting lazily on three flat tires while the fourth clung on to its last few gasps of air.

Rossett studied the gate. It was bound with a thick chain and padlock with a No Entry sign hanging from it.

He tested the path with his toe; it was gravel, so they walked on the grass next to it.

"Do you know now?" Rossett held Jacob's head an inch from his mouth and whispered in the boy's ear. He felt Jacob nod his head and took his hand again.

It was then that the front door of the lodge opened.

Rossett swept Jacob off the ground, twisting and standing up to his full height for the first time since they had entered the cemetery. The Webley came up from his side, and he drew a bead on the silhouette of the man at the door, maybe thirty to forty feet away.

"Puss puss?" the man called.

Unmoving, Rossett was just another statue in a graveyard, except this one had a gun.

"Puss?" the man called again.

To his left, Rossett saw a will-o'-the-wisp cat run past. The animal suddenly stopped, and their eyes met, the cat's reflecting white so bright that Rossett thought they would throw enough light to give his position away.

The cat waited, unsure, one paw rising in the half-light of the door. Looking over its shoulder at the intruders in its territory, trying to decide whether to get in where it was warm or stay and watch.

Rossett bared his teeth at the cat, willing it to go.

It did, dashing to the door and slipping past its owner, who was already halfway back into the house, no idea how close Tiddles had come to getting himself killed.

They stood watching the house for a few moments, slowly letting their eyes adjust back to the darkness and listening to the night as the mist thickened around them in the still air.

After a while, Rossett lowered Jacob to the ground, and the boy took his cue and started to walk slowly alongside the path.

Rossett's feet felt damp as they made their way through the thick grass, and he wondered if he should carry Jacob, realizing that the boy's feet would be soaking. They had crept past maybe ten or twelve rows of gravestones, thicker into the mist, when Rossett felt Jacob veer sharply to the right, leading him away from the path and quickening his pace so that Rossett had to pull back and rein him in.

After another ten or twelve graves, Jacob stopped and rested his free hand on a cold gray granite block.

"Here she is," the boy whispered as he pulled his other hand from

Rossett's and rested it on the stone, gently, as if not to wake his mother.

Rossett looked down at the gravestone. It rose maybe eighteen inches out of the overgrown grass, and he could barely make out its chiseled writing in the darkness.

"Are you sure?"

"Twelve down and nine across."

"What do we do?"

Rossett saw the boy kneel down, and for a moment he thought he was about to pray. Instead, he heard the sound of ripping grass. He crouched down, resting his hand on the cold granite in an attempt to see what Jacob was doing, but it was too dark and he didn't dare to strike a match.

Rossett looked around the cemetery while he waited. He couldn't make out anything farther than twenty feet away except for the odd obelisk or tree, silently sleeping.

Finally, the boy stopped what he was doing. Rossett rested his hand on Jacob's back so as to locate him in the darkness. He leaned forward and whispered in his ear, "Well?"

Jacob held something up to Rossett, tapping it against his arm so that he knew what to reach for.

It was a metal box, maybe the size of a shoebox, wet and cold to the touch. Rossett brushed the soil off of it as he felt for the edge of the lid. Eventually, his fingers found purchase and the lid shifted slightly. Rossett grunted as he pulled again, and the metal lid finally popped off and clattered onto the gravestone before falling onto the grass.

"Shush!" Jacob whispered.

Inside the tin lay balls of rolled-up newspaper, which Rossett probed with his fingers. Almost immediately, his fingers brushed something solid, and he took the item out of the box before resting the tin on top of the gravestone next to them.

He guessed the object to be maybe three inches long and two wide. It felt like a cold pottery cylinder, and the urge to strike a match and inspect what he held became overpowering.

He gave in.

Passing the cylinder back to Jacob, he fumbled in his pockets for the matches. Quickly taking the box out, he paused and lifted his head again to look around him.

In the distance, he heard the dog barking again but nothing else.

All was quiet.

"Hold it up," he whispered as he struck the match.

Jacob held up the cylinder, and Rossett saw it was a sealed earthenware jar with a wooden stopper jammed tight in the end. He took the jar from Jacob and lifted both it and the match to his face so that he could inspect the jar close up.

That was when he heard the shout.

CHAPTER 50

CHIVERS HAD GONE back to eating his fish and chips in the van when he first noticed the headlamps in his rearview mirror. He watched them approach and slowly wrapped the chips back into their paper, sliding down slightly into the seat so he could duck out of sight if he needed to.

One Mercedes pulled in behind while the other slowly eased past the van, stopping just in front.

He waited, heart thumping, wondering whether he should get out of the van and approach one of the cars. His silent question was answered when all their doors opened almost simultaneously, and the occupants fanned out along the wall, equally spaced about ten feet apart, and all seemingly staring at him.

He eyed the machine pistols and rubbed his fist against his chest, suddenly aware that he was getting heartburn.

Out of the car behind, the familiar sight of Ernst Koehler emerged, all blond hair and perfect cheekbones under the streetlamps. Koehler walked to Chivers's window, tapped politely on the glass with the barrel of the MP40, and waited for Chivers to open it.

"Hello, George," Koehler said warmly. "What a surprise."

"Major Koehler, sir," Chivers said nervously.

"Where is the sergeant?" Koehler looked into the back of the van over Chivers's shoulder and then back at the old man.

"'E's gone into the graveyard with the boy, sir, lookin' for the kiddy's mum's grave."

"How long ago?"

"Couple of minutes, sir."

Koehler turned to look at his squad and then back to Chivers.

"How have you been keeping, George?" Koehler asked, as if he were merely passing the time of day.

"Not good, sir. Royalists picked me up, near bleedin' killed me."

"Was that you and the sergeant down at St. Katharine Docks?"

"It was, sir. Me and 'im and the Jew. It was a close thing for me down there, I think the royalist lot was getting fed up with me."

"So the sergeant saved your skin?"

"If it 'adn't been for ol' Rossett, I don't think you'd've 'eard of me again, sir."

"That was a stroke of luck for both of us, George."

"Things is goin' to be 'ard for me, sir. I've seen some faces in that warehouse, and I might be able to put names to 'em." Chivers played his cards close to his chest, wise enough to know that confession and cooperation were two very different things, and, more important, that cooperation paid while confession didn't.

"You might?"

"If I 'ad a bit of time, sir, maybe looked at some pictures."

"Maybe I could just have you run in and you could chat to one of the men in a cell?"

Chivers shifted again in the seat, very much aware he was playing a dangerous game.

"Not much point in that, sir, is there? You know I do my best out 'ere for you. I can't do nothin' in a cell, now can I?"

"You could rot, George."

"What good will that do, sir?"

"It'll at least make me feel better, and I could do with cheering up," Koehler sighed.

Chivers swallowed hard as he looked into Koehler's eyes, then at the German troops behind him, weapons unslung.

"I do my best for you, Major Koehler, sir, you know that."

Koehler frowned and then leaned back from the window. "I need to get along, George. Thank you for your help tonight. You will call me tomorrow and we will speak. Understood?"

"Yes, sir, I'll call, sir, I swear."

Koehler stepped back and looked at his men, aware now that Werner was waiting for orders.

Chivers wiped his hand across his mouth.

"I'm a bit strapped sir. I don't suppose . . . ?"

"Of course, George, here." Koehler fished in his pocket and produced a five-pound note, passing it to Chivers through the window but holding onto it when Chivers took it. "You will call me tomorrow, won't you?"

"Of course, sir. We can have a debrief, sir."

Koehler released the note.

"Wait here. Don't drive away or even start your engine. Just wait here, understood?"

"Yes, sir. Thank you, sir," Chivers replied as Koehler turned away.

The old man folded the fiver and slipped it into his jacket pocket, feeling lower than the bodies in the cemetery on the other side of the wall.

KOEHLER HADN'T REALIZED it would be so dark once they were on the other side of the wall, or that the graveyard would be so big. He looked off to his left and then to his right, squinting into the darkness, then opening his eyes as wide as they would go. Nothing worked. He couldn't see the men he knew were on either side of him, thirty feet away, picking their way, like him, through the graveyard in the silent search for Rossett.

Fuck, he thought to himself, feeling a cold dread now that he was leading eight green troops across a pitch-black, foggy graveyard into a potential confrontation with one of the most dangerous men he had ever met.

It had been a long time since he had been involved in a combat mission. He'd forgotten so much, not least that he hadn't put in place an effective method of communication. He couldn't signal his flanks without talking, and if he talked, he lost any element of surprise and also opened up the squad to danger.

He wanted to stop his men from moving forward, but couldn't. He had to hope Rossett was taken by surprise and that the darkness hindered him as much as it hindered them.

Not much of a plan.

That was when he heard the shout.

He dropped to one knee and brought the machine pistol up to bear on the darkness ahead, glancing left and right for some indication of who had shouted.

"Oi!" came the shout again. Koehler isolated it off to his right and shifted his position slightly, arcing his weapon through a forty-five-degree sweep so as to not engage with the men on his right.

"Who shouted? Who was that?" Werner called off to Koehler's left, the NCO trying to take some control of an operation that was rapidly falling apart.

"What's your game? I'm phoning the police!" The shout again, and Koehler realized it was an English voice. He stood up and took a few paces to his right toward the voice, then tripped on a low gravestone, sprawling across the ground and into the wet grass.

He cried out as his shin struck a sharp edge, and his weapon almost fell from his hands as he slammed down.

"*Was ist das?*" This time it was a panicked German cry from his left.

Light flooded across the graveyard from the lodge, illuminating the Germans and exposing Koehler, much to his embarrassment, lying on the gravestone clutching his shin. No sooner had the floodlamp turned on than someone opened up on it with his weapon. A long burst of gunfire rang out, hitting the lodge and shattering a window but missing the lamp, which remained obstinately blinding them.

It was a wide, panicked spray that whistled over the heads of half of the soldiers to Koehler's right, all of whom dove to the ground and started shouting in disarray.

"Stop firing!" rang out around the graveyard from various quarters, and the shooting ended as suddenly as it had started.

Nobody moved except for Koehler, who rolled off the grave, clutching his shin.

All was quiet for a moment until Koehler called out through gritted teeth, "Who the fuck shouted?"

No reply.

"Do not fire unless you have a threatening target! Understood?"

He looked up from behind the gravestone and studied the scene. His men crouched in an almost straight line stretching the width of the cemetery, illuminated by the bright light, looking for leadership as much as a target. He turned toward the light.

"Who turned on that light?" he shouted.

No reply.

Werner appeared at his shoulder, the old soldier crouching down behind him, eyes on the lodge.

"Who the fuck started shooting?" Koehler hissed.

"One of the lads panicked with the light, sir."

"Take three men and check it. We'll cover you."

Without reply, Werner drifted forward at a crouch, tapping three men on the helmet, one after another. He moved toward the house using the graves as cover. Koehler signaled for the other men to move forward and take up a line parallel to the house.

He didn't want someone opening up again behind him and cutting him in half.

He watched as Werner covered the final twenty feet of open ground to the lodge. Werner crouched down in the grass, then turned to Koehler and signaled for the rest of the squad to move up.

Koehler jogged forward and joined Werner by the lodge wall. On the floor at their feet lay the cemetery caretaker, blood staining his chest.

Koehler sighed and knelt down to check the body.

"He must have heard us and come out to turn on the lamp." Werner indicated the heavy metal trip switch that was set in the wall.

"Who fits security lights in a graveyard?" Koehler replied, feeling for a pulse with no success.

"An idiot," Werner replied.

Koehler stood up and looked at the young soldiers lined up against the wall and then out into the darkness beyond the security light.

"He's not the only one."

CHAPTER 51

ROSSETT WAS RUNNING now, holding Jacob over one shoulder in a fireman's carry with one hand and the Webley with his other. He was on the path, not caring about the crunch of the gravel as he tried to get away.

He knew from the sound of the gunfire that the weapon was an MP40. Not many of those were in the possession of the resistance, whatever faction, so he was guessing it was a German who had fired.

Which only meant one thing.

Koehler.

It was nagging him how the Germans had found him in the cemetery, but in his flight he didn't have time to think. After a hundred yards or so, he veered right off the path, slowing so as not to fall over a grave. In the darkness, he headed toward the dim lights of the houses that backed onto one of the sides of the cemetery.

He'd decided that climbing over a wall into a garden would be safer than running out into the middle of a road.

If Chivers was out there, he'd have to look after himself. They'd come far enough together, maybe now was the time to part.

They fell twice as they made their way across the graveyard. Each time Jacob merely rolled in the grass, then stood up quietly and held out his hands to be picked up again.

A little soldier, never complaining.

They reached the perimeter wall, and Rossett put Jacob down before chinning up to look over into the back garden of the adjoining house. It seemed nearly every house in the street had back-room lights on with faces at the window, no doubt curious after hearing the gunfire.

Rossett dropped down and pulled Jacob near.

"There is a gate a little farther down." Jacob pointed in the darkness. "It lets you out onto the street. We used to get the bus there."

"Show me."

This time Jacob took the lead, holding Rossett's hand. They skirted the wall until they came to a narrow iron gate. Rossett lifted Jacob onto the gate and then climbed over. They dropped down into an alleyway, barely two feet wide, that ran between two houses.

Rossett slipped the Webley into his pocket, and they brushed as much of the mud and grass off each other as possible as they half jogged along the alleyway to the road that lay at the end.

They found themselves looking over their shoulders a few times as they ran, and both automatically slowed as they neared the bright lights of the main road. Rossett took Jacob's hand again and turned right at a fast walk, heading away from the cemetery as they went.

Rossett looked down the road for a sign of Chivers or the Germans, but the few cars that passed did so without paying them any heed. There was a bus stop up ahead, and he looked around to see if there was anywhere to hide while they waited for the bus.

That was when he heard the racing engine behind him.

The car was traveling too fast and in too high a gear for a winter's night in Willesden. It was someone either getting away from or racing toward the site of a crisis.

He squeezed the Webley and waited, not wanting to turn around lest he attract attention.

Only when he heard the car slowing did he spin, pushing Jacob behind him. He held the Webley against his leg and thumbed the hammer.

The little Volkswagen bounced up onto the curb next to him, and

Rossett took a pace backward and leaned forward to look in, lifting the Webley as he did so.

Kate, Koehler's secretary, smiled back and leaned across to open the door.

"Want a lift?"

Rossett took another step back, lowering the gun slightly in shock.

"I promise not to speed." She smiled again, this time with a slight edge of urgency.

Rossett took another step back and looked up and down the road as he tapped the pistol against his leg, thinking.

In the distance, he heard what sounded like a police siren, then another. He looked back to Kate.

"Come on! I've come to help you!" She beckoned him into the car. "Or do you want to wait for the police?"

"Why?"

"We can sit down and discuss it later, but to be honest, I don't think now is the time!" Kate pleaded, waving her hand, beckoning Rossett into the car.

"Why?" Rossett asked again, this time raising the Webley toward her.

"Because of him," Kate said, pointing at Jacob.

"Not good enough."

A police siren approached and Kate looked up as the car carrying it raced by; she turned back to Rossett, who was rising from the crouch he dropped down to as he had heard the car approach. "Okay, look, I might work for the Germans, but it doesn't mean I like what they do. I heard a phone call tonight, someone called Chivers telling Major Koehler you were here. I wanted to help you, and to help the boy." Kate looked close to tears, and Rossett half lowered the pistol.

"Chivers?"

"That's what I heard. Please, we need to go!"

Another police siren and Jacob tugging on his coat made up his mind.

Rossett opened the car door, folded down the front seat, and very nearly threw Jacob onto the backseat; he sat down in front and stared at Kate, who started to pull away before he had even closed the door.

"Remember the gun," he said, pistol now on his lap, half pointing toward her as they bounced off the curb before pulling a U-turn in the road.

She glanced down at the gun as she drove.

"I've a feeling you're not going to let me forget it."

ROSSETT HAD NO idea where the little Volkswagen was going as it raced along the nearly empty streets. For a moment, he tensed as they rounded a corner and caught a glimpse of two Mercedes staff cars parked up against a high wall. It took him a moment to realize that it was the far side of the cemetery he'd just been in. He twisted in his seat to look through the small rear window.

"That must have been the other side of the bear trap," Kate said, and Rossett turned back to look at her.

"How did you know where we were?"

"I saw Ernst's cars, and I guessed you'd be coming out as far away from them as possible. I just drove to the other side of the cemetery."

"Ernst?"

"Koehler." Kate felt her cheeks blush, and she looked at Rossett quickly to see if he had noticed. He stared back, dead eyed, like a shark but twice as dangerous, pistol still on his lap.

"Are you all right?" said Kate, leaning forward in her seat so she could see Jacob in her mirror. Rossett assumed the boy nodded, because she smiled warmly, beautifully, in the mirror and sat back again.

He noticed they were slowing down as they put distance between themselves and the graveyard. Kate was easing into the nighttime traffic and becoming anonymous in her little car. Her driving impressed Rossett. She turned and looked at him, then it was his turn to get a smile.

"Are *you* all right?" This time she was asking Rossett.

"Yes."

"You don't look it."

"I'm fine."

"You look like shit."

"Thank you."

"Seriously, we can't drive around with you looking like that."

She reached up and turned the rearview mirror toward him, and Rossett leaned forward to see his reflection. His eyes were heavy and dark with shadows, his hair was a mess, and he had mud streaked across his face. He could see some dried blood that had trickled down his forehead, and he reached up and found a tender cut on his scalp.

"I look like shit."

"I know," Kate replied, turning the mirror back.

"Where are we going?" Rossett tried to smooth his hair and failed miserably. He licked his hand, tasting mud, then tried to smooth his hair again, with no luck.

"I have a flat, my mother's. I can take you there."

"What about your mother?"

"She's in Yorkshire."

Rossett noticed for the first time that Kate had a slight Yorkshire accent.

"Why?"

"So you can get cleaned up."

"No. Why? Why are you helping us?"

"I told you."

"No, as I said before, that's not good enough. Tell me why."

Kate looked across at him and then back to the road ahead, not answering.

Rossett watched her, trying to decide if she was searching for a lie or for the truth. He'd often felt that the answer to a difficult question that came quickly was usually a lie. He liked that she was looking for the right words.

"Because I understand," she said after a moment.

"Understand?"

"You're not exactly quick on the uptake, are you?"

Rossett stared at her without expression. Kate blew out her cheeks and tried again.

"I understand why you are doing what you are doing. I . . ." She paused for a moment. "I know what happened to you. I know about your wife and your boy. I've lost someone in this war. I . . . I know we can't bring them back, but maybe we can bring ourselves back. Be human again." She looked at him again, and this time her eyes pleaded. "Do you know what I mean?"

Rossett stared at the road ahead. A minute passed while he twisted and turned what she had said until finally he nodded, wiping a finger and thumb across his eyes.

"I don't believe you, but I do need you, so keep driving."

Kate was about to speak again when Jacob broke the silence from the backseat.

"Stop."

Kate looked at him in the rearview.

"We can't," said Rossett.

"Please," said Jacob.

"We can't, we need to keep moving," replied Rossett.

"I'm going to be sick," Jacob said, his voice cracking.

The car immediately swerved to the side of the road, braking hard and causing Rossett to brace a hand on the dashboard.

"Keep going, we can't stop." Rossett looked at Kate, then over his shoulder at Jacob.

"No," Kate replied.

Both Rossett and Kate got out of the car, and Rossett tilted the seat forward. Before it was fully out of the way Jacob was out of his seat, hand over his mouth.

Once clear of the door, the boy let go, and vomit splashed onto the pavement from his hunched body.

Jacob barked again and then rested his hands on his bony knees and gasped for air.

Kate leaned in close and put her hand on Jacob's back.

"Are you all right?" she whispered in his ear.

Jacob started to cry , deep, gasping sobs mixed with retching breaths. He reached up with his bony hands to his face and then out to unseen terrors as he howled the cry of the lost and the lonely. His cheeks were wet and his face twisted in anguish. He tried to pull away from Kate's hand, but she gripped his coat and pulled him near.

"Shush," she whispered. "It's going to be all right."

Jacob reached with his hands, pushing back at the terror again and howling another sob. A lack of oxygen choked it off and his shoulders shook under his duffel coat as his hands fell limp at his side, giving up their fight.

Kate held the back of his neck and pulled him close for comfort.

"Shush, it's all right, it's all right," she whispered to the boy, her face resting against the top of his tiny head, her arms enveloping it.

Jacob's sobs started to subside. His hands lifted and fluttered a moment before they settled, and then he held Kate close, quietly crying into her chest. Occasional shudders rippled through him like after-shocks, but his tears became muffled and the sobs were eventually replaced by sniffs.

He was coming back.

Rossett looked around. An old man and woman were walking along the pavement toward them, smartly dressed, on their way to an evening engagement.

The old lady smiled at Kate and tilted her head.

"Is he unwell?"

"He's got a little flu, we think, don't we, darling?" Kate replied, looking at Rossett as she held Jacob close, covering the yellow star on the boy's coat.

"He's not well" was all Rossett could think to say.

"It's the time of year," the old lady replied. "Poor tyke."

Rossett looked at the old man, who stared back, taking him in and apparently realizing all was not as it should be.

"We'd better get going, darling," Rossett said, aware that the words sounded stilted, forced.

Kate seemed to see what Rossett saw and smiled warmly at the old lady.

"We'd better get him home."

"Yes, dear, best place for him," the old lady replied.

"Will you drive, darling?" Kate said to Rossett, and he moved around the car as Kate shepherded Jacob to the backseat, holding him close and skirting the vomit on the ground. She turned Jacob in her arms so that he faced the car, making sure that she remained in the line of sight of the old couple as she did so, and eased him into the back. She pushed his head down as if he was a prisoner before she too slid into the backseat and pulled the door closed.

"Have a nice evening," she said to the old couple as she pulled the door shut.

"I hope he feels better soon," said the old lady, muffled through the closed window.

Rossett nodded to the couple and then climbed into the driver's seat. His knees were cramped, and he couldn't get comfortable, but he didn't try to adjust the seat. He merely fumbled with the ignition and tried to find a gear.

"When you're ready . . . darling," Kate said from the backseat as she cradled Jacob on her lap.

Rossett glanced at her in the mirror and then over-revved the car as he pulled away from the curb.

He watched the old couple staring at them as they drove away. The old man was speaking to his wife for the first time since they had turned up.

"He didn't believe what was happening," Rossett said, still watching the old couple in the rearview. "He was suspicious."

"Do you want to go back and kill them?"

"I'm not sure," Rossett replied.

"I was joking," Kate said, and Rossett looked at her in the mirror and saw that she was shaking her head.

"Where do I go?"

"Pimlico."

"How's the boy?"

"He's fine."

"We gave him fish and chips; they must have upset his stomach."

"It wasn't the fish and chips," Kate replied, softly stroking Jacob's short, dirty hair.

"Do you think he's sick?"

"He just couldn't take anymore," Kate said. "Don't you ever feel like that?"

Rossett watched her in the mirror but didn't reply.

Jacob lay like an exhausted rag doll in Kate's lap. "Are you better now?" she said tenderly, and Jacob nodded. "There will be some clothes at the flat that might fit you, and then you can have a bath and sleep, okay?"

Jacob nodded again.

Kate stroked his hair again and looked up to Rossett.

"I do," said Rossett.

"You do what?"

"I feel sometimes that I just can't take anymore."

CHAPTER 52

I T WAS CHAOS at the cemetery. Koehler stood by the lodge and looked at the police, the ambulance, and the soldiers milling around. Several cars sat with engines running, their headlamps illuminating the grave-yard.

On the ground, still lying a few feet from the light switch, was the caretaker. Next to him crouched a Metropolitan Police inspector and two German Kriminalpolizei officers. Behind them, at a discreet distance, stood Schmitt, hands behind his back, no doubt glad that the plan had ensured that he was as far away from the fuck-up as possible.

Koehler lit another cigarette, his fourth in quick succession. He looked down at the ground and saw that the third was still smoking, so he snuffed it out with his foot and looked back to the lodge.

Schmitt nodded to him and gave him a discreet thumbs-up.

Idiot, thought Koehler, and he briefly considered just leaving the scene and driving back to Charing Cross, aware that the whole night had become a farce. It was then the older of the two German policemen wandered over.

"Heil Hitler." The policeman saluted Koehler with one hand while holding up a police badge that identified him as holding the rank of generalmajor. Koehler rolled his eyes. All he needed was a jumped-up policeman, especially one who held a higher rank than him. The police-man nodded sadly. He knew what Koehler was thinking, and Koehler hated him for it. The generalmajor stuffed his hands and his ID into his overcoat pockets, then took up a position next to Koehler, both men facing the lodge.

"Could I trouble the major for a cigarette?" said the policeman with a smile.

Koehler produced the packet, and the policeman took one and then cupped his hands around the flickering match Koehler struck for him.

"Your colleague has told me you were tracking an escaped prisoner," the policeman said once the cigarette was lit.

"That is correct," Koehler replied.

"I would have thought it would be best to flood the area to prevent escape."

"I didn't want to scare him off with three hundred jackboots flattening the grass."

"So you scared him off with twelve?" The policeman looked at Koehler and picked some tobacco off his tongue before looking back toward the cemetery.

"The shooting was unfortunate."

"It was for the caretaker, seeing as he is fucking dead."

Koehler flicked his cigarette away impatiently, and it sailed, high and a fair distance through the night, like a tracer shell.

"That was a mistake by a junior soldier who thought he was under attack. I really cannot see what all this fuss is about."

"It is about the dead man lying over there, Herr Major, the unarmed civilian."

Koehler wafted a hand in the direction of the corpse and fumbled for his cigarettes again before thinking better of it and leaving them in his pocket.

"This was an official operation. As I said, it was unfortunate a civilian got killed, but I was doing my job."

"Forgive me, Major, but if you had been doing your job, the prisoner might not have been on the run in the first place, and, if I may add, he would most certainly not be on the run now."

"This is ridiculous." Koehler waved a hand in the direction of Werner, who sprang to attention and marched over. "Get me a driver, I'm leaving."

Werner saluted, then turned, heading off to the original squad, who had been quarantined from the others pending questioning.

"I'll need a statement from you," the generalmajor said wearily, like a man accustomed to asking futile questions.

Koehler leaned in close to the policeman and tilted his face forward so that he was looking up under the brim of the hat.

"What is your name?"

"Neumann."

"Well, Generalmajor Neumann, you'll get a fucking statement, and you will get it when I am ready. Don't fuck with me, flatfoot, or I'll have you arresting pickpockets in fucking Kiev on Monday. Do you understand?"

The old policeman nodded but didn't look scared; he merely took the cigarette out of his mouth and dropped it on the ground.

"Thank you for the cigarette, Herr Major, and, er, Heil Hitler."

Koehler stomped off to his Mercedes as a young driver jogged past him to open the rear door, then stood briskly to attention.

The door had no sooner been closed for him than it opened again and Schmitt appeared. Koehler sighed and held a hand to his eyes when he saw his colleague.

"What?" he barked.

"Where are you going?"

"I'm going home. I've had enough."

"You can't! What about Rossett?"

"Fuck him."

"What about"—Schmitt leaned in close to ensure that the driver couldn't hear them—"the diamonds?"

Koehler let his head fall back on the seat.

"Fuck them. Honestly, fuck them. I'm sick of chasing. We've got a prisonful of English prisoners escaped and no sign of them. Rossett and his fucking Jew can disappear. I've had enough, Schmitt. So far today,

I've been fucking shot at twice, soaked twice, and interrogated by a fucking flatfoot policeman who thinks I'm dead in the water. I want to go to bed, and then tomorrow morning, bright and early, I want to sit down and spend the entire day writing the report that will attempt to save my career."

"But the diamonds?"

"How do we even know if there are diamonds?"

"I thought—"

"You thought what? You thought that because the resistance think there are diamonds, there are? They are bigger idiots than we are. Why should we think they are right?"

Schmitt leaned back from the door.

"Well, what should I do?"

"Write a letter to your wife, because if I am to be shot, I swear to God, you will be standing next to me!" Koehler turned to the driver and ordered, "Drive!"

SCHMITT STEPPED BACK and watched the Mercedes pull out of the cemetery with a spray of gravel.

He looked back to the lodge and the body and then across to Werner, who was standing apart from the rest of his men.

The old soldier slowly walked across to Schmitt and politely stood to one side. "What?" Schmitt asked.

"I had the men search the graveyard as best they could, sir," Werner said.

"And?"

"No sign of Rossett or the Jew."

"Of course there isn't. They'll be miles away by now."

Werner nodded and then bowed his head slightly, so that he could speak to Schmitt without being overheard.

"One of the men found some disturbed earth, sir, near one of the graves."

"We are in a cemetery. What do you think he would find?"

"He also found an empty tin box that had been removed from the soil. It was resting on top of the gravestone." Werner looked around. "It appears the box was removed from the grave. The lid was on the ground."

"And?"

"Maybe the box was the sort of thing you might put diamonds in?"

Schmitt looked at the old soldier and then out to the darkness of the graveyard.

"Show me where," he said quietly.

CHAPTER 53

ROSSETT FOLLOWED KATE'S directions from the backseat and soon found himself coasting in a narrow side street off a main road he didn't recognize in Pimlico. It was just after eleven and the streets of central London had fallen quiet. Rossett eyed the houses and parked cars as they crept along, aware that if he looked out of place anywhere, with his mud-spattered, blood-spattered head, it was here, in a solidly upscale area of the capital. They parked between two old Rovers, and Rossett noticed that the Volkswagen was the only foreign car in the street.

"Maybe we shouldn't park here," he said.

"Why?" Kate replied quietly, not wanting to wake the now sleeping Jacob.

"The car, it will attract attention."

"It doesn't when I park it here every night. Why should it now? For God's sake, Rossett, just relax. Here, help me with Jacob."

Rossett looked up and down the road and rested his hand on the door handle.

"Don't you ever switch off?" she said.

"No."

"You should. It's not good for you living at the edge of your nerves all the time."

"In my current predicament it's switching off that isn't good for me.

Which one of these is your place?" he replied, looking around at the houses now, checking them for flicking curtains.

Kate pointed at a door that was no more than twelve feet away across the pavement.

"Flat 4B, fourth floor. Wipe your feet before you go in."

Rossett looked up at the Georgian building through the windshield. He counted off the floors and studied the fourth floor. It was one floor from the top, with big windows and small wrought-iron balconies.

"How many ways out?"

"There's a fire escape at the rear; you climb onto it through the bedroom window. It leads onto the alleyway that runs behind the houses and comes out at the end of the street. Or you could just jump out the window, but if you do, could you try to avoid my car on the way down? I haven't finished paying for it."

"You're sure there is no one else in the flat?"

"For God's sake, just get out and take Jacob, will you?"

Rossett looked at the building once more and then opened the door. He stepped out onto the road, bent back into the car, and pulled Jacob out. The boy whined at being moved and tried to hold on to Kate, who shushed him as she pushed him toward Rossett.

Rossett hoisted Jacob up onto his shoulder with one arm, putting his free hand into his pocket to take hold of the Webley as he did so. The boy smelled of sick, and Rossett half turned his face away before Jacob reached around his neck and pulled him closer for comfort.

Rossett paused.

"It's okay, son, you'll be in bed soon."

Jacob whined again, more softly this time, squeezing Rossett with his stick-thin arms, then releasing him slightly.

Comfort for them both.

Kate passed them and fumbled with some keys before hopping up the four granite steps and opening the big blue door. Rossett followed her quickly, looking left and right once more as he went.

All was quiet.

He stepped past Kate, who was holding the door open, and into a long narrow hallway that was lit by a solitary bulb in a dusty fabric shade that had remnants of silk tassels hanging down. At the end of the hall was a dark staircase. Along the hallway he saw four dark wood doors leading to flats beyond. Kate closed the front door and squeezed past them before heading up the stairs, her heels echoing far too loudly for Rossett's liking. He grimaced and then followed her, looking up into the dim forty-watt gloom and suddenly feeling vulnerable.

He let her go on ahead. At each landing, he took the stairs slowly, leaning back to afford him the best view through the shadows. The house smelled of other people's dinners and was silent except for the muted sound of a radio playing martial music behind a closed door on the third landing.

On the fourth-floor landing, Kate was waiting for him, her flat door open, hand on hip, impatient.

Rossett made eye contact with her as he approached.

"Put the light on."

Kate rolled her eyes and turned, flicking on the switch behind her. Rossett looked through the doorway along the hall, about fifteen feet long with five doors leading off it, three to the left, two to the right.

"I'll need to tidy up. The living room is on the right. Put him in there. I'll make us some tea."

Kate entered the first doorway on the left. Rossett stepped slowly into the flat and closed the door with his heel. He waited in the hallway a moment, listening. All he could hear was running water, the bang of a pipe, and the clang of a kettle lid. He took a step forward and looked into the kitchen where Kate had gone. It was small but functional. At one end, there was a small window where Rossett could see his own reflection.

Kate struck a long match, lit the stove, and plonked the kettle onto the burner.

"You can relax, you're safe."

Rossett nodded, not totally convinced, before backing out of the kitchen and into the hallway.

The first door on the right was a closet. The next room was in darkness, and he slid his hand along the smooth cold wall looking for where he guessed a light switch might be. He found it and flicked it on.

The living room was huge. Rossett realized it must run across nearly the whole front of the house. The floor-to-ceiling windows had plush gold and green drapes tied back halfway down. He counted five windows, and guessed the room to be thirty feet long and fifteen feet wide. At one end sat a grand piano and a heavy brown leather sofa.

The other end, the one nearest to him, was more homey, with soft fabric sofas and a thick cream woolen rug nestled around a dark iron fireplace that was taller than Jacob. The room was lit by two huge chandeliers, and as soon as Rossett had placed Jacob on one of the sofas he set about drawing curtains and lighting the two small table lamps near the fireplace.

He turned off the main lights and checked the curtains again for gaps.

"Can you light the fire, please?" Kate called from the kitchen, her voice accompanied by the clatter of cups and cupboards.

Rossett found a bucket of coal and some balls of newspaper next to the fireplace. He knelt down and started to build the fire, aware now of how cold and damp the flat felt. He looked up and saw some iron radiators against the wall. Their thick black paint reminded him of elephant skin covered in wet mud.

He guessed they were cold.

"Maybe you should light the boiler as well," he called out.

"What boiler? It hasn't worked in years!" Kate shouted back, a light chuckle in her voice.

Rossett struck his match and fired the newspaper under the coal, watching it catch and leaning forward to blow some soft encouragement. The fire let off some reluctant crackles. Rossett leaned back on his heels and watched it grow. He reached his hands out to the flames to warm them and then stood up, letting go a soft groan from his slowly relaxing but still aching body.

"You sound like you're getting old." Kate entered the room behind him. She was carrying a silver tray crowded with a teapot, cups, and some toast, which she set onto a small coffee table in front of the empty sofa, opposite the one where Jacob lay silently sleeping.

"I feel like I'm getting old."

Kate crossed to Jacob, who was lying with his face toward the back of the couch in a fetal position, dead to the world and still fully dressed.

"I'll fetch him a blanket. He must be freezing."

"The fire will warm the room soon," Rossett replied.

Rossett watched Kate leave the room, then turned back to the fire. He stepped back, wiping the dust off his hands onto his coat and looking at the pictures on the mantelpiece, on either side of an ornate china clock that showed the wrong time.

Broken like the boiler.

He picked up a photo in a twelve-inch gilt frame and held it toward the lamp so he could study it closer, just as Kate entered the room behind him carrying some woolen blankets, which she draped gently over Jacob.

"My father," she said, looking up at Rossett while still kneeling next to Jacob, her hand resting on the blankets.

The picture showed a dashing young army officer in full dress uniform standing next to a large plant on a small table. It was the typical formal portrait that proud young men had had taken prior to going overseas during the Great War. Many homes had them, but not many had them in frames as expensive as this. Rossett could see that the young man in the photo had the swagger of someone who was born to lead. There was also the sly smile of someone buoyed by the certainty of youth.

Rossett did some math in his head and looked down at Kate, who had turned and was now sitting on the floor in front of Jacob's couch, basking in the glow of the fire, staring into it, cheekbones sharpened by the lamps and the flickering flames.

"He made it back then?" Rossett asked.

"He did. Well, most of him did."

"He was injured?"

"Not as such. Nothing you could see, anyway, but Mother said he was different when he came back."

Rossett looked at the picture again and wondered if there was anyone who went to war who didn't become a casualty of some kind.

"Where is he now?"

"He's dead."

"I'm sorry."

"He was killed in the first days of the invasion. He was in Kent somewhere, with the Home Guard, when the Germans broke out of Folkestone. Apparently, they were trying to hold a crossroads, six of them standing up to six hundred."

"He was brave."

"He was a bloody idiot. Do you have a cigarette?"

Rossett put the picture back on the mantelpiece and looked in his pockets for his cigarettes. He crouched down in front of Kate, who had the sort of faraway look that coal fires in dark rooms often cause. Kate smiled at him as she took the cigarette he offered, lightly resting her hand on his as he lit it. He allowed himself to enjoy the soft touch of her smooth fingers for a moment longer than it took to light the cigarette, then lowered the match and extinguished it with a flick of his wrist.

Kate pulled her head away and blew a long plume of smoke up to the high ceiling as Rossett stood again and took his place next to the fire. Kate rested her hand with the cigarette on her knee.

"I read about what you did in France and during the invasion." Kate looked up at Rossett. "Are all those stories true?"

She drew on the cigarette again, watching him.

"Most of them."

"Why did you do it?"

Rossett frowned. Nobody had ever asked him before why he'd done the things he had done. They had only ever been interested in telling him he was a hero or trying to get stories out of him. He looked at the picture again.

"I don't know."

"What were you thinking?"

"I . . . um . . . I don't know. I suppose . . . I suppose I wasn't really thinking anything."

"A bit like you and Jacob?"

"What?"

"You didn't think then either, did you?"

Kate studied Rossett for a moment. Rossett felt his legs growing uncomfortably hot through his trousers, and he stepped away from the fire and sat down on the other settee. The silence filled the room and he felt uneasy.

"Will this tea be brewed?" he asked, staring at the pot.

"You be mother."

Rossett busied himself with pouring two cups as she watched him from the floor, cigarette hand resting against her chin. He stood and passed her a cup before retreating to the couch again, suddenly awkward in his movements and not sure why.

"Mummy was very angry with Daddy. She wanted him to stay in London, away from the fighting. She said it was all a waste of time charging off. She knew the Germans were here to stay. He didn't even have a gun. Can you imagine? Not even having a gun?"

Rossett didn't reply, as he tried to slip a finger into the dainty handle of the teacup he was holding.

"Such a waste, taking on the Germans when you haven't even got a gun," Kate said to the fire, tucking her knees up to her chin and wrapping her arms around them, making herself small.

They sat in silence for a while until Rossett spoke again.

"What is your mother doing now?"

"Not much."

"Retired?"

"Mummy died three years ago."

"You said she was in Yorkshire?"

"She is, buried."

"I'm sorry," replied Rossett, aware that he hadn't seen any pictures of a woman in the flat.

"She couldn't take it."

"Your father's death?"

"Hmm, that, and all this." Kate raised her eyes to the ceiling and waved a hand around the room. "All this damp, despair, grayness. She was sick for a long time and then . . . well, she couldn't take anymore."

"Did she . . . ?"

"Yes, she killed herself."

Kate sucked on the cigarette and stared at the fire; she swallowed down the smoke and then let it leak from her nose, slowly and less dramatically than before.

Rossett watched her and then followed her gaze to the fire. "It was a picture that started all this."

"All what?" she asked.

"Jacob and me. It was a picture, in another house, different from this one but with the same kind of picture. Someone else who died fighting the Germans. Made me realize."

"Realize what?"

"That I was wrong, that what I was doing was wrong. I'm trying to make it right."

"By helping Jacob?"

Rossett nodded.

"What about the diamonds?"

Rossett looked up.

"How do you know about the diamonds?"

"I'm Koehler's secretary. What he knows, I know." Kate shrugged, smoking again.

"Koehler knows about the diamonds?"

Kate nodded.

"How? Chivers?"

"They captured a resistance soldier. He cracked, told them the lot, plus whatever your friend Chivers told them."

"Fucking Chivers." Rossett shook his head sadly.

"The diamonds, did you get them?"

"That's why you came for us, isn't it?" Rossett looked at her.

"No, I told you, I came because of the boy." Rossett shook his head as Kate continued. "You're taking the moral high ground here, but *you* were looking for diamonds, weren't you?" Kate lifted her chin, a flash of hurt crossing her face.

"I don't care about the diamonds," Rossett replied.

"What were you doing in the cemetery then, cutting the grass?"

"Getting them for Jacob. He'll need them."

"Won't you?"

Rossett shook his head.

"What are you going to do?" Kate probed, softly.

"I need to get the boy out."

"And then?"

"I don't know."

"You could go with him."

"After what I've done?" Rossett shook his head again. "I don't think so. They'd have me at the end of a rope in no time."

"Not necessarily. You could say you were forced to work by the Germans. If you escaped, they could use you for propaganda."

"The way the Germans did?" Rossett glanced at her and then back to the fire.

"You'd be alive. You'd be free to start again, and maybe you could look after Jacob, help him rebuild his life."

"After I took it away?"

"You didn't take it, this occupation took it."

"I wish I could believe you, and I wish I believed the free government would believe it."

Kate swirled her teacup slightly and stared into it.

"You could tell the free government about Chivers. That would buy you some brownie points."

"Rat out one double agent? I doubt that would help much."

"He's close to the leadership of the communists. He's been under suspicion for a while now, by both sides of the resistance. He's important to them."

Rossett thought back to Dracula at the wood yard pulling out the Browning in the office. The communists had obviously come to the same conclusion as the royalists.

"The fish-and-chip shop, that must have been when he telephoned," Rossett said.

"Chivers has been working for us, the Germans, for over a year now. He was picked up in a raid at the docks, and Koehler turned him. He'd always been a go-between for the two resistance groups, a sort of fixer. He was perfect for Koehler and easily swayed with the chance of making some money."

Rossett put the cup down and rubbed his hand across his forehead.

"I should have left him in the warehouse."

"For selling you out?"

"For being a traitor."

"We're all traitors. It's just that you and I are more honest about it."

Rossett leaned forward in the chair and rubbed his temples with his fingertips.

"Who was in the picture, the one that started this?" Kate asked gently.

"A boy."

"Your son?"

"No."

"Who?"

"A young man who went to fight the Germans and who never came back, someone else's son and another wasted life."

"And that made you go and get Jacob?"

"That and a pint of whiskey, yes."

"You were drunk?"

Rossett nodded behind his massaging hands.

"Would you like a drink now?"

Rossett shook his head. "I need to sleep."

"You can use the spare room."

"I'll stay here with Jacob."

"I'll get you a blanket."

Rossett nodded, his head pivoting on his fingertips. Kate stood up and watched him for a moment before leaving the room. Once she had gone, Rossett looked at Jacob, then at the fire, before slowly sinking to his side and lying down on the couch. He kicked off his shoes and let them fall to the floor. His feet felt cold and he crossed them over each other and drew his knees up to his chest. A sudden urge to cry pushed behind his eyes and he squeezed them closed tightly, sliding his hands in between his knees and clamping them tightly together.

"Are you all right?"

Rossett opened his eyes and looked at her as she held the blanket like a beautiful undertaker ready to cast a shroud.

He nodded, unable to speak.

"Are you sure? Maybe I should get you a drink?"

He shook his head.

She laid the blanket across him, letting it cover him from the feet up until only his head and shoulders were visible, a mirror image of Jacob on the opposite couch.

"Will you be all right?"

Rossett nodded.

"I'll be just across the hall, if you want me."

"Thank you for your help." He finally found words.

"You don't need to thank me."

"I need to save him," Rossett said softly.

"You will."

"I lost one little boy, I won't lose another."

"Your son?"

Rossett nodded again, aware he hadn't spoke of his son for years until these last few days. It was as if Jacob had breathed new life into long-buried memories. Kate knelt down and rested a hand on Rossett's shoulder, squeezing it through the blanket. He looked at her, saw how beautiful she was, and felt the weight in his chest again. Kate tilted her head and smiled the softest of smiles. Rossett closed his eyes. He couldn't bear to look at her and fight his emotions at the same time.

He felt her hand touch his face, that softness again, so soft in a hard world. He moved his head a fraction so that his cheek filled her palm and his lips brushed her fingertips. He felt the solid thump of his heart, one, two, three times, and then he breathed in through his nose and enjoyed her scent.

"I can stay here with you," she offered.

"No," he said quietly.

"Just to sleep . . ."

"No."

"Why?"

"It isn't safe for you." Rossett opened his eyes, and he could tell that she understood.

"If you need me, I'll be just across the hall."

IT WAS MAYBE three hours later when she heard Rossett cry out. She got out of bed and opened her door. Rossett shouted again, as if he was in pain, like an animal caught in a trap and longing for freedom.

Jacob opened the living room door, sleepy eyed. Holding his blanket over his shoulders like a shawl, he stood in the half-light looking at Kate, a drowsy ghost.

"He's having a bad dream," he whispered.

"I know, come here," said Kate, holding out her hand and beckoning Jacob. The boy sleepily padded across the hallway, and she took him into her room and lifted him into her bed. Jacob moaned softly as she pulled the sheets over him. He rolled onto his side and with a soft smacking of his lips buried his face into the soft white pillow, an angel at rest.

Kate lay on top of the blankets awhile, listening to the silence that had crept back into the flat after Rossett's shouts subsided. But she couldn't rest.

Half an hour after Jacob had joined her, some nighttime rain tapped on her window and wind crept under the frame, causing her curtain to rock back and forth a fraction. Kate watched the curtain for a few moments and then slid off the bed.

She tiptoed along the corridor to the tiny kitchen to make tea. She worked quickly and silently, glancing up at the window as another flurry of rain rattled against it, urged on by the wind.

That was when she saw him.

Rossett stood silent, a ghost in the reflected glass of the kitchen window. Kate turned and looked at him face on, standing in the doorway.

He looked terrible. A man who found dreams harder than reality. His eyes were heavy and his shoulders hung low. His right hand was resting on the doorframe, and Kate saw his bruised knuckles and bloody palm for the first time.

"Can I have a cup?" Rossett whispered and nodded to the teapot.

Kate nodded, and before she could speak, Rossett turned away and walked silently back up the hallway to the living room.

She found him kneeling in front of the half-dead fire. He was prodding it with the poker, so she set down the cups of tea and sat on the couch where he'd been lying, pulling the blanket she had given him earlier over her nightdress and lying down to rest her head on the arm. Kate saw that he had opened the curtains on the nearest window. A streetlamp outside shone a dim light into the room.

Everything was black and white except for the dark red in the fireplace, and Kate was reminded of a dream she'd once had.

She shivered.

Rossett finally gave up with the fire and turned toward her. She smiled and gestured at his teacup, which sat on the carpet next to the couch.

"I've put some more coal on, but it's damp. It'll take a while to catch," Rossett said.

"Everything is damp in here. I hate this place," she said, her smile gone.

Rossett sat on the floor, propping his back against the couch, and sipped at the tea.

"Thank you."

"There are biscuits if you—"

"No, I don't mean the tea. I mean thank you for helping us."

Kate nodded. They both turned to look at the window as the rain lashed against it, and Kate shivered again and drew her knees up under the blanket.

The fire popped as a solitary flame rose an inch or two and danced behind the damp coal. They sat silently for minutes, Rossett cradling his teacup in his lap and Kate watching his profile, silhouetted against the embers.

"You were crying out," she finally said. Rossett only nodded in reply. "It woke Jacob. He's in my bed."

Rossett remained silent.

"What was the dream?"

Rossett shook his head.

"It might help you to talk."

"It won't."

"You can't put your whole life on hold, John. You're not a machine. You have thoughts, feelings. You have love. It's okay to think and talk and be human again, you can't mourn forever." Kate's voice was barely a whisper.

"I have a dream, a bad dream." Rossett paused. "I'm trying to stop someone bleeding to death."

"Who is it?"

"My wife . . . and my boy."

"Oh, John."

"I can't find the wounds. No matter how hard I look, I can't find where the blood is coming from. They're screaming and crying and I can't help them. I keep tearing at their clothes, and the blood keeps coming. I'm soaked in blood. We're soaked in blood." Rossett put the tea down.

"I keep looking, slipping and splashing through blood, until I realize . . ."

"What?"

"That they are dead. The blood is my blood."

A silent tear burst from Rossett's left eye. He squeezed his lips together and looked at Kate, then slowly shook his head and turned back to the fire.

Fighting.

"I can't stop it, the blood. I drown in it. And when I wake up . . ." Rossett paused. "I'm still drowning in it."

Kate reached out and rested her hand on the back of Rossett's neck. He flinched at the first stroke of her fingertips, then closed his eyes and allowed his head to fall forward.

"You poor thing," Kate whispered, fingertips still on Rossett's neck. His head rolled and he found himself turning to face her.

They stared at each for what seemed like an eternity, listening to the rain and the pop and crackle of the fire behind them. Kate's hand gently stroked his face, and Rossett turned his head and kissed her palm. She rolled forward on the couch, firelight dancing in her eyes, her lips an inch from his, so close he could feel her breath on his face.

"You don't have to be alone." Kate barely made a sound. "Not anymore."

Rossett kissed her and Kate slid off the couch until she was next to him on the floor. They lay together in the fire's orange glow and made love.

Afterward, as they lay naked under the blanket, the fire settled down to a shifting glow and the rain eased. Rossett stroked Kate's face with one finger as he stared into her eyes.

"What happens next?" Kate whispered.

"To who?"

"To us, all of us. Jacob, me . . . and you?"

"Nothing's changed. I have to get the boy to safety."

Kate lay silently, watching Rossett's eyes in the darkness, unable to see what they were saying.

"And me?" she asked.

"Do you want safety?"

"I want you."

"I'm not safe."

"You can be, with me."

"Do you want safety?" he said again.

"I do."

"Then you'll be safe, I promise."

They slept as the fire died. The rain came and went and, as somewhere across the city Big Ben struck three, Kate slipped out from under the blanket, stared at the sleeping, twitching Rossett, and left the room to return to her bed.

KATE'S EYELIDS FLUTTERED, opened, then closed again. Sleep was slow to lift. She blinked a dream away and tried to move her arm but found it pinned to the bed. She licked her lips, blinked again, and focused on Jacob, who was lying like a dark bruise in her white sheets, his face turned away so all she could see was his jet-black hair resting in the crook of her arm, still dreaming.

Safe.

She rolled onto her back and looked down the bed. Rossett was sitting by the window on a spindle-legged wooden chair, arms folded, sad eyed, watching her.

He smiled.

"Morning," said Kate, her voice croaking.

"I'm sorry if I woke you."

"What time is it?" Kate stretched her legs under the sheets.

"Seven thirty," Rossett replied without looking at his watch.

He settled back on the chair, turning his head to look out the window at the breaking of the morning.

"What are you going to do?" Kate asked.

"I need to find Chivers."

"Revenge?"

"Escape."

"You trust him?" she asked. Rossett replied by shaking his head, then looked at her.

"No."

"So why go and see him?"

"He knows people, people who can help Jacob."

"What if he won't help you?"

"He will."

"How will you find him?"

"You will." Rossett looked back out of the window.

"I will? How?"

"Your boss will know where he is."

"Koehler?"

Rossett nodded, still looking out the window.

"What if I won't help you?" Kate asked.

"You will. You already have and you will again."

Kate shook her head. Rossett's face softened, and his eyes flicked from her to Jacob.

"Do you think this will ever be over?" Kate asked him, closing her eyes.

"When the boy is safe, it'll be finished then."

"I meant the games, the lies, the occupation. Do you think life will ever be simple again?"

Rossett shrugged, and they were silent for so long he wondered if she'd gone back to sleep. Eventually, she said, "You were shouting again last night, after I left you."

"Shouting?"

"In your dream, you were crying out."

"I'm sorry.

"You sounded scared." Rossett looked back out the window at the houses opposite; a few lights were on as London yawned its way into another day.

"I wondered where you had gone when I woke up," Rossett said.

"I was worried about Jacob. I didn't want him to be scared."

"You're starting to sound like me." Rossett smiled, and Kate found herself smiling back.

"You're smiling."

Rossett nodded and looked back out the window, his breath misting the glass.

"Would you go if you could?" Rossett asked, the smile gone.

"From London?"

"From England."

"How? How would I get away?"

"Would you go if you could?"

"It would be impossible. I don't . . ."

"Would you go?" Rossett looked at her this time, driving the question home.

"Yes."

Rossett nodded but didn't reply.

Kate paused, then said gently, "I've never seen you smile before."

"Maybe I've had nothing to smile about."

"Have you now?"

"I hope so."

CHAPTER 54

"**I**'M NOT SURE, Kate. I could get into trouble."

"Please, Anne, the key is in my desk. I'll be in a right fix if I don't get this report finished, and I haven't got time to come in and get it."

In Charing Cross, Anne twisted the phone cord in her fingers and rolled her eyes as she chewed her lip.

"What if someone comes in and finds me in his office?"

"They won't, and if they do, just tell them you are getting the address for me."

"Can I just do the report for you and add the address when the major comes in?" Anne was doing her best at wriggling out of Kate's request that she enter Koehler's office and unlock his filing cabinet.

"It's pages long, Anne; it would take you all day. I've been working on it all night and I just need this one more thing. It's just an informant's address for the end of the report, nothing important."

"I could get sacked . . ."

"Don't be daft. Please, come on, do a pal a favor?"

Anne paused, then asked, "Where is it?"

"Top drawer of the filing cabinet in the corner of his office. The keys are in his top left-hand drawer. I'll explain everything when I come back to work, so he'll understand."

"Don't you dare! Don't tell him I've been in his office. What is the name of the informant?"

"George Chivers."

"Are you going to wait on the line?"

"Yes."

Anne put the phone down and looked toward her own office door, already regretting her decision to help Kate, but reluctant to stand and finally commit to the act. She hovered half out of her chair, looking again at the phone before finally rising and opening the door to Koehler's office.

Anne moved quickly once inside. She felt like a nervous cat burglar. When she reached Koehler's desk, she paused and looked once again at the door and then at the dark wooden filing cabinet in the corner, like a coffin stood on its end. Heavy and solid, a keeper of secrets.

Anne pulled open the desk drawer. It was cluttered with pens, pencils, loose documents, and scraps of paper, contrasting with the desktop, which sat as smooth and as clear as a becalmed sea.

She riffled through the drawer until she touched the butt of a small pistol, causing her to jump and withdraw her hand as quickly as if she had found a snake. She sighed and rested her other hand against her chest, briefly pondering telling Kate that she couldn't find the key, but then she remembered how much she relied on her friend and supervisor. It was a tough life working for the Nazis, even after all these years of occupation, and she needed Kate as a friend in a big city like London. Steeling herself, she continued searching the drawer until she found the small bunch of keys.

At the filing cabinet, Anne tried the first key and got lucky. She pulled the top drawer open and inspected the folders. There were about thirty in total, some thicker than others, but all neatly filled with papers and photos.

She quickly deduced that they weren't in name order, so she danced her fingers across the tops of the folders with a ballet dancer's precision until she found the one labeled "Chivers, G." She opened it on top of the open drawer, removed the first page, and scanned it quickly. She dashed to the outer office and picked up the phone, holding the cover sheet to her chest.

"Kate?"

"Yes?"

"I've got it. You do promise not to tell the major, don't you?"

"It's our secret."

"He has a gun in there, did you know?"

"He's a soldier, Anne. Of course he has a gun. What's the address?"

Anne suddenly felt stupid and felt herself blush. Kate had cut her off in the manner she did so often.

"Do you have a pen?"

"Yes, what is it?"

"14A Cheshunt Road, London."

"Is that all it says? Does it not give any directions?"

"Yes, other than his date of birth and stuff, that's it . . . Oh, hang on. Someone has written 'Off Green Street, East End.' Does that help?"

"Off Green Street?" Kate repeated. "That does help, Anne. Thank you. Thank you very, very much."

"Why do you need directions?"

"What?"

"Why do you need directions? If it is just for a report, why do you need directions?"

"I don't. It's just for the report, so I don't leave anything out."

"What is it about?"

"I can't tell you. You know what the major is like, everything hush-hush. You don't want him getting that little gun out and coming after you, do you?"

Anne teased the phone cord with her fingers and tried in vain to swallow the sense of dread that was creeping up her throat.

"Are you sure, Kate? This isn't anything funny, is it?" She tried to keep her voice flat, but a quiver escaped at the end of the sentence.

"I've got to dash, Anne. Don't worry, everything will be fine."

The phone clicked in Anne's ear, and she slowly lowered the handset as she raised the cover sheet from Chivers's file. The door behind her opened and she almost cried out in alarm. Koehler smiled at her quizzically.

"Anne?"

"Oh, sir . . . I think I've done something very silly."

CHAPTER 55

KATE PARKED THE Volkswagen on Cheshunt Road and watched Rossett stroll along the pavement in her father's suit. He looked every inch the gentleman, with a necktie, shined shoes, and neatly combed hair under the wide-brimmed black felt hat. She thought back to the night before and the mud-stained, bloodstained apparition that had spun and stared at her, ghostly in the headlamps.

She marveled at his ability to shrug off the bruises that she had seen when she gave him her father's clothes. He looked as though he had been run over by a bus. Jacob leaned forward and pulled on the back of her seat as he tried to get a better view of Rossett on the sidewalk. He'd been silent ever since his guardian had left his side.

"He won't be long," Kate said.

Jacob just kept watching.

Rossett counted off the houses. He'd already identified number 14, and he'd been studying it as he approached from the end of the road. He hadn't wanted Kate to pull up outside in case Chivers saw her and became spooked. He'd given specific instructions to stay well back in the car until he came back out of the house, and if she heard shots, or if anyone else came out, she was to drive away without looking back.

She didn't know it yet, but in her father's overcoat, lying in the footwell, was the small urn that Rossett had dug up the night before. That morning he'd sat in the bathroom, prized out the cork stopper, and found nine cut diamonds, each the size of a little fingernail. He'd stared at the stones in the palm of his hand, rolling them a fraction, side to side. They had caught the light, and his breath.

Rossett had sat on the toilet, unable to decide his next move and to think straight after looking at the dancing light in his hands.

Old Galkoff had taken the risk that an honest man would dig in the dirt.

Rossett wasn't sure the old man's faith had been repaid.

As he walked to number 14, he thought about the diamonds again and looked back at Kate once more, checking to see that she was still there. He wondered why he hadn't told her about the diamonds being in the car. It was as if they infected you with doubt and distrust.

He wondered if people called them stones because they dragged you down while you carried them in your pocket?

He hoped he could swim long enough to get rid of them.

Rossett stopped at number 14 and looked up at the old Victorian house. He tapped the knocker three times, firmly but not too firmly, a postman's knock, not a policeman's.

He watched through the old, distorting glass, looking into the hallway beyond, trying to make out if anyone was coming to answer the door. After a moment, a telltale shaft of light pierced the gloom as a small, shuffling shape approached and worked the lock.

Rossett had been expecting a child, so slight was the shadow. Instead, a tiny old lady opened the door, dressed in black, with hair the color of London smog, pulled back so tight it smoothed her brow but left her face a plowed field of wrinkles.

"Yes?"

"Mr. Chivers? Does he live here, please?" Rossett smiled, convivial and warm, giving no hint of the Webley tucked into the back of his trousers.

"He's upstairs," said the old lady, already turning away from the door and heading back to her room.

Rossett now understood the "A" part of the address. The old lady must have been letting out rooms to make ends meet.

"Is Mr. Chivers at home?" Rossett said to the rapidly disappearing landlady, who raised a wrinkled hand over her shoulder in reply.

"They've been fighting all night. I'm sorry I let them in here. No respect, no respect at all," she said, not bothering to look around before closing her door and leaving Rossett to explore for himself.

He cast a quick look back at the car, then stepped into the hall, shutting the front door behind him but making sure the latch was up so it didn't fully engage. He stood in the dim hallway and listened to the house. Somewhere a bird was singing, a songbird in a cage in one of the downstairs rooms. He couldn't hear anything from above.

The house was smarter than he'd imagined. Even a top-floor flat, he guessed, would be beyond an old docker's means.

The Germans must be paying well, he thought.

He crossed to the stairs and looked up into the gloom. He couldn't see a front door to a flat, so he guessed that Chivers merely rented the upstairs rooms and that the staircase acted as demarcation.

He tested the first step with his foot and stepped near the outer edge of the stairs, moving quickly to the top.

On the landing he paused again, looking at the doors. Each had a small hasp and staple to secure them from the outside, a cheaper alternative to a proper lock in a converted house. He could hear voices behind one of the doors, what might once have been the back bedroom. At least they wouldn't have seen Kate. He stepped to the door and considered taking out the Webley, but decided against it. If Chivers was stupid enough to try anything, Rossett knew he could handle the old man, whatever happened, and if Chivers wasn't behind the door he didn't want to give someone a heart attack.

Well, not yet, anyway.

He put his hand on the doorknob and listened again, hearing only soft voices. Rossett checked down the stairs and then took a deep breath. One, two, three . . .

He flung open the door and stepped into the room. Years of being a policeman had taught him that dominating a room by speed and confidence often served you better than having five coppers backing you up. If you could make the occupants think you should be there and that they shouldn't, the battle was often half won.

The room was a fair-sized converted bedroom. A small four-seater wooden dining table sat against one wall. On a brown leather sofa sat Chivers with a woman Rossett took to be his wife.

Both looked at him in shock, and Rossett realized the voices he'd been able to hear were coming from a wireless that was chatting to itself on a bureau in the alcove next to a tiny fireplace that would have struggled to heat a rabbit hutch.

As Rossett stepped into the room, half closing the door behind him, he didn't take his eyes off Chivers, who stared back, fingers gripping the arm of the settee and feet twitching, unsure whether to stand or not.

His wife, rising from her seat, didn't hesitate.

"'Oo the bleedin' 'ell are you? You can't—"

Rossett struck her with the back of his left hand across her face without taking his eyes off Chivers, who, in turn, didn't react to his wife's spinning to the floor at his feet. She cried out and tried to rise again, then sank back down, blood already dripping from her nose.

"Stay down," said Rossett, eyes still on Chivers.

"Stay down, Gloria," Chivers whispered, leaning forward a fraction and resting his hand on his wife's back gently.

"Ooh, George!" she wailed. "What 'ave you done now? What 'ave you done?"

Rossett's hand stung and he risked a glance at the woman before lifting a finger and putting it to his lips.

Chivers stared at Rossett, licked his lips, and shifted in his seat.

"Try to be quiet now, old girl, shush now," Chivers said to his wife, then turned back to Rossett. "Sorry I 'ad to leave you with the Germans. I stuck around as long as I—"

"Shut up," Rossett replied, his voice flat. "Get your coat."

"George?" Gloria spoke from the floor, her voice thick with the bloody nose.

"Shush, girl, it'll be all right."

"Don't go, George."

"Get up."

"I can't help you, Mr. Rossett. I would if I could, I swear I would, but I can't, see? I'm cut off. Nobody will touch me now. They think I'm in with Jerry, they think—"

"I know what you are. I know you sold me out, me and the boy, to Koehler. I know all about it, George, all about your file. Now get up before I kill you where you sit."

"My George isn't no collaborator! My George fights the Germans!" shrieked Gloria.

"Time is running out, George. This is your last chance." Rossett reached around and pulled the Webley from his belt. He leveled it at Chivers and cocked it. The noise of the gun filled the room and seemed to suck the air out in its wake. "You've got one chance to get through this alive: take it."

Chivers held up his hands like a bad actor. Rossett saw that they were shaking, and he briefly considered just shooting Chivers and walking out of the house, leaving him to bleed out on the settee. Being in the same room with him made Rossett feel dirty, rotten, by association. He raised the gun to arm's length and looked straight down the sight into the old man's eyes.

"Flanagan! Pat Flanagan will help you!" Gloria shouted.

"Who is that?"

"He's a boatman! Tell him, George! Tell him about Flanagan!"

The old man was breathing hard.

"Flanagan," he repeated, in a muffled voice.

"Who is he?"

"He's a boatman."

"How can he help us?"

"He sails out of St. Katharine. He's IRA, sort of." Gloria did the speaking again, still on the floor but becoming more assured, causing Rossett to wonder who actually ran the show that was Mr. and Mrs. Chivers.

"Sort of?"

"He'll do anything for money, run anything and anybody. He'll get you to Cork for the right price." She looked up at him, defiance given foundation by her knowledge and his need.

"'E'd punch the pope if you gave 'im a fiver." Chivers found his voice. "If you found them diamonds and we wave them at 'im, 'e'll get you out, Mr. Rossett, you and the boy, as far as you want. If I tell 'im, that is; 'e trusts me."

"Diamonds?" Her bleeding nose forgotten, Gloria looked from her husband to Rossett and back again.

"Take me to him," said Rossett.

"Diamonds? You never said nothing about no diamonds, George." Gloria groaned, trying to stand.

"'E might not be in town. 'E's a sailor, 'e comes and goes," Chivers said, watching his wife, but not helping her.

"You said they was just escaped." Gloria was suddenly more of a threat to her husband than Rossett.

"What if 'e's not in town, Mr. Rossett? What then?" Chivers asked.

"You'd better hope he is, because he's your only hope, George."

CHAPTER 56

ROSSETT MADE CHIVERS walk down the stairs in front of him, the gun in his waistband but eyes still on his back. Gloria leaned over the banister of the landing when they reached the bottom of the stairs. "Don't you hurt 'im! You make sure 'e gets back here all right, else you'll have me to answer to!"

Rossett carried on down the stairs, the words bouncing off him.

Chivers opened the front door and looked left and right.

"Which way?"

"The Volkswagen, parked in front. Get in."

Chivers stepped down onto the pavement and then half turned to Rossett.

"You're goin' to kill me, aren't you?"

"Maybe."

"Why should I 'elp you?"

"To stay alive a little longer, George, buy yourself some time, and maybe redeem yourself."

Chivers looked up at Rossett, who remained on the doorstep behind him.

"I'm sorry for tellin' Koehler."

Rossett motioned in the direction of the car.

"I ain't no different from you. I take the German pay packet same as you do. We're just the same, you know that?" Chivers continued. "I'm just tryin' to survive same as you, doin' what I 'ave to do. Lookin' after those that love me, same as you."

"Get in the car, George, now," Rossett said.

"I just want you to remember, we're the same. If it wasn't for you, I wouldn't have 'ad to sell out the kid. 'E'd still be in 'is bleedin' 'ouse with 'is family if it wasn't for you."

Rossett stared into the gray sky that was shaded light and dark with heavy rain clouds, then at Chivers.

"Get in the fucking car, or die here, right now. Your choice."

Chivers walked toward the car wearily, Rossett following him, almost as weary.

Chivers opened the passenger door and pulled the front seat forward, noticing Kate as he did so.

"Mr. Chivers!" Jacob cried and held out his hands to the old man, who smiled weakly.

"'Ello, boy! 'Ow you doin'?"

"We found the diamonds!" Jacob burst out, as he shuffled across to make room for Chivers to squeeze into the backseat.

Rossett dropped the front seat down on Chivers's legs, sat down in front, and closed the door.

"So you got 'em then?" Chivers asked. Rossett ignored him.

Kate started the car and pulled away from the curb, heading for the end of the road.

"Where are they? Can I see them?" Chivers tried again.

"Where is Flanagan?" Rossett asked.

"Let me see them, can I have a look-see?"

Rossett reached up and adjusted the mirror so that his eyes met Chivers's without having to turn his head.

"Flanagan," Rossett repeated, a statement of fact that demanded an answer.

"The Prospect of Whitby pub, near the Wapping docks. 'E'll be there, or someone who knows 'im will be."

Rossett glanced at Kate, who nodded silently, affirming that she knew the route. Jacob sensed all wasn't well and looked at each of the

adults in the car before reaching his little hand toward Chivers and tapping his leg. Chivers looked down at the hand and then at the boy, who
smiled. Chivers took the boy's hand in his own before returning to his
thoughts.

They'd driven some fifteen minutes before Chivers spoke again.

"You keep some interestin' company, Mr. Rossett."

Rossett looked at Chivers in the mirror, but didn't answer.

"Drivin' round London with Sir James Sterling's favorite niece
wouldn't be so bad, assumin' 'e hadn't been interrogatin' you in a cell a
few nights ago, of course."

Rossett looked at Chivers, then at Kate, then back at Chivers.

"What?"

"Oh, 'adn't you told 'im, love? Didn't you know 'oo she was? You
should watch 'er, she's a rum sort if there ever was. She pumps Koehler
for information all the while 'e's pumping 'er."

"Shut up," said Kate.

"And all the while she's passin' information one way, there's plenty
going the other way, as well, so as I 'eard. You play all those blokes a
pretty game, don't you, my darlin'?"

"It's bad enough having you in the car with the windows closed. I'd
rather not put up with listening to you as well," Kate said, adding to Rossett, "Pay no attention."

"It doesn't matter, just drive." Rossett stared at Chivers as he spoke,
and the old man smiled back before looking out the window again, still
smiling.

THE PROSPECT OF Whitby pub sat among warehouses on a narrow
road along the bank of the Thames. It was still early, and as they drove
past the first time, it appeared to Rossett that the pub was closed. He instructed Kate to stop and turn the car around before they headed back,
slower this time.

"It'll be open, I'm telling you. They never really shut," Chivers said
from the back.

"Pull over," Rossett instructed.

Kate pulled into the curb, keeping the engine running as she looked at Rossett.

"Maybe there is another way? Someone else who can help us?"

"Flanagan is your best chance," Chivers said from the backseat. "He knows everyone and everything that moves on this river, plus, you can trust him."

"Like we can trust you?" Kate said, turning in her seat.

"You're one to talk," Chivers replied, sticking out his chin to her.

Rossett said nothing. He opened his door and stepped out of the car onto the pavement. Resting his elbows on the roof, he looked up and down the street. A few old-fashioned carters led their flea-bitten, half-knackered horses along the cobbles, and the odd pedestrian crossed here and there. It was a normal dockland street.

Rossett tapped his hand on the roof of the car nervously and lit a cigarette while watching the pub, some one hundred feet away, for signs of life. After a couple of minutes he saw two dockers cross the road and approach the front door. One of the dockers cupped his hands to the glass and looked in before banging on the frame with the palm of his hand. After a moment the door opened and the dockers slipped inside. The door immediately closed behind them.

"See," Chivers said, "I told you, you can get a drink twenty-four hours a day in there."

Rossett bent down to look into the car and said to Kate, "Lock the doors. If anything looks strange, or if I don't come out, just go. Don't wait, don't come looking, just go, do you understand?"

Kate nodded. She was about to say something, but didn't. She just started the engine and looked at Rossett.

Rossett pulled the seat forward and helped Chivers out, pulling him through the door and positioning him on the curb next to him, close enough to grab if the old man attempted to run.

Rossett looked back at Kate. "Will you be all right?"

Kate nodded.

"Stay with Kate, Jacob. I'll not be long."

"Do you promise?"

"I promise."

The boy smiled and looked out the window at Chivers, who gave a little wave and a watery smile.

"Be careful," Kate said softly.

"I will. We're nearly there, it'll be fine. If anything happens, if you have to leave, I'll call you at the flat tonight. I've got the number."

"I'll wait for you."

"I want you to have these. Look after them." Rossett passed Kate the urn with the diamonds. "If I don't call, you'll need them."

Kate slipped it into her handbag on the floor.

"I'll give them back to you when you come out," she said.

Rossett nodded, stepped back from the car, and closed the door. He looked at Chivers, who shrugged apologetically and then shoved his hands in his coat pockets.

"If you fuck this up, George, I will shoot you in the face and then kill your wife. If you do as you are told, arrange for Jacob to get to Ireland and then on to Canada, the slate is clean between us. You'll live and that will be that."

"I'm riskin' a lot takin' you in there, Mr. Rossett. If these fellas don't like it, I could end up in some serious trouble. I think it's only fair I get something for that trouble."

"You get your life, George. Now get walking."

Chivers shook his head and rocked on his heels a moment before finally setting off with Rossett toward the pub.

CHAPTER 57

AS THE DOCKERS had done, Chivers approached the doors and cupped his hands to the glass. He waited a moment, then stepped back and banged the palm of his hand on the door.

"Could you try to not look so much like a policeman?" he said to Rossett.

Rossett took an involuntary half step back when he heard a heavy bolt sliding, and the door opened two inches. A woman looked at him and then at Chivers, only half her face showing.

"What do you want?" she said to Chivers.

"A pint and a word with Pat."

The woman looked at Rossett, then back at Chivers.

"Who's he?"

"A friend. We've got some business. Open the door."

Rossett thought about just shoving the door open and walking in but decided to let Chivers continue the negotiations.

"Pat won't be happy with you bringing coppers calling." The woman stepped back from the door and it swung open just wide enough for Chivers and Rossett to step in.

The pub was dark, very dark. The curtains were drawn on the windows that opened out onto the street.

Rossett squinted into the gloom and saw that behind the door sat a heavyset middle-aged man who had forearms like hams and a neck that would have graced a prize bull. The man stared blankly at Rossett with the confidence of someone who had a simple purpose in life. Rossett hoped he never found out what that purpose was.

The woman slid the bolt back into place and hurried past them toward the bar. She lifted the flap and took up her station behind the pumps. Chivers ambled over and Rossett noticed that the old man had regained some of his swagger. Whether it was for show or because the old man knew something that Rossett didn't worried him slightly, but the weight of the Webley against his back reassured him.

He joined Chivers at the bar and watched as the woman poured two pints of bitter, setting them down with heavy thumps.

"I ain't got no money," Chivers said, lifting the pint to his lips and gulping a third of it in one voluminous swallow.

Rossett tossed some coins on the bar, picked up his own pint, and turned to look around the pub. His eyes had adjusted partway, but dark corners still hid the identity of the shadows that sat in them. The pub smelled of stale beer, and the sawdust on the floor was dotted with cigarette butts.

There was a time when Rossett would have strutted through this sort of pub roistering undesirables and those outside the law, and it struck him that he was now hiding in the shadows with the members of the underworld he'd once terrorized.

Chivers nudged his elbow and flicked his head toward an empty table in a dark alcove.

"Come and sit down. They don't want folk at the bar when it's closed."

Rossett followed him to the table and sat with his back to the wall so he could see the pub and anyone who might choose to approach them. Chivers took the seat next to him, and Rossett placed his nearly full glass down and took out his cigarettes. He took one out and offered the packet to Chivers, who took one and nodded thanks.

"Does Flanagan even know we're here?" Rossett said quietly.

"Someone will have told 'im."

"What if he's at sea?"

"'E won't be. That bastard 'asn't set foot on a boat in years. 'E just organizes things, cargo, people. 'Ee's a fixer."

"You said he was IRA?"

"'E is, or 'e was. Most of them headed into southern Ireland after the occupation. It's a different proposition fightin' the Brits than it is fightin' the Germans."

"Will he be able to get the boy out of Ireland?"

"'E'll be able to get 'im a passport, probably American. 'E 'as contacts. It'll take a few days, but with a passport 'e'll get the kid out."

Rossett took another drink and tapped his lit cigarette against the side of his glass. Chivers watched him and then leaned in close.

"Listen, I'm sorry. I didn't want to drop you in it. I like the kid. I like you. I just 'ad to do what I 'ad to do. You understand? I'm tryin' to get by, tryin' to survive. This ain't easy, the way I live." Chivers shook his head sadly before continuing. "I'm up to my eyes in shit, shit from the Germans, shit from the resistance, shit from me missus. I'm just tryin' to survive, do you know what I mean?"

"We're square for now, but do it again and you'll be sorry. Understand?" Rossett looked at Chivers, who nodded back.

"Yeah, I understand."

They sat in silence for a few minutes before a shadow appeared at the door and the flat knock-knock of a fist echoed round the pub, which fell silent as the barmaid crossed the floor and pulled back the bolt.

Rossett watched the big man behind the door drop his hands out of sight as he waited to see who came in. The barmaid stepped back and a tiny figure followed by two hulking dockers entered the bar. Chivers nudged Rossett's leg under the table.

"That's him, the little fella."

The tiny figure patted the barmaid on the behind as she passed him and the three men followed her to the bar. The murmur of voices resumed and Rossett watched as the men took their drinks and looked around the pub. Rossett wasn't fooled by the seemingly relaxed nature of the group. He knew he was being sized up, so he attempted to affect an air of relaxed disinterest, taking another sip from his pint and occasionally flicking his cigarette with his thumb.

He knew he was a bad actor, but realized Chivers was worse as soon as the old man pretended to take a drink from his empty glass and then gave a hearty "aah" of satisfaction.

Eventually, the three men broke from the bar and headed toward Rossett and Chivers.

Flanagan sat down opposite Rossett at the small round table while the two other men pulled up seats behind their boss. Flanagan took a drink from his pint and then gestured to the empty glass on the table in front of him.

"Could I get you fellas a pint?" he said with a hard Northern Irish accent. Although the question was friendly, the tone wasn't.

"No," said Rossett.

"Yes," said Chivers.

"I should have known better than to ask you, George. Here, get these fellas a pint now," Flanagan said without looking around, and the younger of his two lads stood up and went to the bar. Rossett looked at the remaining heavy, who stared back, dead-eyed like a shark, sipping at his beer and licking the thick mustache that was asleep on his top lip.

"How've you been keeping then, George?" Flanagan asked.

"Not too bad, Pat. Duckin' and divin', you know 'ow it is."

"Ducking and diving, you say? I heard the only thing you've been ducking is Sterling's boys."

"We 'ad a misunderstandin', that's all."

"I heard there was a misunderstanding down the timber yard, as well." Flanagan looked at Rossett as he said this and Rossett stared back, giving nothing away, although he felt sure that there were no secrets left around the table, and that Flanagan knew all there was to know.

"Was there? I've not been around, Pat." Chivers bluffed it and failed badly, his quavering voice giving the game away.

Flanagan chuckled and took a sip of his drink, and the three of them sat in silence until the younger heavy returned with two pints and three glasses of whiskey on a tray. He placed each of the drinks down without speaking and then resumed his seat behind his boss, putting the tray on the floor.

Rossett looked at the whiskey and made a silent vow not to drink it.

The vow lasted for less than three seconds. Flanagan picked up his drink and held the glass up.

"To old friends and new friends," he said. Chivers picked up his glass and chinked it against Flanagan's, then looked at Rossett, waiting for him to join the toast. Rossett frowned, picked up the whiskey, and chinked his glass against the others, and all three men took a drink.

The whiskey was harsh, and Rossett grimaced and twisted his head on his burning throat before putting down the glass and reaffirming his oath to not drink anymore. This time, he meant it.

"So, what is it you're after, George?" Flanagan sat back and clasped his tiny hands on the table in front of him, adopting the pose of a bank manager chatting to a customer.

"My friend John here needs something taken out of the country."

"Would that be the Jew?" Flanagan turned to look at Rossett, who suddenly felt less assured than he had a few moments earlier. The little Irishman smiled at Rossett, baring pearly white teeth that looked slightly too large for the face they sat in. "Oh, sure now, there's no se- crets round here, Detective Sergeant Rossett. We're old friends, you and me, from before the war. Do you not remember?"

Rossett dropped his hands into his lap and regretted putting the Webley in the small of his back. The closeness of his chair to the wall would make drawing the pistol difficult; he'd have to push the table over with one hand while reaching for the gun with the other. He eyed the two men behind Flanagan and saw they too had dropped their hands out of sight.

The odds weren't good.

"I don't recall us meeting," he said.

"Sure now, and why would you? It was a long time ago, water under the bridge," Flanagan replied, waving his hand to assure Rossett.

It didn't work.

Chivers looked from Flanagan to Rossett and back again. Rossett stared at the little Irishman and a dim flicker of recognition stirred in his memory of an arrest a long time ago, back in his beat days at Wapping.

"I think I remember, was it theft?"

"Money with menaces. There were no charges, and you played a fair hand, Detective Sergeant. I'm sure we're among friends now."

Rossett remembered there had been rumors of a crew of Irishmen demanding protection money from local businesses. Rossett had stumbled across a beating being handed down one evening at a shop near the docks, cracked a few skulls with his truncheon, and dragged a few lads to the cells, but the shopkeeper hadn't pressed charges against his assailants and they'd walked the next day.

Rossett recalled that the Irish had moved on to new pastures. He guessed they had spread back into the area once the invasion was complete. There was a lot of money to be made smuggling to and from a neutral Ireland, and the IRA was looking for new income streams after things had tightened up in the north.

"So what can I do for you, Sergeant? Is it the Jew boy?"

Rossett nodded.

"I hear you normally use other methods to get them out of the country." Flanagan smiled at his own joke, and Rossett saw one of the men behind him chuckle and glance to his partner before returning his gaze to Rossett.

Flanagan took a drink and then shifted his gaze to Chivers, slowly, taking his time.

"What's your end in this, George?"

"I just want the kid sorted, that's all."

"Forgive me, George, but I've known you a long time, and you don't do anything for nothing, so what's in it for you?"

"His life," Rossett said, and all eyes turned to him.

Flanagan nodded and took another sip of whiskey.

"So you've found out about George's little line in selling information, Detective Sergeant? I would have thought that would have made you two bosom pals?"

"How he earns his money isn't my concern. My only concern is the boy. Can you get him out of the country?"

Flanagan smiled warmly and then took another sip of his whiskey.

"I can get anything out of the country, and, for that matter, anything in. You don't need to worry about whether it can be done. You just need to worry about if you can afford it."

Rossett nodded and reached into his coat pocket. Both men behind Flanagan seemed to flinch as Rossett moved, but Flanagan merely smiled that smug smile, waiting for the bargaining to commence.

"How far will this get him?" Rossett placed his handkerchief on the table and nodded his head toward it.

Flanagan broadened his smile.

"I do like a good surprise. Now, I wonder what we have here then." He reached forward and unfolded the handkerchief on the table carefully, one fold at a time, until he exposed a solitary diamond in the center of the white cloth.

Flanagan's hand hovered over the stone. His fingers reached out to it but seemed unable to pick it up, as if the stone was pushing him away. The Irishman looked up at Rossett and then back down at the diamond before finally picking it up off the table.

"Would you look at that now?" he said softly to himself, leaning back so as to hold the gem up in front of his eyes.

The two heavies behind him strained to see what Flanagan held. Rossett took the distraction as an opportunity to shift in his chair and reach around his back to pull the Webley free of his waistband and slip it into his pocket. Once the gun was secure he took a sip of his beer and leaned back in the seat again.

"I take it that will get the boy to Dublin?" Rossett broke the spell.

"That it will," Flanagan replied.

"And any papers he needs to get onward out of Ireland?"

"Aye."

"Will two of them get someone else out?"

Flanagan lowered the stone. Gradually regaining some composure, he focused again on Rossett.

"Two of them?"

"The boy and his female guardian."

"Getting two people out is much more difficult than one." Flanagan gave the smile again, and Rossett noticed that he had folded his fist around the diamond and was clutching it to his chest.

"'Ow much to get three people out?" Chivers spoke this time, waving his hand at Rossett, who looked at him, concerned.

"Three? At this rate we'll be evacuating half of London." Flanagan was now leaning forward, his glee barely contained.

"It's just two," Rossett said.

"It's three," Chivers looked at Rossett. "You're goin' too, man. There's nothin' left 'ere for you."

"What'll it be, gentlemen? Any more for anymore?" Flanagan smiled, took a drink of whiskey, and swilled the glass under his nose, raising his eyebrows with the slightest of winks at Rossett.

Rossett looked at Chivers and shook his head.

"We need a minute," Chivers said to Flanagan and stood up from the table, grabbing Rossett's sleeve as he went. Rossett rose and followed the old man to the bar.

"Whatever you think of me, whatever I've done to you and the boy, all of it doesn't matter right now. None of it was personal. I just did what I had to do, understand?" Chivers leaned in close to Rossett. "So what I'm sayin' to you now, I'm saying as someone who's lived a bit . . . both sides of the law. Someone who's survived, yeah?"

Rossett nodded.

"Right. Then you've got to think about this. You've got a chance, better than any chance you'll ever get, and you've got the means to start again."

"I can't go. I'll be slung in prison as soon as my feet touch the soil in Canada," Rossett whispered, leaning in close to Chivers while looking over his shoulder at the three Irishmen sitting some twenty feet away.

"Don't you understand? When you get to Canada, you won't be John Rossett; you'll be whoever these fellas 'ave put on your passport. This is a new start for you. If you want, you can be the boy's father, and you can even be married to the bird! You can be anything you want to be. This is a new life, another chance. For God's sake, you don't even have to go to

Canada, you can head to America." Chivers grabbed Rossett's arm as he spoke and Rossett found himself dumbly staring at the old man as the realization struck home.

"But I . . ."

"I what? You've nothin' 'ere, and now you've a chance. Use the diamonds to get away!"

"But they're Jacob's."

"'Is grandfather wanted them used to look after the boy, so use 'em. Go with 'im, be with 'im, 'elp 'im grow up and start again."

Rossett slowly started to nod in agreement.

"I suppose . . ."

Chivers gripped tighter on Rossett's arm and led him back to the table, dragging him down into his seat. Flanagan leaned forward again, and Rossett noticed the little man had poured some of Rossett's whiskey into his own glass while they had been away.

"Could they make it to America?" Chivers asked Flanagan, who held out his hands in an open gesture.

"For the right price they can go to the moon."

"What about papers?" Chivers probed again.

"I can get U.S. passports from Dublin, and we have brothers in Boston who can arrange things at that end. Like I said, I can do anything for the right price."

"What would that price be for three?" Chivers leaned back and took a sip of his drink. Rossett watched and saw the old man in a new light.

Flanagan rubbed his chin theatrically and then placed the diamond he was still holding on to the handkerchief in front of him on the table. As he thought, he carefully folded the handkerchief back over it, as if putting a child to bed.

"Well, I'll have to have this thing looked at by a friend, but assuming it's genuine . . ."

"It's genuine," interjected Chivers.

"Well, assuming it is, and the others are of similar quality . . ."

"They are."

"I'd want five of them, one for the boy, two each for the adults."

"Does that include the necessary papers at the other end?"

"That's an awful lot to ask for."

"Papers included or no deal, Pat."

"Jesus, George."

"You're making a packet 'ere, Pat, and you know it."

"Aww, go on then, papers included, for five stones, all the same size as this beauty."

"Deal," said Chivers, sitting back and slapping the table with the palm of his hand, making the glasses jump.

Rossett looked back and forth between Chivers and Flanagan, who sat smiling, waiting for some confirmation from him.

"All right, five diamonds," he said after a pause. "Two up front, three on completion. We all travel together, and we go quickly, as soon as possible."

"Is tonight soon enough?" Flanagan replied. "I've a boat crossing to Cork on the tide, the *Iris*. She has the necessary amenities to get you out of London. Once in Ireland you'll have to wait a few days, but things will be quieter there. I have friends who will look after you."

Rossett beckoned Flanagan in close and leaned forward.

"If you double-cross me, or let me down, you'll wish you'd never been born, Flanagan. I'll take you apart bit by bit and make you eat yourself, do you understand?"

Flanagan smiled and raised a calming hand to his two men, who had by now stood up behind him defensively.

"Detective Sergeant, let me assure you, I know all about you and your reputation. I also understand your concerns as to placing yourself and your . . . charges . . . in the hands of others. But you can rest assured, I trade on my reputation. I'm a man who cannot afford to let his customers down. Not because I'm scared of them, far from it, but my failure to deliver on my promises would be an issue for future business. Do you understand?"

Rossett nodded.

"I've worked with Pat for a long time," Chivers said placatingly behind Rossett.

"Just so we understand each other," Rossett said.

"We do." Flanagan drank the last of his whiskey, then set the glass down with a bang on the table like an auctioneer's gavel. "Until tonight, gentlemen. George, you know where, at the stairs. I'll see you at eleven. Don't be late now. Time, tide, and Pat Flanagan wait for no man."

Flanagan stood up and walked away from the table with purpose. His two men sat and stared at Rossett for a moment before slowly rising to their feet, nodding to Chivers and following their boss.

It was only after they had gone that Rossett noticed his handkerchief and the diamond had disappeared with them.

"That's it, boy, deal done."

"Can we trust him?"

"'E'd cut your throat for a fiver, but if 'e says 'e'll do somethin', 'e'll do it. 'E's never let me down in all the years I've known 'im."

Rossett glanced at the old man and raised an eyebrow.

"So, if I can trust you, I can trust him. Is that what you're saying?"

"I'm your security at this end," said Chivers. "If I don't 'ear from you, I'll let it be known Flanagan 'asn't delivered."

"And if he takes you out as well? These diamonds are worth a lot of money. They can make a man do things he wouldn't normally."

"If 'e lets me down, if 'e comes after me, 'e's got the communist resistance on 'is tail. If 'e lets down that bird you're with, 'e has the royalist resistance on 'is tail. Don't forget, I can get word to Sterling to let 'im know where 'is niece 'as gone and 'oo she's with if I 'ave to."

"Sterling wants you dead."

Chivers waved a dismissive hand.

"A crate of machine guns and ammo will sort 'im out. 'E likes to think 'e's in charge, but I know what strings to pull. You're on your way, son. You're gettin' out of it."

Rossett sat back in the chair and looked around the pub before lifting his beer.

"We'll see, George. We'll see."

CHAPTER 58

"**W**HERE HAS HE gone?"

"Where has 'oo gone?"

Koehler wiped a weary hand across his face and then looked back at Gloria. "Your husband, Gloria, where has he gone?"

"I ain't seen 'im in weeks, Mr. Koehler, I swear. All's I've 'eard is that 'e's been down the docks, up to his usual. You know what 'e's like; 'e's always up to something."

"Gloria, I'm tired. Please, stop this, and just tell me. Where has he gone?"

"I swear down, Mr. Koehler, I swear on my—" Gloria broke off as her landlady was roughly pushed into the room by Schmitt. The old lady looked around at the assembled soldiers and then fixed her watery eyes on Koehler, who cocked his head at her and then at Schmitt.

"She heard them arguing last night. Then a tall man came this morning and left with Chivers," Schmitt said.

"Did you hear where they were going?" Koehler asked her.

"No, sir, but he looked a terrible man who took Mr. Chivers, a terrible fierce man."

"Rossett," said Schmitt, redundantly.

Koehler waved a hand, dismissing the old woman, and Schmitt swung her around and into the arms of a soldier by the door. The old woman almost fell, and Koehler frowned at his colleague before turning back to Gloria.

"So, we know now that you are a liar."

"Please, sir. Please, my George is a good man," Gloria sobbed, and Koehler held up his hand.

"Stop, please."

"This brute came in 'ere and dragged 'im off. 'E 'it me, 'e did, like I was a man, just 'it me in the face, just like that!" She waved a fist at Koehler, who rubbed his eyes. "My George done 'is best. 'E tried, lord help 'im, but 'e's an old man. Sick 'e is, all those years in the cold they've ravaged 'im, ravaged 'im."

"Can I shoot her?" Schmitt said in German to Koehler, who shook his head.

"Gloria, please." Koehler held up his hand again to bring the lament to an end.

"My George wants a quiet life. We need to enjoy our retirement, quietly like . . ."

Koehler finally signaled to one of the guards, who roughly shook Gloria, raised his hand as if to strike her, then tilted his head, putting a finger to his lips.

"Shush."

Gloria sobbed, then fell silent.

"Listen to me, Gloria. Your husband is in a lot of trouble, and so are you. Do you understand?" Koehler paused, letting the words sink in. "You have a very small window of opportunity here, very, very small. Once I close this window it is gone, and these men will take you outside into the street and kill you. Do you understand?"

Gloria's knees buckled slightly and she looked at the two young soldiers flanking her, neither of whom looked happy at the prospect of killing her. The younger one looked at his colleague and then back at Koehler, stiffening to attention.

"I can 'elp, sir, please . . ."

Koehler wagged the finger again.

"So, before I close this window, Gloria, you have one chance, and one chance only, to save your life, and possibly that of your husband. I'll ask you again. Where has your husband gone with Rossett?"

"Pat Flanagan. 'E's gone to see the Irishman, sir."

Koehler looked at Schmitt, who shrugged.

"Who is this Flanagan?"

"A smuggler?" Schmitt said, causing Gloria to look at him.

"Guns, sir, guns and other things, 'e can get you anything, but 'e's a nasty man, sir." She looked at Koehler. "You know what those Irish are like, sir, all the same."

"Where will we find him?"

"I don't know where 'e lives, but I know where 'e carries out 'is business. In all the pubs down Wapping way. Dockers' pubs, sir, not nice at all, Mr. Koehler."

"Is that where George went?"

"I think so, sir. I can't say for sure though. That man dragged 'im out before I 'eard tell."

"Take her to Charing Cross." Koehler waved a dismissive hand, and Gloria started screaming as the guards dragged her from the room. Koehler closed his eyes as the screaming went up a decibel on the stairs. He only opened them again once the front door had been slammed behind her.

Schmitt shook his head.

"I would have thought Chivers would want locking up sooner than being stuck in here with that."

"You should use her when you question suspects," Koehler replied, gesturing for Schmitt to give him a cigarette. The other German fished in his coat, produced the packet, and handed it across with his lighter.

"Do we go find this pub?"

Koehler shook his head. He lit a cigarette and passed the packet back to Schmitt, who remained standing on the spot recently occupied by Gloria.

"Waste of time, they won't be there now. We'll set up at the local police station, low key. If we go in heavy we'll make a bigger mess of things than we did at the cemetery. Just get a few men again, plus Werner. I want every informant from the docks spoken to quickly. We need to find out quickly who this Irishman is and where he works; we don't have much time. And don't, whatever you do, make any mention of the diamonds."

"May I speak freely?" Schmitt said.

"As long as you are quick, yes."

"All of this has been handled low key. Pretty much everything except the breakout from the cells has happened off the record so far."

"And?"

"Would I be right in saying, if you'll forgive me, that there is another reason for that secrecy?"

"What are you saying, Schmitt?"

Schmitt checked the door and then leaned in close to Koehler, resting his hand on the arm of the chair so that he was just inches above his superior.

"I'm talking about the diamonds. I think I understand what you are trying to do."

"What am I trying to do?"

"If you can get to the diamonds before anyone else, well . . . let's just say I understand." Schmitt winked at Koehler, smiling.

"Did you just wink at me?"

Schmitt frowned.

"I . . . er . . ."

"I'm trying to keep myself alive, Schmitt. I don't care about diamonds, I care about staying alive. If, and it is a big if, we find these possibly imaginary diamonds, they will be handed in with whatever prisoners we turn up. Is that understood?"

"Of course, sir. I thought, well, with you being so intent on keeping things quiet, that . . ."

"You don't hunt rats with a bass drum, Schmitt."

"Sir?"

Koehler took another drag on his cigarette, then looked around for an ashtray. When he didn't find one, he tapped the end, letting the ash drop onto the carpet.

"Have you ever banged a drum in a barn full of rats, Schmitt?"

Schmitt didn't reply; he merely looked confused.

"They scatter, into shadows and corners. You might kill a few in the rush, but once they are hiding you have no chance of finding them, and to make things worse, all your neighbors will come to see what you are doing, and tell you how you are doing it all wrong."

Schmitt nodded as though he understood, even though he didn't, so Koehler continued.

"The reason I want this low key is to protect us. The less that is known, the less damage it can do us. If Rossett turns up on the BBC in Canada a month before he is due to be given an Iron Cross by the Führer, things will be difficult to explain, won't they?"

"Yes, sir."

"But if we can get him, and a few other players, we will look good. So forget about diamonds, forget about anything other than finding Rossett and the Jew. If you do that, we might just come out the other side with our careers and our throats intact. Yes?"

"Yes, sir. Of course, sir."

Koehler stood up, brushed past Schmitt, and stalked out of the room onto the landing. Werner stood to attention at the top of the stairs and saluted.

"The woman is en route back to Charing Cross, sir."

"How many men do we have?"

"Fifteen, sir, one truck and your car. Plus the others out and about watching addresses."

"Mount up. We're going to Wapping."

Werner saluted as Koehler passed him heading down the narrow staircase. Schmitt emerged from the room, made eye contact with Werner, and shook his head.

"Madness," he whispered as he passed the old soldier without looking at him.

Werner didn't reply. He just followed orders.

CHAPTER 59

FROM HIS VANTAGE point at the top of the road, Rossett watched Koehler bounce down the steps and out of the house. The clouds had let go and the fine drizzle clung to his face like oil as he looked back toward where the little Volkswagen was parked behind him, hidden on the corner among some other cars. Kate had stopped next to a school yard and some children were playing outside, oblivious to the rain. Rossett could see Jacob watching the children, wiping the side window with his sleeve occasionally.

He turned back to watch the troops mount up and the two vehicles pull away. He waited a moment, watching, thinking, then returned to the Volkswagen and climbed in.

"Did you see my Gloria?" Chivers pulled at his shoulder from the seat behind.

"No."

"I need to check she's all right."

"You can't."

"I 'ave to!"

Rossett twisted in his seat to look at Chivers, catching Kate's concerned eye as he did so.

"Look, George, you can't go back to the house yet. They might have left men in there, waiting for you, waiting for us. Where else can we go?"

"We could go to my flat," Kate offered.

"No, you didn't go to work today. If he knows you called about George, he will have put two and two together, and we can't risk that he's having the place watched."

"What call about me?" Chivers leaned forward, looking from one to the other.

Rossett ignored him.

"We need somewhere where nobody will notice us."

"What about the docks?" Chivers tried again.

"We'll stand out like a sore thumb."

"We could just drive around for a few hours?" Kate again.

"Too risky, they might have circulated the car."

They sat in silence for a moment, the only sounds the children playing outside and the odd flurry of rain on the car roof.

"We can't sit 'ere all day," Chivers said.

"Your uncle," Rossett said, looking at Kate.

"My uncle James? Are you mad?"

"Will he be home?"

"I can call his office, but I'm not sure."

"Sterling?" Chivers chimed in.

"He's the only one I can think of. We'll be safe there, for a few hours."

"It might have escaped your attention 'e had his men shooting at you the other night," Chivers said, shaking his head.

"Things have changed. Now someone he loves is involved," Rossett said, looking at Kate.

"I bleedin' well 'ope so," Chivers replied as the car started.

MOST OF THE large houses in Knightsbridge had been commandeered by the Germans in the first few months of the occupation, but a few still stood apart as little English castles. The privileged classes had just about retained a toehold in the most expensive area of London. A few had even managed to regain their properties from the Germans after long and arduous court cases, helped by good lawyers and a lot of pa-

tience. What helped more was being a knight of the realm, especially a
knight of the realm who worked alongside the Germans and had been
a covert supporter of Oswald Mosley throughout most of the thirties,
before he became prime minister, when he'd prowled London in polished boots and a black shirt.

Sir James Sterling's front door had been safe from the German jack-
boot from day one.

Rossett, Kate, Chivers, and Jacob stood in the black-and-white-tiled
foyer of the mansion as the maid went to fetch the master of the house.

Chivers looked around, then up at the decorated ceiling and the
chandelier, and shook his head.

"Bigger than the Locarno bleedin' ballroom."

Jacob stared up, following the old man's lead, his mouth open in
wonder; then he looked at Rossett and smiled.

Rossett smiled back and squeezed the boy's hand.

Down the hall they heard Sterling instructing the maid to make tea.
It was only when he finally saw who was standing at the end of the hallway that he stopped.

"What the hell do you think you are doing here?" Sterling suddenly
charged down the hall, a scrunched-up copy of the *Times* in one hand.

"We had nowhere else to go, Uncle James," Kate said.

"Coming here is madness. You must leave at once."

"I don't think so," said Rossett. "We'll stay a few hours, then go."

"No, no, no. I'll not have it. You must leave and take these with you."
Sterling spoke to Kate and pointed at Chivers and Jacob.

Rossett released the boy's hand and stepped forward to Sterling,
taking hold of his arm and pulling him close.

"We're staying," Rossett whispered.

"I can't allow it. I've too much to lose."

"We're staying," Rossett repeated. "I'm hungry." Rossett stared at
Sterling, who stared back before swallowing and looking at the other
three.

After a beat, he called, "Mary! Where are you, girl?"

The maid stepped forward from a distant doorway and gave a half bow.

"Yes, sir."

"Tea and, I don't know, something to eat in my study."

"Is everything all right, sir?" The girl eyed Rossett and seemed unsure.

Rossett stared at Sterling, who licked his lips.

"These men are associates of my niece's and mine. Everything is fine, dear, absolutely fine. Now run along."

"We'd rather not be disturbed this afternoon," Rossett said to the maid, who looked at her master for confirmation, unsure of the situation.

"After you've brought up the food, we'd prefer some privacy," Sterling confirmed with a wave of his hand.

"Yes, sir."

After the maid retreated, Sterling turned to face Rossett again, his face angry but his voice level.

"Are you happy now?" he hissed.

"You've just saved two lives," Rossett replied.

"Follow me." Sterling spun on his heel and retreated along the hall. Rossett glanced at Chivers, who shook his head and followed with Jacob.

Kate stepped forward and slid her arm around Rossett's, pulling him close so she could whisper in his ear.

"I think this will work," she said softly, watching the other three walk ahead.

"It better. I have to keep the boy safe for a few more hours . . . and you."

Kate nodded, her eyes on Rossett so intently that he felt his heart kick an extra beat in his chest. Kate opened her mouth as if to speak, then looked down at the floor. Rossett felt his head being drawn to her by something stronger than gravity.

He opened his mouth and kissed her. Closing his eyes in unison with hers, he felt her hand tighten on his arm and her body lean into him. His free hand hovered for a moment and then reached up and touched the side of her face.

"We'll be fine, won't we?" Kate whispered.

Rossett nodded.

"Do you promise?"

Rossett smiled.

"I promise," he whispered back, feeling what it meant to lie to someone he loved.

CHAPTER 60

THE TICK-TOCK OF the clock was the only sound in the study except for Jacob's occasional turn of a page. The boy was lying on the floor in front of a cold marble fireplace looking through an encyclopedia Kate had brought down from one of the floor-to-ceiling bookcases that lined three of the walls of the room.

Sterling stood up out of the red leather wing chair he'd been squirming in for the last three hours and flexed his back.

"Where are you going?" Rossett broke the silence, his voice as sudden as a brick through the window.

"Where I am going has got nothing to do with you," Sterling replied.

"Sit down."

"Sit down? Who are you to tell me to—"

"Sit."

Sterling sighed and plopped back into the chair, slapping his hands against the oxblood leather armrests.

"It's been three hours. You've come to my house and made me sit like some sort of prisoner. Don't you think you could at least extend me the courtesy of telling me what is going on?"

"No."

Sterling sighed again and rolled his head around, trying to free up the tension in his throbbing neck, then drummed his fingers on the arm of his chair, showing the frustration of a man who was accustomed to being in control but who was now in the hands of others.

"What is to stop me from just walking out of this room?"

"Me," Rossett replied.

"Is this the sort of man you consort with?" Sterling turned to Kate. "Your father would be disgusted."

"Be quiet," said Rossett.

"Why?"

"If you don't, I'll kill you."

Sterling simply shook his head and looked at his niece. "Do you see? The man is an animal and a traitor. Your father would spin in his . . ." Outside, the gray afternoon was dimming down to darkness, and somewhere in the house a clock chimed four times. A few more minutes went by and a distant telephone rang.

The ringing stopped, and a moment passed before a soft knock came on the door.

"Come!" shouted Sterling, and the young maid entered. She hovered at the door reluctantly, eyeing Rossett before speaking to Sterling.

"I'm sorry to bother you, sir. It's the telephone, a Mr. Wilson, sir. He said it was important. I told him you were not to be disturbed, but he insisted."

Sterling considered the message before looking at Rossett.

"May I?" He gestured that he wished to take the call, but Rossett shook his head by way of reply. "It's a business matter, nothing more," Sterling added.

"No."

Sterling rolled his eyes again.

"Tell Mr. Wilson I am tied up somewhat, and that I'll not be able to make our meeting today."

The maid nodded and backed out of the room, and silence took her place.

Another half hour passed before Chivers got up and wandered across to the fireplace. Jacob was now asleep on the floor, and the old man knelt with difficulty and started to build a fire with some coal and kindling. When the fire was lit, Chivers creaked to his feet and looked around the room.

"Where's the booze?" He looked at Sterling, who shook his head.

"I don't have 'booze.'"

"You posh blokes always have a bottle to 'and. Come on, where's the booze?"

"There are drinks in that bureau, but it most certainly isn't booze." Sterling directed a long, languid finger toward a polished wood drinks cabinet set among the books. Chivers rubbed his hands together and winked at Kate as he passed her. He pulled open the doors of the cabinet, which lit up inside as he did so, and whistled quietly through his teeth.

"Blimey, there's enough 'ere to get me pissed till Christmas." He picked up a bottle of brandy and studied the label at arm's length before pulling the cork and sniffing it, then turning to Sterling and winking.

"That is vintage, man, almost one hundred pounds a bottle," Sterling said, waving a finger at Chivers.

Chivers took a slug straight from the bottle, then tilted his head forward and gasped.

"An 'undred quid? You've been robbed, mate." The old man poured himself a large glass before holding the bottle up and waggling it at Rossett.

"No."

Chivers shrugged his shoulders and poured two smaller glasses, one for Kate and one for Sterling. He handed Kate hers and crossed the room to Sterling, setting the glass down noisily on the small table next to the other man's chair.

Sterling studied the glass and then wiped a small spill away with his hand before picking it up and holding it under his nose.

"Are you not drinking, Sergeant?" Sterling asked.

Rossett shook his head.

"I suppose you'll make something up about being on duty?"

Rossett ignored him.

They had a long evening ahead.

THE ROOM WAS quiet when suddenly, somewhere in the house, a bell sounded once, then once again, and everyone jumped.

"What was that?" Rossett looked at Sterling.

"The doorbell. It must be a caller; the girl will get it," Sterling replied lazily, chin in hand.

Rossett rose from the chair immediately, pulled the Browning from his pocket, slipped the safety, and pulled back the slide, letting it click forward under its own sprung speed.

He looked first at Chivers, who held out a hand to take the gun, but Rossett turned to Kate.

"Here, take this. If he moves, shoot him."

"But—" Kate tried to speak.

"Shoot him," Rossett cut her off. "Shoot him for Jacob. Shoot him for your freedom. Do it for us." As Rossett spoke he pushed the Browning into Kate's hand.

"For us," Kate said, nodding, as she slipped her finger over the trigger.

Rossett left the room. He walked toward the front door, and the maid appeared to his left from some service steps that came from downstairs. She froze and stared at him, so he forced a smile and raised one finger to his lips.

"Just open the door and step back so I can see you. Act normally and tell whoever it is that Sir James isn't home," he instructed. "It'll be all right."

The girl nodded. As she turned away, Rossett produced the Webley from his coat and, holding it behind his leg, ready but out of the maid's sight, he took up his station behind the door.

The bell sounded again and the maid looked at Rossett, who nodded. She took a deep breath and opened the door, stepping back into the hall.

Before she had a chance to speak, two men rushed past her into the hallway. One turned to speak to the maid but stopped when he saw the Webley pointing at him and Rossett staring down the sight.

Nobody spoke. The second man through the door held a Browning at his side, while the first appeared to be unarmed. The unarmed man, whom Rossett remembered from the warehouse, raised his hands slowly, unsure of what was taking place, while his colleague stared at the end of Rossett's pistol, fluttering his empty hand against his other leg, weighing up the odds.

"Drop it," said Rossett, closing the door with his free hand and cutting off any means of escape.

"Our mate is outside in the car. He'll be wondering where we've gone," said the first man. Rossett ignored him and continued to stare at the second, who was breathing hard and starting to lower his brow.

"Don't," said Rossett.

"There is no need for gunplay, Sergeant. We just want to check on our—"

The Webley boomed once and the second man slammed into the wall, the bullet in his chest killing him before his back touched the wallpaper. He dropped to the floor in an unnatural heap as the gun dropped from his lifeless hand onto the tiles.

The hallway seemed to ring with the echo of the gunshot as everyone's ears adjusted to the shock. The maid slowly lifted her hands to the sides of her head and her mouth opened, but no noise came out. Rossett took her wrist in his hand and gently pulled her toward him. The first man looked at his dead colleague and then back to Rossett's gun.

"Is there anyone waiting outside?"

"No."

"If you are lying . . ."

"I'm not. We're alone."

"Gun," Rossett said, and for a moment the man looked confused. Then he gingerly reached into his coat and pulled out another Browning, which he handed over nervously, butt first.

"Go," said Rossett, flicking the pistol, indicating that the man should start walking toward the rear of the house.

The man made his way down the hallway. Rossett gently took the arm of the maid, who gave a low squeak. Still holding one hand to her head, she allowed herself to be led by Rossett back to the drawing room, stepping gingerly over the body of the man.

"In there," Rossett said when they reached the study door.

The man opened the door and stepped into the room, looking around and then crossing to the fireplace. Rossett pushed the maid ahead of him and followed her in.

Rossett turned to look around and saw Sterling, with Jacob on his lap, sitting at the far end of the room. In front of him knelt Kate. The most noticeable thing about the tableau was that Sterling was holding the Browning under Jacob's arm, resting the muzzle against the boy's ribs.

Rossett looked at Jacob, who stared back with watery eyes that hovered uncertainly over thin lips, and then back at Sterling, who looked like the cat who had the cream.

"Drop your gun, Rossett."

Rossett looked at Kate, who lowered her eyes. "Drop your gun," Sterling said again, this time his voice stronger, attempting to take control.

The man whom Rossett had pushed into the room straightened and then took a half step toward him but stopped as Rossett pointed the Webley at him.

"Don't. I'll kill you. Sterling, drop the gun." Rossett didn't look at Sterling as he spoke. He fixed his gaze on the other man, who glanced at his boss and then back at Rossett.

"I'll kill the boy," Sterling said.

Jacob whined, hurt by the words and by the barrel of the gun that pushed into his ribs. Kate made to stroke the boy's hair, but Sterling pushed her hand away.

"Sterling, drop the gun," Rossett said coldly. "It's empty. Put it down. If you do anything but put that gun down, I'm going to kill this man and then kill you. Drop the gun."

Kate placed one hand over her mouth. Jacob whined again and the man at the end of Rossett's barrel opened his hands and made a calming motion.

"Sir?" The man looked at Sterling with pleading eyes, barely able to drag them away from the Webley.

"I mean it, Rossett," Sterling said, his voice less assured.

"Uncle James, please," Kate said.

A moment passed.

Nobody breathed. Minds raced, hearts pumped, and time seemed to stand still.

And then Sterling pulled the trigger.

Click.

Rossett fired the Webley and Sterling's man hit the floor.

Even before the hammer was halfway back, Rossett was pointing the gun at Sterling and making ready to kill again. Sterling clicked the Browning trigger once more, then twisted in his seat, lifting his arm to cover his face.

"John!" Kate screamed as Jacob stared at him, his mouth open and eyes wide.

Rossett paused, jaw clenched, arm straight, and Webley unwavering out before him.

"Please, John," Kate said, more softly this time. "He's my uncle. Please."

Rossett looked at Jacob. The child shook a little and his eyes welled, shocked at what he'd just witnessed. Rossett relaxed slightly as Sterling let the gun slip from his hand onto the floor.

Chivers launched himself out of his chair and crossed the room to take the Browning off the floor as Sterling slumped and pushed Jacob off his lap.

"Come 'ere, boy." Chivers held out his hands to Jacob, who charged across the room and fell into the old man's arms, sobbing.

"He snatched it from me. I tried," Kate said quietly.

"'E's a fast bastard, the bleedin' snake," Chivers said behind Rossett. "She did 'er best."

Rossett reached down, took the Browning from Chivers, and slipped it into his pocket, still pointing the Webley at Sterling.

"It was empty," Sterling said quietly.

Rossett nodded, his eyes on the top of Kate's head, willing her to look up and meet his gaze.

"You was testin' her?" Chivers again, looking first from Rossett to Kate and then back again.

Rossett didn't answer.

He finally lowered the Webley and took a seat, the pistol resting on his knee, as he weighed his options. Chivers led Jacob to a settee and sat with the boy, his arm draped over his shoulders, staring at Sterling.

Kate slowly raised her face and looked at Rossett.

"You didn't trust me?" she said.

"This is the sort of man you're getting mixed up with, girl. He's a killer, a damned murdering traitor." Sterling stared at Rossett as he spoke, using words to mask the embarrassment of having the tables turned on him by someone he considered an inferior.

"I can't trust anyone yet," Rossett said to Kate, ignoring Sterling.

"No, you can't," said Kate sadly.

CHAPTER 61

KOEHLER AND SCHMITT had visited eight pubs in Wapping before they finally found themselves standing outside the Prospect of Whitby.

Across the street, Werner climbed down from the cab of the troop transport and nodded to Koehler as he adjusted the machine pistol across his chest and took up a station at the rear of the truck.

"How many more of these places do we have to visit?" Schmitt said, burying his hands in his pockets.

"We keep going until we find news of this Irishman, Chivers, or Rossett, simple as that."

Koehler checked the Mauser in his pocket, then walked to the bar doors and pushed one open. He squinted into the darkness of the pub and waited for a moment for his eyes to adjust before walking inside.

The fat man sitting behind the door looked up at the two Germans entering and then across to the bar. He stood, picked up his old coat from the back of his seat, and made to leave.

Koehler shook his head, and the fat man sank back into his seat. Koehler walked slowly to the bar, aware that the general noise of the pub had dropped to barely a whisper. He rested an elbow on the brass rail and then turned so that he was facing the customers of the pub, who in turn all managed to not face him.

Schmitt stood at the pub door, hands still in his pockets but eyes alert, holding his Mauser tightly and watching the shadows for movement.

Over his right shoulder Koehler noticed the barmaid moving reluctantly toward him. He turned to rest both elbows on the bar and smiled at her.

"Good afternoon, Fräulein."

"What can I get you, sir?" the barmaid replied politely.

"Is the manager of the pub about?"

"He's upstairs, sir."

"Could you fetch him, please? I'm looking for a friend and he might be able to help me." Koehler smiled again, and the barmaid, much to her own surprise, smiled back.

"I'll not be long, sir."

Koehler gave a half salute and then turned to face the room again. Taking his time to look around, he pulled out a packet of cigarettes and leaned back before speaking loudly.

"I'm looking for George Chivers?" Koehler left the question hanging in the air as he put a cigarette in his mouth and lit it.

Nobody spoke, so Koehler pushed himself off the bar and walked among the tables, smiling at the few customers who dared to meet his eye.

"It's very important I speak to George. So important I'm prepared to pay handsomely for any information that could help me." As he spoke, Koehler stopped at a table around which three men were sitting. He lifted a pint glass out of one of their hands and sniffed its contents, then frowned at the man whose drink it was. "You should try some good German lager, my friend."

The man stared silently at Koehler, who smiled warmly back at him and gently placed the glass on the table before he continued to wander around the bar.

"Can I help you, sir?" A voice from behind him caused him to turn.

Koehler looked at the pub manager, who had appeared behind the bar. The small man smoothed a gray shirt across his potbelly and then nervously put his hands in his trouser pockets and attempted to affect an air of confidence. Koehler smiled and approached the bar, charm personified.

"Good afternoon. Are you the manager?"

"Yes, sir. Alf Beckett." Beckett produced a clammy hand and shook Koehler's over the bar.

"Alf, I wonder if you can help me," Koehler said genially, desperately resisting the urge to wipe his hand on his leg to remove the sweaty residue left by Beckett's.

"Anything at all, sir. Always happy to help," Beckett replied, eyes flicking around the room. Koehler smiled again, leaned against the brass rail, and flicked a finger for Beckett to come closer.

"I'm looking for George Chivers."

"Sir?"

"Come now, Alf, let's not be foolish."

"I think I know the name, sir."

"Think hard, Alf. I don't like asking questions twice." The smile was now gone and Koehler's eyes darkened in the gloom as he leaned even closer to Beckett.

"This is difficult for me, sir." Beckett's voice was barely a whisper.

"Trust me, Alf, it can be an awful lot more difficult than you'd imagine."

Schmitt appeared at Koehler's shoulder and leaned against the bar, his leather coat squeaking as he did so. Schmitt turned and faced the room, causing all those looking to turn away.

"He was in earlier, sir." Beckett was barely audible and Koehler had to lean forward on his tiptoes to hear him. "With another feller I didn't know."

"Describe him."

Beckett squirmed and looked over Koehler's shoulder again. Koehler reached and gripped his forearm, causing him to flinch.

"Please, sir."

"Last chance, Alf."

"Big bloke, angry looking. They met the Irishman."

"Irishman?"

Beckett looked like he might cry.

"I didn't see it, sir, it was only what I was told. I—"

"Irishman?" Koehler repeated.

"Pat Flanagan. Please sir, he's a dangerous man. I could—"

"Alf?" Koehler interrupted quietly, causing the other man to stop speaking and nod dumbly. "You are talking to the most dangerous man in London right now, right at this minute. You are whispering in death's ear. So please, get your priorities straight."

Beckett looked like he would faint. Koehler released his grip and then rested his hand on Beckett's shoulder.

"This could get me shot, sir."

Schmitt sighed loudly and impatiently, then reached into his coat, produced his Mauser, and placed it on the bar. He stared at Beckett but didn't speak before turning his back on the conversation and again looking around the room, which had fallen totally silent.

The pistol sat on the bar like a fat black cockroach, and Beckett found he was unable to look away from it. A bead of sweat trickled down his forehead, and it briefly crossed Koehler's mind that the other man might have a heart attack before he could pass the information that was required.

"Will this Flanagan drag you out into the street in the next two minutes and shoot you in the face?" Koehler whispered, placing his hand gently onto Beckett's arm once again.

Beckett shook his head.

"I will."

"Flanagan is a . . . I don't know, sir. He's able to get you things, anything you want. He has boats."

"A smuggler?"

Beckett squirmed before nodding.

"Chivers was buying something?" Koehler gripped tighter.

"He was. He was buying passage."

"Passage?"

"On one of Flanagan's boats, sir. He wanted out, him and the other bloke, as far as I know, to Ireland."

"When?"

"This is only what I heard, sir."

"When?"

"Tonight, on the tide, about eleven, from the Pelican Stairs, just next door." Beckett pointed to the back of the pub, as if Koehler could see through the wall, then used the same hand to wipe his face.

Koehler leaned back from the bar and turned to look at the other customers. Schmitt picked up his pistol and slipped it into his pocket, staring at Beckett.

"How many customers are in here?" Koehler murmured to Schmitt.

"Twenty-five, maybe thirty, why?"

"Tell them they are all under arrest."

CHAPTER 62

JACOB LAY FAST asleep in Kate's arms, the restocked fire crackled and popped, and the darkness outside pushed against the windows like the sea against a submarine as Rossett listened to the clock in the hall outside chime the hour.

Eight, nine, ten. He counted the bongs, then listened to the heavy tick-tock that had dragged throughout the last few hours like chains around a prisoner's ankles. Chivers must also have counted the chimes, as he moved for the first time in hours and pointed to his wrist, his eyes meeting Rossett's.

It was time.

"Kate, wake Jacob and get your coat and wait in the hallway," Rossett said.

Kate looked at him, then at her uncle, then at Rossett again.

"John, you're not going to . . . He's my uncle."

Rossett ignored her and looked at Sterling, who had straightened on the settee and was staring back.

"She is coming with me. If you or your men interfere in any way, I'll kill her. Do you understand?" Rossett asked Sterling.

"Yes," Sterling replied.

"Don't doubt me, I will kill her. The boy is my only concern. If you love her, you will remember that."

"I don't doubt you."

Rossett nodded, pulled out a handful of bullets from his pocket, and held them out to Chivers.

"Load the Browning."

Chivers took the Browning and the bullets and did as he was told as Rossett stood and walked toward Sterling, stopping just short of the settee and looming over him.

"Where are the sovereigns you took from me?"

"What?"

"At the warehouse, you took the sovereigns. Where are they?"

Sterling shook his head. "I don't know, I left them with someone."

Rossett thumbed the hammer on the Webley and raised it to point at Sterling's forehead. Sterling raised his hands and closed his eyes, then opened one slightly to peek out at the black hole of the muzzle, inches from his head.

"Where are the sovereigns?"

"In my drawer, second one down." He pointed across the room at a small writing desk.

"Thank you." Rossett walked to the desk and opened the drawer. He found the pouch under an address book and took both out. He placed the book in his pocket and tossed the sovereigns to Chivers, who caught them in midair.

"For you."

Chivers's eyes lit up and he weighed the bag in his hand.

"For me? Why?"

"You earned them."

"But . . . I . . ." Chivers didn't finish the sentence, as if he didn't want to repeat his own treachery out loud.

"You did what you did, George, but you were right about one thing. You did it to survive," Rossett said.

Chivers looked back at the pouch and then up at Rossett. He made to speak and then closed his mouth, shaking his head again.

"I need you. This isn't over. *We* need you. Are you with us?" Rossett spoke again.

Chivers nodded and Rossett turned back to Sterling, who sat on the couch, breathing deeply, waiting for the judge's verdict.

"I've a wife and child," Sterling said, his voice a whisper.

"So did I, once," Rossett replied matter-of-factly.

"Please."

Rossett looked at the young maid, who was crying in the corner, sitting so close to death, and then looked back at Sterling.

"Don't follow, don't interfere, or I swear, my vengeance will curse you for the rest of your life."

Rossett turned and left the room.

CHAPTER 63

"**I WANT EVERYONE, EVERY** man we have, down by that fucking pub as soon as possible!" Sterling shouted into the telephone and slammed the glass of brandy he was holding onto the table next to him. "We've only got half an hour before they get there!"

Sterling threw the phone down with such force it bounced out of the cradle and into the spilled brandy. Leigh, who was standing next to him, gently replaced the handset, then watched as Sterling picked up his brandy again and paced a few steps back and forth.

"What took you so long to get here?" Sterling snapped.

Leigh tilted his head.

"I came as soon as you called, sir."

"He had a gun in my face, Leigh, a gun held in my face in my own home!" Sterling shouted so loudly spittle flecked his lips and some landed on Leigh's face.

"Should I get someone to remove Johnson and Wilson, sir?" Leigh finally spoke.

"Who?"

"The men Rossett killed, sir."

"Get your car and get your arse down to Wapping. Johnson and Wilson can wait."

"Do you think it wise, sir, after what Rossett said to you? I'm thinking about your niece."

"There are many victims in war. My niece may end up being one of them. Now get going and fucking kill him!"

CHAPTER 64

A THICK FOG WAS rolling in off the Thames as Kate's Volkswagen made its way slowly down Wapping High Street. Rossett squinted into the gray, trying to make sense of the shadows and shapes that drifted into focus and then melted away again like ghost buildings in dreams.

Chivers had called the wrong turn twice as they crept along, and now he waited until the last moment before pointing over Kate's shoulder and indicating the correct turn into the road the pub sat on.

Rossett spoke for the first time since they'd left the house.

"Park here, I'll go look first."

"Flanagan won't let us down," Chivers replied.

"It isn't Flanagan I'm worried about," Rossett said, wiping the side window with the back of his hand and looking out.

Kate pulled to the curb and shut off the engine and lights. Rossett took out the Webley and replaced the spent cartridges he had fired at Sterling's.

"If you hear anything or see anything you aren't sure about, just go. If I'm not back in five minutes, just go. I'll find you, and we'll try again another time. Understood?"

Kate nodded. Rossett opened the door and stepped out into the cold night air. He looked up and down the empty street as far as the blanket of fog would allow, then leaned back into the car and gestured to Chivers.

"Give me the Browning."

Chivers handed over the pistol and Rossett dropped it into his pocket, before looking into the backseat at Jacob, who sat silently with only his face showing above a thick scarf and coat.

"I'll not be long, all right?"

"Promise?"

"I promise. You'll be safe soon."

"With grandfather?"

"With me."

The boy nodded and Rossett nodded back, both accepting that their fate lay in the hands of others.

Rossett looked at Kate and then Chivers. "Five minutes." He didn't wait for a reply before he closed the door.

Rossett's steps echoed off the pavement as he walked casually down the street. He stopped on the corner of Wapping Wall and lit a cigarette, listening to the night as the flash of the match died down.

On the river he could hear bells and the occasional ship's horn, but from the land side all seemed to be silent. He looked up at the towering warehouses that ran along Wapping Wall and backed onto the river. All were in darkness. Such was the thickness of the fog that he couldn't make out the tops of the buildings or even the far side of the road. A whisper of wind was shifting the odd shadow, and as Rossett walked toward the pub, buildings appeared out of the mist like vague memories.

He stopped short of the Prospect of Whitby and tilted his head to listen. He could just make out voices and laughter, and he glanced back over his shoulder and took a few more paces toward the pub entrance.

"Hey, are you the copper?"

Rossett turned to see a man, wrapped up against the cold, standing at the end of a narrow alley, barely two feet wide, that ran alongside the pub. The man stepped back into the dark as soon as Rossett saw him.

Rossett approached the alley. It was almost completely black except for a narrow band of fog visible at the other end. A horn wailed on the river, sounding closer than before, and Rossett realized that the alley led directly to the bank of the river.

"Yes," he whispered, unable to see the man he was talking to.

"I'm the boatman sent to fetch you. Where are the others?"

"At the end of the street. I'll get them."

"Be quick, the tide's already half turned."

Without replying, Rossett turned and walked back along Wapping Wall toward the car, glancing over his shoulder as he went. All was quiet, the fog providing privacy and comfort for the cautious traveler.

Rossett could hear the car engine running when he reached the high street. The headlamps were still off and he bent slightly as he approached to check that all was well inside.

Kate smiled through the windshield when she saw him, and he found himself smiling back. He opened the door and leaned in, looking first at Jacob and then at Chivers.

"They're there. We don't have long." He pulled the front seat forward and helped Jacob out, then tugged Chivers free from the cramped space and out onto the pavement.

"I was thinking, you and the boy, you'll need these." Chivers held out the pouch with the sovereigns.

"No, George."

"I took a couple, to get home like, but I thought . . . well, the lad, 'e'll need a start."

"No, keep them. You've earned them," Rossett replied. Chivers nodded and slipped the pouch into his overcoat.

"Yeah, well, maybe." Chivers held out his hand to Rossett, who shook it firmly.

"Thanks, George."

"You shouldn't thank me, not the way I've behaved."

"The way we've all behaved," Rossett replied, looking the other man in the eye.

Chivers turned away and bent down to hug Jacob, who stood, confused, on the pavement next to them.

"You write me a letter, boy, when you get to your new 'ome."

Jacob didn't reply. He just held the old man close and reached as far around Chivers's neck as his little arms would allow.

On the other side of the car, Kate stood on the pavement, wearing a white woolen coat with a fur collar. Her blond hair and the white wool made her stand out against the fog like a dash of white paint on a gray canvas. She smiled at Rossett nervously.

"Well?" Rossett asked. "I need to know; the tide is turning."

Kate looked down the street, then back at him. Rossett thought she was crying but wondered if it was a trick of the fog.

"I'm ashamed," Kate said softly.

"Don't be."

"For what I've done, before this."

"I'm ashamed, as well. The tide is turning, Kate. We can catch it if we hurry."

Kate looked down at the pavement.

"Will you hate me?"

Rossett shook his head. "New beginnings."

Kate took a deep breath.

"Okay, new beginnings."

Chivers took a step back, waving at Jacob, who waved back.

"You shouldn't go home," Rossett said to the old man.

"I'll be all right. I've been in worse trouble. It'll be my missus I'll 'ave to watch out for."

"Won't she be with the Germans?"

"They won't be able to put up with 'er. They know they need me outside, doing what I do, and they know I need 'er with me to do it. I'll fix things up."

"Take care."

"Time to go," said Chivers, taking one last look at the three of them and then walking away into the night.

CHAPTER 65

"**A**RE YOU SURE?"

"I think so, sir. It's difficult to see."

Koehler leaned over the shoulder of the young soldier and tried to look out the window at the street below. The fog was getting thicker by the minute, making his idea of having snipers cover the pub entrance seem more and more ridiculous as each minute passed.

"You saw someone walking down the road?" he asked the young soldier again.

"In the wrong direction though, sir. He was walking away from the pub, not toward it," the soldier replied, eye pressed up against the telescopic gunsight, rifle scanning the street below.

"This is ridiculous," said Koehler. "Relocate, one floor lower. Pass the word." Koehler stepped back and out of the way of the young soldier, who jumped up from the burlap sack he'd been lying on, gathered his things, and charged off, whispering to the others dotted around the floor of the warehouse opposite the pub as he went.

Koehler checked his watch again. It was a few minutes after eleven. He looked out the window at the pub, a hundred feet away, and considered the possibility that the manager had been lying, but then discounted it. Schmitt had spent an hour with the man in the cellar of the pub. There was no chance that he wasn't telling the truth. Rossett was coming. All Koehler had to do was make sure Rossett didn't get on a boat, and most important, that the diamonds didn't either.

ROSSETT HAD PLANNED on their walking back to the pub, but at the last minute he decided to drive: if something went wrong with the boat and they needed to escape the scene, a car was quicker than running. Kate drove slowly with her lights off toward the Prospect, and Rossett leaned forward in his seat brandishing both pistols, the Webley and the Browning.

"Pull up so that the pub is on your side of the car, half on the curb by the alley." He pointed into the fog with the Browning, and Kate followed his directions. When she was a few yards away, she killed the engine and coasted to a stop at the mouth of the dark alleyway.

"Are you sure this is it?" Kate asked, looking out into the gloom.

"Get out," Rossett replied. "Take Jacob out on your side and head straight into the alleyway."

Kate opened the door an inch before Rossett spoke again.

"Wait."

"What?" Kate looked at him.

"Here." Rossett put the Browning down in his lap and took the handkerchief containing the diamonds out of his pocket. "Take five, and leave me two. Just in case."

Kate did as she was told and placed the stones inside her glove.

"I'll give them back to you on the boat," she said gently before opening the door fully and pulling Jacob out through the gap.

"THERE! THE CAR by the pub."

Koehler nearly fell as he rushed to the window to look. The sniper pulled at the wrought-iron frame of the window to try to open it, but it held fast. Behind them four other soldiers raced down the stairs for a better view.

Koehler pushed his face up close to the window. The fog bank shifted again so the pub opposite almost disappeared, but then slowly, ever so slowly, a white Volkswagen Koehler knew well shimmered out of the night like a mirage.

"It's them. Get ready."

"The window, sir. It'll mess up the shot!" The soldier was still pulling at the window frame.

Koehler looked at the car and then at the soldier.

"Break it!"

THE SOUND OF glass smashing caused Rossett to turn as he stepped out onto the street. He crouched and made his way quickly to the rear of the car, both pistols out, scanning the warehouses opposite. Some broken glass tinkled onto the pavement and Rossett looked up to see from where it had fallen.

"John?" Kate called from the alley behind him.

"Go!" Rossett hissed.

He heard Kate's footsteps along the flagstones, echoing off the high walls, moving away toward the river. Rossett started for the alleyway.

Then he heard the shot.

"DID YOU GET him?" Koehler squirmed behind the soldier like a child at a fair, desperate to see what was going on.

The sniper chambered another round.

"I don't know, sir. It's very foggy. I think—"

"Has anyone else got out of the car?" Koehler interrupted, but none of the other snipers replied, too busy taking up positions and smashing their own panes of glass. "Can you see him?" Koehler pulled on the sniper's shoulder. The young man shrugged him off, silently cursing his commanding officer for throwing off his aim.

The sniper scanned the front of the pub through his sight and found the car again.

"He went down, sir. I don't know, I can't see him."

CHAPTER 66

ROSSETT LAY ON the pavement and felt a trickle of something wet run down his cheek; he already knew what it was. He touched the blood and traced its trail, finding the wound just above his ear, shallow but bleeding heavily. The bullet had chipped a piece off the pub wall and sent it flying into his head.

He looked at the gap between the car and the alley and wondered if he could make it.

He was still calculating when the pub door burst open feet away from him.

The two German soldiers who came out looked at the car, not at the man who was lying stomach to the pavement next to it.

Rossett shot them both with the Browning.

They both fell heavily, almost simultaneously, such was the speed of his shots. Their machine pistols clattered onto the pavement along with their dead bodies.

Rossett heard the sniper fire again. This time the round slammed into the car, which moved slightly from the impact. He ignored the sniper and kept his eyes on the pub door, less than twelve feet away.

A head popped around to look in his direction and Rossett fired again. Missing the man but hitting the door, he heard a cry, then two more rounds slammed into the Volkswagen.

KATE PULLED JACOB along the alley, blindly flailing at the air with her free hand. The child stumbled, but her pace barely slowed as she dragged him scuffing and twisting behind her.

They burst through to the end of the alleyway and tumbled halfway down the steps that led to the riverbank below.

She heard more shots and managed to stand up, ignoring her bruises. She pulled Jacob to his feet and looked back along the alleyway. She could see the Volkswagen and just make out Rossett lying facedown on the ground.

"John?" She held her hand to her mouth and felt the diamonds through her glove digging into the skin on her palm.

He answered by firing two shots, the flashes from the muzzle answering her question.

He was still alive.

She heard a splash behind her, spun, and, through the fog, saw two men pushing a long rowboat across some pebbles down the short stretch of foreshore toward the river.

More shots behind her, and she felt Jacob tighten his grip on her hand.

Jacob, I must protect Jacob, she told herself. Slipping and sliding across the wet stones, she made her way to the rowboat, which had by now reached the water. One of the men was already in the boat while the second was pushing hard, knee deep in the water, against the stern.

"Wait!" Kate cried. The second man turned and held out a hand. He gripped her wrist and almost threw her into the boat. Jacob appeared next to her, then the man hoisted himself over the side.

OVER THE GUNFIRE and the sound of rounds slamming into and through the Volkswagen, Rossett heard Kate call his name.

He ejected a magazine from the Browning and loaded a fresh one.

On the pavement outside the pub three men now lay dead, and he was sure another two inside were wounded.

The blood from his head wound was leaking into his eye, and he wiped it with the back of his hand. A machine pistol held by nervous hands reached around the doorframe and emptied its magazine high and wide, rising up with the long recoil. Rossett shot one of the hands with the Webley and the machine pistol fell to the pavement, its owner crying out and retreating back inside.

For a brief moment silence fell. Rossett rolled onto his side and rested his back against the bullet-pocked car. He considered using the lull to run after Kate, looked along the alleyway, and slid his feet up closer so that he might crouch.

It was then that he heard more gunfire, this time from farther down the street.

KOEHLER RAN DOWN the stairs faster than he thought safe. He had his Mauser pistol out and cocked. He reached the front door of the warehouse and opened it a fraction. Across the street he could see the Volkswagen, its flank dappled with holes from the snipers, and the pile of bodies outside the pub. From his vantage point, he could just make out through the fog some men hiding behind the cover of the door, unsure of what to do.

He wondered if Schmitt was on the pavement or if he had taken up a position at the back of the bunch.

Koehler cursed.

The operation should have been a simple ambush. He regretted not having stationed men on the riverbank; he regretted not having more men on the scene, full stop.

He realized that in the last few days he'd been regretting an awful lot.

The street fell silent and Koehler wondered why his men had stopped shooting. He listened for voices and heard none. Things had stalled. It was time for him to take charge.

He took a deep breath, kicked open the door, and started to run across the street.

He had made it halfway when the cobbles around his feet erupted in a shower of sparks and flying stone. He stopped, pirouetted, then slipped and scrambled his way back to the door from where he had just come.

Something hit him hard in the calf, and he missed the door and fell against the wall next to it, another round hitting the hand he was using to lean against the wall. It occurred to him that he'd been shot.

He fell through the door and managed to crawl into the building as wood splinters rained down on him from the heavy fire that the door was taking.

Koehler rolled onto his back and looked at his hand. In the darkness it looked black with tar. It took a moment for him to realize it was covered in blood. He tried to count all his fingers but couldn't: they weren't all there.

CHAPTER 67

LEIGH HAD ONLY managed to pull together six men at the short notice that Sterling had given him. He'd assumed he was just going to turn up, shoot Rossett, take the diamonds, kill the communist and the Jew child, and reunite Kate—hopefully after banging her—with her uncle.

He hadn't expected to walk into a full-blown firefight in the middle of Wapping.

He'd left his men on Wapping High Street when he heard the shooting start. His original plan was to just observe what was going on and then pull back. He had no intention of ending up in German custody all over again, especially not over some personal grudge Sterling had developed.

It was only when he saw Koehler coming out of the building that he decided to get involved. He'd already been crouched down behind a concrete bollard, so it had been easy to raise his Thompson and take aim.

The chance of killing that SS bastard was too good to miss.

But, unfortunately, he pretty much had. No sooner had the German fallen back through the doorway than Leigh was making his retreat, changing mags and scuttling backward to the London taxi that was waiting to spirit him away.

Koehler and Rossett would have to wait.

FROM UNDER THE Volkswagen, Rossett watched Koehler fall, scramble back up, then fall again through the doorway and into the warehouse.

He felt a twinge of concern for the German before realizing that the snipers in the warehouse had adjusted their aim toward whoever had shot their leader. Checking the front door of the pub, he rose to his haunches, then to his feet, and dashed down the alleyway toward the river.

Like Kate, he missed the top step, but unlike Kate he didn't stop halfway down. He tumbled hard, hitting the stone and feeling his already fractured ribs fracture even more.

He gasped, forced air into his lungs, and tried to get his bearings. The fog was thicker, almost a solid wall. The only clue he had as to where the river lay was the steps at his back. He struggled to his feet and realized he'd dropped the pistols. He looked around and saw the shingle, just shades of gray, and gave up all hope of finding them.

He lumbered toward the water, into the fog, blood blinding him from his head wound and pain stabbing his side with every step. He stumbled again as the shingle dropped suddenly to a soft sandy shore, his hands splashed into the water, and he struggled in deeper, first on all fours and then lumbering to his feet again.

"John!"

He heard her, and all at once the fog parted. Maybe thirty feet from the shore, he thought he saw her and a rowboat. He could catch it. He could swim. He took a few more steps, stripping off his overcoat and jacket, not feeling the cold, not feeling the pain. The fog shifted again, and he could see that it was definitely her.

"John!"

She called again, this time louder. She waved, and Rossett continued wading toward her. Just a few more steps before he could dive and swim.

That was when he was shot.

CHAPTER 68

WERNER WAS AN old soldier who had stayed alive for many years while many of his old friends had fallen. Some people said it was luck; others, who didn't know him well, said it was because he was a coward.

But Werner knew it was because he was a thinker.

He knew he could think when everyone else was panicking, he knew he could think when bombs rained down, he knew he could think when things looked bad, and he knew he could think when everyone else had stopped thinking.

That was what gave Werner the edge. He wasn't a hero or a coward. He was a thinker.

When Koehler had split his men between the pub and the warehouse, Werner had thought it a good idea, but back then, all those hours ago, the night hadn't been foggy.

He'd gone downstairs to the cellar a few hours earlier to check on the pub customers who were locked up there, and when he'd come back upstairs he'd seen the first few drifts coming in. The barmaid, who'd been allowed to stay upstairs to provide drinks for the troops, had also seen it.

She'd told him that she liked to watch the fog rolling down the river from the small balcony at the back of the pub, and they had stood there doing just that. Watching as the solid bank had drifted with the tide toward them.

When the firefight started Werner thought of that balcony, and as Schmitt sent out the first two young men to get murdered, he considered how best to use it.

He did that thing that had won him so many medals, had earned him the respect of his men and his superiors, but most important, had kept him alive for so long.

He thought.

And that thought, as the bullets flew, told him that if he went to the balcony with a rifle and waited, eventually, if Rossett was as good as everyone said he was, he would show. He would present himself to a good shot with a good rifle.

Werner had waited. He'd watched the girl and the boy go; he wasn't a murderer. He had merely tracked them down the shingle and into the boat with his rifle and then waited.

He knew that the major would be upset that they'd gotten away, but he didn't care. He didn't care about killing Jews, or shooting women, and he certainly didn't care about catching diamonds as they fled the scene. He was a soldier, an enlisted man; he wouldn't get to see diamonds.

All Werner cared about was the job he'd signed up for all those years ago.

Killing enemies.

So he'd sat, cheek resting on rifle, rifle resting on balcony, thinking and waiting, waiting and thinking.

What he did best.

WHEN THE BULLET hit him Rossett fell face-first into the Thames, water swirling around him and drowning his senses with noise and taste.

He wanted to stand up. He could feel the bottom of the river with his feet, and he pushed at the mud and sand, but try as he might, he couldn't straighten his back to lift his head from the water.

He flopped to the side, confused. He felt something hit his face, then realized it was his hand, moving in slow motion, waiting for direction from his brain.

His back hurt. He remembered the sound of the gun behind him.

The realization that he'd been shot seemed a long way away, as if his brain were somewhere else where he couldn't quite hear it.

He tried to stand again, and this time breathed in with the effort. He felt the river flood his lungs, and cursed himself for forgetting he was underwater.

He was drowning, just like in his dreams.

He thought about Jacob, his son, then remembered the boy wasn't his son, and he breathed again.

More water. This time he didn't curse.

He thought about Kate calling his name. Now all he heard was water, drowning her out, drowning him in.

He breathed again.

More water.

He hoped the little boy would be safe and happy.

He'd tried so hard, he'd done his best.

He loved him.

CHAPTER 69

WERNER JUMPED OVER the low rail on the balcony and dropped the ten feet to the shore. He scrambled down the shingle and ran into the Thames, wading to his chest, slashing with his hands, trying to find his balance in the strong tide. He wondered if he'd missed Rossett in the fog and stopped, twisting his head this way and that, looking for a sign.

The flat black river offered sharp contrast to the thick white fog, and Werner listened to the night now that the shooting had stopped. He heard the soft lapping of the water around him, and in the distance a horn sounded.

It reminded him of Hamburg, his home, before the war. He heard another horn, and then saw Rossett, four feet behind him, closer to the shore, drifting facedown.

Werner grabbed him and dragged him to the land, calling out for assistance. When it came, he was already pumping the other man's chest on the sand.

He wasn't a murderer.

ACKNOWLEDGMENTS

I USED TO THINK that being a writer would be a lonely job; well, I couldn't have been more wrong. I'm a lucky man, and this page will show you why.

I really couldn't have written this book without the nudging encouragement of the fabulously talented Tracey Edges, her chivvying kept me working away when I was struggling to see the point. You should buy one of her paintings and give her the platform she deserves. Two others who were there at the beginning are Mary and Kenny; they kept knocking on my door asking me for more, and they helped push me on when I wasn't sure if I could do it.

Sweeney, Terry, Jimmy, and Barry, four likely lads who stood by me when it was dark, who held me up, never doubted, and were always there. You'd be lucky to have one of these in your life; I'm not sure I deserve four. Thanks, lads.

Col Bury, a brilliant writer and a brilliant guy, living proof that there are people out there who will help another for no other reason than they can. You changed my life, mate; it's as simple as that.

Ian Collins, Cash Peters, Jo Hughes, and Jane "StooshPR" Buchanan; early believers who encouraged me and helped spread the word.

Angie Sammons, who opened the door of my cab and led me to a new life. She taught me a lot and occasionally gets me drunk; a special friend who started the ball rolling.

Nat Sobel and the amazing, patient people at my agency Sobel Weber.

They put up with the stupid emails and daft jokes and never complain, they never lose patience and they teach me a lot. I'm a very lucky man to have Nat as an agent. They invented the saying "carrot and stick" for the legend that is Nat; he's perfected it to the extent that he is now able to hit me with both items simultaneously, and I'm very grateful that he does.

The team at HarperCollins and William Morrow: David Highfill, Jessica Williams, and everyone else there behind the scenes. You made the magic happen, you made the dreams come true and the sun come out. You guys changed my life; I hope I don't let you down. Thank you.

There are so many others I should thank: my sister Denise, my brother Philip, John, Tony, Ian, Tracey, etc. This list would be longer than the book if I was to add the name of every person who helped me, encouraged me, and loved me. Rest assured if you're not here and you helped—I love you and thank you for putting up with the selfishness that comes with writing. Christina, I'm looking at you.

Finally, the most important people, the men, women, and children who fought and died in the darkest hours mankind has ever known. Your sacrifice inspired and gave us all a free voice.

I hope I've used it well.

Tony Schumacher
Liverpool
July 2014